"Borregad?" Lyrec called out. "Borregad, where are you? Are you intact?"

A terrible caterwaul answered him.

Lyrec imagined his poor friend lying in the weeds in dreadful pain, or near death. He called out again, but received no answer. Was he too late? "Borregad. I can't find you. Can you hear me?"

Just to his left, a voice said, "Leave me alone, will you?"

Lyrec sat back. "You're not hurt!"

"Hurt!" cried the voice. "What does *hurt* have to do with it? You should see me. It's horrible."

"Now look here," Lyrec said. "There's nothing wrong with you, is there? You're just being vain about your appearance again, like the time before last, aren't you? Come on, Borregad—how bad can it be?"

Then Borregad showed him . . .

Other titles available from
Ace Science Fiction & Fantasy:

A Lost Tale, *Dale Estey*
Murder and Magic, *Randall Garrett*
Tomoe Gozen, *Jessica Amanda Salmonson*
The Warlock in Spite of Himself, *Christopher Stasheff*
Elsewhere, *Terri Windling & Mark Alan Arnold, editors*
The Devil in the Forest, *Gene Wolfe*
Time of the Fourth Horseman, *Chelsea Quinn Yarbro*
Changeling, *Roger Zelazny*
Unicorns!, *Jack Dann & Gardner Dozois, editors*
Bard, *Keith Taylor*
Daughter of Witches, *Patricia Wrede*
Harpy's Flight, *Megan Lindholm*
Jhereg, *Steven Brust*
The King in Yellow, *Robert W. Chambers*
King's Blood Four, *Sheri S. Tepper*
Runes, *Richard Monaco*
Pavane, *Keith Roberts*
Sorcerer's Legacy, *Janny Wurts*
Annals of Klepsis, *R.A. Lafferty*
Citizen Vampire, *Les Daniels*
An Unkindness of Ravens, *Dee Morrison Meaney*
Songs From the Drowned Lands, *Eileen Kernaghan*
The Anubis Gates, *Tim Powers*
Ariel: A Book of the Change, *Steven R. Boyett*

LYREC

GREGORY FROST

ACE FANTASY BOOKS
NEW YORK

To my father, who let me take less traveled
roads; and, in memoriam, to my mother, who
laughed the best

LYREC

An Ace Fantasy Book/published by arrangement with
the author

PRINTING HISTORY
Ace Original/February 1984

ISBN: 0-441-51010-8

Ace Fantasy Books are published by The Berkley Publishing Group,
200 Madison Avenue, New York, New York 10016.
PRINTED IN THE UNITED STATES OF AMERICA

♭Prologue.

PINK dawn light wedged itself between the great gray clouds that spread like mountains across the sky. The low forest scrub—thistled, foul-smelling, yellow freminiad that the leather workers used in tanning—cast off a thin mist that rose in smoky vines like departing ghosts. A flock of birds took wing suddenly, fleeing from the approach of forest invaders. The invaders were preceded by the noise they made: by the clank of armor, of swords, and the slap of reins; by the creak of leather; by the exasperated blowing of horses that disliked being bridled so early. The warning was clear: men had entered Boreshum Forest. One king, his daughter, a cluster of soldiers, and a few trusted servants.

Dekür, the king of Secamelan, rode near the head of the party, with two soldiers before him. His daughter, Lewyn, rode by his side. He looked toward her, saw her proud head tilted back, revealing a strong jaw and slender neck. She was pale and blonde, with her cheeks brightly rouged by the chill air. Seeing the birds take wing, she turned to him. Her blue eyes were wide with an excitement he could not share this early in the morning. He felt stiff and tired, and a little hung over. "Beautiful birds, aren't they?" she said, and he answered, "Yes, very," then turned àway.

Lewyn looked at him covertly in a way that children sometimes do, but he did not see.

He knew some of what she felt for him; her adoration was plain enough. But the depths of it—how she compared him to a great winged *corrut* and such—escaped him. When Lewyn sat straighter in her saddle, adopting what she took to be a more adult pose, Dekür did not notice and he would not have known her pose for what it was if he had chanced to glance her way. He had no notion that his daughter remained tongue-tied around him. He understood more of what her brother, Tynec, thought and felt, and Tynec was only eight—a boy who still played swordfight with sticks and walked with fantasy companions. Lewyn, at fourteen, was intelligent, with a mind for strategy, if often given to the most absurd flights of romantic fancy about life and the world. He loved her dearly; but there was—and always would be—distance there. She looked far too much like her mother.

Dekür thought of his own father, Ronnæm, whom he had just left back in the village of Ukobachia. At one time Ronnæm would have denied the very notion that he might someday live anywhere near—much less with—the Kobachs; but that was before Dekür had defied his parents and (his father would then have said) all decency to marry a Kobach woman: Leyanna. But in the end, the old man's bigotry had proven no match for Leyanna's quiet determination. So successful were her efforts to erase his prejudices against the Kobachs that when she died, it was the pitiless old warrior Ronnæm who needed the most consolation, who had locked himself away and wept for hours.

The love Dekür had for his father caused him to smile. The old man, for all his faults, had taught Dekür well. The king wondered if he could pass as much wisdom and humanity to Tynec and Lewyn as Ronnæm had to him. Perhaps when they returned to Atlarma he would consult a soothsayer. That decision made, Dekür closed his eyes and let his horse do all the thinking.

As they rode, the ground rose on the right into grassy hillocks. The trees on the left grew close to the road, the dirt track shadowed by their overhanging branches. Dekür's horse shied. The king opened his eyes, raised his head.

The attacking soldiers, their clothing green and muddy brown, seemed to rise out of the hillside. They sprang before Dekür could shout a warning, sweeping down on the party like a flock of harpies, hurtling into the nearest riders, stabbing with the spikes on the tops of their helmets, impaling, killing many in that first instant. Shouts of surprise and pain rang out from Dekür's men; the attackers uttered no sound. Horses fell, screaming, crushing their riders. Swords grated, drawn from scabbards, and the fight began.

Having no chance to draw his own sword, Dekür ducked low, took his attacker across his back, then reached around, grabbed the lip of the soldier's helmet and flung the body around him. With both hands he twisted the helmet to break the soldier's neck as he dropped him to the ground. Then Dekür leaned out from his saddle, grabbing blindly for the reins of Lewyn's horse. He missed them. Lewyn sat petrified with fear. He reached again, clutched her reins and pulled them free from her limp grasp. Beneath him, the soldier he had thrown off scrambled up. Dekür cursed the man's strong neck and kicked out at the helmeted head, catching it in the visor; kicked again, knocking the soldier back against the flanks of Lewyn's horse. The soldier grappled for his foot and grabbed onto his ankle. Dekür kicked his horse into action. It leaped forward, knocking down a second soldier. The reins of Lewyn's horse passed over her horse's head, then jerked against Dekür's grasp, wrenching, nearly dislocating his arm, and shredding the soft leather of his gloves. But he held on and her panicked horse took to the gallop behind him. The enemy soldier, still clinging to his ankle and stirrup, dragged along with them.

Both hands full, Dekür could not draw his sword. Ahead of him, his two pointsmen fought wildly. The nearest one had taken a terrible gash in his shoulder from a spike. He fought with his sword uncomfortably balanced in his left hand. Absurdly, Dekür thought, Have to teach them to fight with both hands.

He charged the pointsman's enemy, rode him down. But, glancing back, he saw the enemy soldier spring up again like a trampled blade of grass, as if nothing extraordinary had happened.

Dekür's guts went cold.

Lewyn screamed, "Father!" She had come out of her shock and had seen the soldier dragging along with them.

"Don't worry about *him!* He can't hold on forever!" But he was not so sure, and his ankle was on fire from the other's viselike grip. "If we get separated," he shouted to his daughter, "you hug to Gafrey's mane and ride all the way back to Atlarma. Don't stop!"

"Father—"

"Just do it!"

"I will! Oh, gods!"

He never heard her speak another word.

The air around him began to sparkle and everything seemed to slow down. Dekür tried to kick his horse, but his legs moved sluggishly, as though through syrup. The sparkling lights dizzied him with their bobbing.

And then his horse was gone and his left hand was empty, and Lewyn and Gafrey had vanished. He fell slowly, slowly to the ground, felt his ankle twisted sharply. He cried out at the pain. The enemy soldier had not disappeared.

Dekür landed on his face, dirt in his mouth and eyes, the air punched from his lungs. He choked, spat. The grip on his ankle relaxed. He knew what that meant and rolled over, found himself able to move with speed again.

The soldier, standing, pulled a bone dagger from his belt, and leaped. Dekür threw his hands up, caught the other's wrists and tossed him to one side, then scrambled to his feet. His ankle buckled, but he forced himself to stay upright, fighting off nausea. He pulled out his sword and struck at the rising soldier, swept the blade in an arc beneath the soldier's helmet. The severed head flipped up bloodlessly and bounced on the ground. The body dropped at his feet. Then it exploded. Dekür raised his arm in protection as bits of the body spattered against him in a blast of wind. He expected blood and entrails, but what hit him were twigs and thorns and tightly wound sprigs of long grass.

Dekür stared agape. All that remained of the infernal soldier was its helmet. He limped to it, prodded it with the tip of his sword. The helmet rolled over and stopped against a stone. Empty. No head, no body, a thing of dry grass; a straw man.

Dekür wiped the dirt from his face. He looked back down the road. A few of the straw men had broken away from the fighting and were now walking purposefully toward him. He saw no more than two of his own men still standing. Even as he watched, one of them took a blade in the ribs and fell.

Dekür cried out: "Lewyn!"

Far away in the forest, he thought he heard a distant echo of his name. "Lewyn," he said and started off into the trees. He tried to run, but his ankle would not hold him and he fell into bushes that jabbed and gashed his face. Stumbling to his feet, he hobbled on into the deeper gloom, making a path where none had been.

He called his daughter's name again, was certain this time that he heard her reply, and moved ahead as quickly as he could.

After a while, he leaned against a tree to rest his ankle and his frayed wits. Far behind him, something moved cumbrously along the path he had made. The infernal creatures would not allow him to rest. Dekür stood, tears of pain squeezing from his eyes, and then headed deeper into the forest, grabbing onto small trees he passed for support.

As he moved on, the plants and trees around him began to change. It was a subtle change at first, and in his agony he failed to notice it until it was complete. Then he looked up suddenly, startled.

The plants had acquired an oily sheen. The trees were all bent, deformed; their leaves were no longer green but red and maroon, and hung as if in heavy fatigue. Dekür sniffed and smelled a sulfurous rot on the air. The king thought to turn back then, but behind him came the crashing of men or things like men through the brush, much closer now than before. And ahead, somewhere, was Lewyn. So he moved forward.

His ankle had swelled. It rubbed against the inside of his boot with each step. No time to stop and bind it. He moved on with his teeth clenched against the urge to vomit.

The forest threw off sharp, acrid odors that made his eyes water. The inside of his nose burned and his throat felt raw. Wiping at his eyes, Dekür paused, blinking, to look ahead. There, where a gap showed between the trees, the forest appeared to have turned black.

He moved toward this area cautiously, his sword at the ready. As he closed on the blackness, he saw that it was a wall, an enormous black wall. He touched it: cold, the rough stones wet. Dekür looked up. The wall ended smoothly above the trees—no battlements or windows graced its heights.

What was this? And why was it here in the middle of Boreshum Forest, where no man lived? Perhaps he no longer stood in Boreshum, however; perhaps he had walked out of his world and into . . . where? He knew of no such place, not even in legends.

The wall extended in either direction as far as he could see. It seemed to curve away on both sides, although trees grew right up against it, so he could not be sure of this. He wondered in which direction to go, if there might be a way out of this place.

He wanted to call out to Lewyn again, but held back for fear of giving away his position. Dekür heard the straw men crashing through the brush off to his left. That made up his mind: he went to the right as quickly as possible, pressed against the wall for support. Soon his left hand and sleeve were soaked with cold moisture from the wall. Dekür held the sleeve to his head. Drops of water drizzled from it down his face and neck. He closed his eyes and groaned, then he wiped his palm along the wall and rubbed it over his face. He wondered if he had a fever.

Dekür maneuvered around the trees that grew too close by the wall for him to thread between them. The wall must be old for the forest to have grown in on it, yet there were no vines on the black stones and no apparent fault or places where old stones had collapsed. Almost, thought Dekür, as if it had erupted out of the ground that morning. He wondered who had built it, what it hid. Of the ancient and now united tribes, not one had the capabilities to raise such a wall. Not one. His own city, Atlarma, had taken twenty years to finish, and its wall was far smaller than this.

The forest, the straw men, and now this black wall—the awesomeness of the power that had created these things terrified Dekür. He wanted to flee from this place, to run to the nearest town and take comfort among normal surroundings and people whose greatest concern was gathering enough wood for a cold night's fire. He did not want to know any more about this wall or what lay behind it. He just wanted his daughter back.

Leaning more heavily than before against the towering black barrier, Dekür shambled on. The wall ended so abruptly that he nearly fell. The opening was an enormous arch some twenty feet across. Above him, a gargoyle face glared down, its jaws opened wide and its tongue stuck out at him. He could almost smell its rancid breath. Beyond the arch, the ground sloped up gently. At the top of the rise stood a titanic black castle. Its towers spiraled into spikes that recalled the helmets of the straw men. They reminded Dekür of antlers atop some squatting dark demon—a bestial horned god waiting to suck the marrow from his bones. Dekür hobbled back a step.

Then he saw Lewyn.

She stood on the edge of the hill. Behind her was a second figure, much larger, taller, wearing an unnaturally bright white robe with a cowl that hid the figure's identity. The figure waited for him.

Dekür was no coward, but every instinct told him to run from that place as fast as his legs would go. This was the work of demons and you cannot do battle against demons with a sword. A wise man flees such an enemy. But the thing in the white robe had his daughter, and he would have her back before departing. Dekür concentrated on that fact, fighting off his fear and superstition. He made himself angry enough to raise his sword and start forward. The chiseled gargoyle face leered down at him as he strode beneath the arch. The ground opened and Dekür fell, tumbling down a long shaft.

The sword slipped from his grasp as he plunged toward red magma that bubbled and smoked; falling ever faster, his hands clawing at the smooth sides of the shaft. He screamed, "Lewyn!" knowing he would die when he hit bottom.

Yet he thudded into the magma and lived, unbroken and alive. The shaft, the fall, the pit had to be illusion. He tried to seal his mind off from the treachery, banishing all phantasms from his sight. And even as he did, the fire melted through him. He looked up to see his own sword come tearing down toward him. The blade drove through him, the hilt thumped against his chest with enough force to splinter his breastbone. With his dying breath he cried out at the wrongness of these events. Illusion could not kill!

♣Chapter 1.

A MIRIAN minstrel, dressed in gaudy clothes with puffed sleeves and tight orange pantaloons, walked lackadaisically along the narrow road to Tandragh. He was thinking of a song.

The air around him was cool and sweet with commingled scents and just-opened flowers whose identities were hidden in the long shadows of morning. The minstrel strolled into a small copse. A gentle breeze drifted after him, touching the trees overhead, their branches realigning the arrows of sunlight that fell across his path.

He would have preferred company on his journey, but no one had been going this way from the tavern where he had spent the previous night. Tandragh was at the end of a road that led nowhere else, and Tandragh was small. If the finest maker of cymrallins had not lived in Tandragh, the minstrel would not have been going there either. And so, alone, he chose to work on a song. It would be a love ballad, he had decided. The first line—"Your face, more soft than cat's fur, my love"—was evidence of this. It was a line he had worked on for well over an hour. The rhythm was as he wanted it, but the imagery felt a tad forced. Nevertheless, he chose to keep it for the present. He was not the most renowned of composers in Miria. His magic tricks (for he had performed as a magician since his cymrallin had been stepped on) were little better.

With his mind bound up in the fundamentals of song, the minstrel was slow to react when the brightest light he had ever seen suddenly flared before his face and the air in front of him seemed to solidify. The light struck him, and he stumbled back, clutching at the polished hilt of his sword. The sounds of the forest grew to a roar, then vanished in a thunderclap. A gust of wind like winter's breath poured over the minstrel. The light grew larger, took shape, became a huge silvery globe floating above the ground. The metallic sheen of the globe did not mirror its surroundings, but reflected ripples of white folded against black like shadowed drapery. Within it some dark shape moved.

All of this—the light, the globe, and the minstrel's awareness of it—took place in seconds. He turned to flee and came up against a second sphere. He backed away with a shriek. The second sphere was smaller than the first and was deformed by holes and lumps on one side as though hot wax had been poured over it. The minstrel looked back and forth at the globes, then cried out, "Gods! I'm in the presence of gods!" He fell to his knees, averting his eyes.

The larger globe shot out a white tendril that coated the minstrel from head to foot with a glossy clear sap. It trapped him, bowed down, paralyzed, between thoughts, between breaths, between moments in time.

The second globe, too, attached a tendril to him.

The first globe began to alter. It compressed; its perfect roundness disappeared. The form within it stretched, filling in the changing proportions of the globe like molten metal in a mold. There came a sound—a crackling, hissing, white-hot sound. The globe thinned and elongated further. Its sides began to ripple, and a roughly humanoid form appeared within it. The silver mold redefined itself, first expanding, then contracting; with each apparent breath a new feature emerged beneath the silver: first arms and legs, then feet and hands. A torso was carved out, then clothing on this torso. The top of the figure stretched out to each side, becoming the brim of a hat.

When all else had been defined, the area beneath the hat was still blank. Images were drawn from the minstrel's mind, and their shapes flickered across the silver surface, each face lasting for a split second, instantly replaced with another and then another face until, at last, a set of eyes remained, and then a mouth, a nose, a beard. When the face had been sculpted, a shining silver statue of a human stood beside the minstrel, but its features still reflected a place that was not the surrounding forest.

The silver began to shrink away and colors—material and flesh—appeared. A brown leather hat, and the dark brown fur of a jerkin; a maroon shirt with loose sleeves; black leggings, shiny black boots, and a heavy black cape that was chained to the jerkin. The face was square-jawed, the dark beard trimmed close. Had the minstrel been able to look up, he would have recognized in the face some familiar aspect.

The last few threads of silver pulled away from the man beneath. All of the sphere's outer shell was now collected over his left hand, a silver ball at the end of his arm, hanging from his wrist like an enormous teardrop.

The air swirled and a great roaring echoed through the copse. The man trembled as he passed into the reality of the place called Secamelan.

The man sighed, his head hung forward, then tilted back as he drew a deep breath. His eyes opened. The irises were black; around them the whites were so shiny as to seem almost porcelain. He looked around himself and smiled. He had come through the doorway another time and survived. How many more passages could he withstand? Happily, this world appeared to be intact. "You may have finally arrived in time, Lyrec," he said to himself; then he cocked his head and repeated, "Lyrec." How strange his name sounded on these lips, in this manner of speech. He glared down at the minstrel and reflected on what knowledge he had acquired from the hapless creature. The fellow had either not been very bright, or the society here was not much to speak of—the rudiments of language, a sense of the world that could only be called dim, and a handful of concepts that as yet made little sense. Beyond that, the minstrel's mind had been closed to him, if there were anything more inside.

The weight on his left hand drew his attention. His crex, reduced in size and shining silver, still encased his hand. That would not do. It would have to be disguised entirely. He looked the minstrel over again. There, near the man's waist, was a

thin leather scabbard ending in a short shaft with a semicircle
of woven metal around it. Lyrec was not sure what this device
was—the concept of weapons had not been one that he had
elicited from the minstrel. Nevertheless, it was perfect for his
needs. He closed his eyes.

The silvery crex fluctuated for a moment. Then it sent out
two shining strands that slowly colored and altered to become
leather, ending in a sheath. The remaining portion dropped
down and fit itself into position, assembling above the sheath
into a grip with full-basket hilt.

Lyrec flexed his freed left hand. He looked down. The thing
strapped around his waist was not quite the same as the one
on the minstrel. The sheath was scarcely more than the length
of his hand. There had not been enough material left for the
crex to extend further down his leg. It would have to suffice.

Quite suddenly Lyrec realized that he was alone. He searched
the copse, but saw no one else. "Borregad?" he called out.
"Borregad, where are you? Are you intact?"

A terrible caterwaul answered him.

Lyrec envisioned his poor friend lying in the weeds in dreadful pain, or near death. Borregad's crex had been so damaged
that he could never assume a form on the same level as Lyrec's,
and Lyrec was forever fearful that his friend would accidentally
incarnate into an object—transform into a table or a boulder.

He called out again, but received no answer.

The grass was very high in the copse, and it was impossible
to tell where Borregad might be. Lyrec got down onto his knees
and began prying through the grass, expecting at any moment
to find the twisted, dying form of his friend. As he crawled
about, he scuffed up clouds of dust from the side of the path.

"Borregad. I can't find you." Was he too late, had his
companion succumbed at last? They never should have under-
taken these journeys. What did they know of this kind of travel?
"You'll have to make some kind of sound, direct me. Can you
hear me?"

Just to his left a voice called out: "Leave me alone, will
you?"

Lyrec sat back on his haunches. "What?" he asked. "What
did you—you're not hurt at all!" He got to his feet.

"Hurt!" cried out the voice. It had an odd, nasal twang to
it. "What does *hurt* have to do with it? You should see me.
It's horrible."

The high grass shook. Lyrec crouched down again. He saw a dark shape move behind the wall of grass, and he dove forward. "Bo—ah! What's this?" He withdrew a feather the size of a writing quill from the bushes. The feather was brown and blue and green, and opalesced into gold when the light lay directly upon it. Lyrec twirled it, and a memory not his own passed through his mind. "Good luck charm," he murmured. The exact meaning of this escaped him. He removed his hat and placed the feather in its band. He held the hat out to admire it, but his eyes focused on some movement in the bushes beyond and a look of exasperation came over his black-bearded face again. He brushed a hand through his silvery hair and scrunched the hat back on his head. With a final tug on the brim, he stood and began slapping at his clothes, raising dust like a plague of gnats.

"Now, look here," he called out. "There's nothing wrong with you at all, is there? You're just annoyed at your appearance again, like the time before last, aren't you? I'm sorry for you—you know I am. You know I'll do what I can to help you. But that doesn't include sitting here by the roadside until you see fit to reveal yourself. I'm going. Right now."

"Wait a minute!" the nasal voice whined. "You can't leave me here! Where is this place? What kinds of things live in these woods?" A large freminiad shook momentarily, as if itself terrified of the prospect. "I could be killed!"

"So could I. There really isn't anything else to say. You can stay in the forest and meet some ignominious end at the mercy of a—a rabid squirrel. Or you can come with me. We may be too late, you know. He had a good lead on us and I'll be damned if I'll waste any more time on your conniptions. Goodbye, Borregad."

The yellow bush was jostled again. Then the voice cried: "Drat! This thing's covered in some kind of sap. It's all over my pal—paw. Paw! Lyrec! Don't you leave, you hear me, wait a minute, I'm coming with you!"

From behind the bush a huge black cat appeared, waddling on its hind legs. It was a punchinello of a cat, its coarse fur standing up as if in anger. Its blue eyes were twice the size of a normal cat's eyes.

The cat frantically rubbed one forepaw against the other as it waddled up to the man named Lyrec. Its tail dragged in the dirt. "Here," it said, and thrust out its afflicted paw, "do you

have a cloth or something? I can't get this stuff off." The cat
stumbled and caught its balance. "How do these creatures man-
age to *walk?*"

Lyrec shook his head. "Borregad, you're a waste, do you
know that? In the first place, you don't need a cloth, you just
lick it off. If you weren't so damned busy flapping that tongue,
you'd realize that it has certain other properties. In the second—"

"Lick it off? Do you have any idea what it tastes like?"

"I won't until *you* taste it."

The cat gave him an up-from-under look of distrust, then
tentatively brought its paw to its mouth and licked the rough
pads. Its lips smacked and its eyes narrowed. "Nuh, fuine.
Nuw is snuck nu my nungue." Its whiskers twitched angrily.

"Oh. Well, maybe I got that part wrong. But I do know
that you're what they call a f-f-feline. Your family group walks
on all fours. You're not meant to walk on two legs alone."

The cat spat. "I refuse to walk on four legs. It's demeaning."

"Fine. Maybe we can find a little wagon to put your front
feet in and you can just trundle along behind me."

Borregad's upper lip curled back, revealing very long, sharp
teeth. His lips smacked again. "I don't like this incarnation.
And why do I always end up some second-rate brute while
you're always a paragon? Hmm?"

Ignoring the question that they both knew the answer to,
Lyrec bent down and lifted the minstrel. The body relaxed as
he touched it. He carried it into the high grass.

"The minstrel sleeps very deeply," observed the cat. "Are
you sure he's alive?"

"Are you questioning my capabilities? Of course I'm sure."

The cat clicked his tongue, secretly pleased with himself
for having rankled Lyrec. He tried waddling a few more steps,
then finally gave up and dropped onto all fours. "I hate this
incarnation. Why couldn't that minstrel have thought of some
less restrictive life form?"

"What a distempered little monster you are. Get up on my
shoulders."

Borregad crouched, then leapt up to Lyrec's right shoulder.
"Well, at least this body's good at something. How far do we
have to go?"

"I don't know. There was something about 'steys'—some

measure of distance, but I don't get anything definite. There seemed to be a point where his mind was blocked off. Some sort of interference."

"Probably atmospheric."

"Probably you."

"That's a rotten thing to say, 'pon my soul."

Lyrec kept his comment to himself. He started down the road to the south, and hoped that they had come to the right place.

Borregad muttered, "Rabid squirrel?" and then fell silent.

♭Chapter 2.

GROHD the tavernkeeper manufactured his own grynne, aged it in casks that he built himself, and probably drank as much of it as any two of his regular customers. That may have accounted for his resemblance to a grynne keg and certainly accounted for the veined flush of his cheeks and nose. His patrons frequently asked after the private stock in his special keg. Grohd would just pat his stomach and smile warmly in reply.

By rights he should have been a happy man. He had built his tavern at a crossroads which led out of the kingdom of Miria in the south to Dolgellum and other points north, and through Sivst to Atlarma in the west. Because the crossroads occurred just at the northernmost tip of Kerbecula Forest where it bordered on Mormey Marsh, no town had grown up here— not enough arable land to support more than a handful of farms in whatever direction one looked. Grohd's was the sole tavern for thirty steys in any direction. He had a stable large enough to accommodate two coaches and the accompanying teams of horses, and enough beds in the outbuildings for a full company of travellers. He made ample money, saved a good portion of it; owned a piece of a neighboring farm someone else worked and that kept him in food the year round. He would never be a land baron, but he would never starve.

And still he was unhappy. His perfect life contained a flaw.

The flaw travelled the road from the east—the road that led out of Secamelan and over the Mormey Tors into the small country of Ladoman. Ladoman was the domain of a fat, oily cutthroat named Ladomirus. Although Grohd had never actually seen Ladomirus, he had encountered enough trouble on the villain's account to loathe the very mention of that name. Many people, in flight from the harsh laws and crippling taxation in Ladoman, had stopped at Grohd's tavern. Following them Ladomirus's soldiers had come, had time and again ransacked Grohd's buildings in search of fugitives. The soldiers were filthy, foul, and vicious. They threatened him, baited him, once even beat him. Some years back, one of the outbuildings had mysteriously burned. But he expected no less from the privileged spoilers from Ladoman. Half of their kingdom was mire; the rest was barely tillable land. The people there were kept like slaves, watched over with great care so they would not escape to more enviable lands—to Miria and Secamelan. Fugitives were punished with death, and anyone found harboring them was pressganged into service in their place. Grohd had been careful, but his major advantage was his occupation. Should he be led away in chains, there would be no more grynne and hot food for the Ladomantine soldiers after their cold ride across the marshes.

Lately, though, the soldiers had intimated a change in the murky kingdom, leaving Grohd with the distinct impression that they were now merely waiting for the chance to break him. Something was happening in Ladoman—something frightening and insidious. Grohd smelled war in the air and grew more frightened because of what he had always thought was the impossibility of that; Ladomirus lacked the manpower or the brains to conquer his enemies. He had survived this long only because no one wanted his shabby little kingdom.

Grohd's anxiety over the soldiers' changing attitudes fed on itself; he grew wary of anything out of the ordinary. Anything at all.

When the door of his tavern creaked back to reveal a tall, broad-shouldered silhouette filling the doorway, and when Grohd squinted into the afternoon light to see that four eyes stared back at him from beneath the figure's hat, he gave a little yelp, and considered quickly the distance from his hand to the double-bladed axe he kept beneath the bar; he decided it was too far.

He cleared his throat, swallowed, and said, "Hello?"

The tall figure entered and closed the door behind him. With the sunlight blocked off, Grohd saw the man clearly, and, to his relief, saw the sullen cat perched on the stranger's shoulders.

The stranger himself seemed pleasant enough, although he was a massive figure, nearly a giant by Grohd's standards. His forearms were bare and roped with muscle, but he wore no weapon, unless you considered a silver sword hilt in a truncated scabbard—not a very imposing weapon to Grohd's way of thinking. The man's hair beneath his feathered hat was shaggy and silver; his trim beard was jet black like his cape.

The stranger was smiling. The cat also seemed to smile at Grohd; an unnatural expression, to be sure. Its teeth were extraordinarily long.

The man walked to the nearest table and set the cat down on it, then moved languidly toward Grohd while dusting himself off. "Hello," he said. "Warm afternoon, isn't it?"

Grohd suddenly recognized the stranger for what he was— a pilgrim. His voice gave this away; its silky accent was not local, but it was vaguely familiar. After a moment's deliberation, Grohd recalled where he had heard such a voice, and he wondered if this fellow, too, was a Mirian minstrel. He said, "Warm? Oh, for this time of year it's hot. Wouldn't want to be out on the road all day in this heat—*I'd* need something to drink." He patted his belly. "On the other hand, you wait and see how cold it gets tonight—why, a man'll shiver to death without a hot meal and a hot drink to keep his blood pumping. And, of course, a place to stay."

"Well then, isn't it fortunate that we've discovered this tavern here. And you're right, too. This heat's parched my throat. I certainly could use a cup of—" The man looked deeply into Grohd's eyes. The taverner felt a tickle inside his head. He reached up and scratched at it, above his ear, where he had some hair left. The tickle stopped, and Grohd was left with the unaccountable feeling that more time had passed than he was aware of. "Where was I?" the stranger said. "Oh, yes, a cup of your grynne, sir." His smile grew.

"A...a cup. With pleasure, sir." Grohd moved to where he kept the cups beneath the bar. A pilgrim all right, he thought. He hoped the stranger's thirst matched his size and that the man had found wealth wherever he had been.

A moment later Grohd placed a full, frothing cup on the

bar. "There y'are. That's one plentare."

"One . . . plentare." The man's smile faded for a moment. "In advance?"

"If you don't mind," Grohd said with practiced casualness. "What if you were to drink it and then refuse to pay? Now how would I go about wrestling with the likes of you? And over one plentare. That's not to say I don't trust you or—"

The stranger waved his hand. "Not at all. But, first, might I borrow a plentare from you to show you a bit of magic?"

"Oh, a magician, are you? And I'll bet you play music as well—there'd be a coincidence right enough. Well, I love a good trick." He bent down behind the bar.

"I'm relieved to hear it."

"Here." Grohd slapped a coin down on the bar. "That's a ten-piece. Will that make a difference?"

"I shouldn't think so—except of course that you'll lose ten instead of one."

Grohd's smile spread like a white stain. "Oh? Well, I can afford it."

"All right." The man carefully placed his hands over the coin, then moved them around in opposing circles on the bar top. "Tell me when you want me to stop."

Grohd looked him in the eye. "Stop," he said.

The stranger looked at his hands. A smile flickered on his lips. "Now, do you know where the coin is?"

The taverner shook his head and began to laugh. "You're all alike. Did you teach that one to the minstrel or did he teach it to you?" Grohd lifted the stranger's drink and swept up the ten-piece from beneath it. He held it up between thumb and forefinger. "Your friend was in here just yesterday, playing the same game on me for a drink. You *do* know who I mean, don't you? Of course, you don't dress anything like him, but you both talk so much alike you could be brothers."

The stranger's face flushed. "Just yesterday?"

"That's so. Now, about paying for the drink."

"W-would you care to try it another time?"

"What happens if I win? What do I get?"

"Another ten-piece."

"I might point out that I've not seen the first one yet." He scooted a coin across the bar top. "But I'll trust you that far. You still pay for the drink, though."

Lyrec put his hand over the coin and closed his eyes very tight as he moved his hands around. Grohd watched the hands more carefully this time. When he was certain he had spied the hint of movement that meant the coin had been palmed away, he said, "Stop." Then he reached across the bar and into the stranger's left jerkin pocket. His brows knitted as his fingers encountered nothing but a bit of dirt. He withdrew his hand, rubbed off the fingertips with his thumb, then reached into the opposite pocket. That also proved to be empty. Finally, in desperation, he lifted the stranger's hands and then the drink. The coin was gone. Exasperated, he met the stranger's amused eyes.

"Where is it?" he asked. "I saw you palm it, now where'd it go?"

"My cat has it."

Grohd leaned around the stranger. The cat sat placidly on the table, staring off into space. Grohd looked at his pilgrim. "Go on. What did you do—throw it to him?"

"Sort of." The stranger turned and walked over to the table. Suddenly, there came a crashing as if a full purse of coins had been spilled onto the table. The big man turned. He held up two gold coins. On the table behind him the black cat squatted amidst a pile of a few dozen more.

"Thank you," the stranger said. He laid two coins on the taverner's palm. "That's yours and the one you won." He added another ten-piece. "And that's for the drink and more to come." He started to turn away with his drink, but paused. "Oh, yes. I'd like a cup of grynne for Borregad."

Grohd looked around the tavern, puzzled. "Who?"

"Oh, sorry. The cat. Borregad is my cat. And Lyrec is my name."

"Pleased to meet you . . . I think." He shook his head slightly. "Grohd's my name. Drink for the cat, is it?" He stared at the table in a state of pecuniary lust, which is to say it was not the cat his gaze fell upon. "Anything else?" he asked hopefully.

"As a matter of fact, yes. I seem to have ripped my purse. It was an old thing, anyway—do you have one that I could buy from you to replace it?"

"Buy? Your purse . . . oh!" Grohd closed his fist over the three gold coins. "A spare, yes, I have a number around some-where. Certainly you may buy one. Yes. Just let me get your cat his cup—it *is* a he, isn't it—and I'll get you a purse. Just have yourself a seat." Grohd patted his arm, then went to fill another cup.

Lyrec walked back to the table and sat down. Borregad reclined with his paws beneath him. His blue eyes sparkled with amusement. He stared in silence at Lyrec until the tavernmaster had left him his cup and disappeared into the back in search of a purse. Then, quietly, he said, "So we didn't know about money, did we? We were so busy being rude to our foully transformed friend—weren't even going to buy him a drink!—that we didn't think we might need money to survive in this rotten new world, just like in all the rotten parallels. Gracious, did we make a mistake?"

Lyrec glowered into his cup.

"No answer? Tell me, then—who do you suppose that minstrel was that he mentioned? Nobody we know, I'm sure. It's a good thing I came with you or you might never have acquired any money. That innkeeper has probably seen every variation on that game that's ever been."

"Borregad," Lyrec snarled. Then he sighed heavily. "Thank you for your assistance."

The cat blinked, and leaned one paw up under his chin, spilling some of the coins around him. "You're welcome."

Grohd returned from the back room. He held a purse in each hand. "Here. I brought you two because I don't have one that's big enough for all that money." He set them down beside Borregad. "Hey, I've never seen a cat sit like that before."

"Unusual, isn't he?" Lyrec drawled. "A dreadful example of inbreeding, I'm afraid."

"Oh," Grohd replied, and nodded, though his face was a mask of confusion. "Too bad." He patted Borregad on the head. "Does that mean he won't live as long as most cats?"

"Very likely."

"Ahh. And he's such a big fellow, too." He wandered off into the back room again.

Borregad stuck out his lower lip.

Lyrec smiled back. "Want me to ask him about a little wagon for you?"

The cat's whiskers twitched, and he turned away to his drink.

♭Chapter 3.

As twilight settled over Secamelan, Lyrec was still at the same table in the tavern, drinking and chatting with Grohd. His cheek was rosy and his gaze distant, but these were the only signs that the incredible amount of grynne he had drunk had affected him at all.

This swilling of the grynne impressed Grohd. He could have accepted anything about Lyrec, any dreadful truth, in light of this bibulous capacity. Secretly, he was pleased with the biographical information he had heard—that it tallied so closely with what he had guessed originally. He had no idea how many of the place names and notions Lyrec had acquired from the tavernkeeper's own thoughts.

Lyrec's story unfolded slowly: that he had been abroad for much of his life; passing through so many lands, he had forgotten most of his native knowledge, customs, nuances. The blood of many cultures ran together in his veins. When asked, he informed Grohd that the minstrel of the previous day was not known to Lyrec. Their coincident accents were the result of common location rather than familiarity—so Lyrec claimed.

None of the details of the story surprised Grohd. He had heard many strange tales of men who had journeyed off in search of promised riches, and he had never met one who came back with anything to show for it save the skin on his bones, and sometimes not even that. He himself was no traveller, and he relished all the tales of lands he had heard of in legend or myth, but Lyrec had one tale of a land he had never heard mentioned before, a land decimated by grim plague which Lyrec and the cat had barely survived. More than that—they had come away rich!

Grohd matched every story with one of his own, and also matched the pilgrim for every drink. Lyrec insisted on paying for them all—and for the big cat's as well, whenever the black beast seemed so inclined. Grohd put up an argument at having his own drinks bought; but not so strong an argument that he won it.

Borregad, being so much smaller than the two men, required little of the heady brew to reach his plateau of insensibility. Within the first hour his blue eyes had glazed; by the second hour his eyelids had drooped almost shut; and after the third, his eyes had sprung wide open and thereafter remained crossed. Now he lay with one hind foot dangling off the table, sleeping peacefully, head propped on forepaws, a single stalactite of tooth on either side of his mouth protruding over his lower jaw.

A handful of locals had wandered in late in the afternoon, their field work done for a while, left with a few hours to kill before drifting off to their evening meals. They needed no encouragement to join in the discussion, adding tall tales more often than solid knowledge to what Lyrec had already learned. He kept them supplied with grynne until they were in their cups, and probed each one as the opportunity arose. Finally, toward sundown, they stumbled off together in a single pack.

Grohd looked after them. "Drunken louts," he proclaimed amiably as the door closed. Then he belched deeply. "Ahh. Time for me to make supper. You staying awhile, Lyrec?"

"I'll stay the night and another if you have the room." He downed the last of his drink, then placed the cup in the center of the table to indicate he was finished and would have no more. He had learned this custom from the farmers.

Grohd said, "Never seen anyone drink so much and look so sober as you—except me." He took the cup. "I have room all right. The coach from Dolgellum is due in here tonight, though—not that they'll fill the place. But you take a bedroll from that pile in the corner and carry it around back to the first hut. Go in and pick yourself a bed." Then, speaking slowly, with drunken difficulty, he added, "If you look hard enough, you'll find a loft up the stairs—suit you and the cat well enough."

"The coach to Atlarma—it does go through day after to-morrow?"

"That's so. There's just the one, up out of Miria. You could've waited for it, saved yourself the walk. There's no coaches to Ladoman, in case you hadn't reasoned that from what the fellows said this evening. Only thing coming out of there is trouble." One of his favorite sayings.

"Indeed. Why isn't something done about it?"

"Oh, well, now, King Dekür's not about to start a war over a few minor incidents like that. There's maybe six or seven a year, not enough to justify a war. And it's mostly those who house the Ladomantine fugitives that get involved. Dekür's a good king and all, but he's not out to champion every piddling cause. We know where we stand in Secamelan." He paused thoughtfully for a moment, then said, "If you think of it, you might take time to set a fire in the hearth back there. Winter owns half the day now; pretty soon, the old man'll have it all." He waddled off into darkness.

Lyrec said softly, "Borregad," then gave a mental call: *Borregad.*

The cat's eyes opened, then closed quickly. "Um, too bright."

"Never mind that. How much did you get?"

Borregad put his paws over his head. "You won't like it. Either they're all dense with barely a thought between them, or these creatures can't be probed." Squinting, he opened one eye again.

"Then why was I able to pick so much from Grohd? Why were we able to probe the minstrel?"

The cat raised his head petulantly. "Who says we probed him? All we extracted from him was language—with the exception of a few memory images near the surface, like his magic tricks and my wonderful form. Didn't even get a money concept. And can you play any of his songs? You said yourself he seemed blocked off or stupid. Besides, if you doubt me, then why don't *you* do some probing?"

"I was trying to," Lyrec admitted. "I couldn't get anything, either."

Borregad smirked. "So. It works on some of them and not

on others. Mostly, not. That won't make things easier for us."

"No, it won't. Why should it be so?"

"Chemistry, quite probably. I'd be more precise about it if we'd had more races to experience—if most of them hadn't been annihilated by the time we arrived. It may be like this on every one of these worlds. From what those farmers say there doesn't seem to be much going on here out of the ordinary. Their biggest gripe seems to be that Ladomirus character."

"He does come up in the conversation, doesn't he? Still, he hardly sounds like more than a local gadfly. Borregad, you don't suppose we've made a mistake, do you?"

"Do you mean do I think we're sitting in the wrong sphere while he's elsewhen? Sequestered in the wrong parallel? 'Pon my soul. I thought you were immune to such doubts." The cat stood and arched his back, stretching to his claws. "Just the same, no, I don't believe so. At most we've arrived too soon. You worry too much, you know."

"Do I?" He pushed back his chin and stood. "If there were just some sign . . ."

Borregad moaned. "I'm going to hurt come morning."

"That's not quite the omen I had in mind." He walked across the room and returned with a bedroll. "I'll go pick out a space for us. You might just as well stay put."

"Fine," said the cat, slumping back down. "In that case, I'll take another cup."

"Idiot." He withdrew a coin from his pocket and set it beside the cat. "Grohd," he called out. "When you have a minute, Borregad needs some help with his suicide attempt." Then he walked out the door.

Outside, the air had a chill upon it and Lyrec's arms turned to gooseflesh. Surprising, he thought, how quickly the cold had moved in. The gold and green trees rocked in a wind which, because it was blowing from the northwest, kept the sound of approaching horses from Lyrec's ears.

He went casually around the tavern and into the first of the two conical huts.

It took Grohd a little while to understand exactly what Lyrec had meant, but he and the big black cat finally reached a state of mutual understanding if not communication. The tavern-keeper brought another full cup of his brew to the distraught cat, then went off into the back room again to chop up more vegetables for his stew.

Borregad embraced the wooden cup with the passion of a lover. He sat, hind legs around its base, his forepaws straddling its lip, bending farther and farther over as the level of the grynne descended.

When the tavern door opened, he was bent almost double. His head was practically upside down, his muddled brain swimming as he lapped the last of his drink. He was too busy to look up and see who had come in.

Then the cup was tugged sharply away from him. Borregad reacted with a cat's instincts; he blindly slashed at the hand pulling the cup. His long claws dug into flesh and tore four deep gouges in the back of the hand.

The grynne thief yelled in pain. The hand jerked up, tossing the cup in a spasm that sent it sailing over the bar, splashing dark brown liquid across two tables. Borregad realized he had probably just wounded his friend. With sudden sobriety, he raised his head meekly to apologize.

His head was immediately driven back flat against the table by the same hand he had cut. Borregad looked up and wished suddenly that it *had* been Lyrec he had hurt.

The man holding him down growled, "You rotten little *fekh*. I'll have your guts on a plate." The man was tall and broad-shouldered. His thick beard grew high on his cheeks, almost to his bloodshot eyes. He wore an orange and brown tunic, tied down by a wide belt that hung low under the weight of a sword, an axe, and two sheathed daggers. There was a second man behind him, but with his head trapped against the tabletop, Borregad could not make him out except for one arm and a leg that came within his range of view.

Borregad gulped, then tried forcefully to pull his head out from under the hand. The grip tightened on his throat, nearly choking him. He stopped fighting and lay on the table, his eyes bulging, his heart racing.

"Innkeeper!" the bearded man bellowed.

Peripherally, Borregad saw Grohd emerge from the darkness of the back room. The tavernkeeper started to move toward the back of the bar, but the man said, "No. Come here first. We'll drink after we've dealt with your cat." Grohd hesitated. Borregad wondered why he wanted so badly to get behind the bar. Probing, he saw an image of a double-bladed axe in Grohd's thoughts. He tried to think of a way to help the keeper get to the axe. "Come *here!*" snarled the man in orange and brown. "Now."

Reluctantly, Grohd came to the table.

"Good." The man shifted, and dragged Borregad a little toward him. "Do you remember me, little man?"

"You're called Fulpig," answered Grohd. It was nearly a whisper.

"You have a good memory for a fekh of an Atlarman. If you know my name, you remember what happened the last time I was here and you gave me trouble. So I know you won't give me trouble now." He shook Borregad's head, raised it, then slammed it against the table. "You see my hand, keeper? See what your cat did to it? Now, how're you going to make up for that? Hmm?"

"You can—you can drink all you want for free. No charge for the whole evening."

"And our meal?"

"That, too. Free."

"What will we be drinking?"

Borregad heard Grohd swallow. "Grynne."

The man snorted. "Grynne. How about that, Abo?" he said to his companion, who giggled in response. "Well, that's not good enough, keeper." The pressure on Borregad's neck vanished, but before he could react, he was picked up by his hind legs. The room swung around; then the soldier jerked him up at chest height. Borregad saw the man's free hand reach down and withdraw a dagger from the wide belt. "This animal here is good enough to drink grynne. You serve it to stupid animals! I know you don't think of us as animals, so I know you'll offer us something better than what the cat drinks." The edge of the dagger touched Borregad's throat. Borregad closed his eyes in expectation of death. "Otherwise," said Fulpig, "I'm going to open up this animal."

"Yah," agreed Abo. "We don't drink with dumb animals."

Grohd said, "I have only grynne. There isn't anything else."

"Then, I hope you weren't too fond of your fat ugly cat, fekh."

"Please. I won't cause trouble. Please, put him down."

Abo moved forward suddenly and backhanded the keeper.

Grohd fell back against a chair. "Don't give us orders. Bring us drinks."

"Shut up, Abo," snapped Fulpig.

Borregad panicked as he felt a terrible urge brought on by the pressure in his head and by the dizziness of hanging upside down. He fought it back, but could not stop it. His mouth opened and he vomited. Grynne and bile poured over Fulpig's boots. As he heaved a second time, Borregad knew he was dead—the man would surely kill him now.

The outer door suddenly swung back. A cold wind gusted through the room. A tall figure, wrapped in a black cape, came stumbling in. He seemed oblivious to them and busied himself at trying to find the door so that he could close it. From the way he swung his arm and the way he lurched at the door, it was obvious he was drunk.

Lyrec kept his knees bent beneath the cape and let his shoulders sag. He wandered into a table, then backed away, giving the table a look of reproach. In doing so, he bumped into Fulpig. Turning around, he looked up into the bearded face scant inches from his own. "M'gods! There's a bear in the bar!" He stumbled back. Then, squinting, he smiled loosely and said, "I am ever so sorry, sir." He belched and continued on. The second man blocked his way, and Lyrec looked deeply into Abo's brown eyes. Abo was much younger than Fulpig. His face was shaven clean, but the chin was covered with tiny scars. Lyrec reached up and touched the chin. He clicked his tongue. "Poor boy. I, too, have had hiccups, but never while I was shaving. It must have been terrible." He patted Abo on the shoulder. It was a thin shoulder, without much muscle. That one would give him less trouble. He lurched back then, and sat down heavily in a chair beside Fulpig. Borregad hung within easy reach, and Lyrec smiled at his friend. Then he slapped the table and hollered, "Tavernkeeper! Drinks for everybody!"

Grohd looked at him, then at the soldiers. Fulpig nodded, and he walked quickly around to the back of the bar.

Lyrec looked back at Borregad as if seeing him for the first time. "Ugly little beast you have there," he announced to no one in particular. He lowered his gaze to the floor and Fulpig's boots. "And sick, too. What are you going to do with him?" He raised his head and met Fulpig's angry gaze for the first time.

"We thought we'd eat him." He glanced over at Abo; when he turned back, there was a vague smile on his lips. "Want to join us?"

Lyrec rubbed his beard, pulled his lower lip down, then let it snap back. "Oh, dunno. He looks a little tough."

Fulpig laughed. "Listen, we've been camped on Mormey Marsh for a week—out on the Tor. It's been raining nearly every day and all we've had to eat is saddlegrain. You know what happens to saddlegrain when it gets wet? You spend your whole meal picking maggots off your plate. So we don't care if he's tough as a plank."

"Mormey Marsh, eh? You're from Ladoman, then."

Fulpig snorted, then spat. "You're not from around here or you'd know that just by our colors. Who else wears orange and brown?"

Lyrec pursed his lips. "Pumpkins do."

"What?" Fulpig's mouth hung open. No one spoke to him that way.

"Put the cat down," Lyrec said. The drunkenness was gone from his voice.

Fulpig moved the cat over so that it hung between himself and this insolent drunkard. Then he leaned down and twiddled his dagger around the cat's head. "You got a reason?" He would have added "fekh," his favorite insulting term, but this time the word died in his throat.

"Always. He's mine. Besides, as if you haven't noticed by now, he's an alcoholic—you'd get sick off him."

"Is that right?" Fulpig twisted Borregad around and sneered into the large blue eyes, now almost completely black in anger.

"I'm trying to do you a favor. Put him down now." Lyrec waited. When Fulpig made no move or reply, Lyrec leaned one arm on the table and cupped his chin and said, "I tried."

Borregad snaked up suddenly. He swung out one splayed forepaw and stripped the skin from one side of Fulpig's nose. Fulpig howled and flung the cat away. He clutched both hands to his nose, blood flooding between his fingers.

Abo had his dagger out, but seemed uncertain as to whom he should attack. He looked from the cat crouching under the table to Lyrec, then at his partner, who stared at him furiously and bellowed, "Kill it, you bastard!" though the effect of this command was somewhat lessened by the twang in his pinched nostrils.

"Where'd it go?" Borregad was no longer under the table.

Fulpig, still holding his nose with one hand, pointed his dagger at Lyrec. "Where's your cat, damn you?"

Lyrec reached up and fiddled with the feather in his hat. "I did warn you. No one here wanted trouble except you two."

"Answer me!" Fulpig thrusted the dagger at Lyrec's eyes.

"All right. He's on your"—Fulpig shrieked and twisted madly around—"back."

Borregad leapt from Fulpig toward Abo, back arched, screaming hate, claws extended like tenterhooks. Abo fell back against a table. He stabbed uselessly at the cat; Borregad dodged the dagger with ease and closed his jaws over Abo's wrist. Then he dropped to the floor before the soldier could act and darted into the darkness of the back room.

Fulpig cursed. He turned back to Lyrec, this time to cut his throat. But Lyrec's hand closed over his wrist.

"All right," he said, as if admonishing children. "Borregad's had his fun, now it's time for everybody to go home." The Ladomantine soldier tried to free his hand, then to stab Lyrec against the force of his grip. His eyes met Lyrec's again. He saw a terrible promise there. The eyes had become silver, like mercury. But his anger was beyond sanity or safety, and he tried to stab again.

Beneath Lyrec's hand, Fulpig's wrist made a quick sound like ice cracking on a pond. His face turned chalk white behind his black beard, his eyes bulged, then rolled, and he fell in a faint beside his dagger.

Abo began to edge toward the door.

Lyrec said, "Put your dagger away and see to your wrist, Abo." He stood with a great sigh and bent down, lifting Fulpig with ease. He set the body down on a table spattered by blood and grynne. "You came in on horses?"

Abo nodded. "In the stable."

"Go get them and I'll help you load your friend."

"But we haven't *eaten*. We're hungry."

"And you'll stay hungry for the trouble you've caused. Try Tandragh or Llendid, soldier. Of course, you won't reach them before morning...."

The soldier scowled. He rubbed a finger up and down his long nose and stared sulkily at Lyrec. Finally, he turned and hurried out the door.

Grohd whooped in delight. "Where's that cat of yours? I

want to give him the biggest bowl of grynne he's ever seen. I'll give him a keg of it."

Borregad came out from the shadows and leapt onto the bar. He sat expectantly.

"By Voed's black beard, I've always wanted to see them bested. They were going to kill you, you poor fat pussycat"— he tugged at the cat's ear—"d'you know that?" He glanced at Lyrec, noted the rueful inward look in those black eyes. "What's the matter with you?"

Lyrec shook his head. "I'm sorry we had to do that. I was hoping to get them out of here somehow."

"Well, you did get them out."

"No. In a day or two when we're gone, this one at least will be back. I'm afraid of what he'll do, even with a broken arm. At the very least he'll burn down all of your buildings. I could see it in his mi—his eyes. You must know that."

Grohd stood mutely and considered this for a time. Softly, he said, "Well, we'll see. We're a tough people, we Seca-melaneans. No one comes around burning our homes without a fight." He reached under the bar and brought out his small double-bladed throwing axe. Hefting it, he said, "I can take off his ear from across the room with this. We'll see who gives and who gets."

The door opened and Abo entered nervously. He had wrapped a piece of brown linen around his wrist. He skirted Lyrec as he came up beside the table where Fulpig lay.

Lyrec said, "Here, I'll help you load him."

Abo took a step back. "Forget it," he said. "I can carry him myself." He rolled Fulpig over, placing a dangling arm around his neck then hoisting the body up. But Fulpig's dead weight dragged him down, and both bodies disappeared beside the table with a thud. Grohd snickered.

Lyrec moved around the table and pulled the unconscious body off Abo. He waited for the youth to stand, then helped to drape the body over Abo's shoulder. Lyrec held the door open while Abo lumbered out with his burden.

"They'll be back," Lyrec muttered. He had heard it in the boy's mind, too. How long? he wondered, how many? Silently, he addressed the cat: *Borregad, you stupid drunken oaf.* He sat down and removed his hat. "What happened to dinner, Grohd?"

The bald taverner replaced his axe and moved off to gather bowls and utensils.

Lyrec looked to Borregad. *I'm sorry. It wasn't your fault, I'm sure. I just wish we could avoid trouble.*

Noble sentiment. But we're here to find trouble, remember? It's not the same.

It is. They're mortals. They're more like Miradomon than they are like you or me. Furthermore, we didn't come here to save lives, to save their world. We came here for revenge. And that makes us all the same.

No. It's different.

Borregad's blue eyes closed. *We'll see.*

♭Chapter 4.

THE moon was creeping above the trees when the coach rattled and bucked across the rutted tavern yard. The coach made a "J" at the end of the yard and drew up outside the stable. Grohd and Lyrec came out of the tavern before the coach had quite stopped. Grohd's lips parted in a wide grin as he saw Reeterkuv, the driver, atop the coach, handing down luggage.

"We'll have good times tonight," he promised Lyrec. "The stories you'll hear . . . Reeterkuv can keep you laughing all night with his tales about the people who've ridden on his coach. Ask him to tell you about the fat woman and the cheeses!"

The coach was little more than a box on four wheels, drawn by four horses. No ornamentation or scrollwork added to its frame. The windows were drapeless holes. It creaked and rocked as the passengers disembarked. They seemed gray in the twilight, like statues. A peculiar silence hung over the scene. People getting off coaches usually made a great deal of noise: they cursed their aching backs, or grumbled about the horrible roads, or praised the driver for getting them to their destination alive. These people might have had no tongues. They said nothing. Nor did they acknowledge their companions. They took their luggage as Reeterkuv handed it down and they walked in silence toward the huts.

Something had happened. Grohd had no idea what, but it had to have been very bad. Thank goodness, he thought, that Reeterkuv was driving. Grohd would learn the truth, the story, in a moment. He waved to his old friend.

And Reeterkuv ignored him. The tavernkeeper gave Lyrec a troubled look, and began unharnessing the lead horses. He shot glances at Reeterkuv, but could not catch the driver's attention. They might never have met before. Grohd sighed. His breath, a cloud, rose into the night.

Lyrec worked on the wheel horses. The driver was right above him. He saw the man's chiselled features drawn tight, making a skull of his face. Lyrec said, "Certainly is cold," then waited, looking up, forcing an answer.

Reeterkuv glared at him. He flexed his stiff fingers. "Aye," he answered. His voice creaked like dry leather. "A chill on tonight." He glanced quickly at Grohd, then climbed down the opposite side of the coach and was lost from view behind it.

"He seems to have run out of stories," Lyrec commented.

Grohd muttered under his breath as he led away his two horses. Lyrec took the other two by the rings in their bits and followed behind. Together, the two men put the horses in their stalls. Lyrec went down the row and closed the doors on the stalls, then waited near the stable door. Grohd poured feed grain from a dark coarse sack into the trough beside each door. His disgruntlement was apparent in the way he slung the sack and strewed the grain in and over the troughs. He mumbled about the passengers, that they were "lively as corpses," and he called Reeterkuv an ingrate for keeping the account of it— whatever it was—to himself. By the time he had roped off the neck of the sack, Grohd had decided that Reeterkuv was no longer his friend and would no longer be welcome in *his* tavern.

He turned to go, gesturing to Lyrec—now, there was a fellow you could depend on—to go on ahead of him. They both moved one step toward the doorway and stopped at the same time.

There stood Reeterkuv, leaning against the doorjamb. His head was bowed, though he looked at Grohd. He spoke suddenly, his creaky voice a whisper. "I didn't *think* you'd heard."

"Heard what?" Grohd had forgotten he was angry with his friend.

"About the king."

"What are you talking about?" Grohd demanded.

"Grohd . . ." Reeterkuv tried to smile. "Ah, Grohd, let's go have a drink together. For the sake of the act, what d'ya say?"

"Reeterkuv! What's the matter with you? What about Dekür?"

"Dekür. The king's been murdered. His daughter's taken—disappeared." He pushed back from the doorjamb and began to rub his palms together to warm them, then became aware of what he was doing, stopped and looked down into his hands. "They're goin' to crown the boy." He turned away then; the sound of his footsteps scraped across the yard like shovels catching the last toss of dirt for a grave. A few moments later the tavern door slammed shut.

Dinner did not go well.

Before the food was even finished the argument began. Two of the passengers, a young man wearing a physician's medallion and an older, bellicose, red-faced man, began bickering at one another, and it soon became obvious that this was a continuation of an argument begun during the journey. The older man announced to the room at large that the king's death was so unnatural that no one but the Kobachs could be responsible. Then he leaned back in his chair and waited with folded arms. Tension rippled through the room like waves of heat.

Lyrec looked at the foul-tempered man uncomprehendingly. He looked at Grohd across the bar, expressing his question without words. Grohd frowned and shook his head. Some people were like that, what more could he say?

"Idiot!" The word cracked the silence. The red-faced man had been waiting for it; he had already leaned around in the chair to face his adversary. The young physician drew himself halfway across his table. "How blind can you possibly be? The king came out of Ukobachia that very morning—where he had visited his father. His *father*, damn you. How many times must I shove the facts under your nose? Do you mean to tell me that Ronnæm was in on a plot to murder his own son and kidnap his granddaughter?"

The other, though he had stirred the conflict, spluttered and grew redder still in anger. "Of course not, you young fool! Just because he lives there doesn't mean he has to know what goes on. They plotted behind his back."

In the far corner of the room, Reeterkuv put his head down on his table and crossed his arms over it; the old woman sitting by herself in the opposite corner looked down at the floor in disgust; and the florid man's own wife took her drink and very quietly crept from the table to sit farther back by herself. She tossed her husband a black look.

The physician tapped the side of his head. "Your brain's gone feeble. You should move to Trufege, old man, where they're all as dim-witted as you. A child drowns in a creek—the Kobachs caused it. The crops wither from a summer drought—the Kobachs pulled down the sun to scorch their fields."

"What about last winter's plague, eh? The rats from the forest? *That* was Kobach work. Everyone knows it."

The young man fingered his medallion. "Tell me, you dung-minded imbecile, do you have some idea what this represents? What it means? It means I'm a physician—I had to tell you, I couldn't wait all day for an answer. And as a physician I study and treat illnesses—including plagues. So let me tell you something, let me push some knowledge through those ears of yours—"

The old man began to make loud snoring sounds.

"—Let me give you some fact instead of myth!" His angry voice rose into a yell. "A hundred years ago the same plague slew the Bracknils, wiped out an entire tribe!"

The other sat up straight in his chair and pointed an accusatory finger. "That wasn't rodents!"

"So what?"

"And it wasn't in Boreshum—it was in the south, around Lake Raen."

"Exactly." The physician smiled in triumph. "Disease is natural. It happens in different times, in different places, for different reasons—all of them natural!" He slammed his fist on the table. *"No magic."*

The red-faced man's lips crimped together. "So what? That's disease, that's Trufege—"

"Where you ought to live."

"But that's no answer for the king. Dekür didn't die of plague. He died with his own sword hammered through him. He was burned. All his men were dead save the one rider who escaped to tell the tale, and they say he's gone mad. His daughter is gone without a trace, and not one clue as to the identity of the murderers. Tell me that's natural, O wise man of medicine."

"Well, obviously that's the work of Kobachs," the physician agreed sarcastically. "How could anyone doubt it?"

The other man missed the irony of the physician's voice. "Well," he said happily, "there you are, boy. That's what I've been trying to tell you."

"You stupid old hoarhead."

"You're *both* fools," rang out another voice. The old woman, sitting alone, had heard all she could tolerate. Her puffy eyes glittered with anger. "You know nothing. Neither of you. Why don't both admit that and have done with it? And leave the rest of us to our misery and prayers. Stop screaming about it." Her voice trembled. She looked away, and covered her face with one hand.

Reeterkuv stood up to leave. He paused by the door, however, and looked back upon the room. "I have an idea," he said with soft sarcasm. "Why don't you get a cymrallin and you can set it all to music." He nodded to Grohd and Lyrec. "Begging your pardon, forgive me for delivering such a pestilence into your house. I'm going out to be with my horses, where there's some sense to be found." He closed the door quietly. The wife of the red-faced man fled the room.

The others watched her leave, then, one by one, followed her. The old woman left behind her a full bowl of stew. A cold skin covered its surface. She hadn't taken a single mouthful.

Grohd sighed heavily when the last of them had departed. He went around the bar and began clearing off the tables. In the back room, the cooking fire played shadow-ghosts on the walls. Lyrec stared through the doorway with unfocused eyes, and the shadow-ghosts seemed to him to be dancing figures.

Grohd kept silent and he returned to his stool behind the bar. He stroked Borregad. The cat had somehow managed to remain asleep despite the charged atmosphere. His lips smacked, then his mouth opened and his tongue unfurled in a long yawn. He sighed back to sleep.

"Grohd," Lyrec said. "Tell me something. There was a word that came up just now which I—"

"Kobach?"

"Yes."

"Aye, that's not surprising. They're sort of a special case. A village disliked and distrusted by half of Secamelan, though the king's father lives there and the king's wife grew up there."

"But the way they said it. There's a stigma on the word itself."

"Yes. It means 'witch' or 'sorcerer.' Ukobachia's a village of witches."

"Witch." He let the word sink in. "Why are they so hated?"

"That I'm not so sure of. There's a legend that the Kobachs were a tribe that wanted too much power. They wanted the secrets of the world, of the gods. So Voed decided that since they wanted to know those secrets so much, they could have them, but they'd pay for them by being forever suspect by all other tribes."

"And are they?"

"By some. The king, though, didn't believe it. There was a lot of noise about the kingdom when people found out what he'd married."

"You mean 'whom'?"

"No. What. She was a witch. People thought there'd be trouble between the king and the Hespet, the oracle-priest of Voed's temple. But there wasn't. Seems the Hespet didn't believe in witches, either. Some people still think the Kobachs are trying to take over. You hear all kinds of stories. None of 'em has ever come to pass. I stopped listening years ago."

"And that other place? Trufege?"

"Trufege's the nearest town to Ukobachia. They're always saying the witches did this, the witches did that. They blamed this plague they had on the Kobachs, too. But the Hespet looked into it, found that they'd desecrated Voed's temple and broken with the church. Their priest died in the plague, so the Hespet sent them a new priest, and that one—ho—that one's a fanatic, a raving madman if half the stories are true. He has them kissing the ground first thing in the morning and shouting praises to the sky at night, burning down trees inhabited by demons and throwing away good grain if he says it's impure. Impure— now, what can he possibly mean? He says the plague was the gods' punishment to the village of heathens. And they're all agreeing with him. They're all out of their minds."

"You know a great deal of what goes on in this kingdom, don't you, Grohd?"

He gestured modestly. "Well, if you want to find out news, try a tavern. The fellow who pours the drinks has heard everything worth hearing."

"So I see. What else can you tell me of your country?"

"Well, let me think." And he pondered, opening the pathways to his thoughts and recollections. He looked at Lyrec, drawn by the feeling that he was being watched intently, looked up into eyes of silver. He continued to stare for some time, while a thousand bits of information were read and replicated. Then the eyes were black once more.

Lyrec took his hat from the bar and placed it on his head. "Never mind, Grohd, I think it's time for me to say goodnight. And thank you."

"Lyrec," murmured the taverner. He turned a laggard half-circle and shuffled into the back room. A large blanket swung down behind him to cover the doorway.

Lyrec shook the fat black cat. "Wake up, Borregad."

The cat's blue eyes opened, but rolled around independently of one another, and quickly closed. "Uhh, my head is cracking."

"Shh! It's time to go back to the loft. Everyone's gone to sleep except us."

"But we don't sleep."

"That's a remarkable observation coming from someone who's done nothing else all day."

The cat raised his head with great delicacy into an imperious pose. His eyes remained shut. "A stupor is not the same as sleep. It's the fault of this ghastly beast that I've become. Ooh." His head lowered.

"And how would you know all this? You've never remained in mortal form for half this long before. How do you know if you and I sleep or not?"

"Why do you have to ask me so much? Why do you taunt me so? Can't you let me be? Go away and pine for Elystroya or . . . I'm sorry. That wasn't supposed to be spoken. I didn't mean it."

Lyrec's lips pinched tight, but his anger was brief. "Of course not. I know."

"Anyhow, you shouldn't grieve for her yet. She's still alive somewhere." When Lyrec made no answer, the cat opened one eye. Lyrec was staring down at the bar. "She is alive," Borregad insisted, mustering all the belief he could into his voice. "You've told me so yourself."

He was silent for a moment, then said, "Odd, isn't it, Borregad—that both of us think of her as *her*."

"Here she would be a feminine principle."

"Is that so, do you think? Perhaps. . . . Anyway, come on."
He started away.

The cat sank back. "Nooh. Leave me here. If I move, I'll
be sick, I swear."

"Borregad, my dependable ally. All right. Sleep here. But
I tell you now you've had the last grynne you'll taste in this
lifetime."

"Ennh," the cat replied.

He was asleep by the time the tavern door latched.

Chapter 5.

THE Hespet, Slyur, knelt on one knee. His head hung low—an amber fleece-covered egg that protuded through the blue web-work of his robe on a skew neck. The robe was draped over his body like a sea-soaked fisherman's net on an ancient piling.

The words he spoke meant little to the small clustered family. They knew that he was petitioning Anralys, the goddess of health and of beauty, in her own language, asking her to cure the scrawny girl who lay at the Hespet's feet.

Slyur lifted aside the child's rough skirt, revealing a thin and unwashed leg. A rancid yellow crust stuck in places to the skirt, broke off crisply when he tugged, and a thin pus seeped out. The wound was a purple crescent, raw, ugly. A gangrenous odor poured from under the skirt. Slyur cringed and tried not to vomit, pressing his tongue against the roof of his mouth.

The child, no more than four, had been playing in the fields where her father and brothers worked. And while her brother swung a scythe too large for him to wield, she had sneaked up impishly behind him. A surprise. A slip. And the scythe had opened her thigh to the bone.

Slyur looked into the girl's fevered eyes. She was dying. Nonetheless, he held up his good arm and made signs in the air, calling upon the goddess to renew the child's life, to make

43

her whole. He saw the girl's eyes follow the movements of his
right arm. Slyur smiled crookedly to her and ended his prayer.
He held the stump of his right wrist nearer her face.

"I lost my hand when I was your age. A scythe took it—
just like your leg. And I lived." He doubted she understood
him, but went on, "So you see, child, there is hope." All lies,
but harmless enough.

"Sleep now," soothed the Hespet. He touched her puffy
eyelids closed.

Prayers ended, Hespet Slyur stood, knee-joints popping.
This capricious weather would be the death of him. Perhaps
he would become like the last Hespet and refuse ever to leave
the temple. He drew marks of blessing in the air before each
of the family members present, then backed out of the hut. In
the shadow of the doorway he found another child staring up
at him, and Slyur caught his breath. She was identical to the
girl he had just prayed over. She looked at him as if she could
see _into_ him. Suddenly she drew near enough to take his blue
net robe in her hands. She kissed a strand and said, "My sister
will die, won't she?"

Slyur started to answer, but the lie caught in his throat. She
seemed so calm. He grimaced and hurried through the doorway.

The ground beyond sparkled where early morning sunlight
had not yet melted thin pockets of ice. Slyur plunged blindly
through these; they cracked easily. His feet splashed in chill
water beneath the ice, but he barely noticed.

He passed one of his mounted escorts close enough that his
abruptness made the man's horse shy. The door swung back
on his coach. He tumbled in and called, "Take me back," to
the driver. "This instant!" The coach lurched forward. Slyur,
magistrate of all the priests in Secamelan goggled back at the
conical hut through the window of his ornate coach and hissed
in fear.

From behind him came a wintry voice: "Frightened of children, is it?"

Slyur jolted against the door. The violence of his reaction
nearly pitched him from the coach. His uninvited passenger
sneered, revealing sharp ebony teeth. The figure was painful
to look at. It wore armor of blinding alabaster fire; the hair of
its beard and brows was white flame. Its eyes were shrunken
blood oranges.

"Ch-Chagri," Slyur stammered, " Great God, I didn't expect you *here*."

"Slyur . . . I'm everywhere. I appear in chapels and temples to please priests. It suits me to be convenient."

The Hespet recovered himself somewhat and tried to slide casually from the doorway to his royal velvet cushion. "Yes," he said, "of course. It's simply that for years I prayed to you— to all of you—and never a sign. I know that I'm no great visionary, not like the oracle in Spern—"

"That oracle is a madman and a liar."

"What?" He almost cried out "heretic!" but caught himself. This was a god here, a god of war. What was he thinking to call the god of war a heretic? Though his voice cracked, Slyur managed to say, "Is—is he?"

"Yes. But we tolerate him, knowing that he can't help what he is. He believes that he speaks with us. Just as you do, Slyur." He laughed, a sound to churn bowels. "Nonetheless, disbelieve *anything* that fool tells you."

"I will, yes," replied the Hespet. But he was recalling how that oracle had foretold of a great and frightening power that was soon to cross Slyur's path. That had been months before Chagri first appeared to him, shortly after the plague of Trufege.

"So, a child frightened you—ha, you mortals. . . ."

"She looked into my mind! She knew her sister would die."

"Of course she did. She's the other's twin. Or," added the silvery figure, "is it witchcraft you suspect her of?"

"Witchcraft? Preposterous." He could not help himself from going on. "There are no witches! It's all fabrication."

Chagri smiled blackly. "Come, come. We know better, you and I. We know what's in your soul. You believe in witches like most people believe the sun will come up, so deeply is it carved in you. How much of you is witch, do you know, Slyur?"

The priest had grown pale. His teeth drew blood from his lower lip.

"Don't worry, Slyur. Who would I tell? I have more important business with you. The gods wish to act on your mortal plane once more, Slyur. Your king is dead, murdered—an act so detestable that even the gods loathe it and cannot sit still. You represent us. I've chosen you to act for us."

"Of course, of course. What would you have me do?" He

straightened himself proudly, so overcome that he scarcely considered what the request might be.

"It's a simple thing. The priest you have placed in Trufege..."

"The one you told me to dispatch there."

"I want you to send a message to him to gather the people of his town together and lead them to Ukobachia."

"To the... witches?"

"Precisely. To the witches."

"Why, lord?"

"Because the Kobachs slew your king."

It was a moment before the impact of this hit Slyur. Then he cried out, "But that's not possible, they—"

"You argue with me?" A sizzling skeletal hand emerged from the glowing figure, reached across the cushion and grabbed Slyur's empty wrist. Pain shot through the priest and he shrieked and flailed his arm until he had jerked free. He closed his good hand over the heavily scarred stump.

"I am Chagri, Slyur, and you'd do well to reacquaint yourself with that fact. I speak for all the gods. And you will obey me."

Slyur bowed his head. "Of course. I didn't mean—it was the surprise."

"Surprise.... If you'd think for yourself you'd know the king's death was no act of common assassins. It was unnatural."

Slyur tucked his throbbing wrist beneath his robe. "But how would I know that? The men sent by Cheybal haven't returned with the body yet. I've heard the report from the survivor, no more than that—"

"—Who mentioned soldiers that couldn't be killed."

"He was out of his head, lord. Feverish."

"He was *not!*" The god's armor smoldered. The light it cast off intensified, and Slyur protectively averted his eyes. He swallowed nervously.

"He spoke the truth," the god continued. "Right at this moment, the body of Dekür is in Atlarma. Go look at it, see for yourself. You'll send out your messenger. I know. And as a favor to you, Slyur—tell one of your escorts to go back to that farm. Have the child brought to my temple and placed upon my altar. I'll see that she is made whole."

Slyur whirled around. "Lord, that would..." He was talking

to an empty coach. The light that hurt his eyes came from the bright morning sunlight that streamed in through the coach door opposite.

He withdrew his arm from beneath his robe. It burned in a prickly way. He began to rub his hand delicately over the stump. This feathery sensation made the pain an almost rapturous ache. He performed it without any awareness of doing so; he had done it since childhood, whenever the arm hurt. He had come to associate the feeling with solace and peace of mind.

Slyur had joined the priesthood to escape his father and older brothers. He had adapted to the loss of his hand; yet, his family still expected him to push a plow and wield a scythe. If he failed to satisfy them he went hungry. He went hungry often.

So he had run away to become a willing acolyte in the brotherhood of Voed. Ironically his remaining hand saved him. He became the illuminator of manuscripts for the priests of Voed. His intricate filigree and sweeping strokes adorned volumes throughout Secamelan. He became irreplaceable. But Slyur had joined the priesthood out of need and, though he learned the litanies well, he believed in none of the dogma. Men had injected too much of their own character into the gods. The gods were reduced—if gods they were—to men.

Slyur was shrewd enough not to mention this to anyone. He understood too well the politics of his new-found home.

Keeping to himself, working scrupulously and passionately, he had moved steadily through the ranks to become the Hespet in his forty-first year. Slyur the silently self-professed iconoclast headed the worshippers of Voed, the order of Chagri, and the sisterhood of Anralys. He accepted the honor without false pride—without the pretentious lust that marked the fools who abounded in the priesthood, whom he counselled every day. Lacking the vanity of their fanaticism, Slyur had learned to play a political game of religion better than any of them. His "visions" were calculated and rehearsed performances; they furthered his goals. Slyur's theological skepticism did not interfere—until Chagri arrived.

One night, as the Hespet sat alone in his bare chamber enduring the "hour of pious petition," the god had simply ap-

peared. Slyur had leaped from his bed and toward the door.
His fingers stretched for the rope handle to open it. But he
found himself unable to reach the rope, to flee or to cry out.
A bewildering calmness settled over him. He turned back and
sat on his bed. Sweat poured from his face. His eyes were wild
with terror. But he sat quietly.

Chagri had begun to speak. The god knew his every thought,
related his own unspoken uncertainties to him. Slyr found himself on his knees and begging forgiveness. The god informed
him that begging would do no good; Slyur would have to find
a way of proving himself.

Since that first meeting Chagri had required only one act of
him; that he send Varenukha—a raver in the priesthood whom
Slyur detested—to Trufege as their new priest. Slyur had agreed
easily, in part because Varenukha's appointment seemed fitting
justice against the idiots in that village.

But now this second command . . . to send Varenukha and
Trufege against the Kobachs. Varenukha would welcome the
opportunity; Trufege would bathe in their neighbors' blood.

Slyur shook his head. How many more vile acts would he
have to perform to satisfy . . . to satisfy whom? There was the
question that haunted Slyur.

Who was Chagri?

All Slyur knew for certain was that Chagri—imposter or
not—would kill him with a touch if angered. And Slyur, no
zealot, had no wish to play the martyr. He was forty-five, older
than most men in Secamelan. He intended to live twice that
long. There were just some things he would have to do. Right
now there was a little girl whose life he could save. A decent
act . . .

Slyur leaned out the window of his carriage and signalled
to his escort.

Through every passage and room in the castle of Atlarma
sounded the deep, sonorous phrases of a melancholy dirge. The
disembodied voices that sang the lament were especially loud
here in the room where the body rested in state. Painted can-
vases had been stretched across the windows. Torches burned
on either side of the door.

The body of Dekür lay on a red catafalque. A thin candle
burned at each corner. The hilt of his sword still protruded

from his chest. No amount of force had been able to withdraw it from the congealed wound. Instead, grimly, the blade had been snapped off where it jutted through his back.

A short, trim man stood over the body of Dekür, his hands held stiffly at his sides, his bearded chin pressed against his leather collar. Cheybal, leader of Secamelan's armies. "What has happened?" Cheybal asked the corpse. "Who committed this act? If you would just open your eyes, Dekür, and tell me who to condemn, who to call 'enemy.'" He waited as if expecting his words to revive the corpse.

Cheybal recalled something he had said to Dekür one evening when the two of them were staggeringly drunk. "The unknown," he had proclaimed, "is a thing you can never prepare for, and it is also the single thing you *have* to prepare for." A drunkard's epigram. They had both laughed. But he had been right and here was the unknown, revealed in its true colors: Dekür dead, Lewyn gone, and Cheybal floundering as temporary sovereign of Secamelan. All problems, however irrelevant to matters at hand, would eventually come before him. His answers had to be the correct ones. No one ruled above him any longer to certify or refute his wisdom.

He hated being king.

Soon enough, though, that would change, and Tynec, at eight years of age, would be thrust into that terrible position. . . . Unless they could find Lewyn. Cheybal held little hope of doing so. Her abductors had gone like ghosts, departing with the dawn to some world beyond this one. So where was he supposed to look for her? Where on Voed's noble world? Where?

The candles around the catafalque flickered. The body seemed to move as their light wavered, bringing abrupt shadows. Cheybal tensed. Someone had opened the door to this vast and empty hall. He turned to see Tynec standing alone inside the door. Cheybal's mouth went dry. Who had let Tynec in here? He must not witness this awful scene. Cheybal wanted to shield him from it, but he could not make himself move between the boy and the corpse. It was, he thought, too late now.

Tynec stared fixedly at the body of his father as he moved closer. His face was set hard against stirring horror; he hadn't known what to expect; the phrase "your father is dead, boy" had somehow passed right by him without giving him any inkling of its meaning.

He chose not to look at the body lying on its candlelit platform. His gaze shifted quickly to Cheybal, but the man seemed aghast; no comfort for him there. Tynec stared instead at the gleaming sword hilt that from where he stood projected like a lustrous silver phallus above the toes of the boot soles of the body. The echoes of the chanted dirge roared in his ears.

He slowly approached till he could see the hands of the body, folded beneath the hilt of the sword. He glanced finally toward his father's face and could not look away. He found himself drawn along the side of the funeral stand until he stood beside the closed eyes of his father.

"Your father is dead, boy." The meaning stabbed him at last. The hardness of his expression crumpled and his face screwed up to hold back the tears, but they came anyway, rolling softly down his cheeks. He sniffled, but did not wipe them away.

He had forgotten that Cheybal was there across from him. "Father is dead," he whispered. His throat ached as he swallowed.

"You're the king now, Tynec," Cheybal said. "There's much we have to do, you and I." He regretted saying it instantly. How much weight could the boy bear?

Tynec made no reply.

Cheybal thought of himself, moments before, wanting Dekür to awaken and sit up. He waited patiently and said no more.

The dirge ended and began again.

Cheybal found Tynec staring at him. "There's a lot to be done," the boy said, echoing him. "We'd better go."

Silently Cheybal led the way.

At the door, they were met by the Hespet Slyur. The priest momentarily blocked the doorway while catching his breath. He looked past them even as he greeted them, to the red-draped block and its lifeless burden. He allowed the man and boy to pass him, mumbled some respectfully sympathetic comment, then closed the door. Gathering his robe in his one hand, he hurried across the room.

The hilt of Dekür's sword cast scintillas of light as Slyur neared the foot of the catafalque. The sword hilt unnerved him. Why hadn't someone removed it? How could they leave it there like that? Disgusting thoughtlessness, letting the boy see his father that way. Awful.

Slyur spread his arms wide. He began to whisper a death oblation that Mordus would accept the spirit of the king and lead it across the crimson bridge to eternal Mordun. He paused and noticed that the dirge had stopped.

The candles flickered and the torches died for an instant. A shadow passed over the king. Slyur, thinking someone had come in, glanced over at the door. No one was there; the door remained closed. When he faced the body again, the head was turned to the side. Its eyes were open and milky. They pierced him with their glazed stare. Slyur cried out. He stumbled back, his hand out to block the sight of those eyes. He tripped over his own feet and sprawled on the cold stones. He scrabbled to the wall, then pressed against it to inch himself up. His cheek scraped against the rough, unfinished rock. He whined and looked over his shoulder, expecting to see the body sit up, slide down and come for him.

Eyes closed, Dekür lay solemn in death. Slyur pushed his hand against the pounding of his heart. Sweat broke out like a rash across his body. He suddenly vaulted, froglike, for the door. There, he looked back one final time; the body had not moved.

"See for yourself." The words of Chagri came to him like a rustle of dry leaves on a wintry breeze. Slyur opened the door and hurried out in search of a messenger.

The dirge began again.

♭Chapter 6.

I<small>N</small> the tavern yard the only sound was the jingling of bridles as Reeterkuv moved among his horses. He patted an impatient bay and murmured his assurance that soon they would be going, as soon as he had his breakfast. He ducked beneath the wagon tongue and checked the harnesses on the lead horses. The next trip could only be an improvement, he thought. By the time he returned from Miria with new passengers, the death of the king would be old news. Most probably the people who would ride with him on his return northward would be on their way to see the boy given the crown.

He did not know exactly what it was that made him pause in his thoughts. Something caught his eye and drew his attention to the dark road. He listened, but heard no sound.

As he began to turn away, the first of the riders appeared out of the shadows on the road. The second one, wearing a shiny helmet, was right behind him. Then a third. They came on at a steady, purposeful canter. Soldiers! Reeterkuv squinted until he could make out for certain the color of their tunics. His eyes widened.

He turned and ran.

Grohd stood over the cauldron. In one hand he held a huge wooden spoon and stirred the pudding slowly. In the other hand he balanced a stack of wooden bowls. As Reeterkuv burst through the door, the carefully balanced bowls tipped from his palm into the yellow concoction with a splatter. He managed to retrieve one of them. The rest sank quickly, and the pudding erupted. Grohd swung around, furious. Then he saw the expression on Reeterkuv's face.

"Soldiers!" shouted Reeterkuv. He flung the door shut behind him. "Orange, Ladomantines! On the road right now. They're coming." He found the presence of mind to address his passengers calmly then. "If you've got valuables—money, anything you treasure—give them to Grohd to hide."

The people hurried to the bar and began to pour out the contents of their pockets and bags. The short beefy-faced man bawled out, "My money's in the hut, beside my bed. In my satchel!" He started for the door, but Reeterkuv caught him with one hand and jerked him to a stop.

"You don't go out. If that's where your money is, then it's gone. That's a pressgang I saw and you could be farming Ladoman muck tomorrow. D'you understand?" He released his hold on the short man. "All of you. Whatever they want, you give it to them. Isn't that so, Grohd?"

The keeper looked at the coins and rings and bracelets piled on his bar. The young physician had removed his medallion and put it on the pile. "That's right," Grohd answered. Then he glanced meaningfully at Lyrec, recalling what the stranger had said to him the night before.

Lyrec, with money stuffed in his pouch, had not moved or spoken. A shiver ran up Grohd's spine as dark eyes met his. For a moment, the breath of a second, they seemed to glow silver. The cat, too, was watching him, as if that black beast shared Grohd's fear, as though it understood that the sounds of horses' hooves rolling like thunder across the yard presaged trouble and death. The tavernkeeper made himself move; he scooped up some of the valuables from the bar and began stuffing them in mugs on a shelf below it.

The tavern door crashed open. It smashed into Reeterkuv, knocking him backward across a table. The door rebounded, its top hinge snapped, and the bottom corner dug into the floor, stopping it barely a hand's width open. Outside someone cursed and someone else sniggered. The door screeched, sending shivers up spines, as it was pushed back.

A short, overly muscular man, a Ladomantine captain, stood

in the doorway, his wet hair plastered against his head and
bunched in a flattened ring where his helmet had sat. His lower
lip protruded in what was meant to be a scowl but looked more
like a pout. One by one, he nailed each person in the room
with his stare; one by one, the passengers looked away. Reeterkuv lay back against the table, not daring to sit up. Grohd
managed to look up as far as the captain's shirt. Lyrec, head
down, seemed oblivious to it all. The captain, satisfied that he
had intimidated them all, swaggered into the room. Three more
soldiers moved into the doorway behind him. One of them,
with his wrist wrapped in dirty cloth, was Abo.

The captain walked to the bar. He stared at Grohd, then
glanced down at the small pile of coins that remained on the
bar. As he reached for them, a double-bladed axe chopped into
the bar top between his hand and the coins. The captain jerked
his hand away. The nail on his middle finger had been neatly
trimmed. His eyes shifted from his hand to the polished axe
and followed the handle back to the hand and arm of the tavernkeeper. The captain looked at Grohd in disbelief. "I'll take
you to pieces," he promised softly, turning away.

"So," he said, to the room at large, and that simple and
meaningless word generated more fear in the group of travellers
than any threat might have done. He paused briefly to enjoy
their terror. Then he moved away from the bar, striding slowly
to each one of them, staring each one in the face. He asked,
"Which of you is responsible for the wounds my men suffered?"
He knew the answer already, but he wanted to watch them turn
on one of their own. The game was to predict who would turn
first. "Well?"

"We don't know what you mean," said the physician quietly.
"What wounds?"

The captain pouted. He swung around, his arm raised to
cuff the physician. At his back, in the cauldron, one of the
wooden bowls popped to the surface. The pudding belched,
flinging free a glob of yellow sputum that smacked the soldier
on the back of the neck. He howled as scalding hot pudding
slid down inside his shirt, raising blisters. He hissed, "So,
you're witches, too, some of you. Which?" He slapped the
physician. "You?" He backhanded the wife of the short fat
man. "Or you?" He strode to Lyrec. "Or is it you, traveller?
You sleep too much. *Look at me, are you deaf?*"

Abo nodded to him: Yes, this is the man.

The feather in Lyrec's hat shimmered as he raised his head. The captain smirked at him. "I know someone just over the border in Ladoman who wants to see you again as soon as possible."

Borregad licked his lips.

Lyrec replied, "I don't know anyone in Ladoman."

"Do you have a horse of your own or do we have to drag you along on foot?"

Lyrec clucked his tongue. "All these questions, and I haven't even had breakfast yet." He idly wiped a splotch of pudding from the captain's tunic. "I see you've had some. Is it hot enough to eat?"

The captain, struck dumb, began to tremble with rage.

Borregad eyed Lyrec fearfully. *What are you doing? You'll get us all killed.*

Probe him, Borregad—he wants them all. I can't let that happen.

We're not here to play hero!

I haven't time to debate this. He's taking me on no matter what happens. If he's mad enough, he may forget the others, and maybe I—

The captain struck him across the mouth.

Borregad scrabbled back. Lyrec seemed not to react to the blow at all. The cat regarded the distance to the door. He wondered how long it would take him to get to the hut, find Lyrec's scabbard, and drag it back here. He didn't think he could do it, and cursed his deformity. Why couldn't he have had a perfect crex to form his own defense? His life-force barely allowed him to maintain form. Damn Miradomon! He was helpless.

The captain placed his hand on the pommel of his sword. "Are you coming with me?"

For a moment it seemed that Lyrec would ignore him again; then he stood and spoke softly, so that only the captain could hear him. "Leave the others alone. You've arrested me and I'll go quietly if you let them be."

"Are you giving me orders?" He looked up into silver eyes that pinned his soul to his skull. The captain's mouth worked silently. Then his voice croaked out of it: "Right, then. You come with us and the rest go free. Outside."

Lyrec nodded and turned. Abo moved in to witness his

captain's unaccountable change of mind. "No," said Abo, "no, it's witchcraft! He made the captain say that. He's *Kobach*."

Lyrec could not control all four soldiers—unlike his race they did not possess communal minds. And he could not control the captain this way for long. With no time to plan further, he walked stiffly across the room like a prisoner. The soldiers parted to let him through as Abo berated them, confusing them long enough for Lyrec to make for the yard. Ladomantine soldiers were not known for their quick wits. The captain fixed glassy eyes on Lyrec's movement and followed languidly after him. Abo stamped the floor furiously, confounding the others all the more—they didn't know who to look to for orders. Borregad dashed between them and out after the captain. Abo railed at them, "Go after him! Protect the captain, you—oh, you idiots!" He shoved his way through them and they followed. Grohd started around the bar. He pried loose the axe, but hadn't taken two steps before one of the soldiers turned back, shook his head, and dragged the door shut.

Reeterkuv and Grohd ran to the windows as someone in the yard shouted.

The captain came awake suddenly to find himself marching along behind Lyrec. He bellowed as he drew his sword. Lyrec had hoped for a few more moments of control, to get to a horse. But now. . . . He ducked as the captain swung a vicious slice at his neck, instinctively struck the captain on the jaw and took the sword from his hand in the same moment. The captain crumpled in the dirt. Lyrec backed toward the center of the yard. The soldiers were no longer confused—their prisoner had become prey.

Abo and another man came at him in a crouch, their swords held up lightly. Another soldier came from around the back of the tavern. Three remained guarding the door to the tavern and, across the yard, beside the coach, the final member of the party sat atop his horse and merely watched. He appeared to be not the least surprised that his captain had gone down—in fact, he looked amused by it. His right hand, crossed over his saddle, rested loosely around the end of a short pole that showed above his saddle pommel. Six men in all. Lyrec stopped counting and took the offensive.

He swung the stolen sword in an arc, desperate to get some feel for it. Obviously it was for swinging and thrusting, but he had never held one before. The balance of it confused him; the minstrel had either never used his or had kept the information locked away with so much else of his knowledge. Lyrec swung the sword at Abo and the other soldier again. They glanced at one another and grinned. They knew. Just from his movements, they recognized his inexperience. He had to get to his crex. His shield had the power to protect him, but it was hanging on a peg in the hut. He would have to get through all six men to reach it. Where was Borregad?

Abo lunged. Lyrec parried as best he could, but his point stuck in the ground for a moment, and the other soldier jabbed at him. He saw his error and barely managed to deflect the sword with the hilt of his own weapon. Abo laughed at him.

"You should never have given us trouble, Kobach. Your magic won't make you a better fighter."

Abo thrust at him again, but this time without force, toying with him. Lyrec swung to block the sword and Abo skillfully withdrew it, making him stumble. "Travellers are the easiest picking, I've discovered," Abo continued. He beat Lyrec's blade aside and could have killed him then had he not wished to finish his speech. "No one ever comes looking for travellers or would know where to look if they did. Where were you last seen? Miria? Is there anyone there who even knows your name?" He whipped his blade under Lyrec's nose. "You should have let Fulpig and me eat and drink."

"You would have killed my cat." He moved back.

"What's the skin of a cat against your life? Today you'll be dead and I'll skin your cat anyway. What did you gain?"

Abo's partner decided to join in the fun. He leaped forward and danced his blade around Lyrec's useless block and into the cape at Lyrec's shoulder. Lyrec twisted away and thudded against one of the horses tethered behind him. The horse snorted and shifted its feet. There were three horses lined up there, with Lyrec pinned against the first.

Abo waved him out from the horses, taking a step back. The game was to go on a little longer. The other soldier glanced around at his friends.

Lyrec grabbed his sword below the knuckle-guard and chucked it as hard as he could. Abo's partner literally walked into it. He clutched it and turned around to the others; he wanted to ask them how this had happened. The hilt bumped against

Abo, knocking the dying man off his feet. Abo looked up at Lyrec. He scowled and jumped forward. Lyrec turned, grabbing the saddle with both hands, and swung himself up and over the first horse. Abo's sword pierced the leather just below its head. The stung horse whinnied and bucked. The soldier's blade was torn from his grip, and he had to fall back to avoid the horse's wild kick.

Lyrec landed atop the second horse. He grabbed the reins and turned the animal away from the tethering post. Where his knowledge of riding came from he did not know, but he did not bother to question it. He wheeled the horse around and took off across the yard.

Even as the animal set forth, the mounted soldier who had sat idly by kicked his own horse into action. His right arm was hidden behind him. Lyrec realized as he passed the man that the pole which had been sticking out of the man's saddle was no longer visible there. He sensed that this was important and reacted on some instinctive level, ducking down. His head seemed suddenly to crack open in white flashing pain and he saw the sky come up in front of him and the world appear upside down. His hat whirled past, the crown curiously dented. He observed it calmly, following its descent to the dirt, where it spun to rest in a rut. He reached out ever so slowly to catch it. . . .

Borregad dragged the scabbard belt to the stairs and started down on two legs with the greatest of difficulty. The hilt and body of the crex hung under his belly. With each step the weight of it threatened to fling him down the stairs.

He cursed Lyrec's self-assurance that had led to his leaving the crex there. It wouldn't be needed, Lyrec had said. The people in the tavern posed no threat at all. Idiot, idiot, oh, Borregad hated him. The first perilous situation that came along threatened to wipe out all they had worked for. What was he supposed to do if Lyrec was killed? He couldn't very well carry out their plans by himself. No one knew how powerful Miradomon was, but he was certainly more powerful than a black cat tripping over a scabbard. Oh, how he hated this—this—

"This f-f-feline thing!" he shouted. What was f-f-feline, anyhow? Where had Lyrec gotten that stupid word? "I'll claw your eyes out, you hear me, Lyrec?" In his anger he took two steps and was pulled over the third by the crex. As he tipped, he dug his claws into the soft wood of the wall and managed to keep from tumbling the rest of the way down. With great care he lifted one hind leg and placed his foot on the next step down and followed it with the other. "What am I going to do? Look at me." His tongue protruded from between his teeth.

Laughter echoed from the yard. It was not Lyrec laughing. Borregad glanced up, panic rounding his eyes. He dragged the scabbard down the remaining steps, hurrying as best he could without falling over it. At the bottom he went back to all fours and tugged himself and the belt out the door.

One soldier stood out from the building with his back to the huts, watching whatever was taking place in the yard. Borregad dragged the scabbard off to one side and behind a tree. From there he peered around at the yard.

Lyrec was in motion, bounding up and over a horse, his legs locked and parallel to the ground. One soldier was down, another—Abo—lunged at Lyrec but stabbed a horse. Then Lyrec reappeared on another horse. Movement to the left caught Borregad's attention. The soldier nearest the coach, himself on a horse, had tugged the reins of his mount and was riding out to meet Lyrec's desperate charge. The soldier drew a short pole from a pocket beside his saddle. The pole had a metal ball on the end of it. Lyrec seemed not to see the weapon. Borregad struggled free of the belt, at the same time shouting a mental warning to Lyrec, but saw the weapon swung up and around in a blur of motion. Lyrec flopped forward against the horse's neck, then back, his hat thrown free. He tipped off the rear of his mount and dropped hard. He did not move.

Borregad pressed back against the tree. Lyrec was dead, he was certain. That horrible metal ball had surely crushed his skull. If only he, Borregad, had stayed with Lyrec, he could have acted as his eyes, warned him, guided him through the various attacks. Now the crex was of no use at all. What could he possibly do with it? As a cat he could not wield it: even if he managed to pull it from the scabbard, he hadn't the right kind of arms to lift and direct it. It was Lyrec's, to be controlled by no one else, part of him. Borregad had no idea what it might do if *he* tried to command it. The thing might kill him. It might even throw him beyond this world!

He peered around the tree again. The soldier with the short pole stood over Lyrec as if to strike him again.

Borregad bounded out of cover, his claws ready; but he
drew up as the soldier turned away and shoved the pole back
in its pocket on his horse. He had seen, guessed Borregad, that
the stranger was dead and therefore did not need to be struck
again.

Two soldiers—one of them Abo—helped the captain to his
feet. He shook off their hands and stumbled over to Lyrec,
then kicked the body in the ribs. Lyrec rolled over and doubled
up to protect himself. *He's alive!* Borregad rejoiced.

"Get him up and tie him behind my horse," bellowed the
captain. He spat at the body, then marched off. As he passed
Lyrec's hat, he paused to stomp on it. The feather snapped
beneath his boot to hang broken from the band.

Standing beside the dead soldier, Abo watched as Lyrec
was dragged past him. "He's a fiend, some kind of sorcerer.
You—we ought to kill him now." He looked with frenzy at
the captain. "Why not kill him right now?"

The captain shook his head. "No, not yet. Fulpig has a
better idea. For now we'll make him hurt." Lyrec's hands were
bound together in front of him. The captain took the rope and
carried it up onto his own horse. The soldier with the pole
picked up Lyrec's hat and crushed it on his head. He slapped
Lyrec to full consciousness. "Get to your feet or the captain'll
drag you on your face. You were a fool to take us on when
you don't even know how to use a sword. When will you
people learn? Get up, his temper's short."

Lyrec swayed on his knees. His head lolled forward, dark
with dirt and the blood that ran from his scalp. He raised his
head to see the captain holding the rope high in preparation to
tying it on the saddle. Lyrec grabbed onto the slack length
leading from his wrists and pulled back, falling onto his side
with the effort. The captain cried out as his arm twisted behind
him and he was hauled off his horse. Lyrec spat blood and
laughed.

Borregad saw what was about to happen and started running
again. He shouted out, "No!" as the pole was raised against
the dawn sky and came down on Lyrec's forearms with a crack.
Lyrec howled.

One of the soldiers, having heard Borregad's shout, looked
back at the cat, then past him, scanning the area for the source
of the sound. The other soldiers lifted their captain onto his
horse and tied the rope onto the saddle for him. He lay against

his horse's mane, mumbling incoherently. The soldier with the pole swung up into his saddle and the other men climbed into theirs.

His face white with pain, Lyrec wobbled up onto his feet. The Ladomantine gang went slowly out of the yard, riding into the rising sun. The rope went taut and Lyrec groaned as his arms were tugged forward. He tripped over the body of the man he had killed and barely managed to remain on his feet.

Borregad looked back at the crex. If he brought it along, he would lose the party of soldiers. But how could he leave it lying in the grass beside the tree? Everything had fallen apart, the simplest bunch of local bullies had ripped up their plans as easily as that. *Damn* Lyrec and his disgusting concern over these semi-sentient creatures. Look where it had gotten them.

He tried to make contact with Lyrec. The only thing that came through was incredible agony, and Borregad quickly severed the connection. They must have broken some part of Lyrec's new body; the pain was unbearable.

Borregad gave the crex one final forlorn look, then hurried off to catch up to the soldiers.

Chapter 7.

SEATED at the one table in his quarters, Commander Cheybal scrawled his name on a curled sheet of vellum. The tip of his long, curved pen was black from a thousand signings. His signature was a temporary seal, potent until the true seal of a new king was stamped molten onto it or until the hands which wore the signet ring tore the document down the middle.

As a rule he found the business of signing documents distasteful, but this particular one gave him pleasure. This paper concerned the rights to the best market stall locations—those just within the entrance to the castle. The old king lay in state, the funeral was tomorrow, and already the vultures vied for position. How effortlessly people lost their veneer of decency when a few coins jingled in a nearby purse.

So Cheybal had solved to his own satisfaction the problem of the market stalls: he had banned them categorically from the yard. The ink of his sharp signature grew pale as it dried. He blotted it, sanded it, cast the sheet of vellum onto a stack of similar sheets and pushed himself to his feet. Perhaps he made too much of the request; why would the people beyond these walls be expected to mourn the week through for someone who had been no more than a figurehead, a name, to them?

They grieved, the moment passed, and they went about their business. The cow still delivered its calf and the fence still needed mending, the lowlands would flood come spring and cold feet would still turn blue in the winter without fires, full bellies, and money.

He rose wearily and walked to a narrow window. Flexing his cramped fingers, he looked down on the low rampart below. Two of his men walked back and forth along the wall, their senses dulled to the dazzling sight of the city sprawling far below along the river, the largest city on the continent. They saw it half a day every day. As the two guards came together, they paused to chat. One gestured wildly for a moment. The sound of their laughter reached Cheybal at his window.

What was the joke? He ached to know, to be down there, bored and unencumbered.

A door closed behind him, curtailing his thoughts.

An old man stood just within the room. His grizzled beard was combed and trimmed, his hair flowed down around his stiff laced collar. His face had been much harder once. Age, and a burden heavier than age, had undermined the sharpness in the face of the man who had once been king.

"Ronnæm," said Cheybal. "Come in, please."

The old man remained where he stood. "I am interrupting your reverie?" he asked simply, with no detectable disparagement.

"No, my lord. I'm resting. A few moments. All of these requests to sign, judgments to weigh."

Ronnæm looked at the stack of cream-colored sheets. A smile crossed his face. "Sit, sit," he said. "This is informal. I am not king anymore, Cheybal."

"Of course," agreed Cheybal. Nevertheless, he remained standing. To sit was to give Ronnæm ascendency. Dekür had warned him of this long ago. During any discussion the old man stood, regardless of how insignificant the matter might be, and always requested most graciously that everyone else sit. In this way if the discussion went against him, he towered above his opponents—the dominant voice, the dominant figure, the victor. Cheybal respected him for his subtlety, but found nothing within that hoary frame to unite them as friends. Even now, after so many years among the Kobachs, Ronnæm was a manipulator.

They might have conducted their meeting like that, facing

off across Cheybal's room, but a knock sounded at the door.
Ronnæm gestured that Cheybal should answer.

"Yes," Cheybal said in a voice that implied "enter."

The heavy wooden door opened and one of his captains,
Faubus, stepped in. Faubus closed the door perfunctorily, caught
sight of the old man as he did so, and immediately came to
attention. Ronnæm nodded and extended his hand. He and the
captain clasped forearms, then the old man glanced at Cheybal.
"To be honest, Commander, I confess that I heard of this
meeting and would like to be party to it. Living where I do
these wintry days, I thought I might be able to add to your
discussion things which neither of you could know. Why don't
you have a seat, Captain?"

The young captain moved stiffly to a chair and sat down.
Cheybal stifled his anger. "Captain," he said, "forgive me for
not speaking to you sooner, but the affairs of state have taken
all my time the past days."

How odd, thought Faubus, that the commander should be
apologizing. Then he realized that the statement, although spoken at him, was not spoken for his benefit. He caught the
whisper of contention, the echo but not the words.

"My main concern," Cheybal continued, "is how you found
things in Boreshum."

"In what regard, sir?"

"In all regards. All of it."

The commander's gaze bored into Faubus; likewise, Faubus
sensed Ronnæm watching him. He cleared his throat.

"We arrived after dawn. Where the attack had taken place.
Two separate camps were set up along the road. The first that
we rode through was made up entirely of people from Dolgellum. The other camp"—he glanced nervously at Ronnæm—
"was Kobach. It wasn't far from their village, the place, so
they had been the first to arrive by many hours."

"That will add wood to the fire."

"Sir?"

"You should know what I mean, Captain. How many fights
had broken out between the two camps? How many wounded?
And dead?"

"Why, none . . . none, sir. There was some name-calling
from Dolgellum as you'd expect, and little of that. No fights.
The Kobach leader was very . . ."

"—Adamant," interjected Ronnæm.

"—about it. Yes, sir. Adamant," Faubus repeated, as if the word had some magical properties for him.

"That leader being you, I take it?" Cheybal's eyes and only his eyes moved to mark Ronnæm. "You were the first to find the body."

The old king nodded.

"How could you do that?" Cheybal asked harshly. "You've jeopardized your whole village by rushing in like that."

Ronnæm said calmly, "We are discussing rationally something that happened in panic and chaos. Initial reports were that Dekür was under attack—not slain. And do you think that I cared—then or now—what people in other villages would think? This was my *son*, Cheybal." His calm broke abruptly. "Let Mordus suck the marrow from those *other* people!"

They faced one another over the desk, until Cheybal conceded. He pocked the wax tabletop with a fingernail. "Yes, I see, of course. So would I say in your place. But, dear Voed, it'll be a slaughter."

"I think the Kobachs know what's in for them, sir," Faubus said. He meant it sarcastically, but the reaction was not what he expected.

Ronnæm snorted. "Do you think he has something there?" He moved in front of Faubus. Cheybal might have interfered, but chose not to. It would serve the captain well to be served a taste of Ronnæm. "And what is it," asked the old king, "that's in for them? Hmm?"

The captain attempted eye contact with his commander, but Ronnæm blocked his view. "Well," Faubus said, "it was obvious to everyone that the death of the king and his party was . . . odd. His clothes were singed but his body wasn't burned, and the sword, and—"

"Spare us the graphic re-creation if you would, Captain Faubus."

"All I meant to say is that there's talk."

"Always."

"The thrust of it is that the Kobachs were responsible for the king's death."

"Naturally," agreed Ronnæm. "Do you not subscribe to such proposals?"

"No, m'lord, of course not!"

"Good. Then you are the perfect candidate to pick the armed force returning to Ukobachia."

"What?" Faubus went pale.

"If you don't mind," Cheybal interrupted, "at present such policy is my domain." He glowered at the back of Ronnæm's head.

"But you have to send someone." Ronnæm's thin hand circled the air.

"That's obvious."

The old man allowed him a profile, just the right amount of hesitancy, the exact portion of determination. "I could lead them," he said.

So that was it, finally and simply. Cheybal was surprised that he had not seen the motive sooner. "I think," he said, then he paused. "I think that your original notion was best. Captain Faubus is the man for the job. He can handpick men who are least superstitious, and least given to idle speculation." He moved to where he could see Faubus. "You might also point out to your men that it doesn't really make sense to accuse the Kobachs. With Ronnæm leading them it would mean he had chosen to kill his own son—who had embraced and even married into their race. Do you see this father killing his son, Captain?"

Faubus stood. "No, sir. And—and that's just the tack I've taken thus far."

Ronnæm murmured, "You are wise beyond your years."

Cheybal ignored him. "Tell that to your men, Captain. And choose your party with care."

"I will, sir."

"Also, I want you to assign a second group to ride a patrol along the Tasurlak border."

"Tasurlak?"

"If the Kobachs are innocent, then consider who could be responsible. Surely not our ally, Növalok. Ladomirus? For all his intrigues, he could hardly assemble a sufficient force that far north and go unnoticed. So we have two apparent choices. The first is the eastern border, the mountains before Tasurlak. A circumspect army could prowl there unnoticed I believe. The second choice is the forest itself." Ronnæm was nodding. "While you are billeted in Ukobachia, Captain, I want you to take some men into Boreshum and have them scour it for signs of encampment or habitation of any sort."

Faubus fidgeted. He glanced warily at Ronnæm, but the old king was lost in thought, still nodding. "Sir," he said finally to Cheybal, "that might be the most difficult task of all."

"How so?"

"The Kobachs claim the forest is haunted."

Cheybal started to condemn the notion, but the words caught in his throat. He saw suddenly a room in his family's home in Cajia: the chairs, stools, the rug, a fire; the family grouped there, discussing quietly his uncle's unfortunate death. Cheybal was nine. He sat nearest the fire. Something brushed his shoulder and he looked up to see his uncle's ghost pass him as it walked out of the fireplace, through the group that had fallen deathly still and silent, and through the closed door opposite. His first and only ghost—but one was enough. He said to Faubus, "The notions of the Kobachs need not concern us." Faubus still seemed uncomfortable. "Is there something more?"

"Ah . . . no, sir. I'll go now." He turned toward the door.

"Captain. If there is something to be said . . ."

Faubus lowered his head, mumbled something indistinct, then turned. "I thought I saw a ghost there. In the Boreshum wood," he said with effort.

"You thought?"

"I . . . thought."

"Whose ghost did you see? The king's?" Ronnæm's head jerked up.

"No, Commander," answered Faubus. "I—I don't know whose ghost. It was a figure in a hooded robe. Like the oracle at Spern, only the robe was . . . peculiar, white—I can't explain it. The face was hidden all the time, in shadows."

"What did this ghost do?" *His uncle, stepping out of the fire . . .*

"It stood and watched us from the forest."

"How do you know it was watching you if its face was hidden?"

"That was my impression. I could feel it looking at me like you're looking at me now—with all due respect. And the feeling of being watched wasn't mine alone." He glanced sidelong at Ronnæm.

"In that case," Cheybal snapped, "I want all the more that that forest be gone through. Find that white-robed figure or the reason for its presence. Find anyone or anything that dwells out of place in that forest. Cut down every tree if necessary, but find me the answer." He then quickly dismissed his captain.

As the door closed, Ronnæm faced him fully. "Well, we all know where we are standing now, don't we?"

"I knew where I stood before this. Didn't you?"

The old king's mouth pinched tight for a moment. "I hope I haven't interfered here, Commander. I know the task of kingship weighs heavily on those not trained for it. I hope that you will remember I offer you my assistance should the burden become too great. My credentials speak for themselves."

Cheybal cursed him when he had gone and was mortified by the act. He had no reason to bear malice against Ronnæm. But there was something in the man that nettled him, and right now Cheybal had no patience for bickering. Yes, the burden of kingship did weigh heavily. Such petty squabbles! For a chance to lead a small armed force to his village, Ronnæm had maneuvered as if vying for a country. Cheybal wondered how Dekür had ever moved the old man out of Atlarma. He could not recall. Perhaps he had never known. He walked heavily back to the window.

Below the same two guards as before stood conversing in the middle of the rampart.

Cheybal leaned out of the window. "You men there!" They both started in surprise. "That's right. Up here. Both of you stop idling or I'll have you scraping moss off the walls with your teeth!" He withdrew back into his room and began to pace. His fingertips flicked against his thumb.

Kobachs. Ghosts. And whispers of violence, possibly even of war. All on his head; all to be transferred to a child. Ronnæm could dominate the boy, push him into bloody decisions, and even break apart the country he himself had assembled.

Perhaps he had been too quick in his judgment. Maybe he should have let Ronnæm lead the armed party back to Ukobachia—if only to get rid of him. He would have to decide that before Faubus reported back to him. In the meantime he was expected to sit here and judge trifles as if nothing extraordinary had occurred. He slapped the side of the table in an explosion of frustration. The container of ink tipped onto its side. Thick black fluid poured out across the table. Cheybal looked about for a cloth or a sheet of blank vellum. There was none.

He stood and pressed his hands into his armpits as the ink dribbled slowly and spattered on the floor.

* * *

The low sun cast Lyrec's shadow the length of the rope that
stretched out before him like a lifeline. If that was his destiny,
he did not have to look far to see the abrupt end to his future.
Every few steps he stumbled and the rope jerked taut and pulled
him forward again. His wrists were swollen and raw, the skin
had been chafed away long ago. Marsh gnats swarmed like a
simmering black bandage over each wound. The ground had
become spongy hours before, and there was a smell of sulphur
in the air. His boots were sodden and his feet slipped within
them at each step. His legs ached from maintaining balance.

At times throughout 'he day, he had fallen into fevered
fantasies in which he became his original self who merely
observed the plight of this unfortunate humanoid. At any moment he would withdraw from this world and return to his
homeworld of crystal and its faceted blue sun.

His hands swelled and he drifted into a dream where his
body swelled and changed until it was colors and filaments
within the confines of the globular crex. He thought then of
Elystroya and began to weep, though he was unaware of doing
so or of the odd look the soldiers ahead gave him. In his dream
he was united with her again, telling her of all the wondrous
worlds he had seen. But as he spoke to her, the lies disintegrated
and he found himself telling her the truth: he had found no
such living worlds—except for this one, where he was beaten
and tied and dragged behind an animal. The other worlds had
been dead or dying, the creatures who had once populated them
obliterated. The vision of Elystroya broke apart into darkness.

He remembered Caudel then. Caudel, of a race of tall,
spindly humanoids not unlike these but having hard shell-like
patches over their bodies. Caudel, the last of his kind, lay in
the last hour of his life upon an asteroid of his former world.
They found him, Lyrec and Borregad, before the final wisps
of atmosphere drifted away. And, as Caudel died, they lived
inside his thoughts and saw his world reassemble to be destroyed again; saw gods take form and descend from the skies
with armies of nightmarish things out of legend. The war began.
War. Had Caudel been capable, he would have mocked the
term—it hadn't been war, it had been genocide. People of his
race devoured one another in chain reactions of animal violence, ripping one another into unrecognizable flesh. The gods,

having marshalled all sides to their deaths, did nothing but watch. The demonic armies hovered above the fields of battle like seabirds awaiting the leap of a fish. Their world trembled and the ground opened up. Mountains collapsed to be thrown back into the sky by massive explosions as the molten core of the world blasted to the surface. The entire planet burst apart, though it had already died. Only Caudel remained, on a chunk of rock whose atmosphere fell away like a shroud from a corpse, and, moments later, he, too, was gone.

Lyrec and Borregad left him, carrying with them his last impressions of the war—a memory of the many gods rising up, merging into a new being who somehow reabsorbed the wasted energies of the battles and grew with the deaths. It had been this being who had destroyed their world. No gods had ever been there at all. This Caudel had known in his heart, though how he knew remained a mystery. He despaired at how easily his race had been tricked, how quickly they had taken arms and gone to battle for no reason. This most awful of memories did not die with him. Lyrec carried it away, knowing as he did that the ghoulish being had been Miradomon.

Soon a god would descend from the skies into this world— or had he done so already? From Caudel they had learned something of Miradomon's methods—but not enough for them to know where next to look for him.

It hardly mattered now, Lyrec thought. He, the great survivor of an extinct race, had been reduced to the level of these creatures—an animal, a killer. The notion made him close his eyes and hang his head. He would never find Miradomon. Elystroya would never be avenged.

He lagged behind; the rope jerked tight, snapping him out of his dream and into the reality of raw flesh and pain. The captain, feeling the sudden tension on the rope, laughed and looked over his shoulder with cruel joy. Lyrec concentrated on hating that man, promised himself one more death before they slew him—then was repelled by the desire. He had indeed become human. The human mind of this body he had created tainted his every thought and word and deed. The serene being he had once been was no more. By choice he had left it on the other side of a monstrous hole that had opened between his dead homeworld and an infinity of universes where Miradomon walked.

* * *

Not far behind him, a large black cat listened to these thoughts and considered that his friend had much to learn about accepting change. Such introspection was fruitless. What did he have to complain about, anyway? Things could have been far worse for him.

He could have been a cat.

♭Chapter 8.

THE patterned floors in the outer galleries of the temple of Chagri had been swept earlier in the day. The colored tiles were large and smooth, and feet walking across them made a soft, padding sound. But in the central chambers—those around the altar—the floor consisted of large pebbles, and every movement, every shift of weight from one foot to the other, ground the stones together in a grating din that echoed and re-echoed from the high stone walls. Each time the grinding cacophony assaulted him, Slyur winced. He hated the uncomfortable stones under his own feet, but the sound he made was nothing compared to that of the family of the dying girl.

He made them wait in the antechamber while he went alone into the altar room; even so, he could hear them shifting their stances nervously, scared, helplessly handing themselves over to the powers of a god—an incomprehensible god to them, he was sure. Right then he hated them for their stupid, absolute trust.

In the center of the room, flanked by torches, the altar stood at the top of three steps. It was a twice life-size statue of Chagri carved of the purest white *chidsist,* from what must have been the largest block of it ever found. The figure of the god held its shield like an enormous inverted bowl in its hands. Filled with a small pool of water, the shield acted as the altar stone.

Slyur cast a queasy glance at the statue, noting that its expression lacked the loathsome sneer that perpetually adorned the god himself. Nevertheless, Hespet Slyur moved about beneath it with his body hunched up as if the statue were glaring down at him as Chagri always did. He climbed the three steps and looked down into the shield. He dipped his hands into the dark water. This act was supposed to grant one the power of decision—another of Chagri's attested attributes: God of Decisiveness. Slyur admitted to a forlorn hope that some kind of strength would be imparted to him—strength of will most of all. Just once he wanted to make his own decisions and not have circumstance or some demonic being forcing him to turn this way and that, but he did not truly expect to gain the power to take control of his life from the very being who at present manipulated him.

He muttered an invocation, then a few prayers, by rote. He shook his hands out of the water. Falling drops rippled the surface of the water held by the shield. The reflection of the god's face from above took on a cruel smile. The eyes glowed orange for a moment. Slyur looked up in terror.

No. It had only been the torches reflecting in the polished convex eyes. A trick of light.

Slyur wiped his hands on his robes as he returned down the steps. He dismissed the attending priests in the antechamber, who bowed out of the room and went about their various assigned duties. He had told them nothing of what was happening here, and he was certain they would go off and gossip about it. The wide, moist eyes of the child's father drew Slyur's attention. He motioned the farmer to enter the altar room with him, but could not help looking at the girl again, lying unconscious on a rug one of the priests had thrown down for her. Her sister watched him warily, knowingly. Turning away, he practically shoved the farmer through the arch. They crunched to a halt at the base of the three steps. The farmer stood crouched as if expecting a whipping and would not look at the statue.

"Now make your offering to the god," Slyur said.

"What—what do I offer?" the farmer asked.

"Your daughter is worth what to you?"

The farmer looked back at him with pleading eyes. "She is my life."

"Then you should offer—" No! He would not say it, knowing how Chagri would delight in taking the poor simpleton's life in exchange—especially if he could goad Slyur ever after with the knowledge that he, in his priestly role, had inadvertently recommended it. Damned be his white empty soul! "Offer up a calf. Promise to gut it. Bring the blood here for Chagri to drink. Your best calf." The farmer continued to goggle at him. "Well, go on! Every moment your daughter falls deeper into death's well."

He pointed up the stairs and the farmer steeled himself to approach the statue. He started up. The Hespet thought he heard a deep moan, as if something far beneath the floor had begun to awaken. Above him, the statue's smooth eyes watched the farmer bend over the shield and place his hands in the water. Slyur heard the whispers of his prayer. The farmer quickly descended.

Slyur said, "All right. Bring her to me now."

The farmer went out and, after a moment, returned with his daughter held in his still dripping hands. Her head hung back. She might have been dead for all Slyur could tell. The smell of her was rank, like a piece of raw meat that had been left for days in the sun. Her father's face was seamed with misery and despair. He doesn't dare to hope, thought Slyur.

Without getting any closer than necessary, the Hespet reached out with stiff fingers and began unlacing the girl's dress. The farmer had to assist him in removing it, but she weighed practically nothing and he could support her with one hand. Slyur looked askance at her protruding ribs and the hollowness below them. She did breathe, he saw—she was no more than the length of a finger from death, but she did breathe. The Hespet reached and carefully took the girl from her father. The man immediately turned away and fled through the archway to be with his wife and family. The girl's life no longer belonged to him. For a moment, Slyur felt pity.

He turned toward the altar. Torchlight fell across the girl, allowing Slyur to see her wound more clearly. He scowled at it. White maggots crawled within the purple gash. He looked away, and he could feel the worms wiggle onto his arm and move toward his elbow. He bounded up the stairs and nearly hurled the child into the shield before reaching the top. The tickling on his arm was unbearable. He leaned over the rim of the shield and dropped the naked, squalid body into the black water. Then he flapped his arms wildly, but saw even as he did that there was nothing clinging to them: the sensation of maggots had been in his imagination.

One leg stuck out—the wounded one—and Slyur pushed down her knee, submerging it. The water was cold. The girl had not reacted at all to its chill. Her head lay to one side, a string of drool spilling from between her lips.

From the other room came the echoes of a sudden sob.

Slyur turned. He knew the girl was dead now, but he would refrain from saying so. Let them have a little hope and hold it for a while before easing them into the inevitable outcome. He went down the stairs and into the antechamber. Everyone scuffled away from him. Could they read what he knew on his face? He ignored the grating stones and tried to pretend that all was well. The little twin sister stared up at him, reproaching him silently; he could not lie to her, so he concentrated on her father, opening his hands as if revealing that he was free of deceit.

From behind Slyur came a noise. His head snapped around. His breath stopped and he listened. In the altar room, someone spluttered and splashed in water.

Slyur turned and dashed back into the room, kicking up pebbles, which bounced off the farmer and his family as they crowded in after the priest. As he took the first of the steps, the child's head appeared above the edge of the shield. Slyur drew up in awe. The girl looked at him, then at her parents and brothers and sister. She began to cry. Her mother and father edged past the Hespet, who had become like a statue, part of the altar itself. The farmer lifted his daughter out of the water, handed her to her mother. Her shivering body was pink and shiny with water. The thighs of both her legs were smooth; not even a scar remained to show where the wound had been. They hugged her and rubbed warmth into her as they descended. The farmer lingered on the step beside the priest. "Hespet, I—I . . . thank you, Hespet. I'll bring the calf this afternoon and bleed it here on the steps." He saw his daughter below and hurried to be with her.

Slyur continued to stare at the altar. Slowly he climbed the last two steps and dared to look into the shield. The water was dark but clear. Someone crept into the room. Slyur turned to find the twin sister at the base of the steps, her large cloud-pale eyes upon him as if he were all the world encapsulated. Her worship made him sick. He wanted to slap her face. He started down the steps, but his legs had become weak and his knees barely held him. He had to sit: the burden of her adoration dragged him down. He neither knew why he had become so incredibly torpid nor suspected that the child might have powers normally attributed to Kobachs. He got up again with great effort and went down the final step. The child bowed her head, and the pressure of her worship lifted.

The Hespet shook his head. "Stop it." He meant to command her, but the words came out in a weak rasp. He cleared his throat. "Don't honor me. Do not." He grasped her shoulders with trembling hands. "And I don't want your family honoring me, either. It's not me, do you understand. Not me!" He pushed her away, toward the arch. She stumbled on the stones, and looked back at him, eyes brimming with tears of confusion. She ran away.

Slyur listened to her retreat. She could not possibly understand why he had grown angry and rebuked her, although the reason was simple enough: he still did not believe. A child had been healed miraculously as promised. Why? he asked. Why? "She was dying, she's been saved," he whispered and raised his head to the statue again. "Yes, but why, then, were none saved before?"

If the Hespet doubted Chagri's powers, he was alone in all the kingdom. The word spread faster than a fire through At-larma. By the time the evening torches had been lighted, every crippled or afflicted person in the city was on his way to the temple of Chagri. They camped outside the gates and, when the yard had been filled up, spilled out across the road, blocking it for coaches and other normal traffic. Soldiers came but could not make the people leave. At first they did not know why these people were here, but word quickly came to them.

"A little girl was brought back to life here."

"No, it was a woman and she had her severed leg reattached by drinking the altar water. She was ugly, too, and it made her beautiful."

"Not so! It was her head that was severed and replaced."

"Then how did she drink?"

Laughter poured forth from the crowd. But when they had
quieted down again, no one went away. Whatever the truth
might be, something *had* happened. They would not leave. The
soldiers finally gave up and went off to reroute traffic onto
other roads. In the morning the poor deluded fools would find
out that there were no miracles to be had, and then they would
go home. A few would discover that their pockets had been
picked, but as far as the soldiers were concerned that was just
punishment for such stupidity.

In the morning when Slyur arrived at the temple, he would
have jumped from his coach and escaped into the alleys if the
crowd had not seen him first and rushed out to surround the
coach. He pressed back against the cushions as dozens of dirty
hands, some of them deformed or maimed, reached in through
the windows on both sides and a hundred voices shouted prayers
and supplications and promises and absurdly fantastic rewards
if he would let them accompany him into Chagri's temple. The
hands stretched in farther as people climbed onto the coach.
They wanted to touch the Hespet, to make contact with his
magic and have it act on them. Slyur slid down and curled up
on the floor.

The driver of the coach beat at the twisted mob with his
whip. The panicked horses plunged through the press of bodies.
The roar of the crowd grew louder as people shouted above
each other to be heard. Above the din, the Hespet heard the
crackling laughter of the white-armored god, whose cruel irony
he had just begun to see.

Had Slyur been granted a look into Chagri's City Celestial,
he would not have recognized his god. If he could have gained
some insight into the arcane plot in which he served as a pawn,
Slyur would have realized that all his greatest fears and doubts
were true: that the white, fire-eyed being who called itself
Chagri was not his god at all.

Miradomon had cast off the war god disguise long before.
All that remained of it was an intense whiteness that was the
natural color of Miradomon's robes. This, his chosen appearance, had been taken from a simple priest he had slain upon
his arrival, just as images of Chagri and other gods had been
ripped from the humble priest's brain at the point of death.
The priest had dwelled in a place called Trufege that Mira-

domon had found perfectly suited to his plans. The people there
were like insects; he had only to put his foot in their path and
they angled off in the direction he wanted, blind to his trap,
oblivious to the moment when that foot came down from the
sky and crushed them to jelly.

Miradomon moved. He did not walk, but floated along in
the blackness of his castle. Beneath the hood of his robe his
face was a mystery—the interior of the cowl was as dark as
if night had fallen forever upon his face, and no living soul
had yet come close enough to him to witness the faint points
of blue radiance deep within it. He continued along, passing
through walls when corridors ended, although both he and the
walls were real. He entered the chamber where the source of
his power was kept.

The chamber was huge, as dark and cold as the bottom of
an ocean. Inhabiting it—or more precisely, positioned in it—
was his army: beings without minds that Miradomon had created, their form transmutable at his whim. At present they
towered above him, twice his height, like monstrous brown
slugs. They were monsters from the legends of a people on
another continent—a southern continent. This past night while
all of Secamelan slept, that race had annihilated itself. By
Miradomon's arrangement, they had waged war against a
neighboring country that had been an ally only a few months
before. As the last few members of that ancient race had fought
and died, his army of hideous slugs had cracked open the bodies
of the slain to feast on their flesh while he feasted on their
death essence. As always he had come from the skies in the
form of a god, bringing his mythic army along to generate
madness in the warriors on both sides; madness produced chaos,
and chaos was how Miradomon lived.

He considered that it was time to change the shape of his
army—to make them into creatures relevant to Secamelan and
Növalok. But that could wait awhile. First he wanted to see
how much his source had grown from last night's carnage. He
floated across the chamber to where the floor ended and the
pit began.

Below him was a vast empty space. Out of it light poured
over him, making his white robe glow like hot metal. Far down
within the void, a single small star hung like a blind white eye
shot through with blood. Strings of plasma exploded from it,

falling out into the blackness, slowing, then falling back into the bloodshot core. The energy of each death the fireball absorbed set off a chain of fusion, releasing more energy in iridescent spouts. Each single death made him stronger and the core greater. Then, when all life had been extinguished, the planet would be obliterated and the death of a world added to all the other deaths.

Here was his whole existence: he had severed the last connection with life long ago. Death now sustained him; chaos was his lover.

He no longer relied on his crex to live. The mutable membrane that had once been the boundary of his life was now the boundary of his world. He had used it as raw material, creating his castle and his world from it, expanding it, adding to it in order to surround that world with it—a vast silver globe which now clung parasitically to the world of Secamelan, its point of contact eternally open, like the maw of some leviathan jellyfish, hungry and eager.

Gazing down upon the death energy he had stored, Miradomon dreamed of the day when all the void was filled—a billion worlds drained dry and empty, ready to be regenerated by his design. One by one, he would open all the corridors between this string of parallel worlds and then release his matter of chaos into all of them. This would take an eternity to complete, but time meant nothing. The source made him immortal in the truest sense: nothing could harm him. What other being even suspected his existence?

Elystroya. Only she. But she was his prisoner, and no danger. He wondered then as he had many times before why he had let her live.

On the day he had condemned his race to death, Miradomon had hung in space and prepared the doorway that would lead him out of his universe. He knew full well what the result would be and did not care. It was sheer chance that the two members of his race—the one who had been sucked through the opening, whose name he had not known, and Elystroya—had come upon him. Their minds were so closely linked to his that he could not hide his thoughts from them. Their horror washed over him in the moment that he split the fabric of his homeworld. Two universes of utterly different properties were forced to meet. The creature who had accompanied Elystroya

had been torn away into oblivion, and the homeworld, simultaneously drawn out and pulled out, had begun to disintegrate.
This would have spelled death for Elystroya, too, had she not
acted in the initial moment. Somehow she guessed that he
would survive the holocaust, that he had in some way allied
himself with the unleashed destructive forces, and she had
responded to this by melding with him before chaos pulled her
away.

He and she became a unity, the most intimate of acts among
his kind. He was disgusted by it, but unprepared for her move
and unable to stop it. For that brief time he swam within her
soul, touching her thoughts against his will, powerless to resist.
She did the same. He hid what he could from her. They witnessed as one the death of every being they had ever known;
shards of agony cut them: he absorbed and thrived on it while
she shut off her mind, blocking the horror, and him, for a
while. Soon she opened up again. Violent nausea permeated
him as the second mind within him realized that her sharer,
her lover, had been slain along with her world. She cried out
to the crystal stars to take her life, too. But even the stars were
shattering. She willed herself to die, but she could not while
she was still attached to him, and her alter ego had absolutely
no intention of dying. She began to withdraw from him again.

Just why he had stopped her, he still did not know. She
meant nothing to him. Less than nothing. Her overpowering
love for her lost one repulsed him. And yet—he could not let
her go. As she tried to escape him, Miradomon doubled in
strength and size from the obliteration of his race. It was nothing
then for him to paralyze her within him. Later, when he had
time, he knew he would find a place for her. . . .

Since that unnatural day he had often pondered why he let
her live. What he found for answers could not be right, were
utterly impossible. How could he envy this dead one of his
kind the love that Elystroya radiated? He wanted worship, but
not love, not what she carried. The answer was incomprehensible, too complex to understand. It made him uncomfortable
to dwell on it. He had far more vital things to do.

Turning from the source, drifting past his nightmarish army,
he went to Elystroya. Her body had been discarded as an un-
necessary burden many worlds ago, but he had found a suitable
temporary replacement.

The place where she was kept lay all in darkness. As Miradomon entered, the walls began to glow with a smoky light. In front of him, in a field of tiny, silent sparks, floated a small, polished black globe. Out of the end of his liquid sleeve, a skeletal and greenish hand appeared. He reached for the globe and lines of gold as thin as hairs reflected from the back of his hand. His hand passed through the field of sparks and they vanished as he touched the globe. He carried it away.

Across the room, encased in a similar but larger field of sparks, the naked body of a young girl hovered. The figure was slender, prepubescent. Straight blonde hair hung to her waist. Her face was blank—the essence of her that had been a personality called Lewyn was absent, extracted and encased like that of Elystroya. He would have discarded her altogether, but there remained a slight possibility he would need her personality at some future time. There were always unforeseen elements in any plan. For the moment, her body was of another use to him.

He held the globe over her head, then let it touch her. His hand drew away, and the globe vanished into Lewyn's head. Miradomon's other hand had appeared, to clutch her in a powerful grip as the sparks disappeared. He lowered her to her feet, but did not release her until her pale eyelids fluttered open and two large blue eyes focused on him.

"Elystroya," he said. His fingers cupped her chin. A blue corona surrounded her for a moment, and her eyes blinked. He let loose her head and the corona faded.

The young face filled with conflicting emotions. The mouth opened. At first she made broken, inarticulate sounds and her thoughts came through to him instead. *This is not my body.*

"It might be," was his answer. "It's young and healthy. Or you could choose any of a thousand others, which I would pick for you in an instant."

"You!" Her eyes widened with dawning horror. "I'm not with . . . you've kept me alive and—and *this.*" She looked down at herself. "What monstrous thing have you made me? Where is my body? Miradomon, where? Let me have it so that I can die."

"Not possible. Your crex is dust. You've slept through a dozen universes, and this is how they look here. No stars of crystal for you to appeal to—the stars here don't listen."

Kill me.

No. His own emotion surprised him. "No," he said aloud. "You chose not to die once." He saw revulsion crawl across her features as she remembered that time. "Now I choose not to let you die."

She appeared to resign herself to this. Her blue eyes studied him, then glanced beyond him to where the globe containing Lewyn's mind floated in its field of sparks. "And *your* body," she said. "You've thrown that away, as well."

"Oh, no. This room and beyond, that globe you stare at, is all part of my body. I surround us. You cannot possibly leave."

"Surround us?"

"That's one of many things you don't know. Would you like to hear about it?"

A name formed in her mind, a loud, desperate shout: *Lyrec!* she sobbed. "Why have you done this cruelty to me?" Her new body trembled. She backed to the wall and slid down it, curling up on the floor.

"Elystroya," he hissed. She did not respond. *Elystroya.* Nothing. His bony hand appeared again and gripped her chin. He raised her to her feet. He looked into her eyes, but found no sign of her there. Something had happened to her—the shock of awakening, he decided, had been too much. Bodies such as this were given to highly charged emotions; he could clearly recall the first time he had encountered them, before he learned how they could serve his plans. Of course. It was his fault. He should have eased her into this new experience. This upset him greatly. He wanted urgently to explain himself to her, to make her understand why he had sacrificed their homeworld. It was imperative she recognize the source as something she could share with him. He could not say why this seemed so important, but he touched her shoulder with his cold fingertips and said: *Come and I'll explain. You need to acquaint yourself.*

He made her say, "Yes, Miradomon." He liked the sound of her voice, and had her repeat it. "Yes, Miradomon." Within, her mind was empty. He pretended not to notice; with time, that might come.

He took her hand and together they floated out of the room.

♭Chapter 9.

THE hooves of the captain's horse thudded on the hard scrubby ground, then abruptly cracked against a stone. A small gray chip flicked up. It glanced off Lyrec's brow, stinging him. Blood, black in the shadows of dust, flowed to his cheek. He shook the blood away from his eyelid, then raised his head angrily. He was about to shout a curse at the captain when he heard a faint call. It came only once, and might all too easily have been his imagination. Nevertheless, what he thought he heard was his name, called once from far away. Lyrec searched the barren landscape. On the hillside just one tree stood, spindly and stooped, its leafless branches low as if ashamed of its nakedness. No one could have hidden there.

He listened for another call, but none followed. Wind raked across the tor, rumbled in his ears. The same wind had buffeted them for hours without stop. How could he have heard anyone call through that? Unless the call had been mental. Who? It hadn't been Borregad, whose contact he knew too well now. He did not dare believe what he wanted to believe; he couldn't afford such hope. Better to assume it was fatigue, hallucination.

If it had been Elystroya, she would call again.

Throughout the day rain poured in brief torrential periods between which a mist sheeted the brown fens. Lyrec began to

itch from the dampness. The soldiers seemed to take little notice
of the weather beyond covering themselves with blankets when
the rain came. They did not complain or curse the sky as he
would have expected and he came to understand that this was
the common weather of Ladoman.

It was through the fen mists that Lyrec first glimpsed the
tors. They rose, black against the sky, a collection of mottled
lumps like the decaying skullcaps of a sunken army of giants.
The soldiers wove a deft path through the marshes and, finally,
out and up the first rocky hillside.

The sun had begun to set by the time they started up the
last tor. Lyrec sensed the soldiers' eagerness to reach the top;
something awaited them there, and he soon saw what it was.

A circle of stones stood like fingers thrust out of the ground.
Lyrec thought again of the image of giants. This was a haunted
land. In the center of the circle he saw the remains of a fire.
Beyond it, the ground became dark with a disturbingly defined
edge—a small jagged crater where part of the tor had collapsed.
The soldiers reined in at the stones and dismounted stiffly.
They strode about to loosen their legs. One of them gestured
at the crater with his head and muttered to the man beside him
about "the buttertub," then gave Lyrec a sinister look.

They built up the fire and then moved in around it to warm
themselves, leaving him tied by the length of rope to the captain's horse. He walked past it and sat down against one of the
outermost stones, ignored as if forgotten. His knee joints popped
as he settled in; his whole body was a collected ache. His hands
were white, too white; he wriggled his numb fingertips and
shook his arms as much as the rope would allow, ignoring the
pain this brought.

The rain began again, softly heralding an evening chill. The
soldiers huddled beneath their blankets and drew nearer to the
fire. Lyrec brought up his knees and bowed his weary head.
A moment later he seemed to have dozed off. One of the
soldiers glanced at him, then looked away, satisfied.

Steam began to rise from Lyrec. His skin flushed with color.
The rain falling around him ceased to touch him, as if a clear
shell covered him. On his wrists, the skin grew purple and
hard over his wounds. Then the pale skin around the wounds
began to spread over them. His breathing became quick and
shallow. He shuddered as with chills and broke out in a sweat.

Soon his excited breathing slowed, and he fell asleep. The protecting shell remained. His body and clothing dried. The skin on his wrists had sealed over the wounds.

He did not know how long he slept. When he opened his eyes, the sky was dark and the rain had stopped. Mist was rising from the sodden ground. At the fire—now as tall as the soldiers around it—the Ladomantines huddled together under blankets. He smelled something cooking that awoke a different pain in his stomach. He wondered idly where they had found something to burn and something to cook. What could possibly live on these bleak tors?

"They might have cooked me," said a voice beside him. Lyrec looked over his shoulder. All he could see of Borregad were two large dislike eyes hung in the black night. "Are you feeling better now?"

"I didn't hear you arrive."

"You were busy healing," replied the cat.

"Yes. Did you hear"—he hesitated—"a call earlier? I don't know where you were then, but we were coming up this hillside. It was very faint. I'm not certain . . . but the more I think about it, the more I'm sure it was real." His voice betrayed his desperate hope. "I didn't expect it, so I couldn't have hallucinated it, could I? I wasn't even thinking of her then."

"Elystroya? She called you?"

"Yes, I'm almost certain."

The cat looked away. For some time he had supported Lyrec's desire to find Elystroya, all the while hiding his own certainty that she had perished. The fiend, Miradomon, had no reason to let her survive. This afternoon he had overheard Lyrec's mad ravings, brought on by pain and exhaustion. He would support virtually any notion his friend had—but not this one. "No," he said, "I heard nothing. No call."

Lyrec nodded with suspicious calm. "It was so weak. And the call was to me, so you wouldn't have heard it if you were very far away."

"Lyrec. . . ." He would have gone on, but could not compel himself. Instead, he added, "We have to get away from here."

"Yes. How are you with ropes?"

"I have paws, what do you think?"

"You also have teeth," said Lyrec.

"Oh, no. The last time I used my mouth at your instruction,

I ate that awful plant juice. If you think for a moment I'm going to fill my mouth up with prickly little pieces of twine— sorry, no."

"Did you bring my crex?"

"Look at me. What am I? A f-f-feline."

"I've never heard you stutter before."

"What? Stutter? That's the word *you* used: f-f-feline. You said it just like that. F-f-feline."

"Did-you-bring-the-crex?"

"No! That's what I'm trying to tell you. I couldn't have kept up with you if I had to lug that all over the countryside. I had to abandon it back at the tavern."

"Then I—"

"Hey, who are you talking to?"

Lyrec swung his head around so quickly that he struck the back of it against the stone. He squeezed his eyes shut in pain.

"You—I'm talking to you." A boot caught him in the side. He groaned, opened his watering eyes to see a soldier standing over him with a wooden bowl. The man crouched down. "Talking to yourself?"

"Not exactly. You've brought food. How am I supposed to eat it?"

"Hungry, eh? I'm going to untie your hands while you eat." He drew a dagger. "But don't get any ideas about crawling off. If I'd been against you this morning instead of Abo you wouldn't be with us now."

"I understand. And I'm too hungry to argue with you."

The soldier sneered while he untied the rope. Lyrec picked up the bowl and looked into it. Chunks of meat mixed with a white grain of some kind. He tipped it so that some of the food poured into his mouth. It was hot, not particularly pleasant, but satisfying under the circumstances. The soldier stood by patiently, his dagger laid along his crossed arms. When the bowl was three-quarters empty, Lyrec leaned to his left with some difficulty and set it down. Baffled, the soldier stepped forward. As he did, Borregad emerged from the misty darkness and sat down at the bowl. The Ladomantine uncrossed his arms and took the dagger by its point, raising it up beside his head.

"You," Lyrec called softly. The soldier glanced at him— and was unable to look away. Eyes, shining like metal in the firelight, caught his soul and took command of his body. He lowered the dagger, sat down, and promptly fell asleep.

Borregad finished the meal. "That was awful," he announced, licking his whiskers. He watched the luster leave Lyrec's eyes, making of them dark pools once again that shifted to meet his gaze.

"They have no intention of taking me before Ladomirus. I gather I'm to be a permanent resident of that great gaping hole over there they call a buttertub. Apparently I won't be the first. It's a pit for disposing of unwanted items. This was Fulpig's request to the captain—they're friends."

"What a perfect place for Miradomon," said Borregad. "These creatures are throatcutters by nature. It's instinct. Me, I'm a lower form—it's expected. I have to live with that. But you're infected with the same instinct. You've wanted to get free and kill that captain the same way he wants to dispose of you."

"I have," admitted Lyrec.

"This entire race is insane."

"Only by our standards. And they're hopeless to maintain. We've joined this race for better or worse."

"Thank you. You've finally come around to seeing things my way. I told you we were just like them."

Lyrec recalled the argument they had had at Grohd's tavern. He admitted, "Yes, you were right."

"Of course I was. Now, do we fight or do we go?"

"Go."

"Back to the tavern."

"No. To Ladoman, to the city."

"You *are* insane! They'd love to have you walk right in, you know. That Fulpig was looking forward to seeing you in a very physical way."

"But, Borregad, think. Everything we've heard so far that's wrong with this whole area has been this character, Ladomirus. And Grohd was afraid of these soldiers—no, more than afraid. Something about them bothered him, something he couldn't account for."

"I never heard him talk of it."

"Well, no, actually I picked it up from the first time I probed him. I had no idea to what he was referring then. Later . . . well, there was no time. But I want to meet Ladomirus."

"You think this Ladomirus might be Miradomon. And you want to meet him without the crex?"

"If we took time to go back for it, the whole countryside would be after us. We wouldn't have a chance to reach the city. They won't expect us to go there straightaway."

"Your plans always sound reasonable when you explain them, but I might point out that the last 'reasonable' plan got you *here*." He glanced over at the soldiers around the fire. The thickening mist made them difficult to see, but they appeared to have bedded down. "What of this one?" he asked.

Lyrec smiled. "He's supposed to guard me until morning. Everyone else is asleep, or will be soon enough. That gives us a substantial head start."

"Then, let's be gone."

Lyrec crouched beside the soldier, and, careful not to wake the man, relieved him of his sword and dagger. Then Lyrec took his own hat and placed it on the soldier's head, drawing the brim down low. In this mist, no one would notice the difference.

"Now, look here," whispered Borregad, "it's not that I disagree automatically with your intentions, but you've already had enough experience with those things to know better. They'll just get you in trouble."

"I've probed this soldier; I now know everything he knows about fighting with one of these. Also about throwing this shorter form."

Borregad looked from Lyrec to the sleeping figure and back to Lyrec again. "Is he good?"

"The best."

"Don't smile like that—they'll see your teeth two steys away. Then you'll have to prove it. Here, let me up." He leaped onto Lyrec's shoulders. "Remember, you're not like them—you're peaceful. No fighting."

"If I can avoid it." He started for the horses, but stopped abruptly. Something had scuffled against a rock. The mist had grown into a wall—the fire was a bright circle and every shape had a cloudy shadow. Lyrec could not see anyone, but he bent low and moved off behind the nearest stone.

"Lyrec," Borregad hissed at his ear, "this is a very good time to start avoiding."

The captain could not sleep.
As he lay beneath his oiled blanket, he could not stop re-

living the disgrace of this morning. He could feel his men's
contempt like heat from the fire. Finally, flinging back the
blanket, the captain grabbed his sword belt and stood. The men
would not respect him again until he had dealt with the pilgrim,
and would respect him more still if he took care of the matter
by himself. He would kill the man and toss him in the pit.
When the men awoke, the pilgrim would be dead.

He peered through the heavy mist, but the firelight seemed
to thicken it. Even the horses, off to the right, were no more
than vague shapes: had he not known for sure what they were,
he would have thought them stones. He used the horses as
landmarks and moved off away from them. His foot skidded
on a loose stone, scraping it under his boot. A hand clamped
on his shoulder. He leaped around, his sword ready. Then,
seeing who had touched him, he straightened and tried to look
dignified.

Elforl stared flatly at the captain. The captain shivered under
his scrutiny. The silver ball of the jeit stick hung loose at
Elforl's side. It, rather than Elforl's hand, could have touched
him, staving his skull in. But the silent mercenary never made
mistakes. He wore his taciturnity like a mask, never betraying
a thought. The captain hated the man.

"Why are you awake?" he asked.

Elforl said, "You make too much noise," then walked away
into a swirl of fog.

Right then the captain would have preferred to throw Elforl
into the pit rather than Lyrec. But that jeit stick stayed his hand.
He had watched dozens of people struck down with it. Under
his rage, he knew coldly that he could not defend himself
against it.

Into the fog he continued, picking out his way to the place
where the pilgrim huddled sleeping. The prisoner shifted, and
a groan came from under the wide hat. Quickly, before the
man could wake up, the captain stabbed out and felt the sword
sink home. The body bucked once. Both hands came up, clawing at the air. They fell suddenly and the dark shape collapsed
on its side. The captain withdrew his blade and cleaned it before
resheathing it. He yanked the body up and shoved his shoulder
under it, hoisted it up, his arm wrapped around the dark cape.
The wide brimmed hat dropped to the ground behind him.
Lumbering beneath the weight, the captain carried his victim

to the edge of the buttertub, being very careful not to walk too far. He could picture the mask of Elforl's face cracking into a broad smile at the news that the captain had accidentally fallen into the pit.

He found the lip of the chasm and flung the body into its darkness. An impact of flesh against rock echoed up from below, followed by the rattle of stones. Satisfied, the captain headed back to the fire. On the way, he retrieved the pilgrim's hat for proof of his deed.

Nearing the circle of stones, he heard a horse shy uneasily. He paused to listen and saw someone move in the fog, sneaking from horse to horse. The captain commanded softly, "You, there. Come here this instant."

The figure froze, then turned around slowly.

It was the pilgrim, Lyrec. It could not be! The man had to be a . . . "A ghost!" shrieked the captain. He threw himself into flight, and smacked directly into the stone at his back. He crumpled on his face. Lyrec went over and picked up his hat.

"Thank you," Lyrec said contemptuously to the unconscious man. "Thank you *so* much."

The captain's shout had awakened the entire camp. Elforl marshalled them, calling them all to him. He counted heads.

"It was the captain who screamed," said Abo. "What's happened?"

Elforl almost smiled. "What do you suppose? The prisoner's escaped, and I wouldn't doubt that the captain caused it, either, the damnable caitiff. We've an enemy out there in the fog. The first thing to do is stop him from taking a horse if he hasn't already. Stay together, whatever else you do—otherwise, he'll take us down one by one."

Lyrec heard them coming and moved off into the darkness. He crouched low behind the stone next to the captain's unconscious body. *Borregad, be careful.*

The soldiers checked the horses, found them all in line, though edgy. They found that one had been saddled. Then one man spotted the captain, and ran over to him. Lyrec leaned out from his hiding place and said, "You," loud enough for just the one man to hear. The soldier jumped up, shouting, "Here he is!" as he charged at Lyrec. He leaped past the stone, landing in a crouch, ready to attack. In that instant a small black shape flew at him from the top of the stone. As he tried to ward it off, Lyrec's blade spun around his and impaled him. Lyrec vanished into the fog, Borregad at his heels, before the soldier hit the ground.

The others arrived fast, but not in time to save their comrade. "It's his own fault," Elforl stated coldly. "I warned you three to stay together. Now both of you stay with me or we're dead men." They nodded. "He wants a horse. We have to make sure they're all tied together so he can't have one so easily. Then we can sit back and wait for him to take one. The alternative is to follow him."

"I'm for killing him," said Abo.

"Agreed," said his partner. "I can't wait in this fog—I'll be seeing him everywhere."

Elforl shook his head at their foolishness. "All right. We go hunting. But stay together."

They started at the campfire, spread out to cover the entire circle, close enough to see one another. The fire crackled, hiding any soft sounds beneath its own. The men watched the shadows with straining eyes. Nothing moved. No one came out to face them.

There was a thump and Abo toppled onto his back. The other two rushed to him. He lay with a bleeding gash in his forehead. The rock that had struck him lay not far away.

Elforl peered into the darkness admiringly. "This one's not interested in heroics—he's a canny one. We should have killed him this morning." He looked at the last man left him. "Well, we can hardly go on or he'll brain us both. We're too slow—we're targets. Same's true if we sit still. No. We go into it fast, together. Come on." He stood and ran forward. The other soldier raced after him, not wanting to be abandoned in the fog. He did not see the small black shape drop onto him from above.

Borregad landed on the soldier and dug in his claws to hang on. Then he lashed out across the soldier's cheek and neck. The man danced in agony. He grabbed at the weight on his shoulder, twisting his face away to protect it. His hand closed on empty space. The weight of the cat resettled on his other shoulder. Huge black eyes stared into his. He cried out and swung his sword up awkwardly to kill the fiendish thing. Borregad dropped away in the same moment that the sword came down, slicing into the soldier's own shoulder. He fell to his

knees, clawed at the ground with one hand while his other
slapped the hilt up, dislodging the sword from his wound. He
rolled over, found the blade again, and lay on his back, ready
for anything that might come to get him. He wondered fearfully
where Elforl was.

At the moment he heard the cry, Elforl turned back to see
his man cut into his own shoulder. *Witchcraft!* "He's making
us kill ourselves." He heard a sound behind him, acted on it
before the realization had even come to consciousness. The jeit
stick whipped the air ahead of him, striking nothing.

The figure stood beyond its reach. Elforl could make out
the shadows of the eyes, the darkness of the beard. He moved
ahead, expecting at any moment to be deceived by some spell,
to see monsters come at him. "I wish I'd smashed in your skull
this morning," he said. The figure did not move or answer.
"The captain was a fool to bring you along. Abo tried to tell
them you were a sorcerer, and they ignored it." The figure
shifted stance, presenting less body to him.

Elforl carefully took out his dagger. He lunged with the
stick, swinging it up at the figure's head from the side, following it with a low dagger thrust at the abdomen. With a
minimum of motion, Lyrec's sword swatted the jeit stick away
and blocked low. The dagger screeched along the blade.

Elforl retreated in anticipation of an attack, but none followed. He was amazed at the precision of his enemy's movements—how could the fellow have learned such swordplay
since this morning? And how was it that he held the sword so
well in hands that should have been swollen and useless? So,
he was indeed Kobach. He must be killed quickly before some
further phantoms appeared.

Elforl lunged again. He brought the jeit stick around in a
spinning circle, nearly impossible to fend off with a sword.

Lyrec stuck his sword straight up, blocking at such an angle
that the blade pared into the haft of the jeit. The two weapons
stuck together. Elforl jerked the stick away fiercely and the
blade snapped in half. He used the backward tug to drive his
other hand, and the dagger, forward. The blade sank into the
center of the shadowy figure. Elforl tried to draw it back for
a second stab, but it would not come free: it had caught in the
witch's cape. Elforl quickly brought the jeit up again. In the
last instant as he braced himself, the dagger pulled free, throw-

ing him off balance. He had to pull back on the stick to remain upright.

Lyrec clapped both hands around the ball of the stick and pulled hard, swinging Elforl past him. The soldier realized just before both his feet left the ground that Lyrec had led him to the edge of the buttertub. "Fool," he called himself, and vanished into the pit.

Lyrec knelt down to retrieve Elforl's dagger, and heard what he assumed to be Borregad approaching. He glanced over his shoulder into the buttertub. "That was a waste. He was very good in his way—master of an art." He turned casually.

The soldier with the shoulder wound stood wavering over him, trying with all his might to hold his sword steady for the killing blow. His face was pasty with the painful exertion.

"Put it down," Lyrec said. "Put it down and stop."

The young soldier's eyes opened wider. With a snarl, he launched himself in a charge. He struck at Lyrec, but Lyrec had already moved. The sword cut into moist ground and the soldier ran up against it. His boot split open. The blade sliced into his foot. He tripped and stumbled to one side, away from Lyrec, who tried desperately to grab him, missing by the width of his thumb. The soldier's scream ended abruptly with a crack, followed by the sound of sprinkling stones.

Lyrec stared down in disbelief. *They're crazy, Borregad. They lust for death, did you see him?* He took the sword out of the ground, and threw the broken one he held into the pit. *He could have put down his sword—he was nearly unconscious and could barely hold it. And I just stood there and let him run into the pit. He preferred to die.*

The cat emerged from the shadows ahead. *And you risked your life for the likes of them.*

Yes. Yes, I did. I don't understand this at all.

Poor innocent. It's simply that—Lyrec, behind the stone! The cat scrambled to one side as the tip of a sword cleaved the ground where he had stood. Lyrec drew back two paces and raised his new sword defensively.

From behind the rock, the Ladomantine captain stepped into view. He watched Borregad fleeing into the fog. "Rotten beast, I'd forgotten about you. . . ." He looked up at Lyrec. "Ah—did you think I was dead? You are too gentle and humane, foreigner, to live in our kingdom. You should have slain me.

Too bad, because that's not the sort of mistake I'm likely to make. I want you."

"Do you?" replied Lyrec. "Perhaps I will enlist. If the likes of you can reach such a lofty post just think of how high someone with a brain could go."

"I'll cut you into little pieces!" The captain charged. His sword swung out in an arc aimed at Lyrec's jaw. Lyrec batted it aside. The captain muttered a curse and came on again. His blade whistled through the air, but his target moved back a step and, ever so lightly, tapped his blade behind the captain's as it whipped past, adding strength to the swing, pulling the captain off balance. He stumbled back into position and made a run at Lyrec. The sword swung down. Lyrec caught it against the flat of his own. The two blades rang, sending shock waves into the captain's arms that nearly dislocated his elbows. His teeth ground together. For a moment his sword touched the ground, his arms had no strength. In that moment of helplessness, he expected to die; but Lyrec did not attack. The captain shook sweat from his brow and smiled to himself. An honorable man . . . Well, he had warned the man about showing kindness.

"I—I've no fight left in me," the captain moaned. "What did you . . . my arms, they're so weak."

"Put down your sword and let me see."

"Why would you help me? We're enemies!"

"You're proud of that, aren't you? You enjoy being someone's enemy." He took a step forward. The captain jerked his sword straight up at Lyrec's groin. But it whined against metal and stopped. Lyrec held his dagger parallel with the ground. The sword had driven against its haft. Lyrec glared at the captain. "And a liar, as well."

The captain saw death in the black eyes. He pulled back, then thrust quickly to impale Lyrec. He watched, unable to believe his eyes, as his opponent's blade skimmed around and nonchalantly moved his out of the way.

Lyrec slammed his dagger into the captain's breastbone. The captain convulsed and choked. The sword fell from his grip. He looked imploringly at Lyrec and saw all the humanity erased from that face. Using the dagger as a handle, Lyrec hauled the captain off his feet. "Wait!" the captain sobbed. "Wait, wait now, *please!*" The last word became a long scream that pursued him into the buttertub and did not end so much as fade like a ghost in the background of the night.

Lyrec flung the captain's sword into the buttertub after him.
He could hear Borregad trying to communicate with him, but
he sealed himself off. He never wanted Borregad to know how
much he had enjoyed what he had just done.

♭Chapter 10.

ALCEMON, the baker of Trufege, tugged on the jacket of the man going up the trail ahead of him and said, "He's mad to make us do this." He meant this to be a whisper for the ears of his comrade alone, but the night was crisply cold and Alcemon's words carried all the way to the man about whom he was speaking: Varenukha, the priest of Trufege.

Hearing what was said, Varenukha stepped off the trail and motioned the others to keep going. He watched the short, swarthy baker approach and considered how to deal with him. It was imperative that he defeat Alcemon's doubt, quash it before it spread like disease through the group. They had almost reached the top of the ridge—in a few minutes they would look down on the valley of Ukobachia.

Weighed down by the bundle of torches he carried, Alcemon trudged up to Varenukha without even seeing him. The tall, thin priest reached out and simply pulled the baker out of line. Before Alcemon could react, Varenukha drew him close and said, "Did I hear you say I'm mad?" His scowl sharpened the lines of his face and was repeated in the fine line of his mustache.

The unnerved baker surprised Varenukha by defending his statement. "We're going to do murder."

The priest shook his head, then patted the baker on the shoulder. "No, Alcemon, no. That's where you're so wrong. These are not people—they've defied their humanity through their irreverence to the gods. Do you think I lied when I said Chagri came to me in a vision? This is our god's work we do."

"What about the messenger who came to you?"

This question so shocked the priest that, for a moment, he could not speak. Alcemon had seen the Hespet's messenger. Probably they all had. But he had perceived a relationship between that and what they were about to do; and if Alcemon, no gifted thinker, recognized this, then it was likely the whole party of villagers suspected it. Varenukha spoke loudly, so that the others passing by would overhear what he said. "That man brought a message to me from the Hespet—an invitation to Lord Tynec's coronation. I told him my duties here are too pressing. His appearance and our undertaking this night are utterly unrelated." He scanned the faces going by, faces that made a point of not looking at him. They must believe him, and Alcemon must be convinced so that he in turn would convince others. Varenukha climbed more than a mountain this night—he climbed a notch higher in his quest for the Hespetacy. More significant by far than being assigned priest to a village of heretics, a victory here would be something the Hespet never forgot. Varenukha had succeeded in taking control of the foolish villagers and he would now prove how great was that success by leading them into Ukobachia. Judgment was at hand for the witches. Turning back to Alcemon, the priest produced his fiercest gaze.

The baker was not ready to be intimidated yet. "I want to know, then, what is the word of Voed?" he asked. "You mention Chagri—you *always* speak of Chagri. What of Voed?"

"It's Chagri that your village—*our* village—has offended. His word, his visitation is synonymous with the word of Voed. Do you reject that? Are you willing to blaspheme further after all the infidelity you people have served up?" Spittle shot from his mouth, he was so angered. He kept his voice steady with great effort. "You lost your wife the last time, Alcemon. It's your own existence that hangs in the balance now!"

The baker cowered at that: whatever else he doubted about the priest, he believed completely that Varenukha could have him killed. He reached out to touch the priest, but pulled back, afraid to make contact. "Forgive me, I didn't understand." He

backed away onto the trail where another of the villagers shoved
him on his way up the mountainside.

Varenukha followed the last of his villagers up to the ridge.
He took satisfaction in having silenced Alcemon, but thought
that it might do for the baker to suffer some misfortune on the
way back home. Perhaps one of those torches he carried would
accidentally ignite, setting him on fire. An obvious rebuke from
the gods. Yes.

The trail emerged in a clearing, which ran along the top of
the ridge in either direction. The villagers gathered there, awaiting further orders from their priest. Stars twinkled down on a
valley that was like a bowl carved into the mountains. The
peaks directly across from them were slowly being devoured
by a thick ledge of cloud.

Varenukha arrived in the clearing and took stock of the
situation. The village lay directly below them. Barely a dozen
lights shone to mark its location. Off to the left perhaps half
a stey and on down the hillside, torchlight pinpointed the bridge
on the main road into the village and gave him a better account
of their position. The priest moved through the group to lead
them down. He smelled suddenly the acidic sweetness of mulcetta. As the last members of his party moved out of his way,
Varenukha saw the vines below, mulcetta in endless rows as
far as the eye could see. The plump berries on the nearest plants
gleamed in the starlight. They grew on all the hillsides surrounding Ukobachia: the making of mulcet from the berries
was the Kobachs' primary source of income. That is, he thought,
it was until now. The strong drink even played a part in their
undoing. It was from one of his villagers, who had poached
the berries for years, that he had learned of this hidden trail,
created by the Kobachs to make the harvesting easier. Now he
would follow it down between the rows of vines, to a small
rope bridge across the river. The patrol on the main bridge, if
there even was one, would never suspect this, and would never
know what had happened until it was too late.

Varenukha told his followers, "Sound no alarms. Do whatever you have to do to ensure this. Remember your particular
tasks and perform them swiftly, then make your way back to
Trufege."

The thirty-three heads all nodded in accord. He turned and
they moved after him.

Once in the vines, the smell of mulcetta made their eyes

water. It stuck to their clothing and hair; it would be days before the odor washed away. Alcemon handed out most of his torches to his comrades as they passed. He was not supposed to do this until after they had crossed the rope bridge, but only he and the priest knew that. He followed for a while, but lagged behind until he was forgotten, then stepped in among the vines. He hid there, listening to his comrades move away. The air seemed to darken. Alcemon looked up to see the heavy cloud rolling across his view of the sky. It was scarcely the height of a man above him. He went back out to the path and watched the ridge where he had stood a few minutes before turn hazy and fade away. Alcemon had planned to sneak back over the bridge. Now he chose to spend the night among the vines instead. He couldn't say exactly why, but he had the unshakable feeling that something within that cloud awaited him hungrily. With a shiver, Alcemon returned to the safety of the vines and made sure he could not be seen from above rather than below.

The old man awoke with a start and reached over instinctively to hold and protect his wife. Her nightmare had awakened him: he had heard her calling his name.

His hand brushed against linen and emptiness. The bed, beside him, was empty. A pain entered his chest, as if a rib had snapped when he sat up and now pierced his lung and heart.

A dream. It had been a dream.

He put his palms against his forehead, covering a geometric tattoo etched there, and stared down at the floor. Anralys, he called silently to the goddess, why does the love you represent linger so long in this old soul? It has been nearly nine years, why don't you let me forget? There are times when I lie here and think I can feel her warmth beside me, can smell her and hear the soft snores she made. Sometimes her hair brushes my face, tickling, and I'll shove it away and then realize it cannot be, and sit up to find that she is gone. Of course she is gone. But if so, then why does she keep reappearing for me, Anralys? You're a powerful goddess, make me forget the pain of it. Let me remember her in our daughter. New life and new hope. My Pavra.

The old man peered across the room to where his daughter slept on her bed of straw. So late in life his wife had borne her. Why had it happened that way? After twenty years of fruitlessness, why the sudden fatal bloom?

The old man's name was Malchavik, a costumer by trade to the village of Ukobachia. He had lived a good and quiet life before Pavra's birth, being no maker of laws or director of destinies. He fashioned only clothing, mostly boots and hats and richly embroidered apparel for festivals and weddings. Then his wife had discovered she was pregnant. Forty years old and pregnant. Other shocks followed in ascending progression. The time of birth neared and the midwives had told him calmly that the baby could not come out of its own. His wife had to be opened up. He could still remember the acrid smell of their healing herbs and the odor of her blood that day. The women would not let him enter the room, even when the cries of his wife threatened to drive him mad. Someone—how odd that he could not recollect the person's identity when all else stood out so clearly—took him out to the tavern and sat with him, buying his drinks, which he put down one after the other with barely enough time in between for a breath. He was drunk by the time one of the women came to tell him that his wife, Pavra, had not survived. He had begun to laugh at this, tears pouring down his face—laughing and crying at the same time. What, the woman had asked, did he wish to name the child? All Malchavik had been able to say was his wife's name, again and again.

There were years following that of which he had no recollection. The money he had saved went to drink. He had learned later that many people tried to help him get control of himself, but that he defied each of them and kept to his destructive habit. The women looked after his daughter all the while. One day he had awakened by the quay, stinking of dead fish, lying in muck, and somehow sober. He had cried alone there for hours, despising himself for the wretched creature he was. And he had gone home, as simply as that, to a three-year-old daughter with blonde hair and pale blue eyes. Though her name was that of his wife, he kept the child and mother separate in his mind—as if his wife had died the same night that a baby had been abandoned on his doorstep. He lived his quiet life again and devoted himself to raising his daughter. The village breathed a sigh of relief.

In some deep recess of his mind he cursed the magical

powers of his race for their inability to save his wife. He had stopped using his own powers the day she died, and had never tried them again in the nine years that followed. However, there was a spark of wisdom in him that kept him from curbing his daughter's use of hers. She appeared to have an instinct for reaching out to the source of magic for all Kobachs, for touching and shaping it. She had incredible potential, as he told anyone who would come by, and she needed no emblem to prove this; but Malchavik was from an old family, as his wife had been, and he believed that the Kobachs should wear their heritage proudly. So he had had etched upon her forehead a simple flower in dark blue lines. Pavra, the flower.

Seeing her asleep on her straw bed, his longing became a terrible ache. He could not be with her just then. Without waking her, he dressed and stole out into the night.

The sky was overcast. A chill in the air awoke him completely. He decided to wander down to the river, there to sit and reminisce on favorite times. From the dark side street he could see the quay ahead: oddly geometrical lines of boats and barges moored there, the barge poles pointing into the sky. Two cats darted across his path and disappeared around a corner. He heard one of them growl. Beyond the back of the buildings, the path to the quay extended along the top of an artificial dike built to keep the quay accessible during the spring floods.

Malchavik had reached the middle of the dike when he heard the sound. Like a large slab of tile shattering on stone; like that, but not that. He stopped and looked back at the sleeping village. Probably those stupid cats, he thought. If clouds had not sealed in the valley he could have seen the edge of the village and the bridge farther down the river, much more clearly. He wondered if there was a storm brewing, the cloud cover was so thick. But the air did not smell right for rain.

He was about to turn back toward the quay when a light appeared. It was near the first few buildings closest to the bridge, a small red glow that vanished for a second, then reappeared. A pile of coals and someone moving around them. Who could possibly be up this late and cleaning out their hearth? Anyone else in Ukobachia might have probed in that direction to "hear" the person's identity, but Malchavik had given that up. He set off toward the curious glow.

Before he had reached flat land again, the coals ignited and a bright flame rose up, bobbed about—a torch! Malchavik's heart began to pound. He hurried along the path. A second torch ignited. Then the buildings were between him and the lights, and all he could see were insidious shadows. He would have headed straight for the light but, at the end of the alley ahead, three torch-bearing figures darted past. He called out to them and ran between the buildings and into the road. The figures had disappeared, and he was casting a long, wavering shadow. With a cry he swung around and saw the flames licking up the walls of two buildings.

The sight of the fire was so horrible that for a few moments he could not move or think what to do. Then release came in the knowledge that someone had set the fires. He bolted into the center of the road, shouting, "Up! Up! Fire! Assassins in the village, wake you all!" He sensed a motion behind him, started to turn; his closed-off abilities, re-emerging through panic, warned him of imminent danger, and he raised his arm to catch the thing coming at him, but only managed to slow it down. The club struck him above the ear and he crumpled to the ground.

Shouts, screams and the ringing of a bell all jumbled together in Malchavik's half-conscious state. Some village was burning, but it was far removed from him and too much trouble to devote much time to. Something scuffed near his head and he muttered, "Pavra," and opened his eyes. A bare foot pointed at him, light rippling over it. Fire. He was rolled onto his back and a voice called to him. A bearded face hung over him. He knew that face, if he could just put a name to it. He was pulled to a sitting position. The face wore a look of terror. Why was the man afraid of him? Had they found him drunk again? His eyes focused beyond the man, on flames shooting up as high as trees. Pavra...

"Pavra!" he wailed and wrestled to be free of the man's grip. He twisted his head to see his shop and house—to see them shaped by fire. Throwing himself forward, he tried to crawl along the ground, but the man with the beard stopped him and sat him up again.

"Malchavik, what happened?" The alarm bell stopped ringing then. Somewhere nearby something crashed.

"Assassins ... with torches, to kill us in our sleep." He

raised watering eyes to his house again. "Oh, gods, is she safe? Do you know if she got out?"

"It's chaos, Malchavik. I haven't any idea." The bearded man released him and stood up. Malchavik concentrated past the pain in his head and retrieved the man's name. "Stachem," he said, "help me up. Take me to my home."

Stachem obeyed, helping him to his feet. The roof of the tailor shop fell in and a wall twisted and collapsed on top of it. "You have no home," Stachem said.

Malchavik began to shiver. His voice whined in his throat. He closed his eyes and concentrated. From Stachem he borrowed strength and will, driving back the shock, erasing from the forefront of his thoughts the knowledge of his daughter's fate. His lips parted, curled. "Come," he ordered. His first steps were unsteady, but became surer as he progressed. Around him people ran in desperate panic. He sent his thoughts to some of them, gave them control, direction. They turned and came with him. He choked from the smells that the smoke carried. His eyes stung. But he went on, certain that there was only one place the enemies could go.

Five figures stood in the center of the wide bridge. At either end, blocking them, were members of his village. All three parties were armed, holding one another at bay. At the far end were guards from the pass who had come running at the first sign of fire. They had sealed off the bridge. Those at the other end had guarded the road and, upon seeing the torch-wielding brigade from Trufege escaping, had given chase. Only five members of that brigade had been forced by circumstance to use the main bridge; the others had escaped on the rope bridge that had allowed them access to Ukobachia.

Malchavik and his collected citizens pushed through the guards. The five men on the bridge were strangers to him; one of them was a priest.

The priest, assuming Malchavik to be a town leader, addressed him haughtily. "We're passing through here on church business. It's imperative you let us continue to Trufege."

Malchavik looked at the clubs and incriminating torches some of the priest's party carried, and he laughed in the priest's face. "Is the incineration of so many innocents a scheme of your church? Did Voed come striding down and tell you to kill us in our sleep?" He took another step toward the priest. "That sounds like the work of men to me, unless the gods have become dastards."

"You blaspheme!" shouted Varenukha.

"Do I? I will do far worse than that before morning." He faced his people. More of them had arrived. He looked through their minds but found no knowledge of his daughter. No one had seen her. Tears rimmed his eyes, but he fought off the desire to give up; some of his village still lived. He reached out to the nearest people. They clasped his hands, their own hands trembling. He gripped them hard, imparting his resolve to them. They reached out to others who linked hands with them and then with others still, until the entire group had become a closed chain.

The five from Trufege did not know what the linking of hands meant—what they knew of Kobachs was founded on lies and legends that rarely contained more than a kernel of truth—but the priest could sense this was not in his favor. He grabbed a torch from one of his dumbfounded villagers. He raised the torch to fling it into the midst of the Kobachs, hoping to create a panic situation in which he could escape, even if he had to throw the four others with him to the witches.

The torch sputtered and died.

Varenukha lowered it and then dropped it. He said, "Quick, into the water!" and took one step toward the rail himself.

Suddenly he could not breathe and his legs would not obey him. He heard his men cough and choke. The farthest man back stumbled away and tried to make for the end of the bridge. Varenukha saw him jerk rigid. The body snapped like a dry stick, and fell to the ground. It flopped there, gasping like some dying fish. Varenukha felt as much as heard a pop in his nose. Warm blood trickled down his lip. He clawed at his throat, grabbed the flesh beneath his chin and tried to pull his throat open.

From far away came a strange animal cry. The pressure of Varenukha's throat relaxed and he toppled back into the center of the bridge.

"Look there," shouted one of the Kobach sentries, who had broken the chain to point. They all stared up at the sky. Varenukha tilted his head to see what they were looking at. The strange animal ululation was repeated and then answered from farther off. A swift winged shadow plunged into a burning building; but the Kobachs were watching something above that.

Varenukha saw a second huge shape descending toward a burn-ing house at the edge of Ukobachia. "How is it possible?" someone asked. No one could answer. Varenukha forgot the pain in his throat.

The shape had bulging eyes and great leathery wings. Its arms were short, the legs long and tightly muscled, ending in splayed talons. He could not believe what he saw. It was a thing out of legend, a mythical nightmare. Someone named it even as the word took form in his own mouth. "Krykwyre." The second monster entered the flames as the first one had done. A third emerged from the cloud beyond the village, visible only as a shiny speck. It circled the river briefly, then hovered. In another moment they knew why. Uttering its shrill cry, the Krykwyre changed course and headed for the bridge.

"Run!" The other Kobachs released hands and scattered back to the road. They turned from their vanquished town, vanished into the valley forest—all but Malchavik. The Krykwyre scared him as much as any of them, but he no longer cared if he died this night. He was going to take revenge for his daughter's death.

The priest was getting to his knees as fast as he could and trying to crab his way to the side of the bridge. Malchavik lowered his head, formed his anger and misery into a weapon— an invisible hand that grabbed the priest and dragged him back to the center of the bridge. Varenukha looked up and saw the one Kobach who had not fled. "What are you doing?" he cried to the old man. "It's coming for us!" The monster shrieked, and Varenukha screamed at the same time, as if in answer. The priest's wide eyes stared helplessly as the Krykwyre swooped nearer with every beat of its wings.

Sweat ran down Malchavik's face. His skin was ashen from the effort of holding the priest. He was aging years every moment, but he would not stop. Bending down, he reached out, placed one hand on each of Varenukha's legs below the knee. "For . . . my daughter," he said. The pressure in the priest's upper body subsided, but in that instant he shuddered from a searing agony where the Kobach's grip held him. His hand swiped vainly at the old man who dared oppose him. The air blackened in his eyes. Then the pain stopped.

Malchavik released his hold and limped, wheezing, to the railing. With a last look back at the priest, he pulled himself under the top rail and dropped into the river.

The monster shifted in flight, extended its legs like a hawk about to fall on its prey.

Varenukha rolled onto his side, then with difficulty flipped himself up into a sitting position. With one hand, he felt along his legs. They were rubbery. The bones between his knee and ankle had disappeared. He could not stand! He looked for help, but all of his men lay dead on the bridge, killed by the Kobachs' power. The monster shrieked. Varenukha looked up. Black talons stretched to seize him. He flung himself at the railing. The Krykwyre rose up to come at him again.

Varenukha dragged himself across the bridge, clawing at the dirt, the wood, fingers shredding with splinters that he barely felt as he strained and caught hold of an upright, slapped his other hand around it, drew himself toward escape as the thunder of enormous wings reverberated like the heartbeat of the night. He did not have to look back to see the greenish gray scales and yellow globular eyes with pin-prick pupils and the talons clicking in angry anticipation; in his mind he saw and pulled himself along the harder for it. Then he was caught and screamed and scrabbled madly at the boards, feeling the monster's grip, wildly glancing back to find his robe snagged on a board. He whined as he ripped the robe free and then turned to slide beneath the rail, free at last, staring down into the dark security of the river as the talons of the Krykwyre punctured his sides from above and split him open like the tail of a shellfish.

The icy river shocked Malchavik to alertness, granting him strength through fear. The current propelled him along and down. He let it carry him, and, when it slackened, kicked his way up to the surface. His head broke free not far from the bank and he swam there as fast as he could. Reaching the shallows, he staggered onto the bank and collapsed. His body quaked with each deep-drawn gasp. He lay there until restored enough to take stock of his situation.

The bridge and the land rising to meet it blocked his view of the dying village, but the hidden flames illuminated great chimneys of smoke that reached into the clouds. And as if the smoke had condensed and become sentient, the gray-green Krykwyres rose out of the wreckage. They each carried a blackened, sometimes burning, corpse.

Malchavik stood cautiously, then made his way up the bank.

He could not believe what he beheld. Krykwyres were portrayed in dozens, perhaps hundreds, of illuminated stories and tapestries across the land; he had even once witnessed a festival in Dolgellum in which a celebrant had come dressed as a Krykwyre. He recalled his mother's words from when he was a child: "They wait outside to claim your body and take your soul to Mordus, who owns you in death, for they will eat you when they catch you. Now, go to sleep."

He laughed at the memory, which started him coughing. It was impossible that these things were real—monsters from out of the Grymwyre Mountains? Impossible. Yet there they were.

Then something else caught his eye and he glanced into the sky. The dark cloud that had settled over the valley was spinning like an inverted whirlpool. And far down in that swirling hole lay a tiny ball of fire, larger than a star, but not so big or bright as a moon.

Malchavik ducked back down and considered what he had seen. His disbelief was gone, but this was something beyond anything he understood. He needed to talk with others of his people; he had to go after them. That meant he had to cross the bridge again. He edged along the bank until he reached the corner of the first plank, then raised his head to ensure that no winged horror lurked about—and stared straight into the face of death. Varenukha's eyes looked past him and beyond life itself. His dark tongue dangled from his mouth, touching the boards. The head had been ripped from the body and the body itself had disappeared. A great dark smear across the boards showed where it had been. Malchavik looked down the length of the bridge and saw that all the bodies had vanished. He climbed up, holding the railing for support.

The Krykwyres had lifted the corpses of Ukobachia out of the flames, but had not carried them away. Upon the quay, Malchavik saw bodies stacked, placed there by the monsters. Among the smoldering corpses a bright white figure walked. A total of four Krykwyres—the last just settling on the quay with another corpse—towered over the figure, but were apparently under its direction. They all stood back from it. Malchavik heard a soft purling sound. The white figure grew incandescent. Around it, slowly, one by one, the bodies rose into the air and sped toward the hole in the center of the cloud. They tumbled faster and faster, whirled around the outside of

the vast whirlpool, then shot into its center one after the other.
Malchavik unconsciously stood up, realizing that one of those
bodies had to be Pavra. What would happen to her? Why was
she being taken away? He took a step across the bridge, then
saw what he was doing and stopped. He could hardly go chasing
down to the quay. No. Pavra was dead. What he had to do
was get to his people, perform the proper ritual so that her soul
was protected. The white creature out there on the quay could
take only her body. It would never own the soul of his little
child with the flower on her head. . . . He hugged the post and
began to cry.

His inviolable world was coming apart. Death had invaded
it. Death from the skies. He raised his head. Was he witnessing
the presence of a god? Was the figure on the quay Mordus
himself, as legend suggested? Malchavik wiped his eyes and
looked again down the river.

The quay was empty, the figure gone.

Malchavik trembled. Was it possible the priest had been
telling the truth? That the village had been destroyed by the
gods? If so, why? They were peaceful people. The stories of
their attempts to equate themselves with the gods were all
fabrications of outsiders; surely, omnipotent Voed knew better.
But what if that *had* been Mordus . . . ? Well, suppose it had?
That could as easily stand in their favor. The Krykwyre had
come to slay the priest for his execrable act. No one else had
been slain by them that he knew of. Only the bodies of the
dead had been delivered up. Yes, yes, he vaguely remembered
tales from the early days when his grandfather and father had
been warriors, tales from soldiers who claimed to have lain
near death on a battlefield and actually seen the dark god come
to collect those who were now part of his domain. . . . But the
story went that the god simply *touched* them, leaving the bodies
and leading away the souls. The *dark* god. He was no philos-
opher; he needed help with the contradictions. He also needed
warmth. His teeth were chattering.

Most of the village had burned to rubble. Small fires flickered across the stretch of land. Nothing was left for him there.
He turned and started away toward the woods, rubbing his arms
to keep warm. His legs ached, trying to cramp. Soon he would
be at the end of his energy reserve.

The path was hard to follow in the utter darkness beneath

the trees. Malchavik could not go very far. He leaned against a tree and, after resting a moment, closed his eyes and called out silently to those who had gone before him. From far ahead he received a dim reply. They answered him with energy, with the strength to keep walking; and they would wait for him.

Malchavik pushed off and continued along the trail. It paralleled the river, leading in and out of the foothills. An hour later he had entered the outskirts of Boreshum Forest. The trail he followed eventually led him across the South Road to Dolgellum. He knew precisely where he was then. Not four steys south, King Dekür had been slain. He thought about that as he went along, wondering if perhaps the same cloud that had destroyed his village had opened up and swallowed the Princess Lewyn.

On the opposite side of the South Road, Malchavik paused to contact his people again. The answer was much stronger now, but they entreated him to hurry. The forest swallowed him again as he hobbled off toward the rendezvous.

Within minutes of Malchavik's passing, the dust of the South Road blew up beneath the percussive hooves of a dozen horses. In the forest dimness not one of the Atlarman soldiers saw the trail or the tracks that many feet had made across the road an hour before. They rode in tight formation, Faubus in the lead. Their eyes were wide, glistening in the dark as they searched the depths on either side for Voed-knew-what horrors, and, finding none, imagined their own.

Faubus had deployed one group some distance back to make camp and prepare for a search of Boreshum beginning at first light. Between the camp and the mountains through which they now rode lay foothills where Kobach farms lay; Faubus noted that each one was dark and apparently serene. Neither he nor his men anticipated what they found.

The first streaks of dawn spread above the old, rounded mountain tops, but their first sight of the village was of shadow and darkness. The road made a twist, then widened where it branched toward the bridge. They saw the village clearly from there; the smell of the carnage overtook them even as their weary brains awoke to realization of the destruction.

Smoke hung on the dead still air—a thin and gauzy cloud through which the wan light preceding dawn flowed, dimming the higher eastern slopes to the color of old bones.

No buildings were left standing. Red-hot mounds of rubble indicated where they had been. Faubus raised his hand for his men to rein in.

He selected four of them and sent them across the bridge and up the pass. The rest he sent ahead of him into Ukobachia. As they came nearer, the soldiers saw scavenger beasts slinking amidst the smoke and debris. Most of these figures were animals; but a few were people who moved like animals, whose humanity had been ripped from them. At the soldiers' approach, these creatures paused, lifted their heads in alarm and then fled back into the forest.

Faubus saw nothing that might indicate how this had happened, and he slowly followed his men into the village.

"Captain!" came a shout from the bridge. With a glance at the body of the soldiers ahead, Faubus turned his horse and rode back.

Two men awaited him at the bridge. The other two had apparently disobeyed his order to ascend to the pass. He knew there had to be a good reason. One of the men stepped forward and saluted as Faubus drew up. "Sir," he said, casting a glance at the other soldier, "we have something to show you."

"Yes?"

The soldier turned. "It's over here."

The captain climbed down and tied his horse to the railing, then followed the two men. His legs were stiff. The two soldiers stopped, their backs to him, looking down. As he came up, they moved apart so that he could see.

The head lay on its side, mouth clogged by the tongue, eyes open wide but glazed. Its oily hair stood up like thorny spikes. Faubus thought he knew the face, but, as he had never been to Ukobachia before, could not be certain this was true. Whoever it was, he had died in agony. "I'm afraid I don't know this man—do either of you recognize him? Was he someone important in their village?"

The second soldier, who had not spoken before, said, "Not *their* village, Captain. That is, well—I used to ride patrol round by Chagri's temple. This man was there a lot."

"He's a priest?"

"Sir, this is the priest the Hespet sent to Trufege."

"Trufege." He glanced back at the razed village and let out a short fretful sigh. "Stay by the bridge until the other two have returned from the pass." He turned away and went back past

his horse, walking into the village. Fatty-sweet smells assailed
him again, this time much stronger. Faubus drew back his head
and pressed his lips tightly together. He came upon one of his
men softly entreating a woman who sat cradling something in
her arms. On closer inspection, he saw that it was the black,
charred remains of an infant. His man was trying to remove it
from the woman's inflexible grasp. Faubus went over, tapped
the soldier on the back, and shook his head. "Let it be for now;
come with me," he ordered. The soldier reluctantly obeyed.
The woman began to sing a quiet lullaby. The two men shivered
as they walked away from her.

The soldier said suddenly, "She must have picked it up when
it was still burning—her hands are all blistered, but she won't
let go, she won't—"

Faubus suddenly grabbed and shook him. "Stop it!"

The soldier's mouth worked slackly; then he seemed to find
himself again, and he came to attention. "What should I do,
then, sir?"

"Tell me what you've found. Forget everything but what
goes in your report."

"Sir. We've found virtually nothing. The Korbachs are either dead or have fled into the woods. The few left have, I
think, returned to search through the ruins for someone. But
there aren't any bodies, there's nothing . . . we . . . we had to
kill two of them—there was no helping it, we couldn't save
them."

"Of course."

"But that's no more than five or six people. The rest are
gone. We're still looking."

"Good."

They walked along in silence until they came to another
group of men who were carrying away a survivor, an old man
who was babbling to no one in short, disjointed fits. Another
soldier came up, nodded at the man being taken away, then
said, "The old man said Trufege came down out of the hills.
He sounded sane for a minute there, Captain; then he got on
about hordes of Krykwyre swooping out of the clouds." Faubus
looked up into a clear dawn sky. "Yes, I know," said the
soldier, "that is what I mean, but he insisted all the same. Says
they came and took the bodies to Mordus himself. He claims
the god actually walked through the village, passed no more

than an arm's length away from him, bright as a star. Crazy,
I call it."

Another group of his men called out to him. They were
clustered around one of the mounds of rubble. As he came near
enough to see what held their interest, Faubus stared in wonder.

In the midst of the smoking heap, a small girl lay, apparently
asleep, on the remains of her bed. She had obviously lain there
while the fire raged around her, for the edges of her hay mattress
were blackened; but an unscorched circle surrounded her. Some
fathomless power had protected her. "Maybe we won't all fall
back into the pit," Faubus muttered. Beside him, a man said,
"Sir?" and he replied, "Never mind. Let's take her out of there,
shall we?"

"We've tried, Captain, but something protects her. We can't
touch her or pick her up."

"Try waking her, then. Call out to her."

"What's her name?" someone asked. The laughter that followed was nervous, edgy. Before anyone could call to the child,
another man pointed and said, "Look there!" Above the little
girl, a tall milky figure began to appear. Though they could
see through it, its features were distinct. It was a woman with
the strange designs of the Kobachs on her forehead. She gazed
down at the child reverently and her lips moved, although
nothing could be heard. Then the ghost lifted her face to the
sky and vanished.

The child's eyelids fluttered. She awoke and raised her head
to see the group of awestruck soldiers crowded around her.
She began to shake and, seeing the ruin of her home, to cry
for her father.

Faubus moved past his men and stepped carefully through
the glowing coals. He bent down, but let the girl make the
move to come to him. Her arms looped around his neck, and
she huddled against him. He whispered softly to her, lifted her
and took her out of the ruin. Behind him, the circle of preserved
straw suddenly ignited.

♭Chapter 11.

THE Castle Ladoman—a walled fortress the color of chalk, with squared-off buildings—rose out of a rare expanse of solid ground. Encircling it, trees taller than the castle walls stirred gently in autumnal breezes, but within five steys in any direction, the land turned brown and treacherous and the watery earth stank of sulphur and tar. Lyrec could not believe, when he topped the rise, that an oasis such as that castle could exist in this sodden land.

The owner of the castle was, at that moment, bathing in his lake on the far side of the castle grounds. As lakes go, this one more closely resembled a private pond. However, King Ladomirus would not have it referred to as anything other than *his lake*. His enormous body bobbed, a soft pink island, not far from shore. To the people who stood on that shore attending him, he discoursed loudly about his past achievements—a list his attendants had heard often enough to memorize many times over. The king had only a handful of credits to his name.

His bodyguard, Talenyecis, was among the attendants. She was a fierce red-headed warrior, tanned golden and freckled. Her head rested on a drawn-up knee that was braced against the stump on which she sat looking through narrowed eyes at Ladomirus, imagining the lake around him to be bright fire

rather than water. She contemplated her king cooking in his
own juices while she turned the spit on which he was impaled.
It was a pleasant image and made her deaf to his annoying,
incessant repetition of his deeds.

On the bank between Talenyecis and Ladomirus sat the fat
king's current woman. As with the lake, "woman" was an
inaccurate depiction of his concubine. The flaxen-haired child
was fifteen, if one believed the child herself. The girl pulled
at her wet tangle of hair and tried in vain to comb her fingers
through it. Talenyecis abandoned broiling the king and concentrated on the naked concubine, eyeing dispassionately the
sinuous line of backbone beneath the white skin, a spatter of
pimples on either side of the girl's fleshy buttocks. The girl
was clean, though, and safe, as had been all of Ladomirus's
concubines. Talenyecis always saw to that, just as she ensured
that their physique was to her liking, for the king would inevitably discard her and Talenyecis would inevitably take her.
She could see the time would be soon. The girl had given up
trying to look as if she were listening to what the king said.
He would have noticed that by now. Within a week or two this
would irritate him to action and the concubine would discover
that he had a darker, more unpleasant side to his sexual pref-
erences. Talenyecis did not mind taking the scraps from Ladomirus's table. He took one woman at a time and when he
was done never went to that woman again. Talenyecis managed
much more enduring relationships; from the castoffs she had
built up a substantial seraglio from which to select her pleasures.

Gazing beyond the concubine, Talenyecis was the first to
see two figures coming toward them from the south gate. She
stood, gracefully for all her size, and snapped her fingers. Two
male attendants, who had been ogling the naked concubine
themselves, twitched at the sharp sound and jumped to attention. They looked to Talenyecis for orders.

"Get his cloak ready," she said. "We have visitors."

The attendants glanced back at the people coming toward
them. One was a soldier, striding through the tall grass with
some effort. The other figure, taller and more slender than the
soldier, wore a wide-brimmed hat that cast his face in shadow.
Not far behind these two, the rushes shook as if a diminutive
third party—a dwarf, perhaps—accompanied them. The at-

tendants went about the business of unwrapping a heavy green robe that they were careful to keep from touching the ground.

Ladomirus continued to chatter away, oblivious to any change around him. Then, as he did each time he proclaimed some essential point about himself, he glanced at the shore to make sure his audience was paying attention. He saw the robe held out and took notice of the approaching figures. His gaze met Talenyecis's and he glowered at her for the petty reproach she showed him by not announcing the arrivals. He rolled over and paddled back to shore, his buttocks rising and falling like the bleached humps of a sea monster. The concubine paid no attention to any of this. She continued to work her hair into strands.

The fat king crawled out of the water and shook himself. He accepted the robe and belted it. The attendants, their job done, released it and, as the king strode forward, the embroidered hem dragged along the ground.

The soldier leading the man in the hat had come to attention. Ladomirus looked the stranger over, but spoke to the soldier. "What have we here?"

The soldier went to one knee with his head bowed, then stood. "Lord, this man wishes to join our cause."

"A recruit. Ha!" He clapped his hands. "You see, Talenyecis, just as I said. They know a leader, these mercenaries. Word would get out, I told you, and lead them all to us. And it has, just as I predicted."

"Yes, you did, Lord." *On too many occasions,* she added to herself. She studied the volunteer. He was studying her, too, and looking somewhat surprised, as if he recognized her from somewhere. She hoped he would not prove to be like so many of the others who came here—stupid, rough men with muddy brains who had forced her again and again to prove her superiority as a fighter. Within the castle at this moment were men who wore a scar or lacked an ear on her account. This one, though, seemed intelligent, and observant. A careful man. He made her slightly uneasy in the way he seemed calmly to read the scene and choose his place within it.

Her unease was apparently not shared by Ladomirus. He waddled up to the man and gripped his shoulders. The stranger smiled back.

"Now that's a rare thing," said the fat king. "Good teeth.

You find few good teeth around, heh?" His attendants nodded. "You must do well to stay so . . . clean, yes. And you look fed."

"I get by." That he neglected to add "Lord" to his answer went unnoticed by the king.

"You do of course. Or you'd be dead, in your line of work, heh? So, so. Your name is?"

"Lyrec."

Ladomirus pulled at his numerous chins. "From Növalok, then."

"No, from the south—outward bound from foreign lands. I came up through Miria."

"Yes, I had noted the accent of *course.*" All of the attendants promptly nodded as if to say, "We knew that." Ladomirus continued, "So, word of our needs—our intentions—has spread as far as that." His smile faded as he came to realize the implications of this. He turned to Talenyecis. "If they know in Miria, then we must assume word has reached *Atlarma* as well. What can we do?" Talenyecis continued to gaze thoughtfully at Lyrec. "Did you not hear me?" Ladomirus cried.

"Yes, m'lord," she replied dutifully. "I was waiting for . . . Lyrec to enlighten us."

"Well, traveller?" asked the king. "Our plans are known, are they?"

Lyrec glanced to Talenyecis while he addressed the king. "Not to me, they aren't," he answered. "I came here as a result of a chance encounter with some of your men, who mentioned in passing that you were looking for . . . extra men."

"Ah? My own men are blathering on about this?"

"Oh, no—your soldier was most discreet."

"Was he, then? What do you think of this, Talen, are we safe?"

Talenyecis hated the informal construct of her name Ladomirus liked to use. She glared at Ladomirus. *Safe?* she thought. *We'll never be safe so long as you are king, you pompous whale.* She spoke slowly, selectively. "If Dekür heard rumors he would undoubtedly reject the possibility as ludicrous. However, if for some inexplicable reason he chose to acknowledge the rumors, we would notice his activity immediately, would we not?"

Before Ladomirus could reply, Lyrec said to him, "Excuse me, but you are referring to the king of Secamelan? De-*koor?*"

"King Dekür, yes."

"Then you must be unaware that the king of Secamelan is slain."

The attendants eyed one another, but Ladomirus and Talenyecis stared expressionlessly at him as if he had said nothing extraordinary. Then Ladomirus grabbed up the hem of his robe and ran off toward the castle. Over his shoulder he called back, "Find him quarters, Talen!"

Behind him, the rushes shook again, as if some invisible creature pursued the fat king.

Lyrec asked the attendants, "Have I said something unfortunate?" They made no answer, but ran past him after their king.

"Lyrec, come with me," ordered Talenyecis. She struck off toward the south gate. The concubine began to laugh.

The stairwells of the castle were narrow—built at a time when the king had been leaner and poorer. Ladomirus had to squeeze his bulk like a snail through some of the passages. This annoyed Borregad. He would catch up with the fat king and then have to retreat into the shadows, waiting for the frantic sobs of breath to dwindle far enough away for him to give chase again, up another flight of steps, down another hallway.

Suddenly he heard an inhuman shriek followed by a sharp curse. Borregad rounded a corner and came face to face with a yellow cat, half his size, in flight for its life. Confronting Borregad, it leaped straight into the air and danced back against the wall, its back arched. The cat's yellow fur stood up, doubling its size. Borregad responded by moving to the opposite side of the hall; he had no time or inclination for a skirmish. The cat maneuvered to block him and hissed angrily, flicking one paw at him.

"Bugger off," Borregad snarled.

The yellow cat stopped dead, stupefied.

Borregad hurried past it and up yet another flight of steps. Why did wherever they were going have to be at the top of the castle? He could hear that Ladomirus had now left the stairwell and was shuffling down a hall. But, upon emerging on that level, he was confronted by an empty corridor that branched in both directions, a door at each end. He went left, watching for the green robe, listening for footsteps, finding nothing. Reaching the doorway, he took a look inside. The room was empty, a dark and musty chamber with three old, frayed and discolored tapestries on the walls. One circular window let in light; outside an orange flag could be seen. Borregad's whiskers twitched. There was dust in the air. He moved back, and the light fell across a different section of the floor, exposing an uneven line where the dust had been swept away by something dragging along the stones: the hem of Ladomirus's robe.

Then he heard a voice. Even distant and muffled as it was, the voice prickled the fur on his back. It crackled and sizzled in a way that recalled his passage between worlds.

Borregad crept into the musty room. He followed the dusted trail and the voice to one of the tapestries, then slipped behind it and into a small chamber. The space was all in darkness except for a thread of light spilling in from under a curtain at the opposite end. The voice was disturbingly near now.

It said, "What makes you think you may call me up every time you rattle with fear? The least problem sets you to quivering."

"The least problem?" It was Ladomirus who answered. "The death of Dekür is hardly a small thing. It changes the whole country over there. Why wasn't I told? We could attack this minute, now, while they are without a leader. We could win, couldn't we? Why was I not told?"

Borregad nudged his head beneath the curtain. Ladomirus's back was to him and blocked his view of whoever the fat king spoke to. But a brilliant white light haloed Ladomirus, cast by the speaker.

"Why?" the sizzling voice responded, and that simple word held unplumbed depths of scorn and rebuke. "Because you are a liar and a thief and above all a coward, and because you therefore expect these qualities to govern anyone with whom you deal. Any motives beyond cowardice and greed, especially the particular motives of a *god,* confound you. And you might recall from time to time that I *am* a god, little fat man. We are not equals in anything. If you insist on forgetting that, I shall quite likely melt you down for tallow."

Suddenly the brilliant white light fell across Borregad. He pulled back behind the tapestry then cautiously poked his head out again. Ladomirus had retreated a few steps in fear. The source of the voice was revealed: a tall, silvery white figure, its eyes round and red as blood, its mouth as black as a cave.

Ladomirus stuttered, then said, "I meant no offense. Surely you know that because I am—what you say"—even in his terror, it cost his vanity dearly to admit this—"a coward. But Dekür has died, great god. You must have known."

"It makes no difference to your plans at all. The country of Secamelan is not in chaos from this death. They have banded together against a common foe—an unknown foe, I should add. For you to draw attention to yourself too soon would argue that you were the one responsible for their king's death. If I thought it important I would have told you. We will do what we've planned to do all along. Nothing has changed. The assassination of the foreign king will go on as discussed, and then, when Secamelan is busily engaged in war with Findcarn, we will walk into her unprotected border without a skirmish. Believe in that if you will win."

Borregad retreated into the dark passage. He shivered at the thought of what he had to do next, but he had to be certain. Fearfully, he closed his eyes as Ladomirus began to speak again. The words faded to a buzz. Borregad directed his mental probe into the room with optimum wariness. From a distance he scrutinized the essence of the white being. In this non-physical sphere the being appeared to be a shapeless area of immateriality, as if nothing existed there at all. He stretched the probe ahead delicately. Only the most tenuous tip of thought touched the emptiness.

Its two blank white eyes opened upon him. The true form had appeared, its identity revealed with an intimacy that repelled him. He retracted the probe and, breathless with fear, pressed against the wall. His small heart thudded against his ribs. Those white eyes . . .

"What was that?" hissed the bright figure.

"What?"

"I sense something—someone. Who followed you?"

"Chagri, n-no one. No one would dare, they know the consequences—"

"True. No matter, is it? It would afford them nothing. No mortal can influence my course."

"Nor mine, great Chagri." The fat king laughed uneasily. "I do trust you, great Chagri, I do. You must know I do."

"As evidenced by your actions this day. Do not call me trivially again, Ladomirus."

The air shuddered, then clapped in thunder.

Borregad dared another look under the curtain. Ladomirus was placing a small silver globe on a black iron tripod that ended in a hand shaped to hold the globe. Borregad stared at the globe with grim satisfaction. If further proof had been necessary, there it was for all to see. The fat king came toward him, cheeks flushed, his face shiny with sweat. He shook drops of perspiration from the tips of his bejeweled fingers. He drew back the curtain. The passage beyond him was empty.

"I want to kill him! Let me!" shouted the soldier with his arm in a sling. He brandished a dagger clumsily while attempting to stand, but Talenyecis pushed him down with a sharp blow to the shoulder.

"What problem have you with him, Fulpig?" she demanded. She hated Fulpig more than most others: he was, at any given time, either competing with her for dominance or striving ineptly to seduce her; often he attempted both at the same time. He was a brutish moron and his crippled arm had not surprised Talenyecis one bit. That the new recruit had been responsible for it raised her opinion of Lyrec but made her distrust him more than ever before.

Fulpig spoke through his teeth. "You know what problem! He was to be dropped in a hole on the tors. They *promised* me. . . . How did he get here?"

"Abo brought him in. Apparently, your orders were countermanded by someone wise enough to recognize a potential volunteer."

"Abo? Where is he?"

She was growing tired of answering his questions, but told him, "In the next barrack, sleeping." She hoped he would take this information and leave, but he grabbed onto her wrist and said, "Then come with me and ask him what happened. Ask him where the rest of the men who were with him are, why they didn't come back, too? Ask him, you foul bi—"

She backhanded him across the mouth. "You do not learn, do you?" She poked a stiff finger into his wounded arm, making him wince. *"Never* give me an order. You've no rank that I didn't give you,—Fulpig, and I can take it away with one flick of the wrist. If you have an argument with that man, then you fight him accordingly. You can do it now or when your arm heals—that's up to you entirely. But no one else is to do your killing for you, and there's to be no confrontation within the castle walls. If I even suspect you've involved yourself in something of that sort, I'll dig out your bowels the way I'd scoop out a melon."

Fulpig's lips were pressed together so tightly that all color had been drained from around them. Talenyecis stared him down and he ended the argument by climbing to his feet and marching out past her. At the door, he lingered, then faced Lyrec. "If I can't have you, then I'll take that fat little pig who runs the tavern. *That* is outside this castle and this land, and no one here can govern it." His eyes flickered to Talenyecis. "No one." Then he was gone.

Lyrec took two strides after him, but Talenyecis held out her hand. He said, "Fulpig intends to kill a friend of mine. I have to stop him."

"The same rule applies to you as to him. You'll drive no arguments into conflict here. These are all mercenaries. Some of them I would call insane; the best are barely controllable. I'm more inclined to side with you because I loathe that greasy bastard, but there'll be no fights for you, either. Right now you are assigned to this room and that bed in order to let Fulpig take his partner and his horse and go. Your friend will have to look after himself." She walked over to him. "You've not been in this land long, I think. Here the weak are turned over like last year's topsoil by the powerful. Actually, I'd thought that was universal."

"It's not—not where I come from."

"And where is that?"

"A long way from here. So far that the two places have nothing in common at all."

"Except for you." She leaned down and patted the tattered blanket beside him. "This is your bed and anything you own goes beneath it. Any theft you report to me; but there won't be any thefts."

"No?"

"The last one was over a month ago—a man who decided my rule didn't apply to him and who liked someone else's boots better than his own. You may have noticed him as you rode in—the beggar at the front gate who has no hands."

"I see."

"So do the rest—daily. I don't want them to forget." She

turned abruptly and started for the door, but hesitated before leaving. "I was wondering, Lyrec—Fulpig suggested that I ask Abo about the party who brought you into Ladoman. They were supposed to kill you."

"And?"

"And I know Abo well enough to know he hasn't the mind for story-telling."

"All right. They came and I went with them. They were very adamant about it."

"And?" she asked, echoing his tone.

"We parted company along the way." His implication did not escape her. "I have this notion," she said, "that you are very dangerous, and also very careful. I find in spite of myself that I like you. I think also that the danger you present isn't to me, but to Ladomirus. . . . I see by the look in your eye that this is so. I'll ignore what I know and satisfy myself merely by watching you. In the future we may prove of use to one another."

When he said nothing, she left. One day, she thought, he might be useful, but that day was far off. Tomorrow she would send him out to Maribus Wood and let him ride a border patrol for a week or two. The less he knew of what went on in the castle, the more he would have to rely on her when and if a time for them to join together came. She had never allowed anyone to stand on equal terms with her. That was why she was still alive and not a whore or a peasant. This was no time to change that policy; to stand with men, she had to stand alone.

♭Chapter 12.

A MAN dressed in dark robes and a boy wrapped in a cape walked quickly through Atlarma. The streets were still crowded though it was near midnight. The majority of the multitude were drunken revelers participating in the combined wake and celebration that would continue until after the coronation. None of them reconized the Hespet beneath his purple robes. Nor did they identify the boy with him as their own king-to-be.

Slyur led the way past brightly lit brothels and darkened shops. Tynec dragged along after him, yearning to ask a thousand questions but saving them for the right time and place. Slyur hurried him through dark alleys, taking turns to avoid the crowds, running the risk of meeting up with thieves or worse in one of the narrow passages between shops. Some of the streets were cobbled, but most were dirt. Alleys which served as latrines stung their eyes and nostrils with acrid fumes; the ground there was muck. Tynec had never experienced anything like it and never wanted to again. Though he had spent all the years of his short life in Atlarma, he had never seen its darker side. He had no idea that he was greatly responsible for its filth and congestion.

He slipped suddenly and fell on the stones. The Hespet did

not wait for him, and Tynec had to race past three ugly, indecent
women and into another alley by himself, running to catch up
with the priest, nearly tripping over a body lying there, either
drunk or dead. Tynec ran on, not wanting to know which. He
charged out of the alley. A hand caught his throat and yanked
him sideways into the dark recess of a doorway.

Slyur motioned him to keep still. Tynec swallowed his heart
and obeyed. The new street contained no taverns; dark, deserted
shops and a storage house for community surplus lined the
narrow dirt track. He and Slyur moved quickly, quietly between
two buildings into an alley so cramped they had to walk sideways. They emerged from the alley farther south, then fell back
against a wall as a patrol rode past. Across from them stood
one of the walls that surrounded the temple of Chagri.

Here was the trickiest part of their journey, for the temple
was enclosed also by beggars and cripples camped upon its
yard and down into the ditches beside the road, spilling out
and onto the thoroughfare. The Hespet pressed Tynec behind
him. It seemed to Tynec an hour of hesitation, but it gave him
time to think. He did not like what he was doing. Most of all
he resented that he had not been allowed to mention it to
Cheybal or, at the very least, his grandfather. The Hespet,
coming to him in secret, had forbidden such things and warned
of the terrible dishonor he would bring upon his family if he
did. His grandfather would break under the weight of shame.
A family secret kept for generations would be revealed to the
world, and the source of the strength of his lineage would
collapse—so the priest said.

A commotion began across the street. The people there
began muttering and gesturing. From farther down the road
came cheers and shouts, which swept toward them in a wave.
The coach of the Hespet rolled into view. Caught up in the
drama, Tynec watched spellbound as poor beggars leapt onto
the coach and crawled into the road, narrowly missing being
trampled beneath the horses. Then the Hespet jerked him aside,
dragging him away along the shop fronts. No one in the ragged
crowd paid them any attention. The priest and the boy scurried
across the road and along a short path to arrive opposite the
eastern gate of the temple. A blind man sat against the wall,
weeping. On hearing their approach, he cried out, "Is it you?
I'm ready. I've waited." He hurried to get up. "Great god, I

embrace you; I've always done so! Now let me *see!* No, wait—don't pass me. I'm *worthy!*" His words disintegrated into sobs.

Slyur opened the grillwork door and pulled Tynec inside. The Hespet looked around. As he had anticipated, no priests were in view; most of them were at the front entrance where they would now be prying beggars like barnacles off his coach. He had told the driver that he would be staying in the castle and sent the empty coach back to the temple to distract the crowd.

The temple yard was dark. Light came from the priests' quarters along the south wall. A row of hedges paralleled the walk from the gate to the side entrance of the temple building, and Slyur and Tynec kept close to it, Slyur playing his part, striding boldly along. No one noticed them.

Inside the temple, the night candles had been lit. The Hespet removed his disguising outer robes and took the cape from Tynec, depositing them on a table that they passed on their way into the center of the temple.

The statue of Chagri gleamed in the candlelight. Bits of mineral within the chidsist figure glittered like stars. Candles were hidden on stands in the hollow of Chagri's shield, their invisible fire causing shadows to creep into the unfinished eyes above. Tynec met those shadowed orbs once and did not look up again. He directed his attention to the priest and noted that the Hespet, too, seemed cowed by the statue.

"I will leave you now for a short while, Tynec," Slyur whispered, then coughed and cleared his throat. "When the moment is right we will meet Chagri and you will have bestowed upon you the secrets he gave your father and his—the secrets that will make you as proud a ruler as your—as Dekür was." He left hastily.

Tynec's eyes narrowed. He was almost sure the priest was lying to him. Tynec could not recall his father ever acting through any abstruse powers; his father had always acted openly and honestly. He had rarely mentioned the god of war, and never once in any positive way. His father had disliked the idea that someone could actually worship war.

Tynec listened. In their hiding places, the candles hissed. He could not tell where the Hespet had gone. Uncomfortable with his back to the statue, he shifted so that he could observe it without staring at it directly. This proved to be a mistake;

the statue, seen peripherally, appeared to move with each minute waver of candle flame. Tynec backed away from it. His
feet crunched the stones. The sound reverberated, and he took
some consolation from the knowledge that no one could sneak
up on him here. His fingers rubbed lightly on the hilt of his
belt dagger. His back came to rest against a wall. On either
side of him a candle burned. He relaxed in the bright corner
and waited.

With each passing minute, the boy grew more at ease. The
statue offered no threat, and neither did the Hespet. Although
his father had never brought him here, the temple did not awe
him. His father had worshipped in the temple of Anralys, there
asking guidance, health and wisdom for his family. He never
would have prayed for anything that Chagri might offer.

Tynec reflected on the wretched people he had seen camped
around the temple. He had never encountered so many helpless
and destitute people gathered in one place. He had not realized
that so many of them existed in Atlarma. How did they survive?
Why was nothing done for them? The first thing he would do
upon becoming king would be to pass a law concerning the
unfortunates. There were so many. He would banish them all
from the city. That way—

What had he thought? He hadn't meant that. His brain was
tired, he was jittery, and his thoughts had drifted. Not banish-
ment, for the sake of charity! How ridiculous. Those people
must be helpless. They could not fight to defend the city, but
they could certainly die. When the attack came on Atlarma,
they could be placed out front as a barrier to shield the soldiers.
A human battlement, yes, don't banish them. He could see it
now: bodies adrift like logs jamming a river, carrion birds
circling in the plumes of smoke. Death—the order of disorder,
the element of certainty amid chaos. He so looked forward to
the day of destruction.

"Goodbye, Tynec," the boy said.

The child moved across the room, his puppet-body easily
manipulated as his consciousness was withdrawn and replaced.

The Hespet entered again. He saw the expression on the
boy's face and did not have to ask if the transformation had
been a success. The boy said, "Hello, Slyur—ah, but I mustn't
call you that. You must be the Hespet to me in this form or
someone might grow suspicious." He stretched his arms up

and flexed his fingers. "A healthy little boy. Good. Now you and I can rule well and certainly more wisely than an eight-year-old, eh? You'll have your favorite world of clerics and worshippers . . . soon, more worshippers than ever before. However, as regards the secular world, hereafter you needn't concern yourself with it at all."

Slyur made no answer.

"Oh, and you needn't accompany me back. I can find my way to the castle, and I would just as soon wander the streets a bit, soak up some of the local debauchery. Good night, priest." He marched out past Slyur triumphantly. Chagri's footsteps faded away into the night.

♭Chapter 13.

DEEP within Maribus Wood, Lyrec rode his lone vigil with Borregad draped across his shoulders and trying very hard to sleep. He kept to the trail as instructed. The other two patrollers had parted company with him that morning and he did not know how close they might be or if they rode behind him to ensure his compliance with the orders Talenyecis had given him.

During the earlier part of the ride, he had struck up a conversation with the two riders. They informed him that to patrol through Maribus was an honor; in both their cases, they had been granted it after capturing and returning escaped field workers. Whatever he had unknowingly done, it had obviously won him favor in the eyes of Talenyecis. But this, they warned him, had a darker side he should be careful of. Talenyecis was possessed of unknown but perilous sexual tendencies—a number of men had won the honor of a visit to her quarters, and none of them had ever been seen again. When Lyrec asked to whom this had happened, the soldiers confessed that they had not personally known any of the men but that the stories were far too numerous to doubt. "Don't trust her, ever," both men had warned, "especially when she rewards you. Everything she does has a double meaning."

"Borregad," he called, "are you awake?"

"Mmm."

"When we get back, will you be able to find that hidden room again?"

"Of course, but"—he raised his head suddenly—"you don't mean to face Miradomon *there*, do you?"

"That's exactly my intention. If, as you say, he is called through his crex there, then what better place? We will catch him off guard, expecting Ladomirus. We could never hope for another opportunity like this. He appears in a mortal form—"

"An *im*mortal form, if I might say. Ladomirus called him a god. For that matter, he referred to himself as one. These gods have all sorts of mystical powers, controlling all the elemental aspects of the world. They can make storms and level cities, but they don't live among the lesser creatures."

Lyrec laughed. "You can't actually believe in these gods? When was the last time we visited the remains of a world and saw the gods come down to inspect the damage?"

"What about Caudel's tale? 'The gods came down and obliterated everything.' It could be more than myth."

"All right, it could be more than myth. If it is, then Miradomon started off by killing the gods, because he is presently impersonating one of them and if they were still around they would have taken some action against him by now."

Borregad sat up. "Exactly, 'pon my soul! Look at his power!"

"Then, my notion is still right. The best time to attack him is the moment he appears in that room, in physical form, unprotected."

"Unprotected? From what? What will you do, kick him in the shins? The crex is lying in the tavern yard."

"Well, where do you suppose we've been going while you slept?"

"What? I thought we were riding patrol inside this ghastly excuse for a country."

"We are. We're also headed west. We should arrive at the tavern by tomorrow midday. We will retrieve the crex and ride back to Ladoman, and our long patrol will be up. I only hope Miradomon does not intend to move quickly. But it seems from what you said that he is doing the opposite, delaying, manipulating on a vast scale. If he proceeds as he did the last time, then Ladomirus will assemble an army and Miradomon the god will lead that force into battle and annihilation."

"The army of Ladoman? Those stupid, scabby miscreants against all of Secamelan? And any other nations that band with them? Preposterous. His army wouldn't survive one battle. Miradomon wipes out worlds, whole continents at a time. There have to be more nations involved—Miria, Növalok, these other places. And what about this assassination he's cooked up with Ladomirus? What are we going to do about that?"

"What can we do? We don't even know the circumstances surrounding this proposed assassination. We can't stop it when we don't even know where or when it's to take place. No, the only thing we can do is confront him in that room. The rest of whatever he has planned will have to take care of itself. You were the one who said I shouldn't waste my time worrying about these creatures and their problems. Well, I'm not. I've concerned myself with one thing and one thing alone."

They rode on for quite some time in silence, each of them tangled in his own thoughts. Lyrec had taken sides with Borregad and was forcing himself not to let the problems of an entire race get between him and his goal—a task requiring him to block out any emotional involvement. He found that this was the equivalent of lying to himself.

The sun had nearly set when Lyrec steered the horse off the trail and along the river. They were tired and needed rest and food. Not far downstream of the ford he came upon a clearing and reined in.

The cat interrupted his thoughts. "Lyrec, there is one other thing. I've hesitated to bring it up...."

"What are you talking about?"

"If Elystroya really is still alive, and you slay Miradomon in that castle room before we find his sanctum, you'll lose our one thread to her."

"That cannot influence what we do. We're here to kill Miradomon. And Elystroya is probably already dead. I have to accept that. She's dead. Don't speak to me of her again!" he said fiercely.

The cat said nothing, but jumped down from Lyrec's shoulder and plodded away.

Borregad reached the river and began to pace along the bank. The water drifted by lazily, curling around a sandbar. The cat did not understand himself; why had he brought up Elystroya when he was the one who'd never believed she was still alive?

The cat reached the sandbar and lay down, looking into the water. It slid past him in a ceaseless stream, indifferent to the plans and doubts of men or gods or beings who were neither.

Borregad did not know how long he lay there on the sand, but at some point he perceived that the sky had darkened. He got up and headed back to where he had left Lyrec.

He found a fire burning, but Lyrec, in his Ladomantine uniform, was nowhere to be seen. The cat listened to the forest and heard a soft splashing that might easily have been produced by some large fish, or by Lyrec. He set off toward the sound and soon came upon a narrow path. The river turned back upon itself not far south of where he had lain. A large sandbar peninsula hooked around there, enclosing a pool where there was little current. Lyrec's uniform was piled on the sand and he swam in the middle of the pool.

The huge cat walked out to the tip of the sandbar. He considered how the water seemed to refresh Lyrec; but some deeply embedded emotion caused Borregad to hesitate in joining his friend. Gingerly, he dunked one paw. A wave of dread beseiged him. He backed away and fled to the safety of the shore, there pausing to lick his foot. He cast a series of baleful glares at the black waters.

Lyrec climbed out of the river and sat on the sandbar in the darkness for a while. The swim had charged and awakened him; the chill of the air made him feel keen and tightly strung. Earlier, he had seen the cat watching him from the shore. Closing his eyes, he probed and located Borregad in the darkness not far away.

"Bo," he called out, "forgive me for snapping at you. I'm still unaccustomed to being moved so deeply. It is as you said the first day we arrived: the total sweep of emotions has invaded us just as we've invaded this world." Borregad was silent. Lyrec continued.

"For a while I thought how lucky we were to have come across Miradomon so quickly, but I've changed my mind. We would have found him in any violence anywhere, any cruelty or crime would have led us back to him eventually. I think he basks in the violence these creatures throw off. He loves it— it's part of him. And I am deathly afraid it has become part of me, too. I've hidden most of it from you, but twice now I've been driven to murderous anger; the last time I actually relished it. I looked at what I'd done and I was sickened and thrilled at the same time. This duality, I can't reconcile . . . I'm not even certain I *want* to find Elystroya. What would she be like in this environment? What I recall seems to have been a dream, a fading memory of a life so unlike this one that it cannot possibly have been real. But if we find her, what then? Can we exist in this world? Borregad, I'm afraid of myself."

When, after a few minutes, the cat did not reply, Lyrec got up and dressed in the orange and brown uniform once again. "I don't want to fight with you. We have only us, and both of us must survive."

Borregad sidled down the embankment and onto the hook of sand. "Of course we'll both survive. I already knew about your anger—as a matter of fact, I have been its recipient since we arrived here. If you wouldn't insist on being in control all the time, too, we would get along much better. And stop worrying, will you?"

Lyrec walked up to him, paused, then said, "All right, I'll stop worrying . . . if you stop nagging." He walked on.

The cat looked insolently after him. "Nagging? Me? See if you ever get a drop of sympathy out of *me* again, ever." Lyrec climbed the bank. Borregad stood on his hind legs and shouted, "And instead of being afraid of yourself, you might show a little respectful fear of Miradomon—because I've seen him, and *he* doesn't have a single, solitary reason to be afraid of *you!*" He gestured angrily and fell over.

Embers lay where the fire had been. The camp was silent. Lyrec's eyes opened and stared straight into the darkness. What had awakened him? He shifted his gaze. In the dim red glow he could just make out Borregad lying on his back with his paws stretched in absurd directions. If he was awake, too, he did a remarkable job of concealing it. Lyrec concentrated on listening.

Forests at night are full of sounds that no living being from outside the forests would recognize as natural: dead branches succumb to their own weight after months or years of hanging on and crash to the ground, nocturnal animals escape from nocturnal predators with a dash through brush, various forms of insects sound passionate love calls. Lyrec identified what noises he could and accepted that the rest belonged there. Apparently nothing extraordinary had awakened him. He closed his eyes and shifted to lie on his side.

No more branches fell; the insects subsided. Silence fell upon the forest.

His eyes opened again, and waited. He began to believe that he could see the silence strung like a cobweb around him. Something about it was unnatural. . . . Something entered him. With defensive instinct he closed off his mind.

Someone was probing him.

With his own wall up, he sent out a reciprocal probe, discovering quickly that his inquisitor had remarkably little defense and numerous personalities.

Shh . . . I can't find . . . thistle's in my . . . be quiet . . . someone there . . . feel queer . . . head, my head, must tell someone . . .

A dozen or more voices in all, their thoughts washed over him like river water. He sat up and looked into the darkness, sensing them, a cluster of people, although he could not see them. Gently, he called out to them: *There's no need for this. You are all welcome in my camp.*

Borregad flipped over and stood, his fur bushed out and his ears low. His reflective eyes rolled in panic. "What is that? Lyrec, what's happening?"

"We have company."

"Is it him?"

"No." He stood.

"Then, who—who's coming?"

"I don't know," he hissed. "Why don't you settle back down and let me find out?"

They came into the clearing slowly, one or two at a time. The younger ones assisted their elders, some of whom could barely walk. Lyrec added new wood to the fire, stabbed the embers to raise their heat.

The faces varied in shape and age, but shared a common enervation. He saw in their eyes some wariness as well as wonder and realized that what troubled them was the Ladomantine uniform he wore; beyond that, their gaze contained some collective semblance, as if the same two eyes had been replicated in each face. They were of a cognate stock and, at the moment, a very weary one. As the fire grew brighter, he could trace faint markings on some of them: lines and dots and swirls reshaped the natural features of some of the faces. In the flicker of the new fire, the lines made them seem to be wearing masks.

As one they studied Lyrec, then Borregad, who slunk back beside his comrade, much intimidated by the whole procession.

Seeking reassurance, he asked again, "Who are they?" forgetting in his fear that he spoke aloud.

Someone gasped. Another cried out, "A spirit!" A woman near the front said, "It's a *glomengue*."

"Pardon? A what?" asked Lyrec. Their rush of answers was, so far, meaningless.

"A glomengue," the woman repeated.

"Preposterous," Borregad snapped, "I am a *cat*."

Someone laughed weakly.

"No, Borregad," explained Lyrec. He had begun to understand. "It's a—a spirit—a nature spirit, isn't it?"

A few heads nodded. "The trickster of the forest."

"Trickster? In that case, Borregad definitely is a glomengue."

"And you," said an old man with a bandaged head, "are you not Kobach, then?" The old man's words bore a heavy accent. Lyrec concluded that his native language was not the tongue of Secamelan. He considered carefully how to explain himself. "We . . . have things in common. But I have no Kobach blood in me that I know of."

The same woman who had spoken before pointed at him. "But you had fingers in the darkness."

"F-fingers?"

"He isn't one of us, Belda; you can't use our terms and expect him to know," chided the old man. He then said to Lyrec, "We sensed you reaching out to us just as you must have sensed us."

"He gave me a terrible headache," said a young voice from the back.

Lyrec pursed his lips. "I see. I'm sorry if your head hurts."

"They're Kobachs!" exclaimed Borregad.

A few of the people laughed uncomfortably.

"On top of the situation as always," replied Lyrec. "Yes, they are Kobachs. And all of you are welcome to share our fire and camp. You seem more than a little tired."

"Most tired," agreed the old man. "We would greatly appreciate the chance to rest. My name is Malchavik. I have become a sort of leader for our group."

"And my name is Lyrec. His name you know by now."

"Ly-rek. And you say you've no Kobach blood? How uncommon."

"You're not the first who's thought so."

The old man crouched down slowly, his face showing pain.
"Yet," began Malchavik, "you travel with a glomengue."

"Would you mind not using—"

"Borregad," Lyrec warned.

"Well, 'cat' has proved sufficient for me and I think it ought
to be for them as well. *I* don't care for the sound of that other
word."

Malchavik made a brave attempt at a smile. "Not surprising
behavior for the trickster, eh?" The group murmured to one
another, marvelling at the cat. They had heard stories, but none
of them had ever seen a forest spirit before. Borregad turned
his back on them and watched the old man and Lyrec alone.

"Your village," Lyrec said, "is to the north quite some
distance as I recall. And by your looks I would surmise you've
come nearly that far without much food or pause. Something
must have happened, and it's not good, is it?"

Malchavik shook his head, then began his tale of the destruction of their village by the mob from Trufege, how apparently all those from Trufege and most of his own people
had perished, then described as he had seen it the appearance
of the mythical Krykwyres and the way the sky had swirled as
it sucked up the bodies of the slain. He recounted their flight
from Boreshum, with soldiers hacking paths after them. They
believed the whole country had turned against them and that
the soldiers hunted to kill them. So they had shunned all towns,
travelled mostly by night, and survived by eating things found
in the forests. It was possible that others of their kind had
escaped, and they were following the river to Lake Cym where
a handful of their kind lived in secrecy, certain that any survivors would know to gather there.

"Then we will go south to Myria or east into the mountains
of Tasurlak. There are places in both lands where we could
hide. Tasurlak is virtually uninhabited, you know. Most important, we must keep the elders such as myself sheltered from
sight. My face is difficult to conceal."

"No more so than your accent."

"This is so. Tell us, though, Ly-rek, will we be safe with
other soldiers of Ladoman? We had understood they were quite
cruel, which is why your appearance so startled us. Are many
of your kind here?"

"My kind . . . no. You will find the Ladomantines most unpleasant. You would do well to...kill any who see you or you'll be dragged off to work on their farms as slaves."

"But how do you avoid this? With the *glom*—with the Borregad?"

"Malchavik, I'm not a Ladomantine soldier. The uniform is a disguise. I'm on my way out of here, but I intend to come back."

"You may come with us. You could help us get away from here. Do you know the lands south and east?"

Lyrec, remember why you're here.

Thank you, Borregad.

To the Kobach, he replied, "Some of it I know painfully well, but I cannot join you. And what you've told me makes me more certain of that than ever." Malchavik did not understand, and hung his head. "No, no, not because you're unsafe to be with. I'm searching for someone and I've found him in Ladoman. At least so I thought."

"We did. I saw him," snapped Borregad.

"But we both know as well he dwells elsewhere, and now you have described him, I think, as the leader of the creatures you called Krykwyre."

"That's no surprise to me," said the cat. "He operated on many fronts before—he may even be able to exist in multiple places simultaneously. I'm not sure I like what I just said." He glanced worriedly at Lyrec.

"Excuse me," the old man interrupted, "I am not understanding."

"Well, the story is very complicated. We seek to uncover the location of an enemy we've chased for a long time, who has destroyed many people before and intends to destroy all of you and all of Secamelan."

Malchavik looked back at his people. "Then the omens speak true."

"What omens?" Lyrec asked, hoping for further enlightenment on Miradomon's activities, but the old man disappointed him. "The winds have been for three days from the south, with the smell of the sea upon them."

"I haven't sme—"

"Hush. What else?"

"The monsters that I spoke of, the Krykwyres, are themselves omens, legends come to life. We've felt the breath of

such a creature on our backs since the night our village burned.
At least one of them follows us—they are night creatures, too,
by nature, but a few times we hear in the daylight the flapping
of its wings. And nightbirds are singing at noon. In Boreshum
there have ghosts been seen. All of this, each thing of this list
alone would be terrible, but so much together is a proclamation
of the end."

"Perhaps. But our enemy has slowed down. We have never
come to a place before where he had not already erased the
life. He takes more time now, either glutted with power or
enjoying the finesse with which he manipulates. I would have
expected the skies to open and the thunder to roll, but these
activities are far more subtle and sinister and, I must confess,
more confusing."

"Such a one must be known to the gods."

Lyrec cast a silencing glance at Borregad. "We had thought
of that. It may be that your gods are helpless. Possibly even
dead."

"Is there such a being as that, who could kill the gods?"

"Regrettably, there is."

"And so," said Malchavik, "you have entreated the Borregad
to be your weapon."

"Um . . . I had never really considered it in that light, but
yes, I suppose. He's my ally, most of the time. He has even
seen this enemy, which is more than I have done, and survived
two encounters with him."

"As I thought—you are an avatar. This becomes clear. No,
please, you'll deny it, Ly-rek. We know,
we understand this, Ly-rek. Forgive us for the burden of problems we have delivered to you. We will go on."

"Nonsense. Sleep here, among the rushes, and swim—there
is a pool in the river over that way. I've some food you may
share, as well, although referring to it as food is flattering it.
In the morning I'll direct you to a road that will lead you to a
tavern not terribly far from here—a day's walk at the most—
on the western edge of Maribus. A friend of mine owns the
place and will put you up on my name, knowing that he'll be
generously rewarded for doing so."

"But we cannot pay." Before the old man had finished saying
this, a fat purse landed on the ground by his knee.

"That should keep you in Grohd's graces long enough for
you to recover your health. Then you can send out someone

to Lake Cym and ensure the need to journey there. And you'll need your health against the soldiers of Ladoman. I'll be travelling the same road, and I will herald your arrival and give Grohd a promise of further wealth if he treats you well. He wouldn't turn away that Krykwyre of yours if it paid him."

The old man hefted the purse and slowly shook his head. "How can we possibly accept this?"

"Malchavik, how can you not?"

The old man came to him, took his hand and tried to kiss it, but Lyrec drew it away. The other Kobachs stood.

"You needn't thank me. In fact, most of this—the money at least—is the work of the Borregad. If you've gratitude to offer, offer it to him."

The cat was slow to see what was happening. Then he tried to back away, but the Kobachs had surrounded him. They picked him up and hugged him, stroked him, passing him from hand to hand.

You'll regret this, he silently swore to Lyrec. *I won't forget.*

Lyrec laughed and left Borregad to their attentions. He wandered down to the river and sat back against the bank. In the starlight, the water reminded him in a comforting way of his old self, in swirls and speckles of silver against black. It carried him along and drew off his anxieties.

When he looked up again, it was in response to a sound, that of approaching footsteps. One of the Kobachs. Lyrec glanced over to see a young woman watching him warily, timid but daring in that she came to the avatar alone. The thought made him smile. Off to the left he heard sounds of splashing and talking as the Kobachs, taking his recommendation, waded into his pool. More amazing still, among these sounds he heard Borregad laughing. To the woman, he said, "You should join them."

When she did not answer, he asked, "What's the matter?"

"I don't know why I've come," she replied, so quickly that the statement sounded false.

"Well, neither do I." He admired her sharp features in the dim starlight. But her eyes were in shadow and something about her seemed feverish. He wondered when she had last eaten and asked her.

"Morning past. Some stick-grass pulp."

"You're hungry. Let me get you food." He stood. The woman suddenly hugged herself to him. At the first touch her body jolted as if she had expected to perish upon contact. He stared down at her head, trying to fathom her actions. Her body was warm but she shivered, and he decided she must be cold. He folded his arms around her and began to rub her back. When she stopped shaking, he gently moved her away. "There, now." She wore an odd expression. "Am I what you expected?" he asked.

"I don't know. No. I thought you would kill me for interfering with your solitude. One hears such stories. Or that you would be forceful and take me."

"I don't think I understand."

She shifted her feet. "Well, most of the stories I know about Voed and the others are how he changed form and trapped women when he decided he wanted them. You're a god, and I—"

"Am I?" And he answered himself: Yes, to you and your people I suppose there's no other way of accounting for me. "I don't feel much like a god." He sat down again.

She joined him. "What did I interrupt? Your thoughts are nearly unreadable. Your manner of thinking is not ours."

"It isn't? I don't know about that. You interrupted nothing; some sadness, maybe. My mind had gone home, I guess."

"Is home far from here? We know where gods dwell, but distances never explain very much about it."

"Home for me is eternally far. Please leave it at that—I've dwelled on it all I care to this night. It was as if the river currents pulled memories loose."

They sat in brief silence. The woman plucked up her courage.

"My name is Nydien," she said.

"Nydien. Very nice name."

"The river is cold. I know, I put my foot in."

"Perhaps it is, but you should swim. You would find it refreshing."

"Do you want to?"

"I've swum already. At dusk."

"Will you swim with me?"

He could not comprehend why his mouth went dry. He thought he would cough if he tried to speak. He simply nodded his head. He had meant to shake it. Nydien stood and began to undress, her back to him.

As he watched her from where he sat, strange, incompre-

hensible urgings went through him. What could they mean?
He thought he might be blundering into some trap but dis-
credited the possibility that this woman was from Miradomon.
However, the constriction in his throat and the tautness threaded
through his chest were far more alarming than his earlier, de-
pressed self-analysis. Delicately, so that she would not notice,
he probed her. The astonishing answer weltered near the surface
of her thoughts, rising and falling through them as she fought
to maintain control over her panic.

The Kobach had sent her to him hoping the god would find
her acceptable and favor a banished people by giving them a
child—a hero from his body. The bold proposition awed him.
But he admired Nydien's courage in accepting the honor of
coupling with the avatar. In the old legends, few women were
blessed with a child of a god—and many found death in the
god's embrace.

As the probe receded, Lyrec's other senses revived. He
found tears streaming down Nydien's cheeks. She stood rigid
against the cold. Yearning passed through him again, gently
tugged at him. He stood. "You're cold," he told her and reached
out to wipe her cheeks. Removing his cape, he draped it over
her shoulders. Then he began to undress. Like her, he turned
his back. She saw the leanness of him, the hardness, and her
breathing quickened. He turned around. Her eyes were bright.
"If you like," she suggested, "we could swim afterward."

Afterward. He swallowed. "Nydien, whatever your tales
have told you, I think you should know that I have no idea
what I'm doing. I'm acting on instincts foreign to me," he
added, and wondered for a moment whose instincts they were.

"I've never made love, either."

"Oh. Well . . . let's swim first, then."

Nydien dropped the cape and they entered the chill water
together, but they did not remain long. Here the current had
force and the water, as she had told him, was very cold. When
they emerged, the night air set their teeth to chattering and they
pressed together beneath his cape, huddled on the bank. Lyrec
could not say when the idea first crept into his mind that made
him kiss her. She lay back on his cape and he bent over her.
This time, as desire flooded through him, he made no attempt
to analyze or defeat it.

♭Chapter 14.

CHEYBAL walked the perimeter of Atlarma castle
for the third time that night. His legs ached, especially the
backs of his calves, but most of the pain was attributable to
having stood at attention for the larger part of the day as Tynec
practiced for his coronation. Under other circumstances, the
pain in his legs might have kept him off his feet for the evening.

Guests had arrived continuously throughout the day. Cheybal had missed his midday meal (but had not noticed until the
evening one). Ushering in the diplomats was his duty alone,
but they seemed to appear in an unending parade, all of them
bent upon seeing the new king. Some, with distasteful ob-
viousness, had come for more than that; they brought favors
to ask of their rich neighbor, lists of needs, wants and desires,
which they petitioned Cheybal to deliver on their behalfs to,
as one of them put it, "the child." They angered and abused
and berated him, but most of all they wore him out. However,
they were not the cause of Cheybal's insomniac patrol.

He *was* tired—his eyes itched and were alternately watery
and dry. His mouth tasted like a rotting vegetable. He knew
his head burned and his cheeks were flushed. Were it not that
the sharp air of the cold night soothed him so much more than
the dead air in his room, he would not have been here at all;

but still he would not have slept. There was a problem dogging
him, running his thoughts. He believed he might never sleep
again unless he found a solution. He could not even define it
exactly. But something was wrong.

He entered the castle, wandering past a guard who saluted
him and was dismayed in receiving no response.

Cheybal counted the obvious elements—those he knew—
again. First, the king had been killed and the murderers were
as yet unknown. Faubus was due back at any time from now
to next week—and Cheybal was impatient to know what his
man had found. He wanted answers now.

Secondly, Tynec had begun to act oddly. Very haughty and
willful. From nowhere he had suddenly manifested an impres-
sive knowledge of Secamelan, and, although the notion was
ridiculous, Cheybal had the impression that Tynec had regular
access to information about things going on in distant parts of
the country. He had twice mocked someone's stated opinion
on a subject in a way that, when confirmation of the error later
arrived, suggested the boy had not so much been making fun
as he had been boasting of his prescience.

Third, there was Ronnæm, the old king, still seeking revenge, singling out certain of the arrived guests to let them
know his hand was in the pot and stirring again now that the
son for whom he had abdicated was murdered. Admittedly, he
had become quieter in his habits these past few days. But he
seemed to have taken a particular interest in the activities of
the Hespet; and Cheybal feared that he was only awaiting the
best moment to strike, to cause as much trouble as possible.
Cheybal also assumed that the old man, like himself, waited
for Faubus to return.

By all these threads hung a blade of dread, intangible and
invisible, but nevertheless certain to fall at any moment. No
one else noticed it or understood why he had the jitters. Frankly,
neither did he—never before had he acted this way. In battle
he was known for his calm. Why had it deserted him now of
all times? He thought if he could find the source of his anxiety,
all would be well. It had to be there in front of him, waiting
in plain view. He looked and saw nothing and remained awake.

In this, at least, he was not alone: the castle was alive this
night. People passed him in the halls. He began to take notice
of all of them. They nodded and he nodded back. They bowed

and he said, "Do not." They were people he felt he should have known—cooks and servants and guards, raconteurs and musicians. The halls hummed with their business.

Cheybal came to the great hall where Tynec was to be crowned. Not a week before, Dekür had lain in state here, but all trace of that had been erased. The heavy tapestries were gone. Bright draperies of every color hung in their place. Cloth streamers curled across the room above his head like the waves of a sea. In one corner a group of minstrels practiced tunes which kept everybody's energies up, and a sweet smell he identified as brewing mulcetta came from the large hearth.

The whole scene astonished him. He had not been part of the preliminaries when Dekür had been crowned; at that time he had been off fighting some long forgotten border dispute. At the time of Ronnæm's coronation, he had been a boy in Cajia, training horses with his father and fishing with the old men. He wondered for the first time what a coronation was going to be like.

The people bustling about the great hall greeted him as he passed. He found himself suddenly unable to contain his delight and beamed back at them. The weariness in him went to sleep since he could not; the excited mood caught him up as it had all those working around him.

At the hearth he asked for a cup of mulcet. A woman there warned him it might not be ready yet and still too tart, but she ladled out a mug of the spiced wine and handed it to him. Cheybal thanked her and then asked, "Will it be like this all the night through?"

"Do you mean busy? Yes, Commander Cheybal, we've so much to do."

"Remarkable. You know, in all the years I've lived in At-larma, I've never before seen the celebratory side of it. There have been nights, of course—when some fight was imminent—when we were up and out on the yard. It was as if the yard itself had legs; I remember it was all you could see, hundreds of feet pounding the ground. You could feel the thunder beneath you, like we'd awakened old Kelmod deep in the bowels of the earth and he was threatening us with his stone fists."

"We're equal, then, for I've never experienced such a night as that."

"No, of course not. No battles like that in nearly a decade."

"I'm older than a decade!"

"Of course, but how long in Atlarma?"

She lowered her eyes. "Nearly a year."

"Then this life is still fresh to you. How did you come here?"

"I came from Eyr. I'd hoped to find work in the stables here. I'm very good with horses. But the stables needed no one—they claim not to take on women in any case—so I took this serving post. One has to live."

"Horses; you're good with horses." He smiled at rekindled memories of his childhood. "Nearly a year you say? I wish I'd been restless on an evening before this. For you're certainly someone for whom a late watch ought to be kept." He grinned at the blush he had brought out on her cheeks, then glanced around the room to seem nonchalant in his boldness. "What is your name?"

She said it but the name was lost in the noise of his mug shattering.

With a shout, Cheybal ran forward. The music stopped. All heads turned as he sped past. He saw none of them—his eyes were locked on the small balcony directly ahead. The figure he had seen was no longer there but it had been real enough. The white robe had practically glowed where an unseen hand held back the curtain. He saw Faubus standing in his office, being forced to admit that he had seen a ghost, at a loss for words to describe it: "It was very peculiar, white." Yes, he thought, twice *very*.

He took the spiral of steps two at a time. His hand went to his sword, then he thought better and freed his dagger. In this confined space it would serve him much better. Halfway up to the balcony, a second set of stairs branched off from the first. Cheybal swung around the wall and looked up the stairs. He saw no one, but heard footsteps fleeing above. He charged after them. His legs did not ache at all.

Now the footsteps pounded across the wood beams of the floor overhead. That floor contained private chambers where many of the guests were housed. Cheybal bounded into the corridor. The hallway was empty. He did not even catch a glimpse of a white robe. The footsteps had stopped.

Which way? Echoes in the stairwell had indicated no direction. He took a step forward. Behind him a door closed. Cheybal swung around and ran along the hallway to where it branched left and right. The door had been beyond this intersection, that much he could tell from the sound.

Torches lit both branches evenly. He went to the right. Halfway to the first door he encountered the overpowering impression that someone followed him. He swung about in a crouch, ready to stab out. No one stood there. The hallway was deserted. Cheybal shivered from the unreleased tension, the certainty that somebody *had* been there. Hairs on the back of his neck bristled.

Moving to the first door, he listened against it, but could hear nothing above the sound of a nearby torch. With the greatest of care he drew back the latch and nudged the door open.

A shriveled old man in a white tunic and dirty breeches slowly looked his way and, spying Cheybal in the doorway, jumped up and knocked over his seat—an empty cask. The pins that he had held in his mouth clicked as they hit the floor. One pin remained stuck to the old tailor's lip. He reached up carefully and removed it. Between the tailor and Cheybal stood a wax figure approximating Tynec's size and shape. On it was hung a richly embroidered blue robe.

The commander straightened and tilted back his head. He sighed deeply. He had hired the old tailor himself half-consciously while also arguing with some farmer about dung thieves who had been making off with the man's midden heap, presumably to sell it. He could not so much as recall the tailor's name.

"Excuse me," he said, "I thought I heard rats scuttling about." He closed the door quickly. "Gods," he muttered, "What an idiotic thing to say."

Immediately upon the door closing, the old tailor righted the cask. He reached out his hand and the pins shot up from the floor and stuck to his palm like iron filings to a lodestone.

Cheybal decided to try at least one more door. He went to the next one across the hall. This time, however, he opened the door in a straightforward manner, keeping the dagger out of sight at his side.

On the bed the sole occupant of the room glanced up. He was lanky and dark-skinned, and his eyelids drooped, giving him a languid appearance. He wore his black mustache long with ends that curved like pincers around his mouth.

"Come in," he said in a voice that had never held surprise, "but you might put away the dagger; or can I trust you with my life?"

"Reket!" Cheybal shouted.

The dark man got up from the bed. He opened his arms and the two men embraced. Then they stepped back and admired one another.

Cheybal said, "Is that a sack of grain you're developing under your shirt?"

Bozadon Reket brushed down his shiny stitched tunic and, with a thick lateral accent, answered, "The cut of the material plays a trick. I'm as fit as you, if not more so."

"I doubt that. But how long have you been here?"

"I arrived in the afternoon. You were too busy, they told me, to meet me then. You lord over it all just now, heh? How is it, being king?"

"Do you still long to be a governor in Növalok? Well, I'll tell you, you can have it all! Who do you suppose ever conjured up the idea of ruling over something? It's dreadful."

Reket sat again and hung one leg over the bed. "Yes, well, I admit I now know something of it. I own land now, a great piece."

"A governor? You are a governor."

"For some time, yes." His teeth flashed. Reket's smiles came and went like glints of light.

"Where does it all go, time?"

"Probably out the bladder like a bad humor."

"It is a large tract of land?"

"I said as much, yes."

"Well, why didn't you force your way in, for Voed's sake?"

"You were busy," Reket stated flatly.

"No longer so. And we have a lot to catch up on, that much is obvious."

"Then you had best acquire two bottles for each of us!"

Cheybal began to laugh. It felt good and he let it go on. "I will, of course I will." He started out, then stopped and asked, "Reket—why were you awake just now?"

"Why? Travel. It upsets my internal wheel." He tapped his stomach. "I roll unevenly."

"That's all?"

"Should there be something more?"

"I came up here. . . . Did you hear footfalls—someone running along the corridor?"

"Running? No. But then I did not hear your approach, either. Fortunately I was not, ah, indisposed. In Növalok that is an interruption with tragic consequences."

"How can I allow such a barbarian within our walls?" He smiled and closed the door before Bozadon Reket could reply. Cheybal looked down the long empty corridor. "It's the lateness of the hour," he told himself, though he did not believe this. Nevertheless, for now there was no more to be done. The figure had eluded him. By now the white robe had been doffed and the true countenance had been exchanged for the disguise. He would have to search through the rooms on this floor tomorrow while everyone was busy elsewhere. If only he could find the time.

The four bottles Cheybal ordered were duly sent to the quarters of Bozadon Reket. However, the commander did not return immediately as planned. As he stood apologizing to Imbry, the woman at the hearth, a tired young messenger staggered into the great hall and requested him to follow. Cheybal gave Imbry a look that he hoped she could read as a promise to return, then fell in beside the messenger, knowing whose return the boy must betoken. Before leaving, he looked up at the balcony again. It was empty, the curtains drawn.

Shadows from torches high atop the ramparts crisscrossed the courtyard. Cheybal found the soldiers still mounted. Each seemed cut from the shadows upon them. On closer inspection, he saw Faubus at the head of the group and something inside of him iced over. He waited on the top of three steps, gathering his tired wits to face what his chosen captain was about to tell him.

Faubus dismounted and came forward. "Commander," he said hoarsely.

"Captain. We should retire to my quarters I think."

"As you wish, sir." Faubus eyed the two guards flanking Cheybal. "Nonetheless, the news will be out tomorrow."

The commander also eyed the two guards. They stiffened to attention. "We shall see. Let your men dismount, they deserve a long rest, I'm sure. Come with me."

Once they had reached the chamber and Cheybal had closed

the door, he faced the captain and said, "Now, what news is it that will spread by morning?"

"May I sit first, sir?"

"Would you like some mulcet as well? There's much brewing."

Faubus smiled with weary gratitude and Cheybal called out to a servant and ordered drink and food. "Now, if you would, Captain?"

"Sir. The village of Ukobachia is destroyed. We were too late by a day to save it, even though we made the best possible time getting there."

"You're not being faulted; go on," Cheybal said tersely.

"Few survivors apparently, very few. Some may have escaped into Boreshum, but we hunted them and, if they were there, then they preferred not to be found. I posted men in the village, on the roads, the pass as well. But I thought it far more important to return here myself than to count bodies there. The coronation and all . . ."

"Your actions are prudent, Captain." Cheybal sat down behind his desk. "Now tell me *why,* Faubus. Is it sorcery again? The same death as Dekür suffered?"

"No, Commander. The explanation is much simpler, and the why of it is simpler still. It won't enliven the coronation much, and it's likely to cause a few deaths."

"You dramatize well, Faubus. You might make a poet. But for poetry I have little tolerance."

"And that, sir, happens to be the why of it. Intolerance. The village of Ukobachia was set to the torch by the village of Trufege."

"Oh." He sighed as from pain, then put his fists to his head and fell silent, head bowed. The servant he had called returned with two mugs and a platter of food. The servant normally would not have left until Cheybal thanked him and let him go, but Cheybal paid him no mind. Faubus gestured for the servant to leave.

When Cheybal raised his head again, he was surprised to find the food right in front of him. He told Faubus to eat but took none for himself. "Before I do anything about this, I have to know that you have absolutely *no* doubt in your accusation."

"We found their priest, Commander—I don't know his name, but I'm certain the Hespet could tell you, since, you no doubt

recall, *he* sent him there not so long ago. That seems odd to
me and I'd like to inquire whether or not the Hespet had advised
the priest of Trufege recently on any matters . . . I'm speculat-
ing, of course. There was no evidence of the Hespet's involvement. Whatever the case, the priest got his due. He'd been
beheaded, so I assume the Kobachs gave some account of
themselves before they vanished."

"Then the blame is placed. What astounds me is how quickly
it happened. I want you to look into this business with the
priests, though I find it unlikely that Sly—the Hespet is responsible. He's never been prejudiced against witches. More
likely this other priest incited his followers into the act. Trufege's had its share of troubles, to be sure, but that will not
mitigate this atrocity. The edict will have to be harsh and quick,
or else the murderers will find some plausible excuse for their
actions."

Faubus said nothing. He ate and drank while Cheybal called
out for scribes. When they had gathered, the commander stood
and paced behind his desk. "I want a proclamation drawn up,"
he told them, "against the village of Trufege and all of its
inhabitants. First, they are to be banned from attending the
coronation ceremonies. Any who have come here will have a
day to leave. Secondly, the village is to be ostracized throughout the winter. No coaches are allowed within town limits.
Likewise, no food will be delivered to them should they have
a shortage. Disobedience of this order will result in imprison-
ment, the length of sentence to be set by me alone upon
hearing the circumstances of the offense. Note lastly that the
above orders might be rescinded in part if the guilty parties
give themselves over to me. That's all. Draw it up properly,
I'll put my seal to it and you'll have copies posted here and
sent to Trufege by midmorning."

As the scribes filed quickly out, Cheybal muttered, "If they
think the gods can frown on them, wait until they learn what
an angered tyrant can do."

Faubus, feeling better after his meal, made the error of
smiling.

"You find that amusing, Captain?" asked Cheybal coldly.

"No, sir. I just cannot get over the eternal stupidity of that
village."

"There is nothing more dangerous than stupidity—ignorance and fanaticism being its most exhibited forms. And I tell you this coronation is surrounded by *both* those most murderous aspects. Some of it I can suppress, but there are areas under your hand that you can control and I cannot. Like what those guards and your men will believe about what has happened.

"Faubus, tell your story with carefully weighed words. Make the villains unquestionably villains—and no, please don't pretend to misunderstand me. I have been part of Atlarma's army for too long not to know what gets bandied about in barracks concerning the Kobachs. I rely on you, Captain. You're quick, clever, glib—"

He was interrupted by a knock at the door.

"Enter."

Two soldiers came in, one of them bearing a small dark bundle. Faubus quickly stood. "Oh, sir," he said, "I had forgotten about the child. . . . This is a little girl we rescued from Ukobachia." He took the bundle from the soldier. "Actually, she rescued herself."

"Has someone called for a nurse?" One of the soldiers nodded.

"What is her name?"

"I've no idea," said Faubus. "She has said only that she wants her father. I'm afraid he's probably dead, sir." He regretted instantly having said that. The child began to squirm and cry in his arms. The platter of food on the table suddenly flipped into the air, spilling its contents. His mug poured mulcet across the floor and dashed itself to pieces against the wall. Cheybal leapt up as his chair began rocking back and forth. The door banged open like a loose shutter in a storm. Something grabbed hold of Cheybal and threw him back; he tripped over his chair. The two soldiers were tossed against the wall behind the door. Cheybal clawed his way back up to his table. Every loose object in the room was dancing, shaking, and in the center of it all Faubus and the girl stood untouched in the eye of the storm.

The nurse, an old midwife with her head wrapped in a wimple, came in and gasped at what she found. She started to back out, but Cheybal yelled, "Don't you dare leave, missus! It's the child doing it. I want you to call to her, take her from the captain." The woman held back fearfully. "Well, go on!" The nurse looked diffidently at the commander. He glowered back and gestured sharply with his head. Putting out her trembling arms, the nurse took tiny steps toward Faubus, poised to flee at any moment.

"Call to her, damn you," Cheybal snapped. A wax taper slid across the table and struck him between the eyes.

"Dear," the woman said, her voice fracturing. She cleared her throat timidly and tried again. "Child, you must stop this. Come now, listen to me, dear one, I'm going to take you from these horrible soldiers and show you where I live in the castle. Wouldn't you like that? I'll warrant you'd like a hot bath to soak in, eh? What would you say to that?"

The child's pale blue eyes focused on her for the first time. "I want my papa!"

The nurse glanced at Faubus nervously, not knowing where she was treading. "Oh, he's probably out in the city, you know—celebrating the coronation."

All of the objects hovering across the room began to plummet to the floor. "Can we see him?" the girl asked the nurse.

"Well, later, I think, dear, if the commander doesn't mind. But your papa would probably want you to clean up and sleep first, because it's very late."

The child reached out and put her arms around the nurse's neck, and she allowed herself to be taken from Faubus and carried out of the room.

Cheybal crawled out from beneath the table, climbed up against his chair, then righted it. "Rescued herself, did she, Faubus?" he snarled. "Oh, go away, all of you—go get drunk, just..." Unable to speak further, he turned his back and leaned on the chair. The three soldiers sneaked out quietly. Just as the door closed, Cheybal shouted, "And remember what I said to you, Captain!"

He started to sit down, then changed his mind, surveying the destruction. He stepped out into the hall, told his servant to get someone to clear up the debris, then headed off to Bozadon Reket. If ever he needed two bottles of mulcet, it was now. He had never in his life witnessed anything so incredible as what had just happened.

Halfway up the stairs he began to laugh, and continued laughing in disabling bursts until well after the sun had come up and he and Reket had lost the power of intelligible speech.

* * *

Borregad sat in his accustomed position slung across Lyrec's shoulders, and wondered exactly how large Maribus Wood was. He had thought of little else since he and Lyrec had left those uncommon people behind at dawn. The tavern inspired almost his every thought—he swore that he could taste the grynne on his dry, and surely swollen, tongue.

Somewhere behind them, following the same trail but keeping well into the trees, the Kobachs came along at a snail's pace. If he listened hard, Borregad could hear them like the distant roar of a waterfall, their separate words no longer distinguishable—just a constant, deep, breathy sound. He liked the Kobachs well enough, but meeting them had made him all the more dissatisfied with his present incarnation. Some of the females in that group had aroused certain unique and zestful ideas in him; he could think of nothing better than to have the opportunity to submerge in pleasure, to forget Miradomon for a little while, and all the dead worlds they had chased him through. But his current form had certain limitations—just how many he had barely begun to learn. He wondered, vaguely, if female *cats*—?

He had listened to Lyrec's bemoaning this mortal existence, of how he feared the conflicting emotions that seethed in him and dreaded what he was becoming. Borregad shared none of these reservations. Having been nearly slain and left to hang in eternal semi-consciousness in a world of nothingness, he was all too happy to embrace *any* existence and its attendant foibles. . . . Compared to exile in the void, even death was preferable. So, emotions—good or bad—were things to which he could easily reconcile himself. And he noted that Lyrec had not lodged a single protest against his tumultuous passions since that dark witch Nydien had gone to him last night. Borregad was glad—he had endured enough complaining of how terrible it was to be alive.

The cat stretched out one leg and extended his claws, then turned his paw around and began to lick the rough pads.

A shadow drifted across him. Borregad paused in his ablution; a rush of wind blew across his fur followed by a dull *thump* that sounded like the first burst of a sudden fire. He started to call out, but a terrible stench choked him and the oppressive shadow smothered him.

Lyrec!

Above him, a green-gray monster swooped down, its shiny legs bent, claws extended. It dove too fast for Lyrec to defend himself. He raised one arm to shield his face against the thing coming straight out of the sun, twisted around sharply. In so doing, he flung Borregad from his shoulder. The cat tumbled into the brush. Lyrec tried to shout; the sound became a gasp against the smell.

Shiny black claws sank into his shoulders and tore him from his horse. The terrified horse took off at a wild gallop. Chasing after it, Borregad called, "Lyrec, Lyrec!" not knowing what else to do. His friend was fast becoming a speck against the clouds as a beast of legend carried him away.

♭Chapter 15.

HIS reviving senses lingered at half-consciousness. His head pounded in a blood-flecked darkness and he could barely feel his arms at all. Something nearby smelled fetid, and wind rocked him, lit his body like a torch of pain. The pain awakened him fully. He opened his eyes.

Two black boots—his feet—swung free beneath him. Far below he saw trees and hills and tilled fields. Some terrible clawed gallows held him swinging, hung, this high.

Lyrec raised his head and his neck sparked with pain. He stopped trying to push his head back and raised his eyes instead. The Krykwyre held him with its legs bent. He could see the round scaly belly, the small tucked-up hands, and the crooked hook of its beak. To either side of his head massive talons gripped his shoulders through his blood-soaked uniform, so close that he could see the lighter stripes within the black nails.

Where was it taking him? Did it nest? he wondered. He might well be on his way to feeding a hungry family of the stinking, oily things.

His belt and Ladomantine sword still hung from his hip. When he tried to reach the sword, however, his numb arm barely twitched. His fingers flexed only slightly. They were stiff and cold. He tried working them, opening and closing, more movement each time, until he could make a fist. Then he bent his arm up. It began to tingle. He worked the other one, too, pumping it up and down. The return of sensations to his arms brought with it a new enhancement of his pain. He drew ragged breath through his teeth. The monster saw that he had awakened but paid this no mind. Perhaps no captive had ever harmed it.

Slowly, Lyrec reached across and placed one hand on the hilt of the sword. The huge leathery wings flapped an icy wind across him, but by the time his fingers closed on the sword, Lyrec was sweating. He brought his other hand to it and gripped tightly. Then, by torturous degrees, he withdrew the blade. Holding it against himself, he waited—waited until he had the strength to follow through after his actions. Otherwise he would succeed only in achieving death from a great height.

Again Lyrec brought his head up, agonized and trembling with the effort. His neck muscles corded around his throat. He studied the belly, looking for lines of musculature and bone beneath the slick scales; at last he located a soft hollow and concentrated on that spot, watched the lung cavity swell out, bow in, his eyes blinking but never leaving that spot. He waited, breathed, and braced.

He jabbed the sword up into the monster's belly, drove the blade into the hollow, up to the hilt, crying out against the excruciating pain this brought.

The monster cried out, too, a shriek like cloth ripping. It twisted in flight and tried with its tiny useless arms to reach the sword. A thick yellow blood dribbled out of the wound. Lyrec reached up again, grabbed the sticky sword and tugged it down, opening the belly wider. Viscous yellow spattered and stung his face.

The Krykwyre released him, but he had anticipated this and clutched one of the feet. The monster tried to kick loose, then used its free foot to strike at him. He pulled himself up the monster's leg as the kicking foot raked his side. His fingers began to slide down the oily skin, and he grabbed wildly for a solid grip. The monster screeched again and slowly began to descend. It doubled over and reached for him, round yellow eyes spotted with pupil, its tusklike teeth snapping angrily. He nearly vomited from its breath but struggled higher, aiming for its back. He twisted and kicked out at the arms that tried to grasp him. One foot was caught for an instant, but he kicked again and felt something snap beneath his toe. The Krykwyre shrieked and rolled in the air to dislodge him. Now, for the moment circling its side, Lyrec reached out and found the sword, ripped it toward him. The monster tried to fling him off, tumbling again as it did, but he moved with it, finding purchase on its back between the two great wings. They swatted him, the blows against his shoulders knocking him so hard that his teeth ground together and he thought he would be crushed. He pressed tightly against the foul-smelling skin. Taking his dagger, he began stabbing the monster all along the spine. His whole being seemed composed of pain, his actions directed themselves and he cried out, "Die, damn you. Die!" But the Krykwyre bucked and flipped again, screeching constantly now, and he did not know how it was that he hung on.

Then, suddenly, tree branches cracked and slapped at him. The Krykwyre crashed down through the smaller upper branches. Lyrec was thrown free, against a limb. He wrapped around it as he had around the monster, inching his way inward along the limb. When his head touched the trunk, he began to climb down. This proved hardest of all, for he had to hold himself on the one branch while he probed with his feet for the next level down. His vision was blurry and he feared the thick blood might have burned his eyes, but he had no strength left for panic and went on lowering himself branch by branch in mechanical fashion, not daring to stop for a moment, not even to wonder if he was climbing down to his death. He ran out of energy before he had escaped the tree. Desperately, he called upon his last resources and found them depleted. For a moment he hung there, wrapped to the branch, begging his body to give a little more, wheezing and nearly in tears. Then he teetered and fell.

The ground struck him an instant later—he had been no more than an arm's reach above it. He fought nausea as he rolled slowly over and tried to get to his knees.

A figure moved in front of him. He commanded his throbbing eyes to focus on the blood-red smear of a shape, but they could not obey. The figure loomed larger, coming toward him. He saw a gleam of something—his sword!—and knew that the Krykwyre still lived. He groped for his dagger, but it had

been lost in the fall. He would not die on his back, though—
the indignity of that infuriated him.

Whimpering in torment Lyrec struggled to his knees. The
figure had not budged.

Come for me! he thought he called to it. *Come on!*

The figure moved: it slid up the edge of his vision and then
tilted abruptly as Lyrec crashed, unconscious, onto his side.

♭Chapter 16.

GROHD stepped out of his tavern and stood beneath the overhang of thatched roof to listen. He was not sure he had heard the sound, or heard it rightly. It was probably only a bird call, distorted somehow; but it was still a little odd—a faint tittering cry from somewhere off in the woods. A winter bird come back early? But what bird made a sound like that?

He could hear birds all around the inn but none of these calls corresponded to the strange sort of whining that had awakened him. He yawned widely, then walked back inside. The day was young and there was little to do. The kegs of grynne he had set to brewing outside beside the huts would go on bubbling for another day at least. The fires would need no tending for some time. Grohd returned to the keg on which he had been sleeping before, leaned back against the wall, sighed and closed his eyes.

At the precise point where consciousness fell away and sleep overcame him, Grohd heard the whine again. He sat up. The sound faded into silence. It had not been like a bird call at all, he decided, but more like an axe being sharpened on a whetstone.

He returned to the yard, crossing over the coach ruts and into the trees. He walked in circles beneath the high branches, searching for Voed knew what. The sound was not repeated.

Around he went, kicking through brush, peering under branches, even walking back to the center of the yard and studying the ruts. Aware that he had no idea for what he searched, by the same token he believed he would know it when he saw it. The search led him to the stable, presently empty. No coaches were due in this day, no company and no horses; no one going north, everyone gone west, to Atlarma. Grohd rummaged through every stall. He knew his actions were ridiculous, but the feverous venom of the remembered sound sped him along in search of its source.

He left the stable behind to explore the grounds between there and the outbuildings. He leaned around a tree.

And there it was.

At first he could not move to pick it up, just stared at it and released a great pent-up sigh. He recognized it, could even recall thinking how ineffectual a thing it appeared to be.

How had it come to be here? After Lyrec had been escorted away, Grohd had gone into the loft and found it empty. The cat, too, had vanished. Come to think of it, though, Lyrec had not been wearing the weapon that morning when the fiends had come for him. Bastards, ganging up against a man like that who had obviously never used a sword in his life. . . . This set Grohd to wondering exactly what the silver knuckle-guard was attached to.

He bent down. Some prudent instinct caused him to refrain from touching the shiny guard. He hefted the weapon by its leather scabbard instead. His hand began to tingle.

He called out, "Lyrec?" and felt stupid for having done so. The fellow, powerful as he had been, was surely dead or worse than dead by now. Nevertheless, Grohd waited there until he was certain no one would answer him. Then he headed for the tavern.

Inside, he sat at the first table he came to, then changed his mind and moved to the rear, near his cooking hearth. He used two fingers delicately to slide the weapon out. As he had suspected, it was a broken sword; but the tip where the blade had been snapped in two was polished into a smooth curve. The thing had no edge at all. What a useless novelty, he thought.

At first, he had thought the bell was smooth hammered silver. But looking closer, he saw that it actually had a texture

of fine indented lines running in all directions from the base
of the "basket." He passed his palm over the surface. Lifting
it, he saw for a second the color had darkened where his hand
had touched it. This faded so quickly that he wondered if he
had seen it at all or if the darkness had been the shadow of his
hand. So he brushed it again, watching very closely now. The
silver swirled and spread apart, leaving darkness where he
touched. Grohd drew back from the hilt. He looked up at his
tavern—at the walls and kegs and tables—to reanchor himself
in reality, then at the silver thing again.

Holding it by the end of the blade still, he turned it up. The
inside of the knuckle-guard was ribbed and, in places, studded
with tiny crystalline projections. These did not appear to have
any discernible pattern to their arrangement and left him debating their purpose. Perhaps they kept the hand more firmly
against the hilt. They looked as if they would hurt, though.
Grohd leaned back and pulled at his nose. Whatever the thing
was, it was remarkable, but, all the same, impracticable. He
wished Lyrec were here to tell him how it had come to be
broken, who had removed the edge and polished the tip so,
and what kind of material it was made from. Recalling the
tales Lyrec had told, he expected the truth to be utterly fantastic.
That poor man, coming so far in his quest, overcoming so
many perilous obstacles, only to perish here. If the soldiers
had refrained from slaying him outright (which Grohd doubted),
then Ladomirus himself would have tortured or killed him as
a spy or under some other pretense. Grohd decided he would
mount the hilt and scabbard on the wall above the bar where
it would be seen by all, leading inevitably to tales of the brave
traveller who had taken on seven, no, ten enemy soldiers single-
handedly to protect others. He imagined the battle as one brave
swordsman slew others around him with such speed that they
fell to the ground before their blood knew enough to flow.
Yes, what a story. And there would always be the weapon to
prove it. The remnant of his sword, broken by the angry Ladomantines in their hatred of all the lives it had cost them.
And where was the rest of the blade? someone would ask. And
(grinning as he thought out his answer) Grohd would reply:
No one knows—it disappeared. Perhaps the traveller was no
man at all, but a god in mortal disguise, like in the old stories.
Maybe even Voed himself. And then there was his cat. . . .

So captivated was he by his story, Grohd did not notice the approach of the two men who came along the road. They were on horses but reined in and walked the beasts the last part of the journey. The empty yard, the absence of coach and animals in the stable assured them that nothing stood in the way of their goal. Stealthily, they crept forward, tied their horses, and moved to the door. For a time they satisfied themselves with watching him dream his tale of the man who had bettered them, but this quickly bored Fulpig. He nudged Abo and they went through the doorway. Abo slammed shut the door.

Grohd's head whipped around. For an instant he did not comprehend the situation. Then, recognizing the two soldiers and what they represented, he became paralyzed with fear. His axe was across the room.

Neither soldier brandished a weapon, but this hardly mattered. Fulpig's arm was in a sling, close against his chest. His nose was mostly dark crust, making his entire face look decayed. Abo had what appeared to be the same dirty strip of linen as before tied round his wrist. He did not hold his arm as if the wound bothered him any longer. His expression seemed a trifle glazed, as though he were waking up from a long nap.

Fulpig noticed the abbreviated sword lying on the table and began to laugh. "You going to stick me with that, taverner? Think I'll let you? Why don't you pick it up and let me see?" He gazed around the room. "Where's my favorite cat?"

"Gone." He glanced hopefully at the bar. "Do you want a drink?"

"Soon enough. We'll drink over your corpse." Fulpig started toward him.

Grohd had little choice in what to do—the polished half-sword was all he had. He grabbed it up and jabbed to warn the Ladomantine off. Fulpig drew his own blade, snorting in derision, and casually tapped the shiny smooth tip of Grohd's weapon away. He laughed; this was going to be a pleasure.

Grohd heard the whine that had come to him in his sleep. His forearm began to shudder and a soft pressure applied itself against his hand. It was all he could do to point the weapon again at Fulpig. Neither of the soldiers seemed to notice the whine nor found his look of terror out of place.

The bell of the sword collapsed and flowed over his hand and wrist. He would have tried to shake it off, but the thing seemed magnetized by Fulpig. The soldier shoved a table out of the way—the last barrier between him and the taverner. Grohd saw sparks within the swirling darkling silver, sparks like distant lightning in a steel-gray cloud. He sensed an explosion coming, opened his mouth to yell.

The tip of the blade shot out a plasmatic red stream, whirling around Fulpig, obscuring him from view. The whine that only Grohd could hear became a squeal. The plasma erupted into flame and vanished. It left behind a figure of ash which collapsed in a dusty pile.

The weapon tugged Grohd's arm, redirecting itself at Abo. The Ladomantine pressed back against the door, too horrified to flee. He angled his head away as the weapon took aim at him.

Grohd shouted, "Don't!" as the weapon quivered and fired again. His command produced some effect upon it: the weapon emitted a thread of blue-edged whiteness that strung across the room and wove a cocoon around Abo. The thread stopped abruptly; the cocoon fell away in a sprinkle.

Abo was gone. In his place stood what Grohd could only think to call a shadow. It had Abo's form, but no features. With arms extended, like a blind beggar coated with pitch, the shadow began to move across the room, its footfalls absolutely silent. It came at Grohd. He stumbled back. The shadow of Abo went past him, through the wall, vanishing without a trace. Grohd ran to the window in time to see the shade slide through a tree and disappear into the forest.

He realized then that he still held the unconscionable weapon and also that it had returned to its former shape, releasing his hand. He flung the thing away. It bounced off a keg and clattered on the floor. The scabbard lay beside him, and he bent down to pick it up, but it suddenly came to life and scuttled across the room. Grohd whimpered.

The scabbard slid up beside the abandoned weapon, swung around, and fitted itself into place over the polished blade.

"Where are we going?" Tynec asked Cheybal.

"You don't want me to spoil the surprise," the commander answered as he led the boy through Atlarma castle. "All I will tell you is that you've requested such a surprise before."

"Have I? What have I asked for? A sword—is it my own sword?"

"Of course not. You'll inherit your father's sword at the coronation. I'm appalled you've forgotten."

"I didn't forget. You could have had a special one made for me. One for carrying in battle instead of for knighting and wearing on special occasions."

"Are you planning on going into battle soon?" Cheybal asked innocently.

"Why, no, of course not.... Still, what if I did? It's my prerogative as king, isn't it?"

"Your prerogative?" Cheybal came to a stop in front of the door he had led them to. He placed his hand on the bolt, but paused before opening the door. "What's happened to all you've been taught? You know that war is the last choice a king makes. 'For it obliterates his subjects and savages his lands.' I think those are your grandfather's exact words."

"But grandfather wants war, too," the boy answered haughtily.

Cheybal was overcome again by the feeling of debating with someone he had never known. This side of Tynec had come out of nowhere. "Your grandfather . . . has the same problem you would have if you wanted to make war—namely, identifying the enemy."

"Whoever killed my father—"

"Who *did* kill him, boy?"

Tynec's eyes blazed with anger for a moment. Then a sly smile bent his lips, exposing that estranged inimical aspect which gnawed at Cheybal's peace of mind. The boy *knew* who had killed Dekür—Cheybal saw the knowledge gleam in his eyes, then submerge beneath his false pose of innocence.

Cheybal looked away at a loss for what to do. He had brought Tynec here in part because of these uncharacteristic displays. The witch-child, whose name was Pavra, also displayed extraordinary powers—he had only to count the shattered things in his room to prove this. Later, when he had visited her again, she had surprised him by speaking of the problem that he had been trying to solve. Watching him, she had said, "You mustn't worry. Papa is still alive somewhere. But I am much better and I can wait. I'm sorry for what I did." As simply as that, she had seemed to read his mind. What concerned him now were the contents of another mind.

"Well, Tynec," he said, "your surprise is not a sword, and it's not for making war. It's in here." He opened the door. His eyes shifted between the two faces, wanting to capture any change of expression.

Tynec leaned around the doorway. "It's a girl," he said as he might have identified vermin. "That's not the surprise, is it?"

"Yes, boy, it is," answered Cheybal. He glanced at the girl. She sat perfectly still, her hands folded neatly in her lap, a pose that struck Cheybal as disturbingly other-worldly. "This is Pavra," he continued, playing his part. "She's from Uko-bachia, like your mother. But she's lost her mother and her father and has nowhere to stay, so we've taken her in. You always did ask for a playmate. I'd have thought you would be pleased." Tynec said nothing. "Well, I'd stay and chat, but I have too much to do, and I trust you to acquaint yourselves. Pavra was excited at the idea of meeting you. She's never seen a castle before, either. Why don't you show her some of it?"

"No."

"Tynec, this isn't a debate." He gripped the boy's arm and pulled him all the way around the door. Tynec struggled at first, but then became unnaturally calm, his expression perci-pient. He straightened and strode magisterially into the room.

"Hello, Pavra," he said and climbed up beside her. "Chey-bal, you may leave us now." He gave the commander a bold, even rakish, look. The girl had grown unsure of herself, but was holding to her stiff silence. Cheybal could not glean any-thing from either of them. They were both playing roles. He muttered underneath his breath and closed the door. Had both of them read his intention? Tynec had changed tack quickly, maneuvered around him. The roles the two children played were for each other and not for him. Now he would agonize over having left Pavra alone.

"Would you like to see the castle?" Tynec asked Pavra.

"Are there places to hide?"

"What? Hide from what?"

"I don't know. Are there ghosts or glomengues?"

"Glomengues are outside only. We'd have to play in the yard," he answered.

"So?"

"Well, it's raining," he lied.

"I like rain."

Tynec made a sour face. "I've a better idea. I'll show you where I'm going to be crowned. There's balconies we can hide on and watch everyone without being seen."

"Okay." She climbed off the bed.

Pavra did not care for the balcony once they arrived there. Tynec ignored her and concentrated on what transpired below. In the hall, people were milling about, dressed resplendently— important people whom Tynec must have known, Pavra thought. But, when she asked him to point them out to her, he ignored her request and began to mumble to himself. Something about him was odd. She could not say specifically what it was. He had certain obvious peculiarities, and she did not even have to probe him to sense them. He was like a picture made of tiles— looking like one big thing from a distance, but being something altogether different close up. The discrepancy was sufficient to make her want to go elsewhere with him, where there were other people. She asked him to take her somewhere else.

"Well, where?" he replied with obvious annoyance.

"I don't know. Don't you have a special place of your own, where you like to be?"

"No. Why would I?"

"You must know somewhere that's not so boring."

He dropped the edge of the curtain. The small balcony became much darker. Pavra grew nervous. Tynec said, "I know what. Have you ever seen the statue of Chagri in his temple?"

"No."

"We'll go there, then."

"You said it was raining."

"Did I? We can take a coach." He took her hand. His fingers were hard and cold like stone. "You should meet him. He's the most powerful of all gods."

"Voed's more powerful," she protested.

"How would you know? Have you ever talked to Voed?" Pavra could not see his face, but his tone mocked her. "Maybe I have," she answered. "Sometimes some of us would link hands and our thoughts would touch, and sometimes we could feel this other bigger sort of mind. I always thought it must be Voed."

This reminiscence seemed to make Tynec uneasy. He said, "I don't think that was Voed. It was likely Chagri. Let's go ask him. Come." He drew her toward the stairwell.

For a split second she saw something hideous in the darkness where Tynec walked. Most people would have fled right then, but Pavra kept her wits. "I don't want to go," she said.

Tynec glanced back at her. "You have to. You need guidance. Chagri's guidance."

"Girls are supposed to honor Anralys."

He seemed to think on this for a moment, then said, "We could go there instead. She has the same gift for you. Or could be made to."

"No."

"You're just afraid."

"Maybe."

"No, you are, I can tell. You're a witch and all the gods hate witches." He was smiling cruelly.

"Be quiet."

"I could make Chagri appear here right now, just to come and get you and take you away where all witches belong."

"No!" He let go of her hand, and she ran down the steps and out of sight. People crowded the hall where she emerged. Pavra burst through them, crying, deaf to their calls. The boy smiled as he watched her go, then let the curtain fall back.

❧Chapter 17.

THE talons of the Krykwyre cracked his skull. Lyrec heard it and tried to pull away from the imagined agony. He pushed at its arm. The sharp fingers slipped inside his skull and, pulling free, took half his head away. He saw the horrible result in its fist and cried out as his vision dimmed. Blind, he knew himself to be near death. "Elystroya," he called, "I've truly lost this time." He slept.

The monster attacked him twice more before his fever broke. When he awoke at last, he heard the cracking sound that had been the Krykwyre in his nightmare. Much louder now, it was followed shortly by a shudder through the ground beneath him. Thunder.

With this realization his nightmare receded and he opened his eyes.

A small circular hut enclosed him. Beneath him and above him were dark furs which had a strong musky odor. He lay naked between them. Reaching over the edge of the fur, he dug his fingers into the ground: hard, and cold. His shoulder twinged and itched. He almost scratched it, but saw the swollen, purulent wounds. He was acutely aware of the orbits of his eyes, which felt sunken deep beneath his brows, the fluid around

them drained and replaced by sand. Gingerly, he rubbed at the
eyelids and inspected his environment further.

Not far away a fire burned in a small circle of stones. Lyrec
tried to sit up and a dozen sharp pains shot through his back
and chest and legs. His head thundered like the growing storm
outside.

"Dead is what you should be, you know," said a voice from
behind him. Lyrec stretched back his head and looked over the
fur, seeing an old woman upside down. She was very fat and
her clothes bore stains and patches like skin bears freckles. She
was smiling, but from his point of view her wrinkles ran the
wrong way: the lines of her brow became a grim mouth, and
her matted hair was a dirty beard. Lyrec's eyes began to ache
from straining so far back. He closed them and relaxed his
head. "Where am I?" he asked.

"In my hut," she answered, the "h" coming from deep in
her throat, making the word sound fiery and untamed. "My
name is Hulda." Thunder crashed outside, adding dramatic
punctuation to her name.

"How did I get here? Did you bring me?"

"A Krykwyre died by your hand. Your dagger was still
stuck in its back when I found you. Brave one, I must tell you
that its talons have infected you and no medicine known can
cure you." She touched one shoulder lightly. The swelling was
hot. "I will do what I can to reduce your pain," she said, "and
to make your final hours agreeable. If the agony becomes too
much to bear, you have but to ask and I will kill you." Behind
him where she sat, something creaked as if relieved of a great
burden; then Hulda shambled around the edge of the fur and
paused by his feet. The smell of her—an odor like rotting
mushrooms—drifted over him.

"Do you care for pleasures of the flesh?" she asked suddenly.

Lyrec envisioned with dread Hulda without her clothes.
"No-o, I—must rest." He closed his eyes tight, waited, then
opened one a bit. The old woman still stood at his feet. He
closed the eye and began to shift into accelerated healing.

Hulda saw the change in him, the color flooding his skin,
tiny muscles twitching randomly in his face. "I expected you
would last longer than this, brave one. The poison of the Krykwyre is fiercer than I thought." She sighed. "Well, Yadani
wouldn't be much in a coupling, anyhow." She glanced across

the hut. Near the door, as motionless as stone, sat a figure of filth: Yadani. Her long black hair hung about her smudged face in shiny, clinging strands that stretched to the ground and spread like the legs of spiders around her. Her curled-up feet were bare and her clothing consisted of rags in layers. She might have been absorbed in listening for the storm, but Hulda knew better. Nothing caught Yadani's attention. As a matter of fact, the strongest evidence of a mind the girl had ever displayed had been that very afternoon when Hulda had found her standing over this stranger and holding his sword slackly in her hand. Hulda had thought that the girl had come awake in wild fury and slain the man; but then she had seen his wounds and nearby found the Krykwyre.

Who was he? Hulda wondered. To have defeated such a creature as that Krykwyre... and where had it come from, spawn of legend? Perhaps the Krykwyre and the man were both legend made flesh. She considered it possible that this encounter between some legendary hero and the monster had been repeated in tales so many times that it had taken shape from the words and finally come to pass. People were forever fooling with things they knew nothing about, causing trouble for themselves. And this one, would he return to legend again when he died? "What is this?" She scuttled back to the fur.

Lyrec lay as before, his face darkened as if with rage, his head trembling. Sweat poured off him, and threads of steam rose from him. Hulda bent closer, distrusting her own eyes. She carefully lifted the fur. His whole body was shivering with what seemed a terrible chill. But the wounds in his shoulders... was it possible? The wounds had begun to suppurate, ejecting the poison in rivulets. The swelling diminished. Most of the smaller gashes and scrapes she had treated earlier had vanished already. Steam poured out from beneath the fur as if a fire burned at his feet.

Hulda let the cover drop and rested her hand on her cheek. "I wish I knew the tale of you and the Krykwyre—then I would know who you are. It is certain you are no man of this land." She glanced over at Yadani. Lightning flashed, then an explosion of thunder just beyond the door shook the whole hut. Yadani did not move. "Maybe," Hulda said to herself, "maybe you can help *her* as you do yourself."

She heard the sound of horses approaching fast and went

out past Yadani to see who was trying to beat the storm. They would very likely stop for shelter. They might even pay.

Much later the pattern of Lyrec's breathing altered, his skin lost its dark flush, and his sunken eyes opened again. "So, I'm going to die, am I, Hulda?" he asked hoarsely. There was no answer. He looked back, but her chair was empty. Had his recuperation driven her away in fear? He looked around.

All sorts of objects hung from the thatched walls of the hut. Very few of them made sense to him—nor did the minstrel's memories contain them. He had swept the room with his gaze once before realizing that someone else was there, and he looked again at the figure crouched near the door with its back to him. "Hulda?" he called. The figure did not seem to hear. In the firelight, it was barely more than a shadow.

Lyrec pushed back the fur and got to his feet. He recalled the old woman's proposition and decided he had better wear at least pants. He found them in a heap, torn and stained with his blood.

The storm arrived as he was dressing. Rain suddenly drummed across the hut. Some of it trickled through and ran in a thin stream into an earthenware container on the floor near the fire.

Lyrec tested his body, flexed his muscles, bent and stretched his legs. His toes curled on command, muscles in his feet aching a little. Most of all he was hungry. How many more times would he be able to revive his body this way? He had no idea of the limitations of his current form.

A sound drew his attention to the doorway again. The figure had gone. Lyrec called out to Hulda, then walked unsteadily to the door, having to remember quickly what it was like to move on two legs. Beyond the door, the roof of the hut appeared to reach all the way to the ground, enclosing the hut in a dark curving passage. The door of the roof was not directly opposite him. Considering the present storm, he could see the sense of that. From the sound of the storm he knew where the door was. Moving through the dark passage, he nearly tripped over a pile of rags that lay there, absorbing a puddle.

Through the trees, the sky was green and black. It gave off enough light for him to see the shadowy figure standing not far away. The rain stung and blurred his eyes. Lightning flashed overhead, displaying, for an instant, the figure as that of a woman, naked, standing in water up to her ankles. Her arms were stretched high above her thrown-back head and her fingers moved as if the raindrops tickled her palms. Running trails of mud marked her body like black veins and her hair hung straight—a waterfall of obsidian—to the ground. "You, there," he called. The rain drowned out his voice. He muttered resentfully, then dashed out into the storm.

When he grabbed her by the shoulders, the woman failed to respond. He turned her around. Mud ran from her face and into her hair. Her features were sharp, her eyes black and wide and insensible to the sting of the rain. Lyrec shook her. This had no effect. Finally he grasped her face and turned it toward him. She continued to stare at nothing. Rainwater dribbled from between her lips. He had never seen an expression so empty before; even the Ladomantine captain had been brighter.

Lightning flared in the forest not too far away. Lyrec picked up the naked creature and carried her back into the hut. She rested against him like a sack of grain. They burst into the hut—and there stood Hulda, bent over the fire, her appearance only moderately soaked. She took in Lyrec and his burden and said, "I supposed you did not wish to couple." He started to answer, but she waved him off. "No, do not bother about it."

"She went out on her own." He set her down, then grabbed one of the furs and draped it over her.

"Careful," warned Hulda. "She would set it on fire and never know she burned."

"Why is she like this?"

"No idea. Many years ago I found her, deep in the woods. She was walking just as you see her now: naked, dumb, but young, a child. I cannot even say what moved her limbs then— possibly an instinct from an earlier incarnation pierced the cloud of her mind and took control. Once or twice this has happened since then, but without sense. As to why, perhaps she had been brutalized, or perhaps she was this way from birth and so her parents chose to abandon her. I can only hope that if someone made her this way, they suffer the most cruel and hateful torture for it. But more likely they have prospered."

"Still, she *did* go into the storm alone."

"Once, twice before." Hulda squinted up at him. "Remarkable events seem to accompany you. Dead Krykwyre, odd storm, healing that lies beyond my science. And even the

thoughtless are inspired to move. If I were superstitious—and
I am, as it happens—I would believe you were not a man af
all."

"What else could I be?"

"A hero, at the very least. A *cukordia,* I think—divine,
fashioned by the gods or by tales of men. I have thought about
you."

Lyrec could not help smiling.

"Are you cukordia?" asked Hulda.

He began to wipe the water off himself, wringing the drenched
bottoms of his pants. He was glad that he had not dressed
completely before going out. He could think of no satisfactory
lie for Hulda. At last, he said, "Very well, you've discovered
my secret."

"Of course. As ancient as the Krykwyre in legend, hence
found together, enemies in and out of legend. It is best you
admitted it—I would have distinguished the lie." She smiled,
revealing randomly remaining teeth. "How may I serve you?"

Wrapping the other fur around himself, he asked, "Would
you have any food? Cheese? Bread? Something?" He hoped
that cukordias ate or, that if they did not, Hulda was ignorant
of the fact.

"Of course," she replied and moved off from the fire.

She had only cold food, but anything would have satisfied
him then. As he devoured everything she gave him, the old
woman continued to question him. Most of the answers he had
to invent, having virtually no knowledge of the local legends.
Hulda, like a divine gossip, wanted to know all the embar-
rassing details about the lives of the gods, but in the end she
told him more than he told her. While she prattled on, Lyrec
studied the empty face of Yadani E'Lor, whose name, so Hulda
informed him proudly, meant "shining warmth of the heart" in
the native tongue of her people. Which people? he asked. Those
of Növalok, she answered. He listened to her tell of her life
of destitution here in the forest, and began to probe the young
woman. No resistance met him. There were no barriers, no
walls, no layers of image and memory, no sounds and smells
and voices, none at all. Nothing. He descended far down where
the most ancient of recollections lay and found there some hint
of thought and purpose. On closer inspection, he found it no
more than a mechanical, reptilian set of actions and reactions,

not even something he could call purpose. Mere reflex. He
retreated sadly from her empty mind. Hulda was right.

She was telling him now of the time she had met a magical
being under her bed, but her father had found it and killed it.
To this day, she swore, she did not know what it had been.
She asked him if he could tell her and he answered inattentively,
"A glomengue." Hulda clapped her hands and said, "Of course,"
then began silent rumination, perhaps reliving the childhood
event fully now that she had the identity of the creature under
the bed.

Lyrec took this opportunity to get up from the fire and move
off by himself for a while. The food had replenished his strength
enough for him to attempt contact with Borregad. He leaned
back and closed his eyes.

The darkness became smoky red. Lyrec's consciousness
lifted up and began to fly into the redness. He slipped past
other minds, some strung across his path like cobwebs; a random word or image splashed over him as he crossed each web.
Somewhere, some person would abruptly stop talking and search
for a word which had been right on the tip of the tongue a
moment before. A few minds noticed his passing, but none
saw him for what he was; he became a breeze without wind,
a chill in a warm dry place, a ghostly hair-prickling sensation.
They could never have seen him—his thoughts were aimed at
one being alone who would hear him if hearing were possible
at all. *Borregad.* The name went ahead of him. And the answer
came.

*I don't believe it! Thank you, whatever gods really reign
around here. All I can say is it's about time. How did you
survive? How are you? Did it eat you?*

I'm—

Where are you?

I'm—

Are you dead?

Will you shut up?

*'Pon my soul, is that any way to talk to your poor friend,
who has been grieving so mightily for you these past hours
that he hasn't even eaten? It's been nearly a full day, you
know.*

*Is that all? I thought it must have been two at least. Where
are you, then?*

Well, with you out of the plan, there seemed no point in going back to the tavern, because I couldn't wield your damned crex if I wanted to, so I decided that I might do more good by trying to sabotage the assassination. At present, I'm on the back of a cart headed for Atlarma. The driver of the cart is a farmer, and he eats some kind of root that gives him the most noxious breath. I hope to arrive in Atlarma tomorrow unless he exhales upon me a few more times, in which case I don't expect to have any fur left. Can you meet me there?

I'll try, but I can't say how soon I'll arrive. I'm not sure where I am.

You're north of me somewhere. I know that much just from watching that awful thing take you away. I expected you to be in some afterlife by now.

Afterlife?

It's some fanatical concept this farmer has. He's been brooding over it all day. Worried sick he won't qualify. I've thought of saying something to him about it, but I'm afraid he might die of shock and I'd lose my transportation. Of course, then he would know all about his afterlife.

Tell him to stop eating roots. Borregad laughed at this and Lyrec was immeasurably gladdened by the sound. *So, you say Miradomon hasn't unleashed his plot in Atlarma yet?*

I hope not. Word travels awfully slowly here. If I hear otherwise, I'll contact you again.

I'll try to meet you. Borregad, take care.

Hulda, still seated beside the fire, was staring in amazement at Yadani E'Lor. The dark-skinned, black-haired girl was looking *at* Lyrec. Her face seemed on the verge of expression, of wonder or surprise.

The old woman gathered up her skirt and stood. "You've brought her to life. You were reaching into her mind then, weren't you? You must stay and do so again. Perhaps she will learn to talk."

He looked into Hulda's excited face and something inside him tightened. How could he explain the impossibility of that? Maybe it would be better if he did not try. "No," he said, "that's not possible. I have to get to Atlarma, and right away. I was about to ask you if you had a horse I could buy."

"But this is no way to leave her! You cannot."

"What would you have me do—take her with me?" He saw

immediately what a mistake that proposal was. "Now, wait," he exclaimed.

"I'll give you a horse, two horses, if you will take her to Atlarma with you. At the temple of Chagri you can leave her."

"Why there?"

"A cukordia should know."

"I'm an old cukordia—refresh my memory."

Accepting this, Hulda explained what she had heard of the miraculous cures occurring at Chagri's temple. "If you can do this much, fashioned as you are, then maybe the god can give her a mind fresh altogether. So you take her, you be responsible. Otherwise, no horses."

Lyrec tried to stare her down, but her determination was resolute. "Why is it never simple?" he asked no one.

"You accept?"

"I haven't much choice, have I? I'll take her."

"Good." She stood with surprising speed, then walked over to a large mulcet jug and picked it up. She started for the door, saying, "I will be gone awhile, but your horses will be with me when I come back." Out she went.

Lyrec watched Yadani as he finished dressing in his tattered uniform. She continued to sit, naked under the fur, oblivious to all except, for some reason, him; although even that hint of consciousness fell away when he moved out of her line of sight and she failed to follow. But that deep recess he had touched in her had been alert to his communication with Borregad. He thought about this as he drew on his boots, then moved over beside her and said, "Yadani." She did not respond. Perhaps if he survived his quest against Miradomon he would try to help her. Or, less likely, perhaps some spectacular power did reside in the temple of Chagri. He would have to see.

After half an hour Hulda had still not returned. Lyrec had no patience left and went outside in search of her. He saw another building built on a slope above the hut that had been hidden earlier by the torrential downpour. It was a wider, lower structure with a semi-open front, and it reminded him of another place: the stable at Grohd's tavern.

Laughter burst forth from within the structure. Lyrec crept forward. His feet splashed in the shallow pools of water left by the storm. A faint light came from the building. Lyrec stepped inside, and cold water spilled from the roof and down his back. He edged out from under it, gave the roof an angry glare, but said nothing. A small fire burned in a far corner raked clear of straw. Hulda sat holding the mulcet jug out to a man whose back was to Lyrec, but who wore the brown net robe of a novice priest. The man was saying, "When I woke up, the silver creatures were gone, but I knew it for a vision and could never go back to being what I was. My life was changed, as you can see. *Now* I'll have more mulcet, thank you."

Stealthily, Lyrec crept in behind the man. But Hulda, seeing him, was not wise enough to ignore him. The man caught sight of her wandering gaze and craned his head around somewhat drunkenly. Lyrec recognized instantly the long pointed face. Beneath the robe he saw the puffy sleeves and bright orange pantaloons, now somewhat worse for wear, probably from lying in the dirt beside a road.

The novice priest who had once been a minstrel lurched to his feet and peered blearily at the bearded visage that had been taken from his own thoughts. "I know you, don't I?"

"Too well, I fear," answered Lyrec, and he struck the minstrel across the jaw a short, potent punch. The minstrel twirled around on one foot like a dancer and collapsed against Lyrec. "Poor fellow," Lyrec said, and laid the unconscious man out on the straw, "our meetings have hardly served you well." Then he cast a smoldering glance at Hulda. "Is this the way you go about getting me horses?"

"Well, they are *his* horses." She held up the jug, at the same time starting to slip from her stool. "'F you'd waited, I would have had them in another half an hour." She picked up the jug and sloshed the contents around, listening to it. "Maybe an hour."

"I'm afraid I can't wait. You might as well bind him and keep him trussed up until midday at least. Tell him I robbed you, too. Stole your daughter. But tell him I headed . . . by the way, where am I?"

"On the road between Eyr and Jedemere."

"Jedemere's north, then? Tell him I rode north." He began saddling up the horses. "How long to Atlarma?"

"Oh, possibly as much as a day. Don't worry, brave cukordia, the temple will be there still."

"The temple?" he bellowed, and flung a saddle on the larger

horse. "With all I've been through, the temple is the least of my troubles." Almost off-handedly he added, "I have to kill the god."

♭Chapter 18.

ON the cold uneven stones of her narrow little room, Pavra had drawn a triangle. Setting aside the lump of chalk she had used, she stepped into the triangle and sat down. She stretched her legs out straight. Her toes, together, made the first point. Each bracing arm then strained to touch the other two points. She had drawn the triangle a bit too large; but with effort, her fingertips touched, smudged, the chalk marks.

A pale, hazy wreath of golden light appeared around her head, encircling her temples. A space opened between her mind and body.

Thus released, she began her search for Tynec. In the darkness that surrounded her at first, many minds babbled incoherently. They were dusky flickers of light, unattuned, entering into this plane of thought accidentally. Pavra directed herself to them, sorted through them, and the rooms of the castle materialized around her. She floated, unseen, through each room and wondered as she went how much this journey would age her. Papa had warned her never to perform what outsiders called magic unless the reason was vitally important, because each act taxed the body as well as the mind and could drink years of the performer's life. At one time it had not been

uncommon for a Kobach to die of old age at twenty-five. But
that had been during the wars. Those people had spent their
entire lives struggling against oppressors. All the same, the
thought of being old and gray by her tenth birthday terrified
Pavra.

Can no one help me? Hear me? cried a forlorn voice. It
sounded muffled and very weak. She would not have heard it
at all if someone else had spoken at that moment. Through
dark rooms and rooms full of people, Pavra sailed toward the
voice, seeing without eyes.

Tonight was the coronation; she had very little time.

Please, called the voice, and she moved her invisible body
around and into the room she wanted.

Tynec had obviously been calling for a long time. He had
hardly any energy left. But he knew the plans of his captor
and was determined to warn someone. Pavra saw his body,
dressed in coronation robes, looking proud and handsome. But
his pleading voice and his body were utterly separate: the one
in no way reflected the other. His voice had been imprisoned
within him. Pavra feared that he might have gone mad.

Tynec studied himself in a mirror. Pavra looked into his
disorted reflection. Something hideous overlay his features,
something monstrous, hungry and impossible to appease.

The door to the small chamber opened. Another figure entered. This one, too, had a double countenance, one melded
to the other. She had seen the first face before—it belonged
to the old man who was making Tynec's robes. But the other . . .

The other face was the one revealed in Tynec's reflection,
except stronger here, more malevolent. She was staring at the
source.

The boy turned round to face his master and Pavra immediately sensed the bond: puppet and puppeteer. The true Tynec
had been locked away, unable to do more than call out for help
on a plane where no one could hear him, not even in dreams.
The power of the one at the door was awesome.

She knew she should flee, but she wanted desperately to
contact Tynec, to let him know someone had heard and would
carry his warning. His cries, ignored, continued unabated. The
monstrosity paid them no mind. Perhaps it could not hear them.
Tynec called out and she answered, "Don't worry, we know."
The gentlest whisper of a reply.

The tailor stopped its stride forward and made a hissing
sound. Its head turned by mechanical degrees until it stared
straight at her. The awful eyes that lived behind the tailor's
pulsed with fire. *Who are you?* the puppeteer asked. Its voice
could have frozen the stars.

Pavra broke her contact with Tynec and reeled back as fast
as she could. She heard the crackle of something behind her.
She dared not look back, but raced desperately to the safety
of the triangle. The crackling became a roar.

Her body exhaled sharply as she plunged into the triangle.
Before she could draw another breath, the roaring energy leapt
upon her. The air around the triangle spat and sizzled and
sparked. And although she had protected herself properly and
completely, the flash of pursuant energy burst forth, breaching
her barrier, lifting her up, and throwing her across the room
where she slammed into the far wall like a straw doll.

She slid down the wall and lay still. A tiny trickle of blood
began to form a pool in the uneven stonework of the floor.

The streets leading to the heart of the city were clogged like
a river jammed with debris. Lyrec walked the lathered horses.
The woman-child, Yadani, lay pressed against her horse's neck,
a rope tied around her waist. She had fallen from her horse
twice before Lyrec accepted the inevitable and strapped her on.
The streets were totally chaotic. Music from a dozen different
groups vied for dominance—twelve different tunes meshed and
shattered in continual cacophony. People stared at him in his
uniform, but none could recognize the Ladomantine colors
beneath the dirt and blood. They found Yadani's plight either
disgusting or amusing. Some bellowed at him to set her free,
but they quickly fell silent once his attention had been gained—
dirty and black-bearded, trudging silently through the crowd,
Lyrec did not look like someone who was interested in anyone
else's opinions on anything.

He pushed his way through the crowded avenues, ignoring
the curses that followed him. The temple of Chagri was to the
south and the crowd flowed toward the castle on the north hill.
He had seen it before the rest of the city had appeared—a huge
structure on its hill enshrouded in a pink sunset. The hillside
beneath it had wriggled with life as interwoven currents of
people battled their way to the heights. On entering the city,

he had paused long enough to buy a pastry stuffed with meat for himself. He hoped the priests at the temple would see to feeding Yadani. He had no time to force her to eat.

Away from the river, the crowd thinned somewhat. Fewer bannered stands decorated the edges of the streets and most were unattended. The people here offered him courteous assistance. He took their directions and arrived shortly at a wall with an open gate. Inside, he found a wide dark yard in the center of which stood a surprisingly small building. He had been expecting a fortress at the very least. The yard was thick with trees and sheltered in deep shadows. He failed to notice the people around him until someone coughed. Lyrec's hand went to his sword. He stared hard into the darkness. The beggars lay all around him, some propped against trees. Their eyes remained invisible in the darkness, but their heads lifted and turned at the sound of his approach, following him by whatever senses they had. These creatures would not be attending the coronation; a new king brought no change into their lives. The smell of urine was on the air. This was where Hulda wanted him to leave Yadani?

"Might I help you?" A priest was just closing the inner gate to the temple. Like the gate in the wall, this was black iron. Lyrec could see a hallway lined with candles behind the priest.

"This girl," he said, "she's . . ."

"Is she your wife?"

"Wife? No. A friend—of a friend. Who asked me to bring her here."

"The miracle of Chagri," said the priest sourly.

Lyrec looked around. "I was expecting something, well, more tidy."

The priest shook his head. "These aren't your people, nor are they mine. Would you be here at all except for this unfortunate? Look, you even had to tie her to the saddle. Do you think she is going to mind the company at all? She won't even notice."

"I'm not sure she's staying." He saw faces out of the darkness and they looked hungry in a way that had nothing to do with food. "I made that promise before I saw this."

"Understandable reluctance, I would say. There are probably more thieves out there than hopefuls or penitents. They've been dying in droves nightly. Oh, I know what you're thinking, but *you* try and drive them back to their homes. If they have any. At least with the coronation crowd, most of their enemies are out doing business elsewhere."

"What should I do with her, then?"

"Well, she can hardly stay inside the temple now. No one is here tonight—all attending at the castle, which is where I myself am bound. And I'm late."

"But otherwise she could just go in? What about these people? Can't they?"

"Listen, my friend, let me clear away your ignorance." He started to walk toward the gate, forcing Lyrec to turn the horses and follow. "Each one of these hapless ruins has been in there three times at least. Some as many as ten. They leave a coin or a tooth and touch the fountain and, after nothing has happened, they go out, thieve another coin or pull out another— well, nothing changes."

"Then some have been cured? She could be helped? I have to know."

The priest slowed to walk beside Yadani and view her more closely. "A few, a random few, were cured. Most gave it up. But, you see, Chagri is a god of strength and endurance. He doesn't aid the weak of heart, the cowards. To return again and again doesn't mean you have the strength of heart necessarily—it could as easily mean you are a fool." He lifted Yadani's head and saw her eyes. "Oh. No, my friend, there is no aiding this one. None of *these* have been cured. They don't even know where they are." He turned back to Lyrec, a sad smile on his broad face. "I am sorry."

"What do I do, then? I *must* get to the castle." His urgency was plain.

"I recommend the sisters of Anralys. Their place is not far from here. Back out this gate, but where the road branches there, take the fork away from the castle. It is also a walled place, somewhat larger than this."

"Thank you," Lyrec said and started to go, but the priest stood in the gateway. "Be advised," the priest warned him, "that the sisters are a strange group, rarely associating with anyone, even us, their brothers. We tread with caution beyond their walls and all men are forbidden inside their doors. Even a priest granted favor from Anralys herself must spend the time in a separate building, awaiting a visitation there."

"I'll be careful."

"Yes." The priest looked him over, noting the ragged uniform spattered with mud. "Yes, I'm sure you will be," he muttered as Lyrec led the horses out the gate. The priest looked back at the figures huddled in the yard. "Depraved filth," he murmured. He closed the gate.

The face that beetled through the doorway was stranger than he could have imagined. It shone with shiny metallic paint under which the skin seemed rough and pimpled. The face scowled at him, its red hair drawn severely back into a tight cylinder that stuck up like a horn from behind the head.

"No men." The voice was surprisingly gentle. Perhaps, he thought, the deep scowl was an effect of the paint.

"It's not I requesting entry." He gestured into the darkness behind.

The woman retreated, but returned in a moment with a torch and stepped outside. She was naked to the waist. Her upper torso, like her face, was painted in swirls of color. A terribly sweet perfume followed in her wake. Her dark skirt rustled around her feet. She studied Yadani. "What is the matter with her? Have you gotten her drunk?"

Lyrec shook his head, but realized the woman was not looking at him. "No. She has no mind. I'd brought her here on a promise because—"

"Chagri," the priestess said bitterly.

"Everyone seems to know. Yes, the miracle."

"No miracle. Anralys denies his miracle. She has shown us what a trick has been played."

"How's that?

The painted priestess laughed. "Through our Hespetess. You have come far with her?"

"Yes."

"Too bad. You'll see."

"I've seen already. I don't believe in miracles, either. But a promise was made." And that was a fact he regretted more with every passing, wasted minute.

"Your vow is no concern of mine. We'll take her in, and if any divine power can cure her it will be Anralys, not that false hope raised over there. You should forget the beneficent Chagri, and forget this one, too."

"I can't. I also promised to return her when I leave."

The priestess came to a halt in front of him and stared candidly into his eyes. Finally, she took the reins of Yadani's horse and led it away, around the side of the building.

After a few moments, a second woman appeared at the door to the temple. She was squat and fat. Her head had been shaved and painted with elaborate swirls. "No men," she stated, then slammed the door shut.

"And if I could, I wouldn't," he said to the door, then climbed on his horse and rode swiftly out of the yard and down the narrow streets again, until he reached the river. The hillside above glimmered like a dome of jewels and the castle was a purple silhouette above it.

As he dismounted and started to lead the horse through the crowd a wave of cheering began at the top of the hill and swept down toward him. He asked one of the people what it meant. "The king has been crowned," they told him. "Long live Tynec!" Another wave of cheering descended the hill. "He's up on the balcony," someone yelled. "Where?" cried another, who eagerly strained to see above the others ahead. "Oh, you can be sure he's there from the cheering, but I doubt you could pick him out from here."

Lyrec pushed on up the hill, no longer looking for the road, but taking any possible opening through the crowd. He was tense now, certain that some crime was near at hand as it had apparently not yet taken place. An assassination—where else to look but in the castle?

He was halfway up the hill when the throng turned and began their descent. Again he fought against the tide. They drove him back, and he cursed and shoved people out of his way. They threatened him, shoved him in turn. He gained little ground. Off the road and straight ahead, the crowd parted around a leafless tree. He wrestled his way to it, grabbed hold and brought his horse up close, then waited for the majority of people to go past him. In that period of waiting, he tried to contact Borregad. The crowd destroyed this hope as well— their gathered, swarming thoughts threw a net around him on every side. He had never been in the heart of a throng such as this, and he hugged to the tree, discovering only now the high-pitched claustrophobic tension and terror of being pressed helplessly into so small a space. He wiped sweat out of his eyes.

Fools, he called to them, *your world is on the brink of disaster and you don't even notice!*

Tynec moved in from the balcony as the cheering began again. The gold crown glistened on his head. He descended the steps slowly, majestically, down into the hall. There, the guests continued to applaud as they had since the moment when the crown was placed upon his head. On the landing, halfway down the steps, Cheybal and the Hespet stood across from one another, each with a cluster of their most trusted men around them. Cheybal was still wondering why Tynec had kept the priest near him so much lately when the young king reached the landing. Cheybal hastily stepped out to congratulate Tynec, but the boy swept past him with no acknowledgment whatsoever of his presence. Imperiously, Tynec continued down a few more steps before pausing to regard the crowd.

Cheybal's mouth hung open. He stared straight across at the Hespet. The priest fidgeted under Cheybal's stunned gape, finally pushed through his attendants and retreated down the steps and into the crowd. Cheybal watched him flee from the hall, then saw Bozadon Reket looking up at him. The foreign governor shook his head uncomprehendingly—he, too, had seen Cheybal slighted.

The commander tried to convince himself that it had been an oversight, that he had been preoccupied and stepped out too late so that Tynec, caught up in the drama and excitement, had failed to see him. Of course, he told himself, what child wouldn't get lost in this pageantry? He wondered then how Pavra was enjoying the coronation. What a sight for a child from a small village! He scanned the teeming sea of faces for the little girl. His brow furrowed and he searched through the crowd again. Pavra was not there.

Something is wrong. The thought overpowered him like an ocean wave. Tynec's slight was forgotten. Cheybal pushed through his men and hurried down the steps, waving to Reket. As he passed Tynec, the young king paused and watched him. A slight smile caught at Tynec's lips. He turned away and extended his hand once more for the next subject to come up and kiss.

Of the two guards present at the front entrance to the castle, only one paid Lyrec any regard at all. The other went on

standing as stiffly as before, only his eyes shifting to take in
this ragged annoyance.

"Who is it you want to see?"

"Commander of the guards," Lyrec told him.

"Well, does he know you? Are you expected? You look like
your horse ragged you all the way here. You've missed the
coronation, anyhow." He was careful to be only mildly truc-
ulent until he knew for certain who this man was.

"Yes, I know," Lyrec replied. "I—" He paused, then went
on: "My horse went lame. Slowed me. It is imperative I see
the commander."

The guard looked him up and down. Obviously he had
ridden long and hard to get there. Was he, perhaps, a spy?
"Did you hear me?" Lyrec bellowed. "I said it's urgent. It's
about an assassination—here. Tonight."

"What?" The guard turned to his mate. So far as Lyrec
could tell, nothing was said between them, but the second guard
made a hasty retreat up the steps and through the large wooden
door. Just inside, another guard checked him before opening
it. The sounds of many voices poured out when the door opened.
The remaining guard told Lyrec to sit and wait. "It will be a
while to be sure, what with that hall filled to capacity—it's as
bad inside as it was out here. Who is it that's to be assassinated?"

You great idiot, thought Lyrec. "I don't know," he said,
and moved off to one side, sat against the castle wall with a
torch hissing and fluttering overhead. Until he sat, he had no
idea how tired he was. He closed his eyes. Something tiny
crawled across his chest. He reached under his shirt and removed a black insect, which he ground into the dirt. He needed
a bath, and food and sleep. Leaning back, he tried to contact
Borregad again.

♭Chapter 19.

LYREC awoke in a small curtained room within the castle. He knew that his body still sat outside. For a moment, as he observed the dim room, he assumed Borregad must have drawn him there. Then he discovered that something else entirely had snagged him.

He drew back, shielding his presence as a figure stepped out of the shadows—a translucent figure in the helmet and bright orange uniform of Ladoman. The soldier did not walk, he saw, but floated to the curtain. Pausing, the soldier's head tilted; then the visored helm turned his way. "Are you here again?" came the whispered accusation. "Foolish child, I should have thought one taste enough for you." The implied threat made no sense to Lyrec, but the *quality* of the voice roused dread in him. Too much to withstand, too horrible a being for reality to withstand, the soldier should have been destroyed by its own odious disruption of the natural order.

He had found his enemy at last.

The soldier drew off one glove. Beneath it was a hand like solid shadow wrapped in cobweb strands of gold. Sparkles of light crackled along the filaments.

Lyrec retreated. A wave of panic swallowed him and he spun swiftly out of the dark chamber, into the great hall of the castle, high above the crowd. With no thought but escape, he located his outgoing path, and in the same moment felt the glinting hand discharge its energy—a bright yellow corposant that sped past him and exploded, blossoming like a flower to surround him and blot out the scene below. He reeled in his mental extremities like a turtle pulling into its shell. Part of the energy came with him. On the steps in front of the castle, his body lurched in galvanic spasms. He slapped the wall, pressed against it; his head twisted back and the cords in his neck stood out like tree roots. He breathed short, sharp sobs of anguish.

The guard came hesitantly over to him and prodded him with the end of a pike. "Here, what's come over you?"

Lyrec tried to speak but could only wheeze and choke. By degrees, the pain left him. *And that was meant for a child.*

The guard said, "Attack of the palsy, is it? You know, my brother—Voed care for him—had that till he died. I know about it. You just lean back and rest. The commander will be here soon enough."

Lyrec ignored his advice and forced himself to his feet against the wall. The guard patted him on the shoulder in sympathy. Lyrec turned and struck him across the jaw, then bolted for the castle entrance. Some of the people milling about shouted at him and a few of them jeered. Lyrec ran up the last steps and began banging on the door. People yelled out warnings about this madman to the guard inside. The braver ones threw rocks at Lyrec, which missed him and pounded more loudly on his behalf. The inside guard cautiously opened the door a crack. Lyrec slammed against it. The guard flew back into a small group of celebrants, knocking them all down with him. Lyrec leaped over the tumble and dove into the midst of the crowd. Cries of alarm pursued him, but were quickly lost in the general din. He shoved brightly clothed men and women out of his way. A few angrily picked themselves up and gave chase, which only added to the chaos as they, too, shoved and were shoved in turn.

As Lyrec pried his way into the great hall, heads near the doorway turned and conversations died in a wave away from him. On the landing across the room, Tynec stiffened abruptly and wheeled around to stare at the intruder. The mind controlling Tynec did not know the mud-caked figure, but recognized a threat in the way Lyrec charged through the crowd

directly for the steps leading to the curtained balcony. Tynec
raised a hand to summon a guard; then a smirk crossed the
boy's face and he lowered his hand. But the guard had seen
the signal and came rushing over. "Yes, Your Majesty?" he
asked. Tynec shook his head. "I thought I wanted something,
but I have changed my mind." The guard nodded and stepped
back. Tynec noted a body of pursuers making their way into
the crowd from the hall. He returned to his conversation.

Lyrec took the steps two at a time. At the top he sprang
into the darkness, sword drawn, to find Miradomon. The Ladomantine guise had been abandoned. Lyrec faced the milky
white robe.

The robe chuckled softly at the sword. "You cannot be
serious."

Lyrec struck more swiftly than any mortal swordsman but
the sword melted away the instant it touched the robe, which
absorbed the force of his effort as well, slowing his rush into
sluggishness that was like trying to cleave through water. The
gilded hand emerged and clutched him by the throat. Lyrec
could not move. His arms hung heavily.

"Who are you?" the robe asked. "How did you know about
this? It was the child, wasn't it? What are you, some Kobach
champion? Too bad for you—you could hardly have arrived
at a more propitious moment for me."

A warmth flooded Lyrec and something bright passed in
front of his eyes. Then he was thrown against a wall and held
upright there by some unseen force. A shout and footsteps
echoed from the bottom of the stairwell: the people pursuing
him had broken at last through the crowd.

Miradomon turned away and parted the curtains slightly.
"Ah, there he comes now." His hand emerged from the sleeve
of the robe again. This time it held a small object—a mechanical device shaped roughly like a cross with a spring and
metal crossbar. Miradomon tossed it at Lyrec's feet, then drew
a steel bolt out of the air.

The people giving chase reached the top of the stairwell and
took one step into the room. They stopped suddenly, paralyzed.
Lyrec watched in horror as the black hand lifted up the bolt,
sighting along it at someone in the crowd below. He tried to
scream, but his mouth would not open. In agony he wrestled
against his invisible bonds.

The bolt shot from Miradomon's hand. In the hall below, people began to scream.

The robe turned to him. "I will probably never know who you are. But I do look forward to drinking to your death. Goodbye." He vanished upon the last word; the people at the top step burst into the chamber and confronted Lyrec who, released from his paralysis, dropped to his knees.

Hearing the shouts from below, one of the soldiers in the group crossed to the curtain and flung it back. "Someone's fallen," he said. He would have said more, but the man behind him yelled, "Your sword!" The soldier wheeled around, hand already drawing his blade. He saw a dark-bearded man sitting on the floor beside a miniature crossbow. The man wore a bright, clean uniform—the uniform of a Ladomantine mercenary.

Someone down below yelled, "He's been shot! Up there! Up there!"

The soldier shouted down to them. "We have him!"

The armed group closed on Lyrec. He watched them as if in a dream, barely able to understand what they were saying. He saw a foot swing up at his face but could not move to block it and barely felt the pain of the toe as it kicked his cheek. He tumbled over, cracking his head against a stone. The pain from this released him from Miradomon's spell, but left him dazed by the simple physical violence.

He was jerked to his feet and dragged to the edge of the balcony, revealed to the crowd. They fell silent and stared up at him. Then the men holding him shoved him roughly over to the stairwell and hauled him down the steps. He expected to be stabbed at any moment, but they took him into the hall alive. The assemblage stared at him, some craning to see, as he was led across the room to the steps beneath the throne.

Tynec stood above him arrogantly. Lyrec knew who he was facing, could in fact perceive the energy surrounding the child. "Murderer," proclaimed Tynec so that all could hear. "No one here can doubt it, therefore I decree any trial to be a redundancy. You will be executed at dawn. Your pig of a king will regret having ever sent you."

He was interrupted by a commotion in the crowd. Four men came forward bearing a litter, the people in their path falling back and muttering to one another. The end of the steel bolt

Miradomon had thrown stuck up above the litter. When the four men reached the edge of the parting crowd, they turned about and leaned the litter up. In it lay Cheybal. He was still alive, pale, his glistening eyes half-lidded. The bolt stuck out from the center of his chest. Trailing after the litter came Bozadon Reket in a state of shock; he carried Pavra, unconscious and all but forgotten, in his arms.

Cheybal saw Lyrec, shook his head and tried to say something. Lyrec tried to lean closer, but one of the men beside him grabbed his hair and tugged back his head. Cheybal motioned the men holding the foot of the litter to lower their end that he might stand. Reket quickly passed Pavra to someone in the crowd and hurried forward. "No, no, old friend, don't try to stand. You will kill yourself, sure."

Cheybal squeezed shut his eyes against a wave of pain. He raised one trembling hand and pointed at Tynec. "Not the king," Cheybal whispered. He tried to continue but the pain increased and he fell back with a groan.

Lyrec looked at Tynec. The boy's eyes were wide, but not in fear, rather with some fearful malice directed at Cheybal. At his sides, the boy's hands opened and closed as if squeezing something. "Stop him!" Lyrec shouted, and flung back two of his guards. "Stop the boy—he's killing him!" The hilt of a sword smacked into the back of Lyrec's head and he fell to his knees.

Cheybal twisted in agony now. Reket gripped his hand hard, willing his own life into Cheybal's. Tears flooded his eyes. He bent over and said, "Cheybal, you struggle too much. Let Mordus come, embrace him—remember how we always said we would know the time and give over proudly, remember?" He wiped his nose and face.

Cheybal pulled Reket down suddenly. Through his pain, he said, "The girl. Watch over her. Listen to—to what she says . . . Ghost."

It was all taking too long for Tynec. He came down the steps and strode up to Cheybal. "Poor commander," he lamented, interrupting Cheybal. "Your will is strong. You have served your country with honor." He touched Cheybal's shoulder as if in sympathy. The commander went rigid and was dead. Bozadon Reket, still gripping Cheybal's hand, had his fingers stung by the charge that surged through Cheybal. He dropped his dead friend's hand and clutched his numb, tingling fingers. What had the boy *done?*

The young king saw the accusation in Reket's eyes and had to turn away to conceal his crooked smile. "Well, now," he muttered. Climbing up three steps, he turned and addressed the crowd.

"The best man in Secamelan is dead! Killed by this Lado-mantine assassin—*here!*" He thrust a finger toward the semi-conscious figure sprawled at his feet. "So, too, has he slain all cause for celebration. With the exception of our advisor from Findcarn, I want you all on your way by midday tomorrow. It is time to choose sides, but know that all—*all* enemies of Secamelan will be crushed!" He glanced at Cheybal and added impassively, "I shall need a new commander."

Then he turned and marched back up the steps to the outer balcony.

The guests looked to one another for advice and found only stunned incomprehension, as if discovering themselves trapped in a room full of strangers. Or adversaries.

The prisoner was dragged roughly away.

♭Chapter 20.

THE dungeon was so dark that what Lyrec knew of its shape and size he learned by feel alone. Straw covered the floor of stone. The walls were cold and moist and uneven like the walls of a cave. In one of the walls, a row of heavy iron rings had been hammered; above these, a small shaft—the one potential source of light in the dungeon—let in a chill breeze as well as sounds from the yard above. Feet scuttled past, voices bellowed to one another, and uneasy horses whinnied and trod the ground while their jingling bits and bridles and saddles were strapped in place. More distant than these but more constant was the sound of hammering: the raising of a new scaffold.

As Lyrec stood there, unconsciously gripping one iron ring tighter and tighter, two voices called down to him. They sounded drunk, malicious, and he refrained from answering. There followed a queer spattering sound. Lyrec moved back from the shaft an instant before the pranksters' urine cascaded to the floor. They laughed and called down to him again, this time saying he would do well to kill himself before the soldiers marched him to the noose; if they had their way, the crowd would throw the soldiers aside and rip him to pieces with their bare hands.

A third voice called out from farther away and the two pranksters scurried off.

Another voice called down, "Are you in *this* hole?" It was Borregad.

"I am."

"That's a relief. I have shouted into every grille along this wall. I had begun to think you weren't being kept here at all and I'd have to contact you—no easy thing with all the tension in the air. From what happened, I knew Miradomon was near, and I had no desire to accidentally tap into him, either. By the way, what smells so foul here?"

"You wouldn't care to know."

"This place is mad, do you know? I've nearly been stepped on a dozen times in the past few minutes alone. The whole city is alive with crazy people all dragging sacks of armor—up that hill no less. They hardly say a word to anyone, either. They're busy, but none too happy about it. Be glad they don't know you by name. That fellow you killed, Cheybal—they had a great deal of respect for him. Tell me, was he possessed by Miradomon or what?"

"I did not kill him. I tried to prevent it. He was the object of Miradomon's assassination plot. At the very moment of his death, I came blundering in and Miradomon was all too delighted to let me take the blame. He hung this uniform on me and disappeared."

"'Hung' is a regrettably accurate verb, you know. So he now knows we're here?"

"No," replied Lyrec. "He thinks I'm somebody clever called in by the Kobachs, which apparently delighted him all the more. I suppose he has some plan to link the Kobachs and Ladoman, and probably half a dozen other countries. Secamelan, the strongest, takes on all others." He sat down in the straw. "Oh, it's all my fault. What a dim-witted move to attack him with a sword. He melted it without lifting a finger. What a fool!"

"Well, you know I would be the first one to agree if it were true—but I doubt it mattered what you did. At least now you know him as I do."

"Yes, but—" He stopped as something clanked behind him. It clanked again and he rose stiffly to see a strip of light appear in the wall opposite as the door swung open with a prolonged squeal.

The torchlight stung his eyes at first and forced him to look away. A figure moved into the dungeon with him. Was it time already? He stared at the wall where immense shadows cast by the moving torch wheeled past like the sunlight of a full day compressed into seconds. The door groaned, and Lyrec glanced at it, saw a scowling face look in before the door swung shut. Another prisoner? He squinted across the room, blocking the torchlight with one hand.

The face that looked back at him was fairly young. Light-colored hair was combed straight back from the forehead. The eyes were shadowed with weariness, or it might have been only the harsh delineation of the torchlight. The person set his torch in a wall bracket. It spat flame into the straw beneath it; the man kicked at the straw to clear an area. Then, keeping his hand on the hilt of his sword, he moved toward Lyrec. "Sit," he said. Lyrec obeyed. The young man drew his sword. Lyrec thought, *This is it, then. I'm to be slain by a young executioner.*

To his surprise, the man knelt warily and sat crosslegged, the sword resting across his thighs. For a long while silence reigned while he sought hopefully for some answer in the dark-bearded face across from him. He scratched at his side. "There are vermin in this straw," he said. "You have no idea who I am, do you?"

"No. Should I?"

"I think not," the young man answered. "My name will mean nothing to you, but I will tell it to you all the same. It is Faubus. And I have been chosen to replace the late Lohtje Cheybal as commander of the armies of Secamelan."

"If you came here to thank me," Lyrec said, "you've wasted your time and used up too much of the precious little I have left. Hold me in contempt if you like, but do not act as if I've done you some service, or I'll make you use that sword and cheat the hangman and the crowd above. And I doubt very much that your mad little king would care much for that." Faubus continued to stare at him. "Get away from me, do you understand? I did *nothing* to further your career."

Faubus nodded, then closed his eyes and wiped the oily sweat from his forehead. "I thought not. I know you didn't kill the commander. A ghost did."

"I tried to stop it."

"Is that why you first demanded to see him?"

"More or less. At that point I had no idea he was to be the victim—just that someone was to die by Miradomon's hand."

"Miradomon? The ghost has a name?"

"He has a name, Commander, but he is no ghost. Would that he were."

"Then you must tell me what he is. There may be no way in which I can aid you—I'm to lead the army out at dawn and you are to die soon after. I need to know what I'm facing, who I'm fighting. I know what it is to command—Cheybal taught me himself—but I have no experience with enemies who defy the restrictions of flesh and blood. How do I stop him?"

Lyrec shook his head slowly. "I don't believe you can."

"But *you* could?"

"My most recent attempt certainly declares otherwise, but I know where he dwells. It's a place you cannot reach. And I have a weapon . . ."

"Who are you people? Are you . . . are you gods?"

"It always comes round to defining us. Why is that so important to you? All right, then. Yes, we're gods. Not *your* gods; I fear they've already succumbed to Miradomon's power. We don't make your thunder or rain or cause your sun to rise. But he could destroy your sun if he had a mind to."

Aghast, Faubus said, "Destroy the sun?"

"He's done it before, you see. On many other worlds, some of which—the nearest ones—were virtually identical to this one."

"Other worlds? Like this one?"

Lyrec remembered that no one on this world knew of the other living worlds in their own universe, much less of the parallels connected by invisible doorways and inhabited by intelligent beings whose existences were linked to theirs in a way so beautiful and fundamental that it was impossible to describe. To comprehend even this miniscule amount of reality was asking too much of Faubus.

"Other worlds," the new commander repeated. "Gods from other worlds."

"Specifically from a world that was never supposed to have contact with yours. But Miradomon was—is—insane. He found the means to gain power through destruction, and he . . . he eliminated his own race."

"Except for you," corrected Faubus.

"And me!" yelled a voice from above, through the shaft.

"Who is that?"

"Another of my kind."

"How many of you are there roaming about Secamelan?"

Lyrec smiled in spite of himself. "Just the three."

"And possibly a fourth," Borregad added.

"Wait, please," begged Faubus. "This is too much all at once. Let me think a moment." He looked down into a handful of straw.

They gave him silence in which to assemble what they had told him.

He asked, "How will your Miradomon set about harming us?"

"I'm not certain of all the intermediate steps. At first, as I told you, he was satisfied simply to eliminate worlds by exploding their suns. I can only conclude this bored him, or perhaps he discovered that he absorbed more energy if he set about slowly, meticulously wiping out individual races first. I'm inclined to think it amuses him to do so. The last few worlds have, we believe, slaughtered themselves in genocidal rage. He manipulates you into war even as you sit here."

Faubus crushed the reeds of straw in his hand. "But why? Why does he do this?"

"Because he absorbs death. He thrives on it. He made Trufege go to Ukobachia and lay waste to it—I know someone who saw him there, a huge white-robed apparition. He fed on the destruction like a maggots on a corpse. And now you will go to battle and feed him again."

"And you actually believe he has killed Voed and Mordus?"

"Killed or subdued them in order to take their places."

Faubus resheathed his sword as he stood. "I will do what I can," he promised, "but my allies are certain to be few. So far as I know, not one person besides myself would give you a second thought. And Tynec has the whole city in pandemonium. But I'll try." He started away.

Lyrec stood as well and called to Faubus. "There's something I should like to know. Why did you come?"

Looking down, Faubus smiled as at some private joke. "The guard outside would tell you it's because I am too young for command, that Faubus is a fool. But the reasons are two: First, last night, when you asked for Cheybal, the guard could not

locate him and, so, came to me. We were in the hall when you
burst in and, although most of the crowd separated us, even I
could see the filthy rags you were wearing. And the guard had
said you might be one of Cheybal's secret spies because you
had obviously ridden long and hard to get there—but not in
that uniform they caught you in. Now, that alone might not be
enough to change my mind; but, you see, the commander kept
a private diary designed for the sole purpose of enlightening
his successor about what it was like to be the commander of
Secamelan's armies. There were a good many blank pages left
to be filled." He fell silent for a moment.

"The diary," he continued, "came into my hands last night,
once I had been assigned to his post. I found it in his quarters.
He had *seen* this robed figure of Miradomon on the balcony
where they found you, not three nights before—just as *I* had
seen it in the forest where we found King Dekür's body and
lost his daughter. Just as I saw it again last night after I had
sent those men up to get you. I was standing below, wondering
why it took them so long to climb a short flight of steps and
capture one man. When I moved back to see up there, the
curtain parted for an instant and there was the robe again. I
admit I did not see the bolt fired, but that hardly matters, does
it? Probably half the people in the room saw what I saw, but
Tynec took immediate charge of the situation, and proved so
insistent in naming you the assassin that everyone saw his
fabrication as fact. I knew better than to argue, and I was
proved right. Cheybal believed our young king was possessed."

"And what do you believe, Commander?"

"I? I no longer know anything, except that I am scared to
death. And not of you." He crossed to the door and hammered
on it. The door squealed open and Faubus went out.

"Well, that was a waste," declared Borregad.

Lyrec strode beneath the grille. "How can you say that? He
believes us."

"How perfectly wonderful. You should have taken him over.
We could have used him to guide us out of here."

Lyrec laughed. "Borregad, really. Do you think he could
walk around this castle with us in tow and not be questioned?
And, sooner or later, the king would find out, at which point
Faubus would simply join me on the scaffold."

Disgruntled and refusing to give in, the cat said, "Well, he won't serve any purpose this way. You heard him say he has no allies. What's he going to do now—convert the guards to our cause?"

"I have to agree with you there. It seems you'll have to go on alone, return to Grohd's tavern and use the crex yourself."

"How? I'm only a cat. I can hardly pick it up."

"You're all that's left, damn you! Am I supposed to tunnel out of here through solid rock?"

Then a voice nearby said, *Yes, I've found him, he seems to be arguing with someone, but I cannot make out who it is.* Lyrec looked around the room; the torch revealed all but the deepest corners of the dungeon. No one was close enough to have spoken.

At first, he thought his eyes must be deceiving him as a vague form appeared, growing more substantial by the moment: a small form, that of a child, a girl with pale hair and a strange design on her forehead that seemed to glow. *Hello,* she said somewhat timidly.

"Hello," he replied. "Where are you?"

In another room in the castle. Her words were inside his head, but her lips moved as if speaking them. He found this effect disconcerting. *I won't be able to do this long, as it taxes me.*

"Of course." He recalled suddenly where he had seen her before—in the arms of the one who had held Cheybal's hand as he died. She was the girl the commander warned his friend to listen to.

You must escape. If you die, there is no one else to stand in his way.

Borregad, who was also party to her words, said, "What about me?"

"Pretensions of grandeur," Lyrec said. "Hush and let her speak."

There are two people coming to help you, she said, *but they cannot slip past your guards without a struggle. Can you aid them?*

"Possibly. I don't know."

It must be soon—they left as soon as I made contact.

"I will try."

Good, she said, and faded like the sun behind a cloud. Her voice continued brifely: *I will pray to the gods for you.*

Lyrec pondered for a moment, then walked over to the door and leaned against it, listening, his eyes closed. Borregad grew quickly impatient without any sounds from below and called out, "I could pray to the gods, too, for all the good it would do."

"Shh!"

"What do you mean by that?"

"I mean, if you want me to have a chance at escape, then keep your vicious little mouth shut!" He lowered his head and began concentrating once more. Above in the yard, the cat stood up and marched off in a blind rage. He scrambled back a moment later, having been nearly run over by the wheel of a wagon. He sat down, huffing, beside the grille and waited with what little patience he could muster.

Lyrec strained to make contact with the minds beyond his cell. They were distant, hard to find, but soon he could almost touch them. "What's happening now?" Borregad called down. The contact shattered. Lyrec slammed his forehead angrily against the door. He marched quickly across the cell, kicking over a water bucket in the center of the dungeon and soaking one leg. He gestured up the shaft, though the cat could not see him. "Listen to me, you black thickwit, when I am taken out of here and up the scaffold steps and they ask me as they tighten the rope if I have any final statement to make, I will take the utmost satisfaction in shouting to the crowd, 'I wouldn't be here at all but for my dear friend, whom I rescued years ago just so he could foil my attempts at survival and drive me to commit murder with his unremitting blather!' Do you understand what I am saying?"

"Mmm."

"If you open your mouth again, I'll see to it these creatures erect a little toy scaffold right beside mine and hang you with me!"

Silence came from above. The torch went out.

Lyrec crossed the room again, tripping across the empty, bucket again, then furiously kicking it out of his way.

The two guards stood stiffly at attention though no one was near. Both of them knew who was in the cell, and both knew what Tynec would do if they did not fulfill their roles perfectly.

But neither man knew what to do with the figure that emerged out of the shadows. The figure walked toward them—backwards. They exchanged a look of bewilderment. The one nearer the strange figure said, "Hold there or I'll be forced to cut you down." He saw that the figure wore a Ladomantine uniform, and he raised his sword to strike. In that moment, the figure turned around, faced them with eyes shining a blinding silver. The two guards slid quietly to the ground and lay side by side.

The figure disappeared.

Inside the cell, Lyrec crumpled over in a dead faint.

Faubus and his comrade found Lyrec and the guards still unconscious when they arrived minutes later. At first they thought all three were dead, that perhaps the white-robed fiend had swept through the dungeon. But Lyrec moaned and his eyelids fluttered open. He looked up into a dark face with a heavy mustache and even heavier eyelids. The man seemed half-asleep.

"Who are you?" Lyrec asked.

"That is your question. Mine is 'What in the name of Voed am I doing here?'" said Bozadon Reket. "Can you stand if I let you get up on your own?"

"Yes. The strain of overcoming the guards . . ."

"Especially from within the next room," Reket answered with a hint of sarcasm. He caught Faubus's anxious gaze. "But it has been nothing but Kobach children and demons in white robes and spells and skullduggery since the moment Cheybal was killed. *I* am supposed to be packing and on my way home to tranquility and good mulcet." He glared down at Lyrec. "Instead, because of *this* lunacy, I'm likely to stick my head in the noose next to yours." He sensed Faubus was about to say something and swung around to face him. "If you hadn't shown me what Cheybal wrote . . . and if he . . . and I am guarding a little girl, ostensibly from a little *boy!* Mordus take my soul, I am not responsible for my actions. I refuse. I mean, who *are* you?"

"My name is Lyrec." He stood, a little shakily, dusting himself off. "I'm sorry you've been . . . inconvenienced."

Anticipating another outburst from Reket, Faubus said, "You'll need a uniform so you can ride out with the army. No one will know the difference if we're careful—you'll be one soldier amidst hundreds. Even I won't be able to single you out, which is to say I am trusting you that far."

Lyrec nodded but made no reply.

Chapter 21.

"WHAT do you mean, *'gone'?* Gone where—for a stroll? For a meal?" Tynec gripped the arms of the throne and leaned like a ship's figurehead into the face of the guard. His apoplectic visage made the guard hunch his shoulders up to protect his neck as if expecting Tynec to cut off his head there and then. *"Where?"* the boy repeated.

The guard searched the other faces nearby for a sign that someone might come to his aid, but those around him refused to look at him, afraid that his plight could be contagious. Even his partner, who was too busy praying the king would not execute them, offered him no hope. All hope of salvation extinguished, the guard replied, "I have no idea, my king. He has vanished into the air, *just* Tynec. When we opened the door to lead him out for execution, he was missing, *generous* king."

"He will not be the only thing missing if you cannot account for his disappearance, *idiot* guard." As he drew his breath, the guard imagined a dozen fatal commands. Tynec snapped, "Oh, get away—both of you!" Then, to the crowd: "All of you, out! Scatter and let me be."

The cluster of attendants dispersed upon his word, and were careful not to go in the same direction as the guards.

Tynec sat back alone in the great hall. He thought: they won't find him. He is not one of them—they can't recognize that, but I should have. Perhaps he is a divinity of a sort. Maybe this world could spawn his like, although I would not have believed so. Could he be from one of those other worlds I destroyed, some lingering—but no, I left nothing undone. No one survived my passing. Then, who?

That child, that little witch would know. She alone made the contact. He *could* be a Kobach creation. There are some of them left free and alive. But if they've fashioned him, then I underestimated their powers. I must speak to her... but not as Tynec. That may have been a mistake, driving her away, and I have no time to regain her trust. They're all so ripe for dying now. And my pets await their new transformation and voyage. He chuckled quietly. I shall have to rouse my avenger one more time. The witch is still a child, she will tell a priest everything. And then he can kill her before she summons her savior again.

Tynec's body relaxed, then shuddered. A silver shade emerged from it and vanished in the same moment. The boy, still under Miradomon's control, remained seated, though he looked sad and defeated, old, and weary of life.

"Wake up, my precious priest," hissed the crackling voice. "Much has happened since you crawled back here to cower."

Slyur's eyes opened to see the black mouth grinning down at him and the orange eyes glowing with malicious intent. He arose slowly, consumed by dread. Chagri laughed. "There, you are so afraid of me. That is good for you, and wise.

"I have a task for you to perform, Slyur. I believe it will be the last I have to ask of you. The witch-child called Pavra needs interviewing. You see, while you curled like a fetus in here, Cheybal was killed."

The Hespet's face revealed that word of this ignoble deed had not yet reached him here in the temple.

"Yes," continued Chagri, "assassinated by a man in Ladomantine uniform. Your king has already sent an eager army out to take his reply to Ladomirus. The assassin, however, escaped magically and I believe the girl knows where he has hidden himself. She is an accomplice. I alone am aware of this of course. You I want to question her, and then kill her."

So at last it came, Slyur thought, the task that would damn
his soul to the deepest pits of Mordun. He knew better than to
argue, because he knew it would do no good. And as always,
Chagri sensed his doubt. "Recall, I gave you the life of a child
once. Now you can serve me fairly by evening the score. That
is all I ask. A balance. Think of it that way."

"I shall," answered the priest. "Balance." He knew, however, that he would not harm the girl. He had come as far as
his ability to deceive himself would allow.

The black crescent of a smile split the bright colorless face
again. "You will forgive me for my few lingering doubts." He
grasped Slyur's wrist. The priest's eyes rolled up as if he had
fainted, but he began to rock steadily back and forth. "The
bloodlust has started to trickle in, Slyur, here where your hand
was. Taste it—isn't it sweet? You want to rip the skin from
her bones in strips, make her endure impossible suffering because she is a witch. Make her confess about the stranger she
brought here. And then"—he placed a bone dagger on the cot
in front of the Hespet—"you must relieve her of her head and
bring it here as proof." He released his hold.

The priest stared up at him with sunken, wolflike eyes in a
face no longer belonging to Slyur—a face pulled tight with a
hatred no human being could have mustered. A bubble of spittle
grew and popped at the corner of his mouth. His fingers closed
on the handle of the knife with familiarity and tucked it into
the embroidered ceremonial robes he still wore. He stood and
strode out of the tiny room.

Chagri whispered, "And now I must leave you, Atlarma,
to prepare elsewhere. But fear not, your genocidal night comes
soon."

Then the room was empty, cold and bare.

Bozadon Reket sat with his feet up, across from Pavra, in
her room. He watched as she sprinkled a set of oddly shaped
stones across a board carved with depressions to capture the
stones. He had been present when Cheybal offered the divining
board to her and whispered, "This belonged to the Princess
Lewyn." That meant nothing to Reket, but the child had accepted the gift gravely. Now, however, as he watched her
skillfully roll the stones and saw her reactions to the way they
fell, he concluded that some secret meaning had been conveyed

by Cheybal, for the playing of the stones obviously brought
her no particular joy. All morning, the more she played the
more her expression darkened; sometimes she groaned, other
times muttered seemingly nonsensical things to herself. His
presence was forgotten.

Reket wondered just how long he would have to remain
here like this. Eventually, Tynec would discover he had not
left as ordered and have him put out like a stray cat. And even
if, by the grace of the kitchen staff, he went undetected for
some time, Faubus could be weeks besieging Ladoman. The
child would drive him mad with her occult doings by then. He
folded his arms and tugged on his mustache.

There was a knock at the door.

Pavra looked up. He saw that she was rigid with fright.
"He's come," she said. "All the signs said he would. You
mustn't let him in."

Reket stared at her as if she were insane. Had he had the
time to think, he might have been swayed by her words, but
the knock was repeated, more insistently, followed by a call:
"Hello, is someone within?"

"Why, that is the Hespet," said Reket, and he stood. "We
have to let him in, girl—he's a most important man." He
reached for the door.

"He is sent by the other one—the evil one who killed Commander Cheybal!"

"Child, you go too far saying things like that." But did she?
Was he not peripherally involved in a plot stemming from the
belief that Tynec was possessed by the same fiend? Thinking
this, he was cautious about opening the door. A bone knife
stabbed at him through the doorway. He came on his guard,
blocking instinctively. The knife gashed only his arm and slid
past him.

Reket backed against the wall and tried to get his own dagger
out. Slyur came at him again. The priest was transformed, or
driven mad: his lips foamed. He slashed toward Reket's abdomen.

Reket caught his wrist and shoved the dagger away, but the
crazed priest let himself be whirled all the way around and
used this momentum to slam the stump of his other arm into
the dark man's temple, smashing Reket's head against the wall.
Dazed, Reket slipped to one side, his hands out to ward off

any attack from above. Slyur instead kicked his knees out from under him, then pounded the dagger's hilt down across the back of Reket's skull. For a moment he stood like an animal over his downed prey, eyes lustrous with sweet joy.

Pavra had scrambled off her bed while the two men fought, knowing that it was she the priest wanted. But she was not quick enough. As she neared the door, Slyur spun back and kicked it shut. He brandished his knife at her. "Oh, you aren't to leave, no, but if you tell me the things I have to know about the one who came here last night, then I might let you leave. But your head will come with me at least." He laughed giddily. She saw that he was sweating as if burning with fever. "What was that one to you? Did you call him here? How did you get him to come? I want to find him. I want to know how to call him." He stepped closer to her. She had nowhere to run and could only back up. "Who is he?"

Pavra shook her head. "He is not known to me."

Slyur laughed again. Some of the foam bubbling out of his mouth trickled toward his chin. "No-o, that earns you pain and nothing else. Beginning at the soles and working up, up. And each time you pass out, I will awaken you and begin again. You will tell." He came at her, cackling to himself. He was all she could see, his laughter all she could hear, masking even the sound of her own voice screaming in her mind.

The priest flicked the dagger through her hair. He was so close she could see how large the pupils of his eyes were. He pulled up a long lock of her hair on the dagger, then snapped his arm at the last, jerking on her hair. She tensed at the pain but refused to cry out.

Then all at once the priest jerked up onto his toes. His dilated eyes accused her of some cruel jest. He began to turn away from her, then tilted to one side and collapsed across her bed. The bone dagger skidded off the bed and onto the floor against the boot of old Ronnæm. He held a blood-dripping dagger of his own and wore a grin of feral delight. She saw now that the door hung ajar.

"This one wiped out our village, girl," he said. "On his orders Trufege came."

Pavra found herself crying. She ran to Ronnæm and let him hold her and murmur gently to her.

She did not cry long, and wiped at her eyes when Bozadon

Reket groaned and attempted to sit up. He tipped back over the first time, then touched his head first where the blood flowed through his scalp, and then where a scrape on his brow was beginning to swell. He saw the old king and the girl, and the priest lying across the bed. The Hespet's hand clutched a clump of the coverlet and was squeezing it as if in time with his heartbeat.

"If you allow him to remain there long," Reket observed softly, "he will ruin that fine quilt."

"He's to live long enough for execution," answered Ronnæm. "That is why I haven't killed him. That is the only reason."

Reket pushed himself into a sitting position. When the galaxies stopped whirling behind his eyelids, he said calmly, "If you are expecting Tynec to read out his crimes and pronounce sentence, you are wasting your time and wrath."

"My grandson will make a just king."

"Possibly. If he ever gets to rule."

"And what is that supposed to mean?"

Reket nodded at Pavra. "Ask her. She can tell you what you would know already had you not been dogging the priest these past days—not that I am complaining, mind you. All the same, ask her."

Ronnæm glared at Pavra. "What does he mean?"

She surprised him by meeting his gaze, refusing to be intimidated. "The king is under the control of a force that sees everything. It killed his father and tried to kill me once when I saw it—and now, again, through the Hespet. And last night it killed Commander Cheybal." Reket watched Ronnæm all the time she spoke, anticipating the moment the old king would choke on his disbelief. As Pavra had frustrated Ronnæm now he frustrated Reket by merely gesturing at the priest and asking her, "What do I do with him, then?"

"He is like Tynec," Pavra said. "If he made others go into our village, I think it was not his fault."

Reket was rewarded at last by a growl from Ronnæm. The old king pushed Pavra away; he was willing to accept a great deal, but not the loss of his prize villain. He nudged the priest with his toe. "Let's wake him and see if you speak truly." He shoved at Slyur again. "Let me see your eyes, Hespet, before they lose their shine. And don't warn me of a god's wrath for touching you—I am long past fear of your war god. I have sown the fields he reaps too many times to worry how he likes me."

Slyur said softly, "My back feels cold."

"That is where I stabbed you."

The priest turned half over with some difficulty. "Then it *is* you, Ronnæm. I thought I heard you in a dream." His eyes focused on Pavra. "But it was no dream, was it? Oh, child, what I nearly did. Forgive me."

"For what you succeeded in doing, you'll hang," said Ronnæm.

Slyur lay on his side with his knees drawn halfway up. "It no longer matters," he said. "Once Chagri finds out that I have failed, I won't live long enough to be tried. He may even know already. He knows even what I think."

"Chagri? You see him?" asked a stupefied Bozadon Reket.

The Hespet nodded wearily. "He has been appearing to me, ordering me for months. Whom to assign, whom to promote. Whom to kill. When he ordered me to harm her and I said I would, he knew I was lying and took control of me." He shivered at the memory of being caged within himself. "It was like being a hungry rat. He wanted information about the stranger who—is this correct, is Cheybal truly dead?"

"Yes," answered Reket. In the same instant, Pavra said, "But the stranger is not guilty of Cheybal's murder, and the one who comes to you is not Chagri. It is something so huge and awful that it can be anyone or anything it chooses. It was the tailor who tried to kill me. And it killed Cheybal before I could tell him, I know it did!"

"It isn't Chagri?" cried Slyur. He sat up, numb to his pain—his worst fears had been confirmed. "I have destroyed an entire village, hundreds of people dead . . . and it was all a *lie!* All for promises from a god I never even believed in." He shook his fist at the ceiling. "I never believed!" he shouted. "Oh, you are right, I should be hung. I have murdered a race."

Bozadon Reket reached out to brace the priest, but the Hespet stood, doubling over at first from the sudden effort. "I must seek out the true gods and solicit their help. I have ignored them and they've punished me in kind. I'll go where I have to." Before anyone could stop him, he pushed himself away from the bed and lurched out of the room.

Reket watched the door rebound off the wall and swing

shut. Then he sat down on the bed. "So, what is the next thing
to be done? Who goes mad now?"

"This force or this god or whatever, once it meets up with
the Hespet again, we will be in obvious danger here," said
Ronnæm. "If my grandson is possessed by this monstrosity of
Pavra's, then we must escape before it finds a way to prove
us traitors and have us taken." He turned to Pavra. "The assassin, the stranger whom you defend—did you call him here
as Slyur thought?"

"No. I've only spoken with him."

"Then tell me where is he now—do you know which of
the prisons he has been put in?"

Bozadon Reket said, "He stole off with Faubus and the
army this morning."

Utterly astonished, Ronnæm spluttered, "How do you know
that?"

Reket smiled uneasily. "I . . . I helped him escape."

♭Chapter 22.

THE sacred chamber of Anralys was an octagonal room in the center of the temple. Eight was the goddess's sacred number. Eight benches stood empty on the polished wooden floor. The intaglio panels on the walls were separated by eight stonework columns. In the center of the room a single smooth wooden stand held an oddly twisted black metal sculpture, something like thorny twining branches, each branch ending in a cup containing a candle; eight candles in all.

Being the omphalos of the temple, the shrine contained no windows. Light came from directly over the candles through a single skylight formed of triangular panels of thick glass. The panels were uneven, dark and rippled; the light they let in was dim. A distorted sun crossed the sky overhead and the shadows in the chamber crept from the corners.

This day the shadows took on more life than usual. One shadow rose up and detached itself from the rest, moving clumsily and ponderously into the light. The shadow stepped into the light and took substance, became Slyur, the Hespet. He had entered through a secret tunnel, bypassing all the Sisters of Anralys, who would have forsaken their usual message of "No men" and instead have torn him to pieces on sight. His god and their goddess had always been at the head of the most important religious factions in Voed's celestial city. The Hespet was the Sisterhood's most bitter enemy. Never would they have dreamed he knew of the escape tunnel out of—and into—this shrine.

Pale and drawn, he shuffled past the gnarled candelabrum on legs that were almost numb. He knew he was slowly bleeding to death, but he had come too far to die now before completing this final task that might weigh in the balance against his misguided crimes. He had certainly come too far to be willing to risk being slain by the fanatical women inhabiting the shrine, so he went first to the door and with immeasurable effort hoisted the bar meant to protect the innermost room from invasion and set it in place. His whole body shook, and Slyur had to hold himself up against the bar while his legs recovered enough strength to carry him back to the candles. Upon turning, he discovered that he was not alone in the room.

At first glance the woman looked very beautiful. She had long hair framing her face, and the skylight caused purple highlights to shine through it. Her profile was sharp but not severe. He could not believe she had not heard him enter before now. His gasps of breath seemed as loud as drumbeats to him. He went toward her fearfully, expecting her to look at him and cry out in alarm at any moment. He would kill her if she did...somehow. However, by the time he reached her, the woman still had not revealed any awareness of his presence. Slyur closed his hand over her mouth and jerked back her head, expecting a struggle. She offered no resistance and continued to look straight ahead as if drugged or under a spell. He released her and stepped back, but his legs gave out and he dropped to one knee. It cracked loudly against the boards. Kneeling painfully on his hands and knees as if in obeisance to the woman, he regarded her again. She must be some deficient, mindless creature; she should cause him no trouble. Satisfied with this diagnosis, Slyur got to his feet again and shuffled to the black candelabrum.

He delicately touched the wound in his back, found it sticky with oozing blood, his robe was stiff with the blood he had already lost. More disturbing that that—though he could feel his back with his hand, he could not feel his hand against his back. Soon the numbness presaging death would crawl up to his brain.

Slyur knelt before the candles, his face pressed against the boards. He began to pray for protection and forgiveness. Could she not see how he had been deceived? Could she not forgive him—Anralys, mother of them all? Within her heart was supposed to be a bottomless well of forgiveness. He begged her to pay heed and warn the other gods of this terrible impostor threatening all their children.

A stab of pain bent him. His legs stretched out stiffly behind him. When the pain abated, Slyur lay wheezing, his cheek in a smear of drool. He looked across the room at the woman, who continued to ignore him. Who had brought her here? he wondered. It was inconceivable that she was a recruit for this mad order. Or was it impossible? Could she be someone normal now trapped within a spell by the Sisters? No, he thought not. More likely she was one of the strays the Sisters were widely known to take in—women who had been abused or abandoned, or both. One could see rightly enough *why* she had been abandoned. She had less value than a stone to top a wall. Yet he envied her her plight. At least she was looked after, and she had no fears, no anxieties, no white-robed specters haunting her dreams. Wherever she lived in the recesses of her mind, it appeared to be a peaceful and carefree existence. Slyur glanced down at his scarred, empty wrist and cursed his life for where it had led him.

Then the dark-haired woman did something that amazed him: she turned her head and faced him, almost as if she had heard him thinking of her. Soon he realized that she had not faced *him*, and he turned with mounting trepidation to see what had appeared behind him.

The goddess had arrived in absolute silence. Her face was sculpted of rainbows, inexpressibly beautiful to behold. She stood half again as tall as the Hespet, her naked body as smooth and shiny as hammered copper; the nipples of her breasts were as sharp as black thorns. Her aspect was fearsome despite its beauty, and he thought suddenly that she must be dressed for war against her wicked brother. She had come to help him.

Her gentle voice, as mellifluous as a cymrallin, said, "You have asked for my assistance, priest of the war god."

"Your protection, Anralys. From someone who masquerades as Chagri."

"You accuse someone of impersonating a god?" she asked.

"I do. He has deceived me. We have to destroy him. You, and Voed . . ."

Anralys's rainbows flared brighter. "I have to do nothing. I am not to be ordered, especially by one such as yourself. First we must uncover the truth of your claim."

"Truth?" He could not understand her skepticism. And then it came to him that here he was once more, doing that very thing that he had refuted the possibility of for years, even after Chagri had appeared: he stood before a god, debating as casually as this. But was he standing before a god? "The truth?" he repeated sharply.

"You must face whom you accuse," she proclaimed. Before he could respond, the goddess had turned away—he assumed to leave. But Anralys had no intention of leaving. She started to turn back to him, and the copper of her skin grew brighter and seemed to ripple out in the light of the flickering candles. She grew too bright to watch and Slyur shielded his eyes. When he was able to take his hand away, the figure before him had been transformed, Anralys no more. Chagri stood before him. The war god's evil laugh deafened the priest. Chagri swaggered about and even gave a mildly amused glance at Yadani, who appeared marginally aware of him.

"In the time since I last spoke to you," Chagri began as he strode about, "I have stood on the other side of your world and led two nations, each greater and grander than this Secamelan, to their deaths. They had once been the greatest of allies, and they went to their graves the bitterest of enemies. I am stronger today by a million deaths. Yet, in all that time, Slyur, you could not kill one helpless wretched little girl. Not even with my assistance!"

Too amazed and horrified to speak, Slyur could only avert his eyes. He concentrated upon the whorls and lines in the shiny floor and edged closer to madness with each thud of his heartbeat.

"You do not comprehend any of this, do you? Hespet!" Slyur's head jerked up. He tried then to answer, but his voice had disappeared. Chagri grinned. "Allow me to inform you of some minor facts, most of which you have wanted to know all of your life.

"For instance, there are *no gods*. You weak people create them to fill your needs, to promise you a future where you see none, to comfort you in defeat and death. There is no Voed, no Chagri, no Anralys nor Kelmod. No land of Mordun where the dead are rooted like trees in the soil. Nothing—there is only nothing in the end for the likes of you." The smoldering shape with scarlet eyes shrank and reformed as it spoke. It became the faceless white-cowled figure of Miradomon. "You've served me all you're able, whimpering priest. I fed very well last night—I can afford to give up one so hypocritical as you."

Slyur bellowed in rage and flung himself at the robed form. Miradomon stood his ground, making no move to defend himself. Slyur's forearms punched into the robe as if it were soft dough. Too late he realized his mistake—his arms could not pull free. His head was hammered back so fast that his neck nearly snapped. He howled with pain; more pain than he had ever endured, pain that made the loss of his hand seem a trivial ache. In that instant he went mad and began to struggle wildly, no longer thinking to escape, but to reach his one good hand into the darkness within the cowl and claw to shreds whatever dwelled there. His body turned red. The skin began to blister. His consciousness started to fade, but before he fainted, Slyur lurched forward and sank his teeth into the throat of the cowl. Blackness took him.

In shock Miradomon released him and reached up with fingers no longer black, but green and decaying, to touch the spot where golden fluid leaked from a semi-circular tear. At his touch the wound vanished.

Someone pounded at the barred door and shouted to be let in. Miradomon studied the smoldering corpse of the Hespet, watching the life fade away, unable to absorb what he had directly destroyed. Then he spotted Yadani across the room. For a moment he thought that she had stolen in while he dealt with Slyur and, impossibly, had gone unnoticed. Then he saw that this creature had no more personality than a plant. Miradomon, destroyer of worlds, remembered his desire for a queen to share his immortality. He decided to take this one away with him. What an amusing joke on these creatures, he thought, to have them outlived by one who was useless to them all. He went to her and lifted her by cupping his hands around her chin. "You will see the universe in all its possibilities," he whispered to her expressionless eyes. Together, he and the empty one vanished.

The pounding on the door continued, but there was no one inside who could remove the wooden bar.

Night came slowly, and the army of Secamelan pushed on until the final vestiges of twilight had been erased by darkness. Then Faubus gave the order and the weary soldiers dismounted. The veterans among them knew that tomorrow would bring with it aches and pains in every joint in their bodies from the sudden return to activity. These men ate a light supper and turned in. The younger soldiers whom they could not convince to emulate them remained awake, chatting and joking. They preferred to follow the example of their leader, not understanding that he would have retired already were it not for the necessity of making plans with his captains.

Faubus and his leaders sat around a fire. They agreed that surprise would not be on their side, that border patrols would have sounded the alarm long before they came in sight of the castle Ladoman. It was even reasonable to suppose a spy might be riding away right now with the news of their coming. One of the men jokingly pointed out that there must be dozens of spies in that area: any man with half his senses would have volunteered for the opportunity to dwell outside the swamp and stench of Ladoman.

Faubus hoped that Ladomirus would conform to ancient tactics of honor and send a champion out for single combat against a champion from Secamelan, the winner carrying the day for all. However, too many years had passed since such a conflict had been joined, and the fat king was too great a schemer to be trusted. Therefore, although they could pick their champion, they must still arrive prepared for a long siege. That meant their battle machines would have to be built while they still had decent trees to work with—which meant hauling them from Kerbecula Forest across the treacherous bogs. That would cost them a great deal in time and power, leaving fat Ladomirus to ponder and plot. So Faubus proposed they split into two divisions once Kerbecula had been reached. The first, his, would march straight on to the castle with the best infantrymen and the chosen champion. The other group would erect and transport the siege machines. If things went against the first group, then the appearance of the second squad would, he hoped, suck the fighting spirit out of the Ladomantine mercenaries. In the end he had his way, overcoming the few dissenters, whose voices were those of older men who resented being commanded by one so young. They could not have known that Tynec had chosen Faubus *because* he was young and had had little experience. But Miradomon did not know that he was underestimating Faubus.

The young commander understood the reasons behind the dissension, but said nothing to the men; they were bound to the army and, as they lost and won their rank and eminence in battle, so would their respect or resentment of him be determined on the field. He was sure he would not disappoint them.

Dismissing his captains, Faubus remained alone for a time to reflect upon his plan, reaffirming to his own satisfaction that it was the best plan. Just one path led straight into the murky country, and boldness was the best choice of action. He hoped Ladomirus was as great a coward as the many stories made him out to be.

Unable to debate the matter further but unable to sleep as well, Faubus went off in search of Lyrec and the bizarre black cat. He had not noticed where they settled once camp had been made, and now, in the dark, he did not know for certain if he could pick them out from the hundreds of sleeping or idling men. When he had made two circuits of the entire encampment, however, and found no sign of them at all, he could not satisfy himself that the reason was the night and its shadows. Of course he knew nothing could be done. He could not sound any alarm without condemning himself to death as a traitor. He had no choice but to turn in.

The next morning his fears were confirmed. The horse, cat, and rider had disappeared without a trace.

Chapter 23.

THE yard of Grohd's tavern was deserted. Lyrec's first thought upon seeing it was that the place had been abandoned. He recalled the threat delivered by Fulpig, the Ladomantine bully, to return here and take vengeance on Grohd. Looking over the yard, he found that possibility all too plausible.

Borregad jumped down before the horse had stopped. He ran across the yard to the tree where he had abandoned the crex. "It's gone!" he cried. "Someone's stolen it."

"You had better be wrong about that for everyone's sake," Lyrec replied as he dismounted. He pulled off his helmet and tucked it under his arm after first tying the reins of his horse to a post. Here was the place where he had fought the soldiers, where he had first killed a man. The notion barely meant anything to him now, so much had occurred since then.

He opened the door and looked inside.

The interior was dark, the hearth containing only ashes although the early morning air was cold enough to make a man's eyes water. Cups and bowls littered the tables, as if a breakfast feast had been interrupted and never resumed. "Grohd?" Lyrec called out. Planking creaked beneath his feet. "Grohd, where are you?" He saw the blanket hanging closed behind the bar. He started toward it.

The blanket flipped up suddenly. Grohd peered out from the dark doorway; his face was haggard and his eyes red and puffy as if he had slept badly for many nights. "You!" he said. "I wondered when I would see you again, if ever." He went back into the dark, then returned, tying a length of rope around his trousers. His naked belly stuck out. "I've had nothing but nightmares ever since you left—and it's all because of that thing there." He pointed a stubby finger across the tavern.

"The crex," said Lyrec.

"Is that what you call it?" replied Grohd.

It lay where Grohd had left it, on the floor near the far wall. "You tried to use it?" asked Lyrec, confounded by the implication.

"I *did* use it." Grohd waddled out, then stopped and pointed with one big toe at a black scorch on the floor. "You see this? This smudge is all that remains of Fulpig. Bastard soldier wasn't worth more than a smudge, either."

"Oh my," muttered Lyrec.

"And that's hardly the half—the half I can live with. His partner, the weasely one, is running around here somewhere without a body because that damnable thing changed him into a big black ghost, and he's been haunting me day and night. I'm afraid to sleep for fear he'll pass through me in the dark and suck me right up."

"Oh, he can't do that. You see, he's not truly here any more. Ah . . . I'm not sure I can explain this."

"You needn't bother," said Grohd. "I want no more magic in my life."

Lyrec shrugged, then went over and picked up the crex. "So many times," he said running his fingers over it caressingly, "I thought I would never join with it again."

"There is also the matter of a bill for food and drink for your friends. They used up your purse two days ago. Did they steal it?"

Lyrec shot him a glance that answered his question. "I had expected to be here sooner when I gave it to them. I'll pay— you know that."

Grohd's tone became less severe. "Oh, yes, I knew you would, but I tend to worry these matters a little." The tavern-keeper paused then, and responded to what he had been seeing for some minutes now. "Isn't that a Secamelan soldier's uniform?"

Before Lyrec could answer, a new voice spoke from behind him: "It is, yes—he likes uniforms."

Lyrec looked around. "Malchavik," he said with delight. "You look well—you've recovered."

The Kobach bowed slightly. "I have been expecting you, though I cannot precisely say why. Perhaps the weapon. Grohd has told us what it does—graphic portrayals that become more gruesome in detail with each recital. We have seen the black ghost, so we know he tells some truth. None of us can contact it, either." He came in. A dozen or so people followed after him. Lyrec saw Nydien and smiled to her with rekindled affection. She blushed and could not meet his gaze. The people seated themselves at the tables. Malchavik said, "You have turned true mercenary, then?"

Lyrec had to laugh. "No, not exactly that. I do work for all sides. The time is close now for my battle. I must say your country hasn't allowed me much time to prepare."

"You still pursue the one I saw, the one who brought the Krykwyres."

"Him, yes. It was one of those creatures—the one following you as a matter of fact—that kept me from joining you here."

Borregad, tired now of being ignored, jumped up onto the table in front of Malchavik. "Pleasant to see you again," he said. He had forgotten that all present were not Kobach. Grohd cried out in alarm and clasped his hands to his mouth. Soon he lowered them and eyed the cat askance. "Do that again," he said.

"Do what?" asked Borregad, taking pleasure from the shock he caused. "Jump up on something?"

"He can talk, the cat talks." His doubt was aimed again at Lyrec. "What manner of creatures are you?"

"Outsiders. But you'd do better to think of us as soldiers. It hurts less than trying to understand the real story." He touched the crex and Grohd turned his eyes skyward.

"Where is the rest of your army?" Malchavik broke in.

"By now I should think they've nearly reached the place the Ladomantines euphemistically call the buttertub."

Ladomirus lounged on a bed of down. With one hand he plucked small fruits from a stone bowl beside the bed, while the fingers of his other hand crawled between the buttocks of his concubine. The flaxen-haired girl lay on her face and, though awake, pretended not to notice her master's explorations. It was all she could do not to draw away in revulsion.

A pounding at the door rescued her from further caresses. The fat king pulled his robe across his wide torso and propped himself up. "Yes," he snarled out.

The door opened and Talenyecis strode in. She glanced at the concubine, who had rolled over to one side in order to see her as well. Advances had been made and not rebuffed. "Have you heard the news?" asked Talenyecis, and she might have been asking the girl.

Blind to this, Ladomirus asked, "And what news would that be?"

"The commander of Secamelan's army has been murdered."

"Wonderful!" He clapped his hands.

Talenyecis now devoted her attention to him, and briefly allowed him his delight, the more to enjoy the height from which he would plummet when she told him the rest. "It might be wonderful," she added at last, "except that they believe you were responsible."

The king's glee slid like oil from his fat face. "Who told you this? How did you hear of this, heh?"

"A scout of ours at the outer perimeter was given that message along with a warning for us to pick our best warrior for our champion."

"He was given the message?" When she made no reply, he shook his massive fist. "Who *gave* him the message, damn you?"

Now she was satisfied with his fury. "By the *new* commander of the army of Secamelan, which, coincidentally, happens to be less than twenty steys away. They should be entrenched on the hill by dusk with enough men to blockade our farm routes and starve us to death if nothing else."

"Send for supplies. Dispatch riders to the south immediately."

"I have done so already," she replied. "But they'll not be back before the way is cut off."

"What am I to do?" He stood, dropping his robe, unaware of his nakedness. "I haven't prepared. This isn't how he said it would go—it is we who are supposed to ride into Secamelan and rout them. I must go seek him out, whatever the consequences." He started to move, but Talenyecis kicked shut the door and drew her sword. "No," she said, with utter coldness in her voice. "You are insane—you believe a god holds council with you. I have watched it for months. I had hoped that perhaps some divine inspiration might actually make your strategy work. But you are simply a mad coward." The tip of her sword flicked up at his eyes. "We're coming to war and no quivering madman can lead us from here. You are used up, I'm afraid."

The fat king's eyes showed fear, but he scowled. "You want the kingdom, traitor."

She laughed in his face. "Would any sane woman work to rule this pestilent swamp? Ridiculous. Only a man could see it as a prize." She took a step toward him, forcing him back to the wall. "I care nothing for the kingdom. I want to survive."

"And you suppose I want to die? Let me pass so that I can find out from Chagri how to carry the day."

She repeated her verdict: "You're insane."

Ladomirus moved then with more speed than Talenyecis could have anticipated; he batted her sword away in the instant before she struck. She tried to draw it back for a riposte, leaping away for more room to move; but her elbow struck the door, hampering her. The fat king slammed the top of his skull into her jaw and smashed her between himself and the door. Dazed, she pounded at his head with the pommel of her sword. Ladomirus grunted, grabbed her arm and bent it back, then reached up and closed his hand over hers. Close enough to see the freckles on her nose, he said, "Did you think I was totally unaware of your greed for my kingdom, heh? And, knowing, do you think I'd be unprepared?" He produced a large dagger, seemingly out of thin air. "I've expected a manifestation of your treachery for some time." He nicked her throat with the tip of the blade.

She strained to pull her neck away and struggled fiercely. He pushed harder, mashing her against the door. It was all she could do to breathe. He chuckled.

Something whipped through the air and shattered over the back of his head. Ladomirus's forehead bounced off the door beside Talenyecis and he slid down, hands pawing her for support. A dozen cuts spouted blood on the back of his bald head. He rolled over onto his side, crushing a piece of fruit that squirted its juice across the floor.

The concubine sat on her knees at the foot of the bed and

watched her oppressor lying among the shards of bowl and
pieces of fruit. Half-conscious, Ladomirus saw her there, as if
in a dream. He watched her get up and plant her foot beside
his face. A mist drifted between him and the world. The concubine's face hovered high above him. Her mouth moved and
made noises, but they made no more sense to him than the
buzzing of an insect. He closed his eyes for what seemed no
more than a minute.

When he opened them again, the gelatinous hem of a painfully bright robe hung scant inches from his face. He studied
its odd, leathery contours, his brain awash with fuddled ideas.

"Sit up," a voice hissed. He recognized it and came awake
as if cold water had been splashed over him.

But the figure above him was not Chagri. It had no face.
His attention was drawn to its one visible feature—one hand.
Strange rough flesh, black as if it had burned. The hand sparkled as if some flakes of gold were embedded in the black
skin.

The robed figure made a clucking sound. "No one seems
to be able to do anything today. However, in your case that is
fortunate . . . for me. Had you killed Talenyecis, my battle plans
would have been severely curtailed. I suppose I could exact
promises from you that you won't repeat your attempt to murder
her, but I know you so well—as I have said oh so many times.
I think I shall make a symbol of you that will remind your
soldiers of the alternative to fighting against Secamelan. Nobody likes you, anyway." The hand reached down as if to help
him up. The cowl came close enough that he thought he saw
within it two faint points of light, like two stars seen through
a thin cloud of noxious vapors. The hand closed on his wrist.

A moment later the halls of the entire castle echoed with a
protracted keening wail. It raised the hair up the backs of a
hundred necks and charged a hundred minds with horrific visions of human torment.

♭Chapter 24.

"WAIT!" shouted Pavra, tugging sharply on the reins of her mount. Her horse fretted, wanting to stay with its fellows. The two men stopped their horses, looked back at her, then at one another with annoyance. Neither man rejoiced in what he was doing. Ronnæm believed he might have abandoned his grandson to some terrible evil. He could not have remained or defended Tynec from that force in any case, but the burden of guilt persisted. Bozadon Reket felt that he had run away from a confrontation which he should have been able to win. He mistrusted the ease with which he had allowed himself to be swayed by one little girl and her wild proclamations. Reading passages in Cheybal's diary and hearing what Faubus said had convinced him of the unnaturalness of the situation, but there were still moments when it was easier to believe everyone else was crazy. And cranky old Ronnæm was not the sort of person he cared to be stuck with for days on end.

The two men rode back to Pavra. She waited at a crossroads to which they had paid little attention upon passing—it led north to Dolgellum and they wanted to go east after the army. At least that was what they had understood.

"What is the problem?" Ronnæm asked, barely civil.

Pavra had shut her eyes as if listening to something. "He

has separated from the army—the one called Lyrec took this road. Earlier."

"Now what can that mean?" Reket muttered. "Faubus would never have allowed him to go free. Not by himself."

"Faubus is a child with his hands in a fire," responded Ronnæm. "He has no control in this situation at all. Girl, you had better be right about everything or we will be laughing-stocks and Faubus will be swinging by his chin."

Undaunted, Pavra reiterated, "It's this way," and nudged her horse onto the north road.

Ronnæm could not make up his mind. He wanted to be with the army, in the thick of battle; Reket understood this. "Let's follow her," he advised. "If she is wrong, at least we will be on the right road for Növalok."

The two men set off in pursuit of the child.

Lyrec said, "We have to go immediately."

"We will come with you," answered Malchavik, and he stood. He looked over his people and all of them agreed. Grohd made a sour face and cast his glance elsewhere. He had minded neither the company nor the money delivered by the Kobachs, but magic still had only negative connotations for him.

"I regret it isn't all that simple," Lyrec answered. "We won't be moving through normal space, and I haven't the crex enough for more than a few of you. Your powers would be useful to me, adding weight to my own. Might I call upon you to unify and direct them if necessary? Only if necessary."

"Of course. Gladly."

"Don't agree so casually, Malchavik. You could die in this."

Malchavik smiled ironically. "We recognized that before I answered. None of us would choose to die, but we will not turn our backs on an avatar when he asks us to stand with him. We want to join our own in the high places of Mordun when we come there, not in the pits."

"Avatar?" asked Grohd, but no one noticed.

"Very well," Lyrec answered the Kobachs, then turned to Grohd. "About your payment, my friend—"

"No, no. When you come back, we will talk about it." He could not quite believe he had said this, but added, "And then I'll give you drinks in celebration of the success of your . . . whatever it is you're going to do."

Borregad gave Grohd a dreamy smile.

"You heard what he said, Borregad—when we get back."

The cat looked the room over. "I detest long goodbyes and this one has been going on for centuries. Let's go." He leaped onto Lyrec's shoulder.

The crex quivered in its sheath. Defying gravity, it poured up Lyrec's side, breaking into hundreds of webs that spun around his body so fast no eyes could follow. The cat, too, began changing color, as the webs spun around him. His fur flattened. Silver spread over him.

The two figures became a statue of molten polished silver. Lyrec's eyes opened. They glowed a deep blue, like the tip of a flame. Then the air rushed past the Kobachs, tugging at their clothes and hair, and Lyrec and Borregad vanished. The tavern shook in a thunderclap that knocked people off their feet and split one table down the middle.

Holding onto the bar, Grohd shook one fist at the air and shouted, "I expect you to pay for that!"

❦Chapter 25.

IT began with a gentle flutter of the curtain at the back of the room. A wind blew around the dark unadorned chamber. Dust on the floor swirled up in a spiral, then burst away from its center as a deafening thunderclap shook Castle Ladoman to its foundations.

Soldiers marching in the yard below looked up and wondered if this were yet another omen. Their faces were set, their minds simmering in anticipation of their leader's appearance. She had left them to drill and they wanted war. The thunder clapped again, but the soldiers had ceased to pay it any mind.

In the room high above, Lyrec and Borregad passed into being. Lyrec opened his eyes. In front of him stood the black tripod as Borregad had described it—the three legs ending in a hand that cupped a silver globe. Now they had only to find Ladomirus and force him to summon "Chagri."

Behind him, something pattered forward. Lyrec swung about in a crouch, hands up to ward off a blow. Seeing who it was, he said, "You!" and found that she, Talenyecis, had said it at the same moment. She held her sword drawn, but had not struck. Lowering the weapon and with great control, she remarked, "I did expect you eventually, but not like this—you look like some animated silver idol stolen from a shrine."

"Excuse the appearance—it's necessary." He glanced toward Borregad; the cat concentrated on the woman, content for once to observe a situation without climbing into it. "Why are you up here?" Lyrec asked.

"Why, indeed?" She studied the tip of her sword. "What if I told you it was to kill you?"

"Is it?"

"What are you?"

"The only hope you have against a power you can't even imagine."

"You are not the robed one, then."

"No. We're his enemies," Lyrec said. "Long-standing enemies."

Talenyecis relaxed. She leaned forward on her sword, her head bowed against her hands as if in prayer. "I had thought myself capable of defeating anything that stood in my way. Any soldier, any king. Any force at all." She turned her head; terror was in her eyes. "Gods, but this is beyond me. It came to me and promised me everything if I led the soldiers to battle: I would not die; all of Secamelan would be mine."

"He was lying."

"I know. I knew it then. But he—you say 'he'—believed what Ladomirus believed—that I am power hungry. As well, he knew how much I doubted those barbarians Ladomirus hired. He *knew* this. I thought they would scatter and he told me I thought it. He caused a mist to rise in the yard. Every one of them was seized by such ferocity I thought their hearts would burst. 'They are yours,' he said. 'Yours to command. They will fight until the life has gone out of them.' Then he—he chuckled as if at some secret joke and added that they could even fight beyond death, but that he would gain nothing if he let himself influence them that much.

"I had thought Ladomirus insane with his secret trips to this room and his conversations with gods, hearing voices. All madness—what god would ever side with him?"

"Where is Ladomirus?"

She pointed at the curtain. "In the other room—look. . . ." She could not finish.

Borregad pattered across the floor and beneath the curtain.

Lyrec fairly trusted Taleyecis, but he wanted to know one more thing. "With all he promised, why are you here and not out there marshalling the army?"

She laughed humorlessly. "I'm here to kill him, what else? I have been standing here in the dimness awaiting his reappearance so I could split open his head."

"That was something like my intention, too. Possibly we can accommodate one another. He would destroy you alone."

"He will anyway. I am neither foolish enough nor greedy enough to be blinded by his promises of things to come. No one with him wins. Ladomir—"

"Lyrec!" cried Borregad in a strangled voice from the other room.

Talenyecis refused to accompany him. He ran through the dark passage into the next room.

Borregad stood rooted to the center of an otherwise empty chamber. Lyrec saw nothing to warrant the cat's horror. A few tapestries hung flat against the walls. He said, "Where? What?" Borregad's answer was to glance quickly out the circular window, and just as quickly to turn away.

From where he stood, Lyrec could see nothing unusual outside the window. He walked past the silver cat. The point of a conical roof and the base of a flagpole came into view. He strode nearer, his curiosity building. More of the flagpole appeared, and something . . . he bent over to see, and stopped dead still.

Flying from the flagpole was a thing so grotesque he could never have imagined it. A human skin, empty of bone and muscle and fat, flapped out almost horizontally on the breeze. Distorted empty eye sockets glared reproachfully and a crumpled hole of a mouth seemed to howl at him. He looked away from the window. "Come on, Borregad, we have to think of another way to get Miradomon here."

In the dim room, he found Talenyecis with her sword raised to strike above the black tripod. "No!" he shouted. "It's our only remaining link."

She answered without daring to take her eyes from the tripod. "But it is *shrinking*."

Lyrec raced forward. The silver globe had dwindled to half its original size. "Borregad, hurry up. He's forcing us to chase *him*."

The cat charged back into the room and scrambled to a stop beside Lyrec.

"Let me come, too," said Talenyecis.

"Not wise. If we fail then someone must survive who knows

about him. And you might still have your chance to kill him here. When we met, you gambled on trusting me—now it's I who has to trust you."

She understood. Then, quite suddenly, she smiled.

Borregad smiled back.

"A cat that grins and talks," she said.

"It's a gift," replied Borregad.

From the center of Lyrec's chest, a thread of silver shot out and attached to the shrinking globe. A harsh cold wind buffeted Talenyecis, stinging tears into her eyes. She squeezed them shut, and then heard the cat call out as if from a great distance: "We still have time to change our minds!" She rubbed her eyes and looked, but the two silver figures had disappeared.

Down below in the yard a wild roar rose up. The madmen she was supposed to command had caught first sight of the approaching enemy.

Talenyecis leaned on her sword and waited.

At first he thought he must not have made the transition out of Ladoman because dimness surrounded him still; but Lyrec waved his hand and the dimness swirled around it—thick mist or cloud that had in some way been drawn to him as he arrived. He swished the air with both hands. The heavy cloud parted, letting in a red light like none he had ever seen. With utmost caution he stepped out of the cloud.

A red forest enclosed him. Ugly swollen leaves sagged on black branches as if no wind had ever cooled them. They dripped a gelatinous fluid that had coated the ground under each tree in a translucent mound. Overhead, the same leaves blotted out any view of the sky and what light there was filtered through them. The layer of mist around his feet, the occasional patches of dark ground, even his uniform had taken on the color like a layer of rust. Everything smelled of moist decay.

Dispersing most of the thick cloud with his movement, Lyrec turned around and came up against a shiny black wall. It rose above the trees, as high as Lyrec could see. While inspecting how it had pushed out of the ground, he realized suddenly that Borregad was nowhere to be seen. Lyrec circled through the mist, envisioning the cat arriving in a cloud and scurrying off blindly in a panic. Lyrec thought to call out, but stopped himself: what if Miradomon were near as well? This was where the silver globe had brought *him,* and it held that Miradomon might enter his world at the same spot. He dared not call—not loud or mentally. He and the cat would have to find each other by chance.

Keeping close to the wall, he set off—a silver figure reflected in the uneven, faceted black surface. His image was warped grotesquely, almost as if the fundamental substance of this strange place wished to belittle him.

At one point he came upon an opening in the dense foliage overhead, which granted him a rare view of the sky. As red as the forest, the sky was spattered with hazy black blotches. The sight troubled him, but he could not say why until he took another step and, still looking up, saw some of the black marks change shape and size in a way he recognized. The arrangement of red and black was actually the forest, the wall, and the ground where it showed through. The sky reflected back a distorted view of everything below it, and Lyrec knew that it could be nothing other than the inner surface of Miradomon's crex.

He was inside Miradomon.

More fervently than before he hoped that Borregad had not come to any harm, and he hurried faster along the wall. In this place any law might be called natural: the ground might sense his weight upon it and the pendulous leaves might even now be watching him like a thousand blood-drenched eyes. Lyrec did his best to ignore the wild speculations and concentrated on finding a way through the wall. Unknowingly, he was following·the path of a dead king called Dekür.

The wall became an archway topped by a rude gargoyle face. On the hill beyond the arch, a castle squatted like a charred black tree planted upside down—its body a bulbous, misshapen trunk and its gnarled, twisted spires the bare roots. No doors or windows graced its unwholesome heights.

As he came nearer, he saw that it was not of the same material as the wall. Nothing reflected off it; in fact, the wall of the castle was depthless, like the far side of a line separating day from night. He acted on instinct and walked into the wall. It swallowed him up.

Everything became black. Absolute silence enclosed him. Breathing became difficult because the nothingness exerted pressure. It was, he thought, like a congealed shadow. And he had correctly penetrated its illusion. With great, heavy strides as though he walked on the bottom of an ocean, Lyrec moved through the wall with blind determination.

He passed through it so suddenly that the release made him stumble. The place was a nightmare of conflicting perspectives. A floor sloped down from where he stood catching his breath to an off center low point, then climbed back up again, without a line of demarcation, into another wall. The tiles composing the floor had been stretched out of shape toward the lowest spot. Some of them contained great jagged holes and Lyrec looked up to see a ceiling high above that dripped steaming stalactites. Knobs in the ceiling suggested that some of the stalactites had broken away, which accounted for the holes. He continued to look around, but could find no source for the illumination that allowed him to see the chamber in such detail. Nor were there doorways or exits of any kind. He sensed that the chamber might be treacherous in some way he could not see, and he chose instead to retreat into the wall of darkness again.

Lyrec came out onto a wide ramp that curved out of sight both above and below him. Unearthly cries echoed along the ramp from far away—cries of unimaginable birds or reptiles. Lyrec hesitated, debating which way to go. A king or a tyrant would normally place himself at the pinnacle of the castle so that he could lord over everything. Miradomon would therefore dwell in the deepest bowels of the castle and leave something deadly at the top.

Lyrec started down.

He had taken no more than a dozen steps when he heard, over the distant animal cries, the sound of some unseen dweller in the depths scraping slowly along.

The crex unraveled from Lyrec, flowing over his arm, swelling to a sphere around his hand.

From around the curve, a broad stone creature shuffled into view—a roughly carved statue given life. Lyrec knew it must be out of some legend, but not a legend that had been known to the minstrel of Miria. Perhaps from elsewhere on this world. Or from another.

The stone creature paused to see if the end of its hard climb were any nearer, and it spotted Lyrec for the first time. A dull-witted look of consternation settled upon it. The toothless elastic mouth opened and moved as if in speech, but no sound came out, leaving Lyrec with the undeniable impression that the creature thought it could speak, was attempting to communicate with him . . . and he wondered with horror if this thing might be one of Miradomon's victims. For all Lyrec knew, the bodies of the slain might be transformed into a horde of obedient demons. Then he could sympathize no longer—the creature came for him. Its arms reached up at him, thick fingers flexing in anticipation.

From the silver sphere a sizzling ball of fire burst forth. It rammed into the stone creature's chest and, spitting sparks, seared a fist-sized hole through it and sped on to spatter flames against the tunnel wall farther down.

The stone monster hesitated and inspected the damage done with imbecilic fascination. Then it came on as before, shambling purposefully, groping toward its victim.

Lyrec retreated a few steps up the ramp. Another way had to be devised if he was to slay this thing. His energy was not limitless—he could not pound at it till it was dust. Dust . . .

The crex released an invisible bolt of energy the same instant that Lyrec thought of it: a spinning force that whipped around the monster, a miniature cyclone abrading up and down rapidly like the string on a spinning top. Millions of sparkling granules spattered on the walls and floor. A cloud of dust billowed around the creature.

The force of the crex's wind died out. The dust cloud settled. All that remained of the stone monster was a mound of sand spread across the ramp. Nevertheless, Lyrec kept his fist pointed at the floor as he tread across the grains.

He hurried down the ramp much faster now. His momentum paralleled his growing excitement. Miradomon was very near, he believed. An electrical thrill tingled in his scalp.

The ramp went on and on, down to impossible depths. No more creatures appeared to assail him, but the alien cries never stopped.

The ramp ended in a cul-de-sac. The presence that had tingled before now set off a shock wave of anticipation. He did not even hesitate as he came to the dead end, but walked straight into the wall. The tingling became an ache that sent shivers all through him. He put out his hand to feel when he had reached the other side. His hand passed through the embracing barrier. Instantly, an inhuman force clamped on it and ripped him out the far side.

The dazzling light of a huge fireball blinded him after the solid darkness. The fireball's gravity reeled him in faster every moment. He had discovered the source of his tingling, but not in a way he wanted. He writhed in torment. His skin darkened from the intense radiation thrown off by Miradomon's star. He forced his head away from the white, exploding mass, saw high above him a circle of dim light. The mouth of a well or a rip in spatial fabric, but in either case, Miradomon's joke and his only hope of salvation. Below, the star tugged him faster still and grew to blot out the void.

The crex spun back around Lyrec.

The fireball, like the eye of an ebony giant, glared at him voraciously. The crex sealed off its furious grip. Lyrec slowed, hovered, then began to rise. Against the tug of the red-streaked star, his ascension lasted an eternity. The circle of escape grew by painstaking degrees.

The miniature sun ejected a plasmatic stream as if in a rage at having been foiled. Lyrec closed his eyes, but its pinkish after image remained against his eyelids.

At last the circle opened around him and he rose out of the void and floated over the lip of a well; when he stepped down onto the floor, the crex terminated its field of repulsion and Lyrec collapsed in a heap. If Miradomon had been there then, Lyrec would have been at his mercy. For an unknown period of time he lay helpless, almost unconscious. His reserves of energy had very nearly been drained. Slowly they returned. He stretched his mind to find the Kobachs and drank greedily from their offered resources. Restored, he thanked them and told them to break the contact and escape; but they refused to leave him alone and still in danger. He could not send them away now that they knew where he was.

Lyrec came to his senses lying on his back, staring up at a cavernous ceiling that rippled with the weird light thrown off by the fireball that had nearly killed him. The ceiling, like the walls and floor, had been carved out roughly. Lyrec rolled onto his side and sat up.

The room was decorated with tapestries—long purple and gold banners displaying designs that represented nothing to him: interlocked circles, spirals, and curved figural outlines.

The banners reminded him of a place, however: of the great hall in Atlarma Castle. Miradomon, it seemed, was celebrating. Another world conquered?

Standing, testing his legs, Lyrec wondered what sorts of creatures found the cragged and broken floor easy going. He started across it cautiously, expecting a trap to open beneath him or fall upon him; and so it was some time before he saw the throne.

At first the deep shadows near the wall hid it from him. But the faint, reflected light outlined it against the shadows as he moved. Two raised steps carved out of what had been molten rock led up to a wide stone seat. The light caught on bits of sparkling mineral embedded in the black stone. At the top of the throne, stretching out of either corner, two leafless black branches arched up like scraggy claws. Again Lyrec was struck by a sense of odd familiarity, and he recognized a similarity to Tynec's throne in Atlarma. The banners, the throne—Miradomon had turned this cavern into a parody of that hall in Secamelan. But what of the star?

He moved back to the edge of the well and looked down into its dimension-defying depths. The incipient sun released a string of plasma and sucked it back in. He could feel none of its pull here and assumed he had passed some unseen barrier that blocked off its gravity. His one uncovered hand he found to be burned and blistered. Any mortal who might have succeeded in overcoming all obstacles to reach that pit would have been crisped in a matter of moments. Yet the star had to be more than a simple last defense. Why keep it here? Why make it the center of his world, create what had to be an unstable dimensional bridge just to look upon its light? Why?

Still pondering, he withdrew from the pit—and found the throne occupied. A vague figure slumped in the black stone seat, the shadows playing tricks with its identity. Lyrec, approaching, ready to unleash death upon it, thought at first he recognized who it was, but immediately doubted his senses. Perhaps this was the trap, the last defense. But soon the stygian gloom gave up its secrets; consternation replaced doubt. "Yadani?" he called. She continued to stare straight ahead, blankly, mindlessly. The mystery of the star was minor compared to this. What possible reason Miradomon had for bringing her here, he could not imagine.

Even as he stood baffled, from out of the wall behind the

throne a white robe emerged. It floated forward a few steps before it saw him. "You!" hissed Miradomon. The robe ignited, emphasizing the shock surging through it. In its illumination, Lyrec saw a Krykwyre standing motionlessly behind the throne. Had it been there all along, hidden in shadow? "How did you survive?" The depthless cowl twisted toward the pit; Miradomon drifted across the floor. Light from the star threw his enormous shadow across the ceiling. Satisfied that the star remained undamaged, the robe chuckled. "I forget you haven't that sort of power. And I doubt you could even influence its spin without my knowing.

"I must say I am impressed with you, defender of children. Yet I also regard you with pity for your incredible stupidity. Can you believe you will be able to harm me here at the center of my realm when you couldn't inflict a gnat's damage in Atlarma? Ah, but I suppose it's your duty—your single-minded purpose. When the witches call, you must obey." The robe studied Lyrec carefully and saw the shine of silver at his hand. "What is that?" He pointed, a charred, skeletal hand sparkling with gold.

"Permit me to show you." Lyrec raised the crex.

Fire spat from Miradomon's fingertips; he snagged the crex and tore it from Lyrec's arm. In the split second before it pulled away, Lyrec shaped and released it. A fraction of a second slower and he would have lost his arm. The transformed weapon sailed into Miradomon's hand. He turned it over, analyzing it. "You planned to attack me with this?" He laughed, and held up a tarnished, dented short sword. Then he flung it away, where it clattered and bounced up against the first step of the throne. "The least I can do is arm you decently for your battle." The air in his empty palm began to sparkle and take shape, becoming a thin white sword. "There," he said, and tossed it to Lyrec. "Test it. Try the weight. I think you will find the balance to be exceptional. Yes? Good, then we come to the problem of choosing your opponent."

"Why not you?"

"Too simple. You must *earn* that opportunity. Perhaps we should start you off with a Krykwyre to test your mettle."

"Another? I've already dispatched one."

The cowl stopped moving, and Lyrec had the uncanny sensation of being stared at, though he could see nothing within.

He speculated on what form his enemy had taken. "So," said Miradomon, "that is the reason it never returned. I thought it was simply errant. Well, then, a creature from someone else's legends. What would you say to an opponent of stone?"

"I'm afraid you may have some trouble with that one. Of course, you could always reassemble it, I suppose."

Miradomon said nothing for a while, and Lyrec could sense that he was probing for his stone slave. The crex lay across the room, too far to grab without first maneuvering himself closer to it. He took two small steps away from the robe. Miradomon did not seem to notice. He said, "I see you speak the truth. The *goylem* is destroyed. I had prepared it for my next conquest. I fear it will have to remain a legend.

"You are very nearly a challenge, savior of the Kobachs. Since monsters do not challenge you, let us try something else—one of your own kind. A human being."

The robe turned away, toward the pit, and created two flat stone platforms hovering in the air above the star.

Lyrec ran for the crex then. He took one step, then found himself frozen in position. Miradomon made him turn around.

Out on one of the platforms stood Talenyecis. She stood in a combat pose, expressionless. He uttered her name in a shocked gasp. "You know her, then," hissed the robe. Lyrec called out to her. "She won't hear you—I control her. This should be better than I had anticipated. Will you kill a friend for a chance to save your world? For a chance at me?" He gestured and Lyrec was lifted into the air and deposited on the stone slab opposite Talenyecis's. A white sword identical to his appeared in her hands. "Kill her and you might survive. Fail and, of course, you will not. Her weapon is identical to yours. They're unique, you'll find."

Not much space separated the two platforms from each other, but Lyrec considered the jump from one of them to the rim of the pit would take a good deal more effort.

Talenyecis came to life stiffly at first. Her movements became much more fluid as she drew up across from him, but her face remained expressionless, her eyes blank. The white blade hung loosely in her grip, ready to flick in any direction, defying him to guess which. He retreated to the far edge of his own slab.

She leaped with feline grace and strength, landing halfway

across his square, sword driving up at him from both hands at her belly. He blocked her blade to one side. The instant they touched, the twin swords flared brightly and sent an electrical charge into Lyrec. He jerked wildly and pulled his blade away.

"You see?" laughed Miradomon. "Every time you choose not to kill her, but to parry her instead, you will be electrified. Possibly even electrocuted—I really have no idea how much you can take."

Lyrec tried to throw down the sword but it stuck to his hands. He had to topple backward to avoid Talenyecis's swing at his throat. She chopped down before he could get away, forcing him to block again. The blades clashed together, igniting the air with sparks. Lyrec shook. His eyes rolled up in his head. He could not maintain the contact, and tugged his sword away again. Talenyecis's blade continued down, nicking his shoulder.

He rolled away, at the same time kicking her legs out from under her. Jumping up, he could have killed her then, and he knew Miradomon was giving him the chance. But he could not do it. He leaped across to the unoccupied platform. Talenyecis climbed mechanically to her feet. She stopped. "Too bad," teased Miradomon. "Is it a rule you live by: you cannot kill those you serve? Well, you'll have to bend the rules here or die."

Lyrec took a chance; closing his eyes, he tried to probe Talenyecis, to break whatever force held her. His probe went awry, snared by a highly charged energy nearby—Borregad, coming to save him.

He looked down into the cavern in time to see a silver blur launch itself from out of the shadows, sailing through the air behind Miradomon. The shining cat struck the back of the white hood. Razor-sharp talons raked the spongy material, and yellow fluid sprayed out in a dozen streams. Miradomon clamped his hands over his head, but Borregad had already taken flight, back toward the throne, landing atop the discarded crex.

No, thought Lyrec. *You can't even pick it up!*

The robe swung about, bony green hands pointing accusingly. Sizzling blue flame blasted the floor. Lyrec shouted, but was drowned out by the explosion and a piercing howl that abruptly cut off. A red-hot circle of melted slag bubbled where the crex and the cat had been. No trace of either remained.

Oh, Borregad.

"What was that?" screamed Miradomon. His hands sealed over the last of his wounds. "You brought help? You will need more than an army of silver vermin! You aren't Kobach—*who are you?*"

Lyrec's anger built slowly. "You don't know?" he asked haughtily. "You aren't infallible?" He blocked the anger, shot a probe at Talenyecis, intending to shatter whatever hold Miradomon had over her. What he found stunned him. His eyes opened wide in dismay.

"I asked you who?" yelled the robe.

Talenyecis came alive again, bounding the short distance, sword coming up to strike—Miradomon's way of forcing an answer from him. Before she could bring the blow down upon him, Lyrec stabbed into her. She crumpled at his feet. Her body trembled, then shrank rapidly into nothingness. Lyrec cursed his stupidity—if he had just thought, he would have known she was not real. That was the way Miradomon played with those he meant to destroy.

He backed to the edge of the slab. The same sibilant voice rang out, *"Who?"* Lyrec rushed to the edge and made the leap across the void to the lip of the well, pitched forward on landing, rolling head over heels, ignoring the bruises from the rough floor. He tumbled up onto his feet and plunged the white sword into Miradomon.

"I'll tell you who I am. I'm your executioner."

The robe stood immobile, cowl doubled over as if in shock at finding the white sword impaling its chest. One sickly green hand came out of a sleeve, took hold of the sword and withdrew it by degrees. The other hand sealed up the wound. Lyrec saw the green skin begin to darken again.

"Executioner," mocked the robe. The sword melted away in his hand. "A premature description. Once more and only once more. Who?"

"The last survivor," he hissed.

The meaning of his statement struck Miradomon like a blow. "Impossible. No one survived!"

"As I said—you're not infallible."

"No," answered the robe, "but given my powers I can afford to make mistakes, whereas you . . . that silver weapon was your crex, was it not? Ably disguised, certainly, but you should never have allowed me to disarm you. You hesitated, and now"—he pointed to the melted circle—"you have lost what little chance you might have had. But here I am wasting time teaching you lessons on life when yours is nearly over."

"If that's true, then tell me first why? Why did you commit genocide?"

"Not genocide—genocide implies waste. I wasted nothing. That core of energy down there began with our world. The first hot cinders came from the destruction I caused in stepping beyond our universe."

"Into all of these other, these . . . parallel ones."

"Parallel universes? No, no—again you're wrong. You have followed, but have not understood. Each of those worlds comprised a part of a single universe. In normal space and time they would have been unimaginably far apart, but that corridor we sailed through so many times in our separate pursuits compresses the distance. Space becomes meaningless, an illusion. Parallels, yes, but all within one universe that I will eventually obliterate."

"It will take you an eternity. I've caught up with you, which means you have slowed down considerably. Glutted, perhaps?"

Miradomon laughed contemptuously at the small jibe. "Yes, I did slow down, but out of *wisdom*. At first, you see, I was impulsive, eager to increase my powers, and in my haste I wasted the energy of the life forms on those living worlds by going directly for the energy within the world itself. A mistake when you take into account the enormous energy to be distilled from the population. I tried killing them myself but found their death at my hands blocked my ability to absorb their life force. It trickled away, escaped. Even now I have no idea why. Nevertheless, I was forced to make them kill one another and that involved deception and intrigue. These worlds are all in a similar development pattern and time frame—all young, impressionable, and ignorant. They worship deities as the answer to everything; their faith is fanatical. I simply use it against them, as their own leaders have done for centuries.

"For instance, look at the Kobachs—scorned and hated for offending the gods. Well, who dreamed up that ridiculous tale? There are no gods, no formidable being appeared and told this to someone. No, some person in power hated the Kobachs and was in a position to make others hate them, too. These races are all like that—stupid and violent. Insane. I find it amusing to pare them away by degrees." He floated over to the pit and eliminated the hovering platforms. "I must say, I am enjoying this. I've never had an opportunity of explaining it all to anyone who might understand, in some measure, what I have done. But *you* have to hope I will go on talking forever. Well, unfortunately for you, there is little left to say. I severed all contact with my crex. I no longer needed it. Now it's another utensil, a tool like the boy king. Means to an end. You see, I no longer need its protection as you do. Chaos protects me far better. Come look at all that energy down there. You see how ludicrous it was for you to try and slay me with a paltry sword." The robe turned to him again. "Tell me, now—how did you survive?"

"In the simplest way: I was not there," explained Lyrec. "Distant by three or four stars. I saw the destruction—watched our homestar shattered and sucked out of existence. Of course, distance being what it is, everything had been destroyed even before I saw it. I raced back nonetheless. The area around the rip you opened had attained equilibrium by then. No one, nothing was left. I searched for the cause and for my . . . the word here would be 'lover.' I could not be certain that she had perished unless I entered the hole. I had to see the other side. And there was one survivor, crippled but alive. I saved him."

"He didn't die?"

"Another error on your part. You should have made sure he was dead then." He looked at the blasted circle on the floor. "Maybe that no longer matters. He told me what had happened. He saw you, recognized you. But my lover . . . You either destroyed or imprisoned her. I've come this far to find out which."

Miradomon began to laugh helplessly. "That's why you've come? She is the reason? You must be rewarded for your trouble. I destroyed her. There, now you know—was it worth the journey?"

Lyrec could not reply. To hear it said at last left him devastated. *I destroyed her.* Lyrec had been certain of this all along, he told himself, but hearing it, living it was more chilling than he could have imagined.

"The crippled one you helped—he was the thing that attacked me? The silver creature I destroyed there?"

Lyrec nodded.

"Then it remains for me to dispose of you and get about my business. All this talk has made me anxious to finish what I've begun. What are you called here?"

"Lyrec."

"Then, Lyrec, this is—" He had leveled his hand, palm upward, but hesitated. "What is that around you? Let me see it." As if on command, a thin veil of rose-colored energy appeared over Lyrec. "I see," said Miradomon. "The Kobachs are with you. Have you united their dwindling corps against me, Lyrec?" He chuckled. "First, then we must remove the final barrier." The purple veil began to sparkle. Lyrec could hear the echoes of a dozen souls in agony.

Escape, he told them. *I've failed—don't you die for nothing, too.*

The sparkling web covered him. The Kobachs retreated, and the veil faded out. Miradomon ended his attack. "Their numbers have decreased again. My, what a sorry lot they are. Nobody likes them. Now, as I began to say before—goodbye, Lyrec."

An invisible hand clutched Lyrec and lifted him out above the pit. He looked down at the white seething star and at Miradomon.

The unseen hand released him and he fell into sudden darkness.

♘Chapter 26.

THEY saw the first body outside the tavern. Charred, still smoking, the person had apparently met his end in trying to escape the source of his torment—inside the tavern. In hope and fear, Pavra jumped from her horse and bolted for the tavern door. It rested ajar. She slid through. The people there raised their heads; their leader could not believe his eyes. He stood as Pavra ran to him, crying, "Papa!"

He swept her up and crushed her to him, kissing her face and her tears and saying, "My flower, my flower," his voice cracking in joy and grief.

At the door, Ronnæm recognized Malchavik and the others. They sat in a circle, and Ronnæm understood what had happened. They looked equally grim, terribly weary. Four bodies lay on the floor in a similar state to the one outside. On the rear wall, the outline of one victim had been scorched into the stones.

Over the serving bar one very intimidated tavernkeeper raised his head and watched them.

Malchavik set his daughter aside and stood up to embrace Ronnæm. "Sire," he said, for he would always think of Ronnæm in this way, "we have failed in defending the one called Lyrec from the evil one. We were discovered. The evil one attacked and Lyrec ordered us to abandon him. What else could we do? We were dying. Even so, not all of us survived."

Bozadon Reket had only the barest inkling of what all this talk meant. He slipped away, went behind the bar with Grohd. The tavernkeeper eyed him distrustfully at first, but moved over and let him sit.

Pavra said, "You must not attack him directly—he is nearly all-seeing. Attack through his weaknesses."

Her father tried not to sound conciliatory as he replied, "No one knows if he has any, or what they might be. By now it will hardly matter, in any case. The avatar is surely dead, Pavra."

Grohd muttered from behind the bar. Reket understood none of it but nodded in agreement with the tone.

Pavra pulled away from her father. "What if you were wrong?" She turned to Ronnæm. "And if he is right, will we simply agree that the horrible robe has won and go to our slaughter at his will? What of Tynec?"

Ronnæm stared hard into her eyes. He had looked into such eyes at one other time in his life and had yielded to that other Kobach female—his daughter-in-law. Now she was dead and so was his son. He missed his family. "Yes," he answered. "I swore to avenge my son and I intend to carry that out if it means we *all* burn. You're all tired of this fight and you want to take time for your grief. But what difference can one last try make when our enemy is about to crush us in any case?"

Malchavik solemnly asked his daughter, "What is the weak spot you know?"

"The way to attack," she said, "is through Tynec." She saw all of her people look up at Ronnæm. To add weight to her argument, she added, "The avatar dies more certainly while we argue."

Ronnæm said, "Do what you must."

Two heads peeked over the bar. "I would fight in combat against any warrior," Reket whispered to Grohd, "but this battle isn't for my kind. Or yours."

"Except they claim we'll all die if they lose," replied Grohd.

"We will?" Reket looked from the tavernkeeper to the group of people linking hands. He stared down into his own hands, wondering what secret powers they might have.

*   *   *

Darkness enshrouded the cavern.

For an instant Lyrec thought he had died. Then he decided this had to be some trick of Miradomon's, one last cruel jape. And then he heard the sinister voice booming out of the darkness. "What is *this*? Another trick of the Kobachs? Or have you involved a faction of eldritch power I know nothing about? Who else have you turned against me, Lyrec?"

He began to see again as Miradomon created a phosphorescence on the walls of the cavern. The walls started to glow much as the robe did in the center of the cavern. Farther back, the throne lay entirely in shadow.

Lyrec found himself stretched out on a solid black sheet that sealed off the pit completely, a barrier between them and the star. He got to his feet. The robe floated over onto the reflective barrier, then discharged a blast of heat at it. Lyrec fell back from the intense heat; where it hit, a circle of dullness appeared—the only sign that the heat had any effect at all. "If you think this shield can help you, you're a greater fool than I imagined. What can you possibly expect to gain?"

Lyrec thought he might have heard the tiniest tremor of fear in the question. He stepped from the shield and moved far enough from it to avoid being roasted by any further attacks. "I'm not sure," he replied, "since I have no part in it."

From behind him a female voice said, "It's *my* handiwork."

The speaker climbed down from the throne and came out of the shadows. Perplexed by her identity, Lyrec said, "Yadani?"

Miradomon knew better. "Elystroya," he muttered. He realized from that what he stood on, but not how she had escaped or managed to transform her prison into the shield.

Lyrec stared fiercely at him. "You lied. And I *believed* you."

"You're so gullible, you'll believe anything people tell you," remarked another voice, but one Lyrec knew well. "Borregad!" he shouted.

The cat stood in shadow—only his eyes pinpointed his position. "I'm sorry you had to believe I was dead, but you needed help and I needed the crex to set her free."

Lyrec saw that Elystroya held a silver sphere. He moved out of her line of fire. The sphere ejected a dozen thin rods that impaled Miradomon where he stood on the shield with his arms raised, disabling him from damaging it further.

The robe wrestled against the hindrances. He growled like an animal. One rod began to sizzle and in a moment was gone.

Lyrec reached out and accepted the crex from Elystroya. He stared into her dark eyes. The cat came forward. "Not now," he said. "That shield was her prison; it's of his design—which means while none of us can do much to it, he can probably obliterate it."

The second rod had vanished, and Miradomon concentrated on eliminating the last one holding his hand up. "Your performance is moving," he shouted at them, "but it plays badly here. All you gained was the opportunity to wish one another goodbye."

"The shield cuts off the star—it's the source of his power," Elystroya said. "He told me."

Lyrec understood finally why the star was here. Miradomon was wiping out a universe to replace it with one of his own, the raw material for which was in the bottom of that well. A universe of chaos: his strength.

He turned and charged at Miradomon. The crex whined impatiently.

But the brief reunion, as the robe had said, had taken up precious seconds. Eliminating the remaining rod that pinned his right hand Miradomon pointed at him, creating a flickering ring that girdled and paralyzed him at the edge of the shield. From the cries behind him, Lyrec concluded the other two had been snared the same way.

Casually, Miradomon began destroying each rod. "I warned you not to hesitate. Now you will spend the rest of eternity dying. I'll keep you at the center of my universe, where the powers of its creation will shred you into a billion particles, and every one of them will be alive and thinking and screaming in endless pain. Your deaths will spread and taint every world.

"Even if you had attacked me, you could not have won. Your puny crex is nothing compared to me! Look at her—she could only pin me for a moment. Of course she lacks your bond with that weapon, but you had your chance and didn't take it." His hands were free; the rods had all been eliminated. "You see? I have freed myself and I still have enough resources left without the source to blast this shield into powder." He roared with triumphant laughter.

Sparkling with golden filaments, his hands pointed down to

finish the job of shattering the shield. Twin streams of plasma cut into the surface. A hairline crack appeared and began to spread out toward the center of the shield. The plasma streams withered suddenly, then stopped.

Miradomon cried out in pain and alarm. He clamped the cowl in both hands as if to tear off his own head. "Damn the child," he screamed, "damn the child!" The Kobachs had tapped into him and begun to drain his reserves. In any other circumstance, they would have died, but here he could not replenish himself. "Damn, damn, damn." As his power melted away, the viscous material of the robe started to slide out from under his clutching hands, taking with it the impenetrable shadow that had concealed his features. His hands, still grasping at his head, became pale green and decayed. The gold threads disappeared.

The ring surrounding Lyrec faded. He could have slain Miradomon then, but he stood rooted by what was taking place on the shield. Elystroya and the cat came up beside him. Breathlessly, they watched as the hem of the robe congealed into a glowing mass around Miradomon's feet.

Upon his arrival in Secamelan, Miradomon had stolen the knowledge of a priest whose misfortune it was to be in the wrong place at the wrong moment. Miradomon vaporized the man, but first borrowed his physical appearance. Now, against his will, the effects of his corrosive spirit on that form were revealed.

The whole of his head was gangrenous, the skin swollen and covered with dark seeping sores. The nose had caved in and the faintly glowing eyes seemed impossibly contained in nearly lidless sockets.

Borregad looked away in revulsion.

The cracked and rubbery lips split into a perverted grin as Miradomon summoned desperately the will to concentrate on a single molecular junction in the shield. If he could shatter one or two more points along the crack already formed, he might crack it wide open. He strained with all his might. The robe slipped farther revealing a sunken, skeletal chest.

A shard from the shield suddenly shot up. A narrow beam of light poked through and fell across Miradomon.

"Lyrec!" shouted Elystroya.

He had seen it and already taken his first step. He jumped

onto the shield, both arms raised above his head, bonded into a silver sphere encasing his hands.

Miradomon needed only a few more seconds. He cried out, "Wait, Lyrec. I could give you worlds! I could—"

The crex shot out a beam of disruption, cutting the air like a wave of heat, slicing into Miradomon as if he were a mirage— through the rotting skull, through teeth and tongue to end his final plea. Lyrec stared into the terrified eyes and said, "Wait? You told me *never* to hesitate." He shoved his arms down as hard as he could. The beam drove through the body and bit into the black shield. The mound of white viscous fluid that had been a robe burst into flame. The shield began to crack.

Independent of one another, Miradomon's two eyes rolled in his head. The two halves of his body split apart with a wet sucking sound and toppled back. His putrid flesh sizzled and popped.

His power was ended.

The shield collapsed and the body and Lyrec vanished into the pit.

Elystroya and Borregad ran to the edge. The floor trembled beneath them.

Coated silver once more, Lyrec floated up out of the pit. He landed safely beside Elystroya, and hugged her to him. She made no response. The floor shook again.

The cat ran toward the rear of the cavern. "Hug later," he yelled at them. "This place is coming apart. We brought Lewyn—the princess. In the throne." He vanished among the shadows, his voice echoing after: "Wait for me!"

Lyrec called after him but got no reply. He ran to the throne and found a naked girl sitting there, staring blankly ahead. He picked her up, turned back to Elystroya. "Take my hand," he ordered. She came to him. Where they had been standing, a section of ceiling crashed down through the floor. Elystroya touched him. Silver spun up her arm and over her body. Lewyn, too, gleamed under the polished surface of his crex.

One wall shook and began to collapse.

"Why is this happening?"

"He died," Lyrec explained, "and his force, or will, or whatever, was all that kept this place together. His crex is the boundary of the world here and it's probably shrinking. That star down there—we have to—"

The floor opened up beneath them and they tumbled out of sight. A thin string of plasma shot up through the ceiling, then splashed down, melting through more of the floor.

Borregad reappeared out of the fluctuating rear wall. "All right, let's . . ." He saw that the floor was gone and scrambled wildly up onto the throne. "Lyrec? You better not have fallen in!" Above him, half the ceiling broke loose. "Lyrec!" he shrieked.

A silver hand materialized behind him. It reached out, grabbed his tail, and he was pulled, howling, into nothingness.

The throne shattered and the last of the floor gave way. The walls rippled and exploded. In the pit the white star collapsed in an instant to half its original size.

Then it blossomed.

Talenyecis, standing at the ready, almost killed the first silver figure as it popped into the room.

Lyrec eyed her and blinked at the blade vibrating a hand's width from his head. Beyond her, a single torch burned in a wall bracket, and the fine edge of the sword shone with its light. "Would you mind?" asked Lyrec breathlessly. Talenyecis lowered the sword and replaced it in her scabbard. "Hold her," he demanded and handed Lewyn to her. A coating of silver spread from the princess to cover Talenyecis.

"What are you doing to me?" she asked irately.

"In a minute," he gasped. He tilted his head, eyes closed as if listening to something. Talenyecis heard nothing. He reached out; his hand vanished. After a second, he tugged sharply back and his hand re-emerged, holding a howling mad silver beast by the tail. Upside down, the cat bleated, "I could have died! You left me there, I could have *died!*"

"Why did you run off?"

Borregad showed him the black globe. "This is why."

"What is it?"

Elystroya said, "One of his prisons."

"Lewyn's soul is in here," said the cat. "And let go of my tail."

The castle shuddered. Talenyecis's eyes widened. "What?" was all she could ask.

Lyrec took Borregad in his arms, said, "Stand close," then closed his eyes.

The last thing Talenyecis saw was a huge crack running down the outside wall. Then the room tilted, fluttered, and shrank from view.

♭Chapter 27.

THE tavern looked like a war had been fought in it. Chairs and tables lay overturned or, in many cases, shattered. The Kobachs had surreptitiously taken control of Tynec and, through him, had siphoned off what they could of Miradomon's power. But they could not absorb such adverse energy, and it had spun off them like a whirling stormfront. Confined and forced to rebound inside the building, it had wreaked demonic vengeance on everything outside the Kobach circle.

Grohd sat beside his hearth, where he had started a fire after crawling away from the circle. His pants were soaked with grynne that had poured across the floor when his stored kegs ruptured in the tumult. Bozadon Reket remained seated beside the others. Both he and Grohd had been persuaded in the end by Ronnæm to volunteer. Reluctantly, they had linked up with the Kobachs. Now they were glad they had done so—it had probably saved their lives.

Reket was utterly drained after the experience, but he tingled with a strange light-headed vigor that no previous experience in his life had ever generated. He was reminded of how he felt sometimes after a sexual encounter, except even more awake and alive than that, and he contemplated that being a Kobach might have some advantages . . . but he maintained his reservations about magic.

Thunder shook the floor beneath him. A cold wind swirled, buffeting everyone. Grohd whined, "Oh, no, it's come for us!" and crawled into hiding again behind his serving bar.

Three silver beings—one of them carrying a silver cat and another bearing a sleeping silver girl—appeared in the center of the circle. The wind dissipated. The members of the circle stood up.

Lyrec set to reeling in the crex from each individual of his group. Talenyecis hardly noticed as the silver withdrew from her; her eyes were glazed with the lacquer of memory—a memory of travel between time and space. Nor did she notice as Lyrec gently lifted Lewyn's body out of her arms.

Ronnæm stared in wonder at his granddaughter. One of his group handed a cloak to him. He took it and draped it over Lewyn's naked form. Then Lyrec handed her to him. Ronnæm stared into the untroubled face pressed against him, and tears welled in his eyes. Lyrec whispered to Borregad, "Would you care to do the honors?"

The cat, still annoyed at being abandoned, mumbled under his breath as he strode over to Ronnæm and held up the black sphere in his forepaws. Impatiently, he snarled, "I'm not on stilts, you know." The old king's mouth dropped open. Bozadon Reket gasped. When Borregad saw the tears in Ronnæm's eyes, his tone softened. "I have to touch her head, you see. Could you lower her down just the smallest bit?"

In a daze, the old king obeyed. The cat reached up and put the globe against Lewyn's forehead. It sank steadily from sight. Lyrec said, "Concentrate, Borregad." The cat silenced him with a smoldering glance, then did as he instructed. The globe soon bobbed into view. The cat retrieved it, held it up. Relieved of its contents and no longer bonded by Miradomon's powers, the globe disintegrated in his padded palm. "She will sleep," Borregad told them, "and when she awakens, she'll know of her father's death, so it won't be such a shock. The rest of recent history is too tangled for me to implant—all of you will have to teach her. You should let her sleep somewhere undisturbed."

Malchavik, clutching his own daughter to him, said, "There are two buildings outside. I will show you, old friend. Come." He and Pavra led Ronnæm and his sleeping granddaughter outside. Ronnæm paused and bowed his head humbly to the cat.

Borregad turned to Lyrec. "Did you see that? I could get to like this. Are cats allowed to be kings?"

"This is preposterous," declared Reket.

"You wait," warned the cat, "when I'm king I'll have you executed for that. I never forget anything."

Reket's mouth worked but no sound came out. Lyrec moved in between him and Borregad. "Excuse me. This is Talenyecis. She helped us eliminate Ladomirus. The circumstances, however, have left her a little dazed, as you can see. I thought perhaps you might—"

"Yes!" said Reket, seeing a chance to escape the cat's sharp tongue. He drew Talenyecis sharply away before Lyrec could warn him of her potentially lethal aspects.

"You say Ladomirus is gone?" one of the Kobachs asked. "What of the war?"

"I doubt there will be a war. Your king has his own mind back now that Miradomon is destroyed and will surely order it stopped. In the meantime, I find it difficult to imagine that any loose band of unguided mercenaries will bother risking their necks over a castle that has probably sunk into the ground by now. I'm sure they'll surrender to the superior forces of Secamelan. They're stupid, true enough, but even they have that much sense."

"We can be at peace now," the Kobach said. "We have time for the dead."

Lyrec took Elystroya's hand and said to Borregad, "We're going off for a while. Why don't you get Grohd out from behind the bar and have him give you that grynne he promised. And then you can regale these unfortunates with tales of your brave deeds today."

"Lyrec, there's something you should—"

"Never mind, I know already. But thank you." He headed outside.

"What did Borregad mean?" Elystroya asked him. They stood in the yard near the stable, under a night sky sprinkled with stars. Lyrec found the cold refreshing.

"He meant that you remain unfinished. When he put you in Yadani's body, he had time to give you but the barest knowledge of who and what you were, and who we were. Pure facts, no emotions."

"What are emotions?"

"The instincts that these beings operate with. They have individual names such as hate, greed, yearning. Another, called love. When I embraced you for the first time you made no response because you lack the emotions to do so. You feel toward me as you always did—at least I hope so."

"I do, of course. How could I ever lose that?"

"Yes, but that, I've learned, takes a long while to evolve into its equivalent here. And Yadani was for all purposes a blank. For whatever reason she had never developed memory or thought."

"Is it better? In this form?"

"Better," he said. "Not better. That would be an unfair analogy. They are unalike. These creatures experience overwhelming waves of emotion. I've gone from unplumbed depths of despair to an unmatchable ecstasy."

"Once," she began slowly, "when Miradomon wanted to speak with me, he placed me in Lewyn's body. Those emotions drove me into a corner—I could hardly tolerate existing and I retreated." She sought his eyes in the darkness. "How is it you've survived them so well?"

"Not well at all. But the scars are invisible. There will be scars for you, too. Unavoidably. I have to live with some things that are abhorrent to me—acts that I can never forgive myself."

"Why—"

"Shh. Listen, please. Miradomon used those emotions as his chief weapons. He boiled the blood of race after race until they frothed with hate at the sight of one another. He very nearly won it all. That is how strong these emotions are. But they are also elementary to every one of these beings. To live here, you need them. To reject emotion is to reject the value of life. Which is, after all, what he did."

"We could go elsewhere."

"Perhaps. But our universe is sealed off from us—and you no longer have a crex. You couldn't survive. If Miradomon spoke the truth, then all the inhabited worlds here are similar. His parallels. We might search forever and never find a world without emotion. And I'm not certain I want to try. I searched for you and now I've found you, and you can't imagine what that feels like."

"Finish what Borregad began," she said urgently.

"But do you understand what I'm saying?"

"No. I don't. But how can I?"

He saw that she was right. Taking her hands in his, he told her to close her eyes. Then, closing his, he started to give her the gift that was also a curse.

Delicately he touched her mind, slowly let the emotions he knew enter her. He wished then that Nydien had been available to tap into, remembering her gentleness, remembering their coupling, his pleasant memory passing into Elystroya as a shade of joy. Even as she absorbed that, Lyrec was realizing in shock and sorrow that Nydien had not been among the Kobach survivors. His grief and loss trickled through as well before he could withdraw contact.

Opening his eyes, he found Elystroya weeping. She shared his misery and mourning. They held each other in silence, sharing at last the moment of reunion.

After a while, Lyrec looked up into the night and said, "Right now, somewhere out there a small star is flowering into a great source of light. New worlds are being created. I wonder how long before we'll see it here?"

"However long," she replied, "we will watch it together."

"With Borregad."

She laughed, wiping her cheeks. "He saved us, you know."

"Yes, I suppose he truly did. Rescued the crex, rescued you and me." He glanced toward the tavern. "Oh, oh."

"What?"

"I just realized—once *he* figures that out, we'll never hear the end of it."

"Never."

"'Pon my *soul!*"

Fantasy from Ace
fanciful and fantastic!